Questor
Surgeon to the Republic

Tallis Clark

Published by Leaf by Leaf
an imprint of Cinnamon Press,
Office 49019, PO Box 15113, Birmingham B2 2NJ
www.cinnamonpress.com

The right of Tallis Clark to be identified as author of this work has been asserted by her in accordance with the Copyright, Designs and Patent Act, 1988. © 2025 Tallis Clark.
Print Edition ISBN 978-1-78864-883-7
British Library Cataloguing in Publication Data. A CIP record for this book can be obtained from the British Library.

All rights reserved. No part of this publication may be reproduced, stored in a retrieval system, or transmitted in any form or by any means, electronic, mechanical, photocopying, recording or otherwise without the prior written permission of the publishers. This book may not be lent, hired out, resold or otherwise disposed of by way of trade in any form of binding or cover other than that in which it is published, without the prior consent of the publishers.

Designed and typeset in Adobe Caslon Pro by Cinnamon Press.
Cover design by Adam Craig, inspired by: Surgical instruments of the 16th and 17th centuries. Wellcome Collection © Adam Craig.
Cinnamon Press is represented by Inpress.

Author biography

Tallis Clark is an emeritus professor at a London medical school. Fascination with the ideas and ideals of the seventeenth century and their impact upon the practice of medicine and surgery at a revolutionary time led to this book. Clark is also a published poet, has produced two volumes of poetry and lives in both London and France, near Avignon.

England 1649; the King has been executed. Turncoat army surgeon John Lockyer saves a child and is accused of murder. He must turn spy to discover the truth in the turmoil of Oliver Cromwell's new Republic.

Questor

Questor: One

*London 1649 First Year of the English Republic
Thursday September 13th just after midnight*

They are gaining on me. I'm running hard. I can feel my heart thumping—I gulp a lungful of night air. Now I'm at the top of the hill—the gardens of the old Bishops Palace—there might be somewhere to hide. But the weight in my belly is slowing me, my legs drag. I can see the dark walls and the gatehouse at the back of the military hospital. The men are close although they run so silently—if they had not blundered against another sleeper I wouldn't have realised. I was up and off then. I thought I'd escaped. My last chance now—there's a light in the gatehouse; I can see the porter's head! I'm calling him but they are on me, dragging me down. I am draining... help me... red... pain... dark, redness... redness and dark...

Chapter 1

It began with the woman.

She lay on the table; her dress had been torn apart and I could see movement in the huge curve of her belly. I cut her open, tugging the knife along a rough incision. The pale flesh and fibres were tougher than expected, there was a tearing, a hot metallic smell and blood welled from the wound. I grabbed a linen cloth to stuff in the opening. I reached inside her, felt the sticky stub of a foot and curve of a spine. Then, my hand beneath its back, with one swift movement, I lifted the infant free. The blue cord pulsed as the woman standing next to me tied and snipped it.

'Give me the child' She stretched out her arms for the little red body, sucked at its mouth, then blew gently into its nostrils.

Nothing happened.

I wiped my bloodied fingers as she blew again and rubbed the tiny chest. Nothing.

We exchanged glances. I nodded encouragement and watched as she kept on with gentle movements pressing her palm against the warm wet skin.

To my relief I saw the smallest rise and fall. I hardly dared breathe, but after an age it came—a whimper. The infant still slippery with blood and wax, gasped into life, grunting, and twisting in the woman's arms. Shadows danced on the wall and a thin cry reached up to the vaulted ceiling, cutting the silence of the hours before dawn.

I had cut the mother open, a mortal wound. Even if by some miracle, she could have survived the ordeal of having the baby sliced from her, she had already lost too much blood. She was no longer breathing. Her long brown hair streamed over the table's edge and her arms dangled uselessly, white skin vivid under the streaks of blood. I saw the tips of her nails were already blue, pale decoration to her paler hands.

Never had I undertaken surgery like that yet we had saved the child and it felt like a reprieve. I was startled by a swishing sound behind me as Thomas, my assistant, threw sawdust on to the floor. I had taken a big risk. How big I wasn't sure.

'Say nothing of what you have seen. When morning comes, I'll speak to Colonel Aldridge.'

I turned to the midwife who had wrapped the baby and placed her finger in its mouth. I could see the fontanel in the skull throbbing, the tiny veins flushed blue. Alive.

'Thanks, Hope-Anna. Without your skill, the child would surely have died.'

'You had the courage to cut her. You would have, even without me,' she said as she bent over the child.

She was right. Surgery was my trade where you must act and be quick about it. Some wished it grander but for me the Army was where my skills mattered. In the last seven years of civil war I had seen many men die. Sword, musket, cannon, and pike inflicted their own terrible style of injury. Tired and red-eyed I worked all hours, hacking bone, my ears closed to screams, binding, stitching, staunching—and praying. The work carried neither the fear nor the exhilaration of the field soldier, just exhaustion and sadness for the young men damaged beyond my skill to repair.

But you either do nothing or something:

It was this that had made me open the woman; now I turned again to her body. Her massive wound gaped black and deep. Gently, I pulled the edges together. More blood trickled on my feet as I closed the flap. Thomas was collecting the candle-stubs, his fingers already stained with blackened tallow.

'Thomas—go find a sheet. Get a shroud as well and—you'll have to clean her up.'

'Sir, it's not seemly… can't Mistress Tyler…'

'She's taken the baby,' I said sharply.

At the shadowed edge of the room something gleamed—a fragment of the young woman's dress. It was rich material threaded with silver. I picked it up. Sodden with her blood, it still glittered as it left a red trail across my hand.

For decency, I placed the remnant across her wound and it seemed as if the last breath left her. In the old days, they said that meant the soul was leaving the body but would stay nearby for a few days, a discreet shade waiting admission to the next place on its eternal journey. Was she watching me? Such superstitions were frowned upon now. Out of the corner of my eye I noticed Thomas make the sign of the cross and mouth a prayer. I pretended I hadn't seen. Climbing the damp stone steps away from the smell of blood and candle-smoke I walked across the yard to my bed. I felt more than usual exhaustion. The night sky was turning grey to the east, over the great towers of the cathedral of St Paul and the warehouses, wharves, and airless counting rooms of the City.

Thursday September 13 early morning

When I woke a few hours later it was to the luxury of a basin of warm water someone had thoughtfully brought in. Could they have known that washing my body is one of my great pleasures? I had acquired the refinements of bathing during the time I studied in Padua, and it had served me well in the recent conflict. During battles I'd often spent the day, hair tied back, standing only in breeches and boots as the wounded inside the surgical tent piled up. A damaged leg had to be taken away fast if the soldier was to survive. I tried to work in the open air, especially during the summer. Touch and go whether the flies were worse inside or out. They feasted on the piles of severed limbs, hindering my work. Twice a day I ordered a trench dug to bury disembodied arms and legs. The sight of them exercised a horrid fascination on passing troopers, but like all young men they continued to believe themselves invulnerable.

All day there was blood. Despite frequent dousing, I was always covered in it. Sometimes, if I had a moment, I wondered how many men's characters had been daubed on my body—because according to the laws of war, I treated casualties from both sides. The great Galen had taught that a man's spirit is kept in his blood. How many enemy spirits had I taken in?

Did this double exposure explain the way I finally behaved, while the King and Parliament had fought it out? After the siege of Oxford, I had made the choice that altered my life.

I switched sides.

I abandoned the claret and gold jacket of the Kings Foote Regiment and putting on the plain russet coat of a soldier of Parliament, left behind the years I had fought for the King. Now I was a hard-working surgeon in Cromwell's New Model Army. I was experienced and reliable. Most people thought I was not easy to know. I was a turncoat. No one asked me why. To apply Galen's theory would be a pretty solution. But that was far from the truth.

As I dried myself on a rough towel and pulled on a clean shirt I thought about the waste of life and suffering I had seen over the last six years. Most had been inflicted on young boys and men who, even if they lived, would be changed forever. The war had been long, the King was dead and now there was a new Republic. So many—my Army colleagues especially—hoped to build a different country where virtue and freedom coexisted. For me, in whom belief in great causes had never been strong, the good always lay in practical wisdom that could restore, replace, or relieve. I felt more secure in the outcome of surgical skills than in rhetoric. Reason and virtue would not be sufficient for the enormous task of rebuilding government, and I had seen enough to know talking about the nation's good was no guarantee against the evil or foolishness in men's hearts. My work saw me through the day. At night, my dreams were cruel, still full of the war, confused images of slaughter and voices calling in appeal.

As much as I could, I closed my mind and memory. Perhaps some portion of my heart as well.

There was a tap at the door. Hope-Anna stood there.

'Did you sleep Mr Lockyer?' she asked, smiling. I smiled back.

'Two hours—did you?'

'Not much.' She laughed. 'The baby, you see—needed feeding and it wasn't easy. Just dripping milk and water didn't satisfy his hunger. He is lucky to survive; few babies born that way stay alive. But I kept him very warm. I'll have to find a wet-nurse quickly—I think there's one among the laundrywomen.'

To me, Hope-Anna looked surprisingly fresh for one who had not slept; her red curls bubbled out from her starched cap. Born by Bishopsgate, I knew she came from a family of tooth-drawers and midwives. Her kin stretched across the City and beyond into the surrounding villages of the estuary. If anyone could find a wet-nurse within the hour, it was Hope-Anna.

'Madame O'Brien wants to begin as soon as you are ready—and I notified the searchers as you asked—they are on their way—oh and Colonel Aldridge would have you stop by.'

'Thank you, Hope-Anna—for everything.' But she was gone.

I felt I should get moving, but I paused to look again with pleasure at the chamber that was my newest home. It could not be more different from the smoky, overcrowded field tents, sometimes ankle-deep in mud, where I'd lived during those hard years. It was high up and overlooked the yard. The space was square and light, with an elm board floor. I had a long oak table with a horn inkwell, spindle chair tucked underneath. In the ledges of the walls, I kept my battered volume of Ambroise Paré on battlefield surgery, its leather cover stained and scratched. There was a bootleg copy of Vesalius' classic of anatomy *de Humani Corporis Fabrica.*, and Tom Johnson's latest *Herball.* Next to them, volumes of the new chemical medicine of van Helmont and Paracelsus. In the place of honour stood the great work on the circulation of the blood by my friend and mentor William Harvey: *De Mortu Cordis,* the Frankfurt first edition, bound in black calf and lettered in gold. Here also, in orderly but unbound sheets, were my case histories written up late at night or in the gaps between battles. I hoped to publish them when things quietened. Just now, so shortly after the King's execution—or murder, as many said—the presses were self-censoring, wary of being closed. The wars had not ended with the King's death, Scotland and Ireland remained loyal to the Stuarts and had yet to be subdued for Parliament. It was best to wait.

Looking down, I saw the gates to the yard had opened to admit the morning laundry cart. It trundled noisily over the new cobbles and halted before Mrs Ellis, who was, like most nurses, a war-widow. She supervised the unloading of fresh bedding. She counted and marked off the wicker baskets and her two daughters lugged them towards the arched door of the main chapel opposite, which served as the hospital's Great Ward. Below the chapel was the crypt, whose coolest enclosure served as a mortuary. Then I saw two women climbing stiffly up the crypt steps. One looked up at my window. Damn, I thought, they are here already! The Searchers!

I'd been expecting them, for I'd summoned them myself. The Army had made me questor for Ely Hospital meaning I must keep a tally of the deaths and produce a report every year. The City Fathers, quick to take advantage, for a small additional stipend had extended my duties to cover the local leper house. I also acted as coroner for the area and advised when there was need for a post-mortem. If so—and it is rare, for the causes of death are usually obvious—I would undertake those duties. It didn't pay much and carried more responsibility than power. But it implied that despite my past, I could be trusted. And it satisfied my curiosity.

I could call witnesses and summon the help of clerks and others, often fellow citizens of varied abilities. Two were heading towards me now. I hurtled down the flagged staircase and rushed into the yard. The old women saw me and shuffled forward, beckoning in agitation.

'We need to speak to you, Sir. What has kept you so long? We were on our way to bring you most urgently.'

'Forgive me Mistress Byatt, Mistress Meadows; I have had little sleep. I'm sorry you had to come after me. Let's go down below.' We turned back down the uneven stone steps.

The crypt was vaulted, and dry. In the adjoining cellars the Bishop of Ely making the most of his London palace, had kept his wine in the old days. It lay cool beneath his gardens, where roses bordered strawberry beds. Last night, in one of these dark stone rooms, I had performed the riskiest surgery of my career.

'We put the lavender away, Sir,' said Mistress Byatt, 'for it covers the smell and may hide a poison or plague—although here it seems poison or plague was far from the cause. There is a mighty wound in her belly.' She paused and then stiffened. 'It seems, Sir, you were the surgeon who inflicted it.'

The girl's body now lay under an unbleached linen sheet. And in her opened corpse lay my problem. I would have to report this death, about which I knew more than I wished. As questor, however, I had some control.

Mistress Meadows drew back the sheet. The little light in the room came from a long grating in the wall. The woman lay, her white skin darkening and stiffening. Thomas had done his job well; he had tidied her, and it was even clearer to me now that in life, she had been a beauty.

'The cut I made was to save her infant's life. She was already dying. She was knifed with great force, spine, and heart. Look there for the cause of her death.'

With ease because she was so light, the three of us turned the body over; the wounds were plain. Mistress Meadows looked straight at me. Her eyes were rheumy and cold.

'Sir we must make a report of what we have seen. Those are no ordinary wounds. This is not a plague case, but a far more shocking thing.'

'Yes, Mistress Meadows. If I advise there should be an inquest, you will be questioned.'

Mistress Byatt looked uneasy.

'What about the child, Sir? It will need to be mentioned in our report. Is it alive?'

'Dead. I failed.' It was my instant response. The less they knew the better.

Both women looked at me their eyes full of unspoken questions.

'As I took it from her body, it stopped breathing. It was… er… half formed. Not whole. It has been wrapped for burial.'

'Better that it's dead. Poor girl,' said Mistress Byatt.

Mistress Meadows's mouth tightened. 'No doubt God's punishment for her wickedness. You may think, Sir, you acted for the best but there are others who would question whether the fruits of sin should be a charge on the parish. With the wars come many sins of the flesh, bastard children, women brought to ruin. We must hope for the calm of the Republic and the kingdom of God.'

'The Republic is far from calm!' I exclaimed, thinking that those who believed the kingdom of God would soon arrive are presently disappointed.

She had not finished. 'We need to see the remains, Sir, to confirm.'

I wanted rid of them. They were sharp enough to have suspicions. I needed time; time to sort out the tangle in which I had put myself. So, I got angry, glaring at the pair of them.

'For what?' I roared, 'To satisfy some twisted curiosity? Have you not seen enough? I am the questor for this hospital—there will be no burial charge to St Andrews. And I should remind you goodwives you are here at my invitation as a courtesy to the civil authorities. This is an Army hospital.'

'General Cromwell is in Ireland. The Army doesn't rule us yet,' snapped Mistress Meadows. Her big hands clutched her apron, and she looked ready to argue but a breathless young orderly came hurrying through the crypt's arched doorway.

'Colonel Aldridge wants you Sir—now.'

'Well, I've finished here.' I was thankful to turn away from the two women. I knew their parish pensions depended on making a report. I hoped that having ruled out the plague, they would not go into too much detail. But they were careful, intelligent women—and suspicious. They muttered to each other, and I was glad of an excuse to leave. Now I had to go and explain to Aldridge.

The left arm of Colonel Aldridge's grey worsted uniform hung empty. He'd lost his limb in a skirmish with Royalist irregulars. They had been torturing a farmer to get at his meagre savings. But the grip in his right hand was as strong as ever and now his fist was balled and prepared to strike something.

'Bowels of the Lord, what were you doing Lockyer?' he roared. 'This is an Army hospital! Not a place for whores and drabs! We treat the honest men of our Republic. We keep a midwife to attend their wives, good, clean women whose bellies have not been swollen by lust! We could be closed, and you sent packing to Ireland!'

He brought his fist down hard on the table. It rocked on the stone flags and a plate flew. At the same moment, there was a knock on the door. The young orderly was back.

'Colonel Aldridge, Sir, a man is here. He demands to see you.'

'A man? What sort of man? Is he Army?'

'No Sir. He is foreign and wears livery—er—from a noble house.'

'Noble house, *noble house?*' yelled Aldridge. 'This is the Republic, fellow. We bow to no one.'

'An honourable and courageous sentiment Sir, I applaud you.'

The words came from a tall blond man whose head was bent forward as he filled the doorway. His jerkin was embroidered with the image of a leopard, blue-black spots on yellow. And he was well armed—I could see a pistol and an elaborate dagger in his belt. This was no casual call. He spoke slowly, in a deep, lilting voice. I could not place his accent except that he was not from these islands.

'Colonel Aldridge, I represent my Lord the Earl of Pembroke—as you know a loyal servant to the Republic. And no doubt you will have heard of his cousin Colonel Algernon Sidney who fought so bravely alongside General Cromwell.'

At the name Algernon Sidney, I noticed, Aldridge stiffened and fell silent. The tall man continued.

'I am here on a private and secret matter, Colonel Aldridge. We know you have the body of a young woman in the hospital. I must tell you she is a member of our household. I have been sent to collect her and oversee her burial. My Lord is a member of the Council of State. We have the highest authority. I am to take her to his palace on the river, Baynard's Castle. Immediately.'

'This is a military hospital. We have our rules,' Aldridge snapped.

'Just so, Colonel Aldridge, but Parliament still controls the military, I think? And the Earl has a further request.'

'Which is?'

The big blond man looked at me. 'Surgeon-major Lockyer is well-known for his discretion and skill. The Earl asks he accompany the body and anatomises it before burial.'

Chapter 2

Thursday September 13th mid-morning

I wedged myself in the cart as it jolted across Holborn Bridge. The girl's body lay at my feet, shrouded, and covered in straw and canvas. I was at last beginning to reflect. Last night I had acted on instinct. Now I wondered—as Aldridge had—what had I done?

Who was this girl? Who had told Pembroke? Above all, why had she been murdered? The thoughts swirled to be replaced by others. That man's accent. Not French or Spanish. Not Italian either. Where had I heard one like it? I looked at the blond giant beside me.

'May I ask your country Sir?'

'I was born in the Low Countries but have served my Lord's family for some years.'

The noise of coaches and carts was extremely loud and the traffic so dense as we turned into Snow Hill, I could barely hear my own words let alone the reply. His tone suggested further questions would not be welcome, so we sat in silence during the steep descent, giving way to a slow oxcart and swerving to avoid the barrier of the Old Bailey. We passed into the dark between the twin towers of Newgate prison. The building opposite had recently housed the royal robes of state, rich materials, furs and golden thread, the King's Wardrobe. The Queen had sold the contents to raise an army. Now it was bolted and shuttered. As we headed down St Andrews Hill towards the Thames, I saw that most of the garment warehouses and fabric cutters, once overflowing with silver gauze and coloured silks, were empty.

The huge curtain walls of Baynard's Castle cast Thames Street into deep shadow. Its frontage extended yards along the river, with a jetty and iron water gate. The Yorkist kings had been proclaimed here and the great doors, broad towers and stone-framed windows gave an air of sombre magnificence. But since January this year the days of kings were over, perhaps to be followed by the end of great lords too. And then what? Some prophesied the day of judgment was near, the world would be destroyed and only the Elect would remain. Somehow, I didn't think I'd be among them.

As the cart trundled the sunless street, I was remembering corpse dissection was a messy job at best. Harvey had taught me, we worked on the bodies of executed thieves and murderers in his Oxford cutting room. I began to calculate. In September, the weather was still warm. The girl's death had occurred two hours before dawn. It was now almost midday, some eight hours later. Corruption of the corpse could set in fast. The cart turned through a side gate into a narrow courtyard.

As if he'd read my thoughts, my companion said, 'We can pack her body in ice. My Lord has an ice well inside the walls. It drains to the river.'

A troop of soldiers from a Parliamentary regiment dawdled near the gate. Two were summoned to lift the slender canvas bundle from the cart. I followed them to where a set of cellar steps led downwards. As I made to follow, I felt the Dutchman's firm grip on my arm.

'They have their orders and will set things up for you. My Lord wishes to meet you, and before you do, he desires you take refreshment.'

Not having eaten since the previous evening—everything had happened so fast—I was starving. And I needed to plan the task ahead.

Thick slices of salt pork, bread, butter, a plate of Kentish cobnuts and two mugs, one of beer and one of water, had been already laid. I looked hard at the water then thought a man who had taken the trouble to install an ice well would make sure he had clean drinking water. I drained the jug in one and started on the meal. I had long learnt the soldier's maxim of eating everything when you can. As soon as my plate was empty the Dutchman appeared. I wondered whether the room contained a spyhole and that I had been under surveillance. That did nothing to ease my fears.

But the man relaxed. His long bony face looked friendlier now. He put his hand across his heart and gave a small but formal bow.

'Surgeon-major Lockyer, my name is Captain Tjaard van Prin. I was in the service of the Dutch regiment commanded by the Earl's cousin Colonel Robert Sidney. I came to London from The Hague at the end of last year at my lord's request. He has lost the use of his legs and needs a strong man to move him. His temperament is erratic, so please speak softly.'

'Why does the Earl wish to see me?'

'The Earl doesn't give reasons. Probably because you treated the girl and were present at her death. He wants to give an account of it to her family.'

'And who are they?'

'Not important,' said van Prin dismissively. 'Let's go upstairs.'

The room was large with long windows. I could see the Thames, busy with skiffs, barges and wherries catching the rising tide. The Earl sat in a high-backed leather chair. His trembling left hand grasped its carved wooden knob. His feet rested on a frayed footstool. Long ago some woman had embroidered it with his arms of the lion and leopard.

I hardly needed surgeon's training to see that the Earl of Pembroke was in poor health. His complexion was grey. His right foot drooped and his puffy face was slack at one side. I guessed he had recently suffered an apoplexy. I bowed.

'My Lord. I hope I find you in good health.' Words of common courtesy—they were out before I could stop myself.

The Earl gave a bitter laugh. 'No, you do not, Sir. Not since May when this cursed fit fell upon me. Since then, you surgeons have taken enough blood from me to float a warship. Tell me about last night.'

I hesitated. 'My lord before I tell you anything, I want to know what your interest is in all this and why it is not a matter for the justices that a young woman lies dead. Since the King's execution this is a lawful Republic. You can't make your own laws.'

The Earl's face flushed. 'You talk of laws and the King's *execution*—you—a turncoat! You were a surgeon in the King's forces before you joined with Parliament! Why fellow, by the rule of law *you* should be hanging from a gibbet!'

Countries and did not want to relive it. The Earl was getting ready to leave for Whitehall and required van Prin to attend him. Although silent, I sensed that the Dutchman was disappointed to miss the show.

Their absence meant something else. I could say nothing, and they might not learn of the child's survival. If I arranged her body and shrouded it, no one would know the child was not inside her. But why not tell them? I was a trusted surgeon, a responsible man, I should keep to the law. Yet since I had arrived at Baynard's castle I had felt uneasy. Now my instinct was urging me to finish the job, keep silent and get out as fast as I could.

It may seem obvious that cutting a dead body is different from cutting a live one. But I was not engaged in dissection—my purpose was to establish the cause or causes of death and that was relatively unusual. Whereas the corpses I used were often preserved this was not the case here. A healthy young female less than 20 years old not wasted or wrinkled. I had the uncanny feeling she might wake up. Then I moved the sheet and saw her wounds including the one I had made. I steadied my hand and made my incision. To distance myself, I composed mental notes for my report, as I had learnt from Harvey years ago in Oxford.

'The arms and hands show cuts which are wounds of self-defence. Two further wounds have penetrated deeply into the body and damaged the great organs. One has transfixed the heart, and damaged the lungs, a second lower one pierced the abdominal aorta. The blows bypassed the uterus. There has been a great bleeding into the chest cavity and the belly. Death, although not instantaneous, would have followed within minutes of such an assault. The wounds are not gaping which

suggests the blows were done with precision and deliberation using one or several sharp weapons.'

I stopped. I had noticed a peculiarity. Although clean, each major wound had a single serration. I must be sure to add:

'The blade of at least one of these weapons may display an incision or dent.'

The major organs took time to remove. Some were damaged and ruptured. Yet the tissues of the lungs and heart were healthy, with no sign of previous disease. It was chiefly by an examination of the bowels that something like poison could be found. The Romans used to feed the liver to an animal and see what happened, but I didn't have the means for that and would have to rely on observation.

That produced another surprise.

The liver was spotted with dark blotches, and some of the lower bowel was crinkled and covered with abscesses. The neck of the womb was discoloured. I hesitated. Was this disease or something more? I had to admit I did not know. It was inconclusive but suspicious.

The final task I hoped would be easier: to prepare Lady Derryn Barlow for burial. It was not a job I had done often but I performed it carefully and with respect. I washed her, replaced her organs, padded her belly with straw. Finally done, I pulled the clean linen shroud up over her head and fastened it. As I did, a gust of air made the candle flame gutter. Someone had entered the room.

The woman facing me in the doorway was tall and so thin the dark stuff of her dress hung loosely on her body. She was leaning on a cane and watching me intently with bright black eyes. I could see the high colour in her bony face. Her white hair was piled in elaborate curls and crowned with a velvet cap. A long rope of pearls was looped in three strands over her breast. This was, I knew, Countess Pembroke.

'I see she is already shrouded Major. Open the shroud if you please.' Her voice was sharp and commanding. I hated it. I had to stop her, or my deception would be discovered.

'Your ladyship, I do *not* please. I have finished my work. Leave her in peace.'

The countess halted like a cat tensed to spring but seeing the anger in my face said quietly, 'You have done the Earl an important service, but he did not appoint you as guardian of her corpse. Major, she was my kinswoman. Just open enough so I might see her face.'

With reluctance I undid the rough strings and lifted the flap that covered the girl's head. The countess was standing next to me now and I caught the sweet spicy scent of orange flowers. She stared for a moment at Lady Derryn. Then she bent forward and spat with all her force on that still white face.

'Whore!' she hissed.

'What?' I was outraged and tried to pull her away, but she had already turned towards the door walking swiftly and tapping her cane. The speed of her movement set the candle flames dancing and made shadows dart crazily against the walls.

I watched the countess go. As the door slammed, I turned back to the corpse of Lady Derryn. I bent over her and gently wiped her cheek. Then I pulled the shroud up and tied it over her head.

Chapter 4

Thursday September 13th 1649 mid-afternoon

My encounter with Pembroke's wife had shaken me. Still, I told myself, she had only seen the woman's face. The secret was safe. The Earl had asked for a report, and I must provide one. I raced upstairs calling for ink and paper. I wrote quickly, hoping for no more interruptions or the countess to reappear. I wanted to be on my way back to my life at Ely, far from whatever mess this family had cooked up for themselves.

I confirmed I had indeed found abnormalities in the bowel. There was internal scarring, for which one possible explanation was poison. But this was not proven though I could not rule it out. The obvious cause of death was stabbing. Let's see what they make of that, I thought. Somehow squaring it with my conscience, I did not mention the cut in her belly I had made to save her child. I re-read my hastily written and blotchy script. I could have taken my time. Escape from Pembroke's clan was not to be my fate.

For the moment I felt light and free, responsibility discharged. As I took a last look around the room, afternoon light fell on a huge painting I had missed earlier. Two satyrs knelt beside the white body of a nymph. I did not know how to read their gaze. Lust? Anguish? Was she asleep or dead? I wondered who would delight in such a picture and contemplate a mythical world, when the real one was full of mystery. Leave now, I thought and closed the door. In one hand, I clutched my case of surgical instruments. With the other I tucked into my jerkin the heavy pouch containing ten pounds in Commonwealth gold. It was a relief to inhale the cold fresh air. Turning against the wind, I headed east along Thames Street hoping to put a great distance between myself and the menacing walls of Baynard's Castle.

Colonel Aldridge would complain at my long absence. So would the duty surgeon, Mr Yorke. I'd already decided to give some portion of my fee to Yorke and reckoned that would keep him quiet. Yorke always wanted money—I wondered if he was a regular gambler. A handsome man, my height, but fleshier, he was as much a libertine as he could get away with. A seasoned soldier too, with a good measure of hatred for Royalists—ex-Royalists even more so. It had taken most of my small supply of forbearance to forge a working relationship with him. The money would help.

At St Peters Hill, I climbed to St Paul's towards the book stalls of Paternoster Row. But the rhythm of walking did not calm me as I'd hoped. I had to admit my work at Baynard's Castle and all that had gone before troubled me. I was no expert in poisons. What if my observations were mistaken?

I needed to talk to someone—and there was only one person with whom I could openly discuss my doubts.

I turned left abruptly into Old Fish Street and nearly collided with a dark-haired man in a blue coat. He had his head down, gazing at his fine shoes. They were already stained with dirty liquid which slopped from the overflowing gutters. Foolish to walk in the street with shoes more suited to the dance floor, I thought. Doesn't he know London?

My walk took ten more minutes. Meanwhile, I wondered. Would I be welcome, or have the door slammed in my face? How would I explain myself and ask for help? St Laurence Lane was lined with elegant brick houses. I halted outside one gate, then lifted the latch and entered a paved garden shadowed by a mulberry tree. I felt the fallen fruit crush and leak under my boots. The knocker rattled loosely.

The servant who answered shook his head. 'I'm sorry but Master William is resting, Sir. He spent the whole morning up on the roof making notes and now he's gone to lie down. You can imagine the effort it takes him at his age.'

'Joshua, Joshua, a visitor at last! A sure salvation brings him here, let him in!' The familiar voice made me smile as Harvey's small gouty figure limped towards me, then pulled me to him in a close embrace.

'My ingenious spark, John Lockyer! Welcome, John, welcome! Tell me your news! Here I am in my brother Eliab's fine house, and no one comes.'

Harvey led me into a book-lined room, the shutters closed. A fire glowed at the room's far end and as my eyes got used to the dimness, I made out many sheets of paper in tall piles on the floor. But my eye was caught by something else. Lit by the glow of the fire was a young woman, her fair hair in a long plait.

Harvey saw my glance and said, *'King David was old*

and stricken in years, they sought for the king a young virgin; and the damsel was fair and cherished the king, but the king knew her not. My Shulamite, Letitia Herbert, John.'

Letitia smiled, and I could see how young she was—about fifteen with a clear gaze and gentle face. I bowed. 'John Lockyer at your service.'

'I know you were a beloved pupil of Master Harvey's Sir. He has often spoken of you and grieved that you are absent from him.'

I did not know how to respond to her frankness, but Harvey interrupted. 'Leticia dear child, John and I have a much to talk about—of old times before you were born. Ask Joshua to make us some coffee and leave us to our past.'

The girl stepped gently out of the room and the light seemed to dim.

'You are tired, John, I can hear it in your breathing.' Even in the dark, Harvey was sharply observant. 'The Army works you too hard at the Ely Hospital. Why won't you let me speak for you? A surgeon of your experience would be welcome at St Bartholomew's. From there you could build a practice—perhaps get married.' He chuckled.

'St Bartholomew's is still a nest of royalists, William. Only last week, a nurse was heard declaring she hoped General Fairfax's head would be spiked on London Bridge! She was fined of course.'

'Lucky to be only fined,' Harvey growled. 'The vicar at St Botolph's has been hung for saying that the King's beheading was a crime. Yet many people think so. You remember the great groan that went up the moment his head was cut off—it was heard all along the river.'

Who could forget? It had been a cold January day, the little King, upright and dignified.

'I go,' he had said, 'from a corruptible to an incorruptible crown and to a place where no disturbance can be.' Then the axe fell.

A terrible wind had swept the city, whipping the Thames into waves, breaking trees, as if all hell's witches were loose. At these memories—for we had witnessed the event—the mood between us darkened and we sat quietly.

Finally, Harvey spoke. 'John, what happened in Oxford? You joined the other side. You deserted your King, and you deserted me. You offered your skills to the rebels. Why?'

So, the moment had arrived, more quickly than I'd expected. Keep it simple, I thought. 'Oxford was chaos, William, you know that. The King and Queen lived in luxury; the wounded were lucky to have a bed in the stables. Every church, alms house and bridewell, overflowed with sick men! There was no food, no proper medicine. The streets were awash with filth, after each battle there would be cartloads of wounded. Typhus was everywhere. Many died needlessly.'

'The King had no money. Parliament controlled it all.'

'No money? He and the Queen lived in Christ Church, with fine wines and musical evenings—and could escape before Fairfax's army lifted the siege.'

I saw again the broken and dying men that had been left behind. Remembered the hell in which I'd worked and what I had done.

'When General Fairfax entered Oxford, he found only two other surgeons and me still working with hundreds of men too ill to move. He saw the plight of his own soldiers—Parliamentary prisoners in Oxford castle, starving and sick. Yet he took no revenge. He brought in another four surgeons—and nurses too. There was fresh food, clean sheets, medicines.'

'Yes, I had heard that,' Harvey admitted, 'but as his most trusted physician, I had to leave with the King. His care was my responsibility. I abandoned everything. You know the price I paid.'

I knew. A mob had looted Harvey's house in Ludgate and made a bonfire of his books and papers. Records of dissections, treatments, experiments, all destroyed. Harvey was now living on his brother's charity. He was crippled with gout and no longer able to earn. Although still regarded as a great scholar, he was also seen as a Royalist sympathiser, which meant his movements were watched by the agents of the new Republic.

I took a sip of the coffee Joshua had served. It was hot and bitter.

'William, death had conquered Oxford as surely as if the Four Horsemen had ridden through its streets. I could have left the city, fled abroad. But to where? You had already gone.'

'John, I sent you word—but the King's escape was secret. I could not risk…' Harvey's voice trailed off.

'The surgeons of the New Model Army gave me a chance William. They did not have me thrown into some foul cell. They said I was needed and asked me to work with them. I followed General Fairfax to London and Ely Hospital.'

'So, you saved your skin?' Harvey's words came out sharply.

'Yes, I suppose I did. And here I am. I swear everything

I ever learnt from you has been put to the task of mending what is broken in this country of ours.'

Harvey sighed deeply. 'Yes, it's broken. Was that the King's fault? He was not clever like his father. He loved his family with all his heart. The splendour was not for his pleasure—he simply believed music made men happy in the darkest times and that beauty on earth reflected God. He was the kindest man I have ever known.'

Also stubborn, arrogant, deceitful, and more than a little stupid I thought.

The flames in the fire flared and I saw the grief on Harvey's face. These recollections saddened us both; I had feared as much. To break the mood, I asked him to recount one of his favourite stories. 'Tell me about the princes. The King once entrusted them to you.'

Harvey smiled. 'Yes. At Edgehill. The King brought Charles and James to watch the battle and me to watch them. James is brave and stubborn. Charles is wiser—and wittier. We sheltered under a hedge until a musket ball whizzed past my head—and we scrambled higher up the hill! James was longing to be in the cavalry charge—he was only just nine! I had to stop him running away and he got into such a passion. "Our cavalry could smash the rebels easily," he cried. "Why don't we?"'

I knew the answer—I'd seen it many times. Prince Rupert's Royalist cavalry had ridden from the battle to be first in pillaging Parliament's baggage train. My memories of Edgehill were not like Harvey's. For me there was only the remorseless line of casualties, men torn by muskets and pikes, the enveloping smell of raw flesh and terebinth and the shouts and screams of men. I'd scraped at terrifying headwounds, stitched flaps of tattered skin and sliced through limbs at speed. In a brief respite I'd looked across the battlefield to see Rupert's soldiers already broaching their stolen barrels of beer. My leather apron was stiff and sodden with blood. My hands and arms were red and there had been no water to clean myself.

I pulled myself back to the present. I was here for a purpose.

'William, I need your advice. About poison.'

'Poison? As I learnt in Italy there are many poisons and many medicines. Often, they are one and the same. It is not my field, it's full of superstition—I leave it to the alchemists and wise women.'

'Could poison cause a bowel to be pouched and ulcerated?'

'Perhaps, but so could disease. That is why people use poisons, because they are so hard to detect. Used over time, they may not leave suspicious signs. It is an ideal weapon of murder, for poison can mimic another disease. Can you tell me more? Is this a recent case?' Harvey was giving me one of his piercing looks.

I should tell Harvey everything or nothing. But I feared for the old man. Harvey was watched constantly. Knowledge could put him in danger. So I decided to live with my uncertainty. In the matter of Lady Derryn I reasoned, poison is not proven. There was no doubt about the stab wounds, however.

Harvey had not stopped looking at me.

'John, what troublesome task have you undertaken?'

The door opened and Leticia came in, carrying a candle, which lighted her face and slim shoulders.

'Master William, it is nearly five of the clock. I have brought my drawings of the dog's heart for you to annotate.'

'Ah my dear child,' said Harvey, tenderly. 'See John, Leticia possesses a talent for drawing. I am teaching her to prepare anatomical specimens for engraving. Even now, her work is good enough for a printer to use.'

'Then I'll leave you to your work and go to mine.' I had already stayed too long. 'Goodbye Leticia. Goodbye old friend and master.' I pulled the burly little man into my arms and kissed his wrinkled cheek.

Harvey was animated again.

'God speed John! Is it true Cromwell is going to live like a king in the Palace of Hampton Court?' His laughter followed me through the gate.

The early evening sky darkened over St Pauls. A wind came up, blowing the sheets of manuscripts on sale in the printer's booths. A paper flapped around my feet; I picked it up.

'His Majesty in his Solitude and Sufferings,' I read. It was the title page of *Eikon Basilike*, said to have been written by the King just before execution. I scrunched the page and threw it away. The ball of paper landed at the feet of a man who leant down and picked it up. I recognised his blue coat and badly stained shoes.

It was only a mile back to Ely. The streets were crammed with carriages for hire; some had already lit their tapers. I needed to walk, to feel the nerves of the city, the energy of its people and the palpability of rumour that swept the streets like a busy wind. It had been a risk to visit Harvey. What if my old friend had refused to see me? Even the possibility made me feel desolate for of all men, Harvey meant the most to me. He had made my life possible.

I walked under the arch into the courtyard of Ely Hospital.

Mr Yorke, the duty surgeon passed me heading out. He looked angry.

'Doing favours for grandees Lockyer and ignoring the common men in your charge! Once a Royalist…'

That stung. I saw that Yorke was still carrying his bloodied smock and instruments. He must have worked late, I thought, guiltily.

Then another, sharper voice. 'Mr Lockyer! You have finally arrived! Where in the name of the Lord and his Mother have you been? You were supposed to be the main surgeon on duty today. We have had a new batch of casualties from Ireland. They are all complicated. And work is piling!'

She was tall, dressed in a soldier's cloak and boots. And she was furious.

Getting into a fight with her was the last thing I wanted. I held my hand up, palm outwards. 'Madame O'Brien, I apologise for my absence—it was unavoidable.'

'I've had to manage on my own—your assistant Thomas has gone God knows where. I have only two helpers, and the wards are full.'

'Again, I'm sorry. It was Parliament business.'

'Parliament indeed!' She laughed scornfully. 'What's that these days—a bunch of little squires who daren't say boo to the Army!' Her strong fingers dug into my arm. 'Come with me Mr Lockyer, I need you to see this. The night watchers will be here soon, but this must be settled before they arrive.'

I felt delayed exhaustion wash over me. In the yellow candlelight of the Grand Ward, I gazed at the rows of wounded men. Most slept, there were mutterings and soft cries. The air was heavy with charcoal fumigation.

'Through here.' At the end of the ward was a small room. A curtain hung in place of a door. Beyond I heard a man's voice, high and pleading like the fearful voices in my dreams but in an unknown language. '*Fola, Fola, Fola.*'

In the dark a man sat on the floor rocking. He had overturned his chamber pot and his rumpled sheets lay drenched and soiled. No charcoal could disguise the stench.

'He's been like this since he arrived this morning. His wounds have been cleaned, his fractured arm set but he is insensible to everything and repeats the same word continuously. He'll talk himself to death if we can't stop him.'

At the sound of her voice, the man started to wail.

'I fear I make him worse,' whispered Madame O'Brien. 'Would you agree to give him the strongest draught of the new mixture? It will put him to sleep. I think his body has sufficient strength.'

The new mixture was exactly that—an opium pill dissolved in wine, used sparingly because not all its effects were known. I felt impatient.

I snapped. 'Madame O'Brien you don't need me to decide—you know what to do—why haven't you? You should have quietened him already; the man is out of his wits and will disturb everyone. Tomorrow, we'll move him from this building and when his wounds are healed, if this babbling continues, I'll transfer him to Bedlam. Does what he says make sense? What is that word *fola*—do you know?'

'Yes, I know,' she replied calmly. 'It is Irish. It means

blood.'

Once she returned from the medicine store with the warm drugged wine, the soldier was quieter but still muttered his intense dialogue, punctuated with outbursts of weeping. I felt I could no longer keep awake, but one last effort was needed to get the man to drink the red sticky mixture. Finally, the night watchers arrived, and I could at last find my bed. I pushed open the chamber door and fell on my rough cot without bothering to remove my boots. Yet a thought nagged my tired brain. Something had been forgotten. But what?

Chapter 5

Friday September 14th, 1649, morning

The courtyard was wet from overnight rain. Now thick cloud lay over the city and the wind was loosening the leaves on the old ash tree by the Grand Ward. I shivered as I prepared for the day's work. Cromwell's Irish campaign, begun a month before, already brought its crop of wounded.

There was an iron gate in the courtyard wall into the hospital's herb garden. Beyond was the wild and muddy stretch of land Derryn Barlow had stumbled across the night she was stabbed. It was through that gate porters had carried her. The gate swung open. Hope-Anna came bustling through, followed by a fat black-haired man.

I had an urgent question for Hope-Anna, but she pulled the man towards me. 'Mr Lockyer—my husband, Jonas Tyler. Jonas is here about building the new sweathouse. He's already late—Jonas, hurry!' She pointed him in the right direction.

Jonas ambled off towards Aldridge's room.

Hope-Anna grinned.

'Sometimes he doesn't know if he's coming or going. But he is a good builder.'

'What news of the child, Hope-Anna?'

'The child is well John, settled with a healthy wet-nurse, Mistress Martindale at Chiswell Street. Do you know the place?'

I recalled a narrow street near the north-east gate, lined with poky houses.

'Most importantly, John, he has been baptised. When there is no parent, a midwife must see to that. Mr Barnes at St Giles gave the sacrament. I named him Edward.'

'Well done, Hope-Anna. I'll pay for his wet nurse for now, but I should seek out his relatives. Or take him to Christ's Hospital.'

A turn of fate to be sure, I thought.

'It was my old school.' Like all the orphans I had worn the uniform blue coat.

'Were you happy there?'

For a moment, I was back in the dark rooms of the old Grey Friars monastery. I'd sat on oak benches with other unruly boys to learn Latin and geometry. To each pupil, the governors donated woollen stockings. How they itched! Yes, I had been happy. A handy ability to repair anything, however broken, meant I was always popular.

'Your parents were dead? You had no family?'

'I suppose so. Yes.'

I never opened the door to the earliest part of my memory. Other doors I avoided because there was too much behind them, but this one I feared might open only to emptiness. Until I was seven, I believed Mr Whittier, the apothecary who brought me up, and Elizabeth his housekeeper, were my parents. But then I was told they had died long before. I lost my imagined parents and those whom I had never known existed, all at once. And the memory door stayed shut.

Hope-Anna touched my arm lightly. 'I am sorry indeed to hear of it, John.' I saw the compassion in her face.

'Well, I had a good guardian. I was one of the lucky ones. It was long ago. Ho, here comes Jonas. I'd better get on with work.'

Jonas was trotting alongside Colonel Aldridge. The Colonel carried a sheaf of papers rolled under his arm. The two were engaged in a vigorous discussion.

'It's the materials Colonel. It's a costly business a copper stove and all the brickwork. I can get them more cheaply than the army suppliers—but I will need the cash in advance.'

'We've got money coming in from the sequestrations,' Aldridge replied, 'but there are many calls on it by Parliament. Besides, the Army always pays in arrears. Ask any soldier.' Then the two went arguing towards the front gate.

I climbed the steps to the vaulted ward. Two women were removing sheets and piling them in a corner, collecting the spent candle stubs and emptying the chamber pots. One was Rose, Mrs Ellis' daughter.

'How is the man we had to drug to sleep last night? Is he quieter today?'

Rose shook her dark curls. Perhaps to show them to advantage, she wore no cap despite Madame O'Brien's rule.

'Oh Mr Lockyer, Sir, he's just the same, muttering and crying, shaking and saying words in that savage tongue. We don't know what to do. Dr French has suggested we drench him all over with cold water and then sprinkle him with hot. I think it's a waste of time Sir. But it's not for me to question Dr French.'

'I am no physician, just a simple surgeon. Is this the new water treatment?' Perhaps French was behind these plans for a sweathouse. This was a German fashion I had heard about that involved removing the body's defensive coating with water, opening the pores and then closing them again. It was a way of regulating bodily humours. I did not think much of it.

'I'll leave him to Dr French. Let me start on the men brought in this morning.'

I was doing what I knew best. I could see that treatment of the wounded in Dublin had been summary. One trooper's arm had been bound so the head of the bone was lodged in the armpit. The man could not move the limb and was hunched in pain. He needed a brutal intervention—fast. 'This will hurt, trooper.' He set his face and I called to the orderly, 'We'll have to use the coulstaffe—Thomas—where is Thomas?'

'He was here Mr Lockyer, but he's gone,' replied the orderly.

'Well run and get someone, will you?' I yelled, dragging the coulstaffe from the cupboard.

One assistant at each end held the long pole covered with a pad. Standing on a stool the trooper eased his dislocated arm over the pole. I grasped it.

'Ready?'

The man grinned weakly. 'As I'll ever be.' At a word from me the stool was kicked away as I hung on the arm and turned it. The man screamed as the bone slipped into place. His fellow-patients let out a chorus of cheers.

Fortunately, the other patients did not require me to exercise such strength.

One man's ulcerated leg was not healing. As I examined him, I saw the flesh was corrupted, flaking and full of yellow matter. It needed cleaning and dressing again.

'This time use the salve of rose-oil and turpentine,' I ordered. It was my recipe, and I was rather proud of it.

Things quietened. The soldiers had taken out their pipes and sat smoking, chatting, or playing cards. The morning's rainstorm cleared, and sun streamed through tall windows. I was getting ready to write up my notes when a high-pitched shriek shattered the peace. I ran towards the room where the weeping man lay, but the sound was not from there. More yells and cries followed and now it was clear a crowd was gathering in the yard and the noise came from outside. In the hubbub I heard my voice called and I rushed below.

A crowd of nurses and laundrywomen were supporting a screaming white-faced girl as Madame O'Brien and Colonel Aldridge hurried across the yard towards them.

'Mr Lockyer, Mr Lockyer help! In there!' shouted Mrs Ellis. She pointed to a large oak tub. This was the 'buck' where the dirtiest bedsheets were soaked in lye and beaten free of stains before being laundered. Sometimes the beater, taking care to lift her skirts and protect her feet, climbed in to stamp the soiled linen. I peered over the side of the tub into the filthy brown water. There, amid a yellowish tangle of sheets, I saw an arm. Picking up the laundry pole, I probed and pushed the mass of laundry. With a sudden squelch, the pole dislodged a small body, fully clothed. The crowd cried in horror.

'It's Sally Watts,' exclaimed Madame O'Brien, 'one of the laundry girls. She must have slipped and drowned!'

'Let's get this mess cleared up.' Colonel Aldridge was brisk. 'A couple of men can drain the tub and carry her into the crypt. You'd better oversee this Lockyer.' As I turned, I felt someone tug my arm.

'Mr Lockyer, I must tell you. This is my fault.' It was Rose Ellis. Her pretty face was tearful. 'Madame gave me the buck, as punishment she said for being lazy with the sheets. It's such a dirty job! So, I asked Sally if she'd do it for me and I said I'd pay her—she always needs money, you see. And now look.'

She dabbed at her eyes.

I had no time to console her. I had work to do.

Jonas Tyler's men put the girl's body in the crypt. Now, Hope-Anna stood by with a cloth and warm water. She had already sprinkled sawdust on the floor, busying herself to hide her shock.

'Hope-Anna there's no need for you to be here,' I said gently. 'I must examine her unwashed body.'

'But John,' Hope-Anna whispered, 'she was lying in filthy water full of lye.'

'That's so, the acid has eaten her skin. But the poor girl cannot feel anything now.'

Seeing her pitying look, I added, 'Come back later and prepare her for burial. Does she have family?'

'I don't know. She's only been here a few months. She comes from Mistress Cattell's laundry—most of the laundry girls are foundlings or orphans. A good worker, despite being so small.'

'Well perhaps Mistress Cattell—'

'I don't think so. She does well out of this hospital, but won't extend charity. It looks like a pauper's grave for Sally.' She turned and climbed the steps to the yard.

I folded the sheet that covered Sally's body. As Hope-Anna said, the girl was small—and thin. She looked about fourteen. I noticed her chest was slightly arched like that of a pigeon, so I checked her legs and found that the bones were curved inwards. Dr French had written about similar deformities in the bodies of poor children and young women. She had not been born like that. According to him, it was because of starvation.

I turned to examine the deep bruises on her face. Then I saw her feet. They were bruised and the lye had produced red blotches and bubbles in her skin, but what I noticed now was a line around both ankles as if made by a rope. And a raw wound revealed the big toe of her right foot was missing.

I checked her nostrils for signs of drowning. There was no froth, but that could have been wiped or washed away. I needed to open her fragile chest to see if her lungs were water sodden. If there was no water, she was no longer breathing when put in the tub. She had not fallen in by accident. But who had put her there? Was it the same person who had inflicted such violence upon the poor girl? I reached for my knife.

Sometime later, I climbed up from the crypt. The yard was empty and echoing. The ancient gate of the hospital was closed against the street and the porter was lighting his evening brazier, blowing on the red coals. I glimpsed a tall figure move from the shadows hands outstretched to the brazier's warmth. Before I could duck away Madame O'Brien came striding towards me.

'Have you news on the girl? She must have struck her head as she slipped—odd we couldn't find her pattens, the girls always wear them when treading the buck.'

My mind's eye flashed to the small, ruined body on the table below. No pattens. Hope-Anna removed the girl's brown linen dress and folded it on a ledge by the bench with her collar and chemise. Some unformed unease jigged at the edge of my memory.

I dismissed it because there was something more pressing. My inspection of Sally's lungs confirmed what I had suspected. She was dead when she went in the water.

I faced Madame. 'I have to speak first to Colonel Aldridge but be assured we'll have an answer.'

'I'm glad to hear it. The other laundry girls are reluctant to work now; they say there is something odd about her death. She was always careful.'

No point in letting rumour run riot. I changed the subject. 'I hear the madman was given the water treatment. Has he improved?'

Madame O'Brien lowered her voice. She sounded almost gentle. 'He is still disturbed, but he goes tomorrow to the care of someone I know near Blackfriars. Father Southworth feeds paupers and cares for the sick, especially those with disordered minds. Don't tell Colonel Aldridge, he won't approve.'

'I have seen men rendered speechless by slaughter, never one who raved like that.'

'The news from Ireland is that the soldiers have done terrible things. The man may have witnessed these horrors. Or taken part in them.' She gazed at me, but I could not read her expression. I looked away as shame and nausea swept over me.

I was back with Prince Rupert's forces, riding to relieve the siege of York and on the way taking the Parliamentary town of Bolton. We were jubilant, killing soldier and civilian indiscriminately, screaming and hollering through the streets to loot and rape. A year later under the blazing sun at Naseby, I picked my way amongst the freshly mutilated corpses of women, the wives and camp-followers of the defeated Royalist army. Many of Parliament's soldiers had mistaken their lilting Welsh voices for Irish and slaughtered them accordingly.

What saves me from memories and thoughts? Only work. It makes me feel like a man worthy of redemption. I decided to take another look at the madman wondering if I could unlock what drove him to his pitiful state, but my musings were interrupted by shrieks and laughter from the Great Ward. At that moment, the door flew open and a figure, naked and wet, raced down the steps. Sobbing and screaming, he threw himself at my feet. It was the madman. Some paces behind came three men, one was Aldridge, the others I did not recognise. I gently raised the man and slipped my cloak over his shaking body.

As I did, one stranger, wearing a preacher's cone hat, stepped forward and hissed into the man's face, 'Sinner, repent and pray! Your demons will quit you on hearing the Lord's words!' He raised his voice. 'Asmodeus, I command thee, leave this man! Begone accursed thing to burn in Gehenna!' The man cowered and wept as the preacher gripped him.

I was enraged. 'Let him go man!' I shoved the preacher hard in the chest knocking his hat away. 'Colonel Aldridge who is this? By what right does he interfere with the sick?'

The Colonel was almost speechless, but the words 'Special Army inspection' tumbled out. The shorter of the two strangers was a uniformed captain. To control myself as much as him, I held my patient for some moments until his sobs grew less. What ignorance! What stupidity! I was infuriated at the interference of these interlopers and turned to face the three men.

'This man isn't evil. He is not possessed! You have simply added to his injury. Take him back to the Grand Ward.' Madame O'Brien touched the man's arm lightly.

'Another draught of the new mixture, I think,' she said. She led the madman by the hand. He cringed as he passed his tormentors.

The preacher, hat restored, was already in a fury to match mine.

'Is this what you call a hospital? No space for the Lord, a place without prayer or preaching! Foulness of tobacco and ale present on every hand, each corner a nest of card-playing serpents! Doctoring by a turncoat and a woman who's a Papist! You make Devil's traps against these enfeebled men!'

Aldridge decided it was time to intervene. 'Peace Sir, a moment. Major Lockyer, may I introduce Captain Burrell and Preacher Barebon. They have a duty to inspect us without warning. They say we are ignoring the spiritual needs of our patients. There are no regular times for prayer and preachers have not been encouraged to visit.'

It is a foolish doctor who ignores God. As the great Paré said after the successful conclusion of a difficult case, *I dressed his wound, but God healed him.* So, despite my anger, I steadied myself. I noticed the preacher was sweating heavily and I caught the rank odour of unchanged linen. Cleanliness wasn't next to godliness in his case.

I took a breath. 'Patients are free to worship as they want, but this is a working hospital. Sickness and death do not keep to the clock.'

It was Burrell's turn. He gave a complacent smile. 'Our wounded soldiers should pray regularly in thanks for Parliament's generosity. We give them hospital care, bring them back to health and it costs them nothing! God's Providence has given us victory and they should remember that. There are many deficiencies here, but,' he coughed, 'I will give you time to reform. Colonel Aldridge I am watching Ely hospital. If these vices or absences of piety remain, I shall withhold funds or even close you down. I bid you good evening, Sir. Come, Barebon.'

And the two marched briskly to the main gate.

'What happened in there?' I asked, my eye on their retreating backs. From a distance, one tall and thin, one short and stout, they looked comical.

'Those interfering jackanapeses were in the Grand Ward, heard that poor man's cries and Barebon took it upon himself to pray over him.' Aldridge was frowning.

'They mean it, John, about closing us down. They have the power, although Burrell's nothing but a jumped-up brewer from Fore Street—I doubt if he's ever been in a battle. As for that fanatic Barebon! They'll be back but I can take care of that. But they must *not* discover what's been happening here or they will close us for sure. A murder, a fatal accident—'

'No Colonel,' I interrupted, 'perhaps two murders.' It was time to tell him.

'Sally was taken, tormented, and killed. Hiding her body among the soiled sheets in the wash tub was an attempt to make her death appear an accident.'

Colonel Aldridge sighed, looking troubled. 'Lockyer, I wish you had never taken in that dying woman; I know you had no choice, but it has entangled us with the city authorities and Earl Pembroke—a member of the Council of State. And now this—another brutal death! We do good work John, that's what's important. We must save that above all!'

My work at Ely meant everything to me. Yet I had taken the risk—Aldridge was right—because I had no choice even though I knew there would be consequences. With the same inevitability, I realised what I had to do next.

'Pembroke has tried to cover things up. He may know who killed these women. Perhaps there is a connection between the deaths, but the more we can discover ourselves the more we can be prepared for any threat to the hospital. Let me find out what I can.'

The Colonel clenched and unclenched his fist. Then nodded. 'Do it quickly and secretly. We cannot keep something like this quiet for long.'

The disturbing evidence revealed by Sally's body and the noisy confrontation in the yard triggered bad memories. These were not helped by knowing the threat to the hospital and my future. It was late evening, but I needed to clear my head.

I drew up a list of questions. I wanted to be methodical but realised I did not know where to start. Had Sally been killed at the hospital or dumped there? As for Lady Derryn Barlow, the hospital's involvement had been coincidental. Nevertheless, saving her baby meant I, Aldridge and others at the hospital who had helped might be accused of wrongdoing. Then there was the Earl of

Pembroke. What had he made of my report suggesting poisoning was an unproven possibility? I'd received no response but perhaps the Earl had not yet read it. Yet he had seemed so eager!

One thing I was sure was a lie—the tale that Algernon Sidney told with such an insouciant air—that Derryn Barlow had been stabbed to death by a group of vagrants whom he had executed. How convenient! Hero he might be, but a bad inventor of spur-of-the-moment falsehoods.

I crossed the yard and opened the side gate to the garden. Beyond ran the Fleet, its banks slippery with night soil slopped from the buckets emptied there. Any dry patches were occupied by the outcast human refuse of the city, who though poor and weak, could be dangerous in a pack. There were many there tonight; I could see the light of their meagre fires. A wind blew from the west. It was autumn equinox. I looked up and traced the outlines of the constellation of the Great Bear. Before the war, I had spent a year at the University of Padua. I looked through a powerful telescope there and was amazed at the thousands of stars. It was said there are many worlds beyond our own and I experienced a powerful wish to know more and understand. I gazed up at the blackness.

Then I realised I was not alone. I stopped and turned, hand on my dagger. The figure following behind stepped back. It was Rose Ellis. Her mouth opened in alarm as she saw the glint of my knife.

'Mr Lockyer Sir, it's me, Rose. I must speak to you. Everyone is saying you don't think Sally's death was accidental and—well—I heard something. It might be important.'

Her face in the moonlight was white and urgent.

'When? What?'

'Just after you'd left with that foreign man yesterday morning, Sally was talking to Thomas. They were standing beside the hole dug for the new boiler. He was angry with her and he shook her arm. I heard him say, "You'd better get it back or there'll be trouble. You're a thief".'

'What were they talking about?'

'I don't know Mr Lockyer. Thomas walked off then Sally saw me and ran. Later I asked her to do the buck for me and she said she would. I could see she'd been crying so I asked her what was wrong, and she was surly, not like her at all. And the next time I saw her—well you know, Sir.' Rose sobbed.

I sheathed my dagger and touched her gently on the shoulder.

'It was brave of you to follow me out here. Let me walk you back to the hospital. It's not safe for you to return alone. We can talk as we go. Tell me about Sally. Why do you think Thomas called her a thief? Was she?'

'She was poor, Sir,' said Rose. 'Easy to be virtuous when you've a full belly. But she was no worse than most. Sometimes they find a few coins in a dead man's pocket and keep 'em. Sometimes it's a scrap of lace or a torn shirt that won't be missed. But Mistress Cattell is strict. She searches her laundry girls and keeps what she finds.'

'Where is Mistress Cattell's laundry?'

'Turnmill Street, back of the old Hospitallers priory. They have their own well. Mistress Cattell lives by the laundry and she's building another house there. It's all brick and stone, they say. She's got plenty of money but pays next to nothing. Sally and the other girls sleep in a loft above the tubs.'

We had reached the hospital gate. I nodded to the porter, who winked at me.

'Goodnight Rose. Thank you for telling me about Sally.'

'Mr Lockyer, Sir. I hope I have done right. I'll do anything to help you and that poor girl.' She smiled and looked straight at me, brushing a hand against her cheek so her hood fell back to show her loosened hair. I stood still, returning her gaze for several heartbeats. Then the moment was gone. She turned to the dormitories of the old palace.

The moon had clouded, leaving the courtyard without light. I thought I saw a shape move in the shelter of the main doorway. It dissolved into the darkness.

I called out, 'Who's there?' There was no reply. I'm seeing things, I thought. I need some sleep.

Chapter 6

Saturday September 15th morning

The watery sunrise to which I'd awoken had darkened with scudding black clouds once I dressed. I sighed, bundled my hair under my hat and reached for my soldiers' cloak. The rain was already glistening on the courtyard flags below and I wondered if I should set a flask and catch some of it. The chemical followers of Paracelsus, noisy newcomers in the medical marketplace, argued that equinoctial rain contained minute traces of meteors and planetary dust, and therefore had special powers. Perhaps I should ask Aldridge to let me have one of the outhouses for experiments. Then I stopped dreaming and remembered my mission.

As I hurried downstairs, I made a sketchy plan of investigation. Apart from Rose I had not spoken to anyone else about Sally. Talking to all the staff was a large task, I would need help. But who could I trust?

Reluctantly, I thought of Madame O'Brien. We had arrived at the hospital at about the same time. As was fitting I had kept my distance from her and all I knew was that like most women employed there, she was a war widow. Her husband had been a professional soldier. She had followed him to the wars, so she was courageous and resourceful. As a colleague she was neither pleasant nor unpleasant, but perhaps a little chilly. As far as the men in our care were concerned, my amputations were reputed the fastest and cleanest, while Madame far excelled me in the fine art of bone-setting.

As if I had conjured her up, Madame O'Brien strode towards me, her army coat flapping against her long legs. I smiled a greeting but got none in return. 'Mr Lockyer, a word please. Not here.' She nodded towards the doorway. Her voice, usually modulated, was sharp and for the first time I heard the trace of an accent.

'Madame O'Brien, what is it? I'm supposed to be going out this morning on hospital business.'

'Hospital, is it? There might not be one here when you return! I know what those men said yesterday evening, the threats they made against all of us. Yet later the same evening, you deliberately follow your own foolish desires. You could get us closed for immorality!'

'What do you mean, Madame?'

'I mean you and that young whore Rose Ellis. I saw you come back with her last night.'

'No, but she followed me, she said she had something to tell me…' I was completely thrown off balance by her ferocity.

'Ha! I don't doubt it! You should know Lockyer she has had something to "tell" most of the men around here. If it weren't for her mother, who's a great worker, and her sister, who is a poor simpleton, I'd send her off. She's lazy and a liar and because she's pretty she thinks the world owes her something. She beguiles the men in this hospital including you.' Her face was flushed.

She was mistaken, but she made me feel

uncomfortable so although I thought it demeaning to cross swords with a woman, I wanted to annoy her.

'Rose is very handsome. It's no surprise that the men here admire her. The world likes beautiful women—what's wrong with that? Whatever attributes a woman has, beauty is the most obvious and likely to succeed.'

She gave me a freezing look. 'In the world of men, perhaps.' She looked disappointed. Why couldn't she mind her own business?

I was about to make a sharp reply but remembered I needed her help. 'There was no wrongful behaviour on my part last night—be sure of it.'

'Surgeon-major your conscience is your own, but we are on notice at this hospital and anything that jeopardises its survival is my concern.'

Hoping to pacify her, I nodded. 'You're right Madame. After the Army Inspection we must be careful. They'll be back for sure and before they do Colonel Aldridge has ordered me to find out what I can about Sally's death.'

'Then the rumours are true—she did not die by accident?'

'There's evidence she was harmed and then hidden in the laundry tub.'

'God have mercy on her! There are beggars, thieves and wantons running all over the city, but she was just a poor wash-girl, who'd want to kill her?'

'Madame, that's what I want to discover. Will you help me? Perhaps you could talk to everyone here and see what they know—when they last saw Sally, and if anyone wished her harm. I think she was killed the night before last or early yesterday morning. But whoever killed her had kept her prisoner for some time. Ask if anyone noticed anything in the storehouses, things having been moved, traces of disturbance.'

Madame frowned. 'Surgeon-major, of course, I'll help. I shall speak to the patients as well—they know that something happened. Some sit out in the yard. Who knows what they see?'

'Good. I'll visit the laundry to speak to Mistress Cattell.'

'Rather you than me, she is a close woman. Sharp witted—believe me Mr Lockyer, you'd have to rise early to get the better of her.'

'Thanks for the warning, Madame,' I replied, thinking, *she's not the only one*.

It was raining heavily now, but I had to go to Turnmill Street. I went back to the crypt to collect Sally's scraps of clothes to return to her relatives. Sally's body still lay on the long oak table but covered now. Hope-Anna had shrouded her in a linen sack.

As I looked at the small pile of poor garments, I realised what had been nagging at my thoughts. The other corpse. Where were Lady Derryn Barlow's clothes? In my mind's eye there appeared an image of a fine silk dress, torn and heavily blood-stained. I had been obliged to slice through the delicate fabric, tearing the dress. Afterwards, Thomas had followed my instructions and shrouded Derryn Barlow's body. At Baynard's Castle she had been dressed in a brown linen shift beneath the shroud. That detail had escaped me. So where was her dress and where was Thomas now? I needed to talk to him.

I picked up the remnants of Sally's clothing and rolled them into a ball. They fitted easily into my pocket.

Heading for the back gate, I followed the brick path

though the vegetable garden and came out on the muddy wasteland again. I trudged past a man and woman, who ignoring the rain, sat patiently by a small brook, fishing for eels. Like me, I thought—fishing, not sure what I can catch. But I must catch something and soon, or we'll all be finished.

As I tramped across Cow Bridge, I had a good view of the priory of St John of Jerusalem. Four hundred years ago it housed Knights Hospitallers heading for the Crusades. What had been in men's minds when so much of the nation's wealth and blood had been spent on far-away campaigns? It was claimed to be the defence of the Holy Places sacred to Christianity, but also the trade routes and rich pickings of the Mediterranean for the Pope. How foolish that seemed now, the Knights long defeated by the Moslem Turks. Adventurers seeking fame and wealth were no longer looking east, but towards the great continent which lay westward, spanning half the world.

Turnmill Street topped the slope above the Fleet. I saw a plume of steam curling into the air from a wide-open door. I looked at what had once been the nave of a chapel. A great iron pump stood in place of the font, surrounded by wooden tubs. About twenty women and girls, some little more than children, scrubbed and folded linen and I could not fail to notice that most were stripped to the waist. The noise of crackling fires and the shouts of the women were loud enough to be heard outside. Fascinated, I continued gazing at their bent backs and unceasing repetitive movement, until I was startled by a voice.

'Stop your ogling Sir! These are working women, not a peepshow! What's your purpose here?'

I turned and saw a blonde in an expensive grey silk

dress. Her high heeled leather boots were unmarked by the muddy street. She looked as if she had just stepped out of a carriage.

Embarrassed, I bowed. 'Surgeon-major John Lockyer, Madam—of Ely Hospital.'

She frowned. 'Ely Hospital? Is there something wrong? It's only a week since Madame O'Brien renewed our contract. As I explained, the costs of wood and soap have soared. Thankfully, that charming Colonel Aldridge agreed with me. I hope you are not here to question the account.'

Mistress Cattell was a fine and handsome lady—not at all the grasping harridan I had expected from Madame's description.

'It is not about the contract, but one of your workers, Sally Watts. I am afraid she has been drowned. Burial—'

'Dead? Drowned? How? Well, let me tell you I'll expect repayment. She was one of my best workers. What do you want?' Her voice was sharp, and I was quickly revising my first impression. Don't tell her anything, I decided.

'I have come to enquire about her relations and to talk to any friends.'

'Friends? There's not much time in laundry work for making friends. As to relations, she was a foundling, she and her older sister.'

'A sister! Working here?'

'Here, no. But nearby.' Mistress Cattell hesitated. 'She's at Mistress Graham's establishment in Whitecross Street. Just ask. Now—'

Suddenly she was in a hurry. 'Sally's back wages. How may I obtain them?'

'The hospital will hold a portion to cover funeral expenses.' It was normal.

Mistress Cattell's voice rose a pitch 'What? I think not! That was that Papist witch O'Brien's idea, wasn't it—the hussy! I want what's mine!' The pretty features were pink with anger.

'Madam, you will get what is due to you,' I answered mildly and bowed again, more deeply this time, then looked at her and smiled. I hoped this would have the required effect.

Her face changed. She smiled back and her voice softened. 'I'm sure a gentleman like you Major Lockyer, will ensure I do not suffer injustice. You are obviously used to dealing with ladies. Should I need a surgeon perhaps I could call on you.' She leaned towards me and from her body came a warm scent of roses. I smiled a farewell and turned towards Whitecross Street.

Clerkenwell Road was busy, with overladen carts creaking towards the City gate. The rain had stopped and there were crowds walking purposefully or dawdling, while many stood in animated groups reading the black-print wall posters. One with the ink still gleaming fresh, caught my eye.

'*Where is that liberty that is so much pretended, so dearly purchased? Reade ENGLANDS NEW CHAINES DISCOVERED by Mr John LILBURNE.*' In the swarm of people someone pushed a leaflet into my hand. I read, '*We have not bowed down to the prophets of BAAL! ANNA TRAPNEL, moved by the Spirit will preach this NOON at ST PAUL'S near the Churchyard.*' Asking for trouble, I thought. The pamphleteer was busy pressing her papers on anyone who would have them, and the crowd were snatching eagerly. I glanced down at her.

'Leticia! What are you doing here?'

She grinned. 'Dr Harvey may be as wise as King David, but he doesn't own the Shulamite, Mr Lockyer. Please don't say you've seen me. He would be worried.'

'He is right Leticia. This woman preacher will certainly be the cause of a disturbance. Be careful, apprentices roam the City and will knock her down and prevent her speaking.'

'The Kingdom of Saints is coming, Mr Lockyer, I want that future! I am protected by the love of Our Lord—don't fear for me.' Laughing, she turned and disappeared into the crush of people.

It is my good fortune to be tall—useful in crowds. I scanned the mass of people, but she was gone. Since the events at Baynard's Castle I was alert, but I saw nothing suspicious in the sea of folk who wanted to keep up with the latest news or be about their business. Mine was to find Sally's sister and Mrs Grahame's establishment.

Aldersgate was a busy street that sliced through an ugly part of town occupied by the dirty trades. I was passing the tannery from which Ely Hospital made a tidy income by selling the contents of its chamber pots to the leatherworkers and skinners who softened hides by soaking them in the mess. The porters supplemented their wages by conveying the fetid mix. The stench floated over Aldersgate, but as I rounded the corner into Whitecross Street, I was hit by a stink that made even my surgeon's stomach heave. Beside a shop lay a mound of dead dogs, carcasses glittering with flies. They would soon be butchered to supply hawk's meat for when London's wealthy went hunting. These oozing sacks were headed for the forests of Enfield Chase, where it was said, General Cromwell loved to ride. The yard was ankle deep in blood and dogs' guts that ran into the common drain at the side of the road.

I swerved hoping to avoid the mess, for my thoughts were on Sally and her sister. How close were they? According to Rose, Sally had argued with Thomas about something Sally had taken. Would her sister know anything about it?

Mrs Grahame's house was towards the south end of the street, where pavements were cleaner. It was large, gabled, and timbered, several stories high with freshly painted woodwork. Behind half-shutters, all the windows were heavily curtained. The big oak door was firmly closed. I hammered on it with the hilt of my dagger.

A small grille rasped, and I stared into a pair of unfriendly eyes.

'Surgeon-major Lockyer, Ely Hospital. I want to see Mistress Grahame.'

'No one has sent for a surgeon. There's no sickness in this house. Mistress Grahame is not here.'

'Then I wish to speak to a girl called…' I realised I didn't know the sister's name, 'er… Watts.'

'Finny Watts? Not available! Go away! No one comes in here without an introduction from a known gentleman. Go and sling your hook in the Fleet and be damned!' The grille slammed.

Well, she's called Finny and she lives here. That's something. I knew such houses had several exits to ensure that clients would not meet each other. At the rear was a long garden and an enclosed walkway. It probably led to a back gate near to Aldersgate Street. There, likely, a row of coaches waited for hire.

Another door opened. The stocky figure who emerged was familiar. The man recognised me too and made as if to run but I blocked his escape.

'Good day Captain Burrell. I see you are overseeing the spiritual needs of this house.'

Burrell looked embarrassed, but quickly recovered himself. 'And what of you Surgeon-major, what is your business here?'

'Purely professional, Captain. There are five in there with the pox. Did no one tell you?'

With a curse, Burrell twisted from my grip and fled towards the walkway. The door stood open. I walked in.

There was no one about, although for a moment I thought I heard children's voices. I stepped across a spotless floor, tiled black and white in the Dutch fashion. The air smelt of cedar. I looked above me. Light poured through a transparent dome of blue and green glass making me feel as if I was underwater. This was no common brothel.

The passage was also lit at the far end by a window above the front entrance. From where I stood, I saw a polished ladder propped against the door. Next to it sat the guardian who had spoken so roughly. I saw that despite his adult head, he was no taller than a six-year-old child.

I heard a latch click open behind me.

At the same moment, the little man hurled himself at me with surprising force, whacking me across the shin with a spiked club. I winced and yelling, reached down to throw my attacker as far as I could. Blood trickled from my leg. The little man scrambled to his feet and raised his club again. I grabbed his arm.

'Peace, Dicky, let's find out who he is. You look like a gentleman Sir. Why does a gentleman break in and sneak around my house?'

I turned to look at the speaker. I could not believe what I saw.

Chapter 7

Saturday September 15th late morning

It was Mistress Cattell.

And yet... it was *not* her. This woman was taller, dressed for the outdoors in a high-crowned hat. Pearls glowed in her ears and around her neck. Her skin was not rosy like Cattell's but powdered white with ceruse. Resemblance to the pretty laundry-mistress was unmistakeable, but in this woman the same features formed a strong handsome face.

'Mistress Grahame?'

'You ask me? I should ask who you are, Sir!'

'He slipped in here Mistress, came around the back.' Dicky was enraged. 'I told you to go away, Sir!' I decided to act the gentleman and bowed.

'Madam, Surgeon-major John Lockyer of Ely Hospital. Late of Colonel Fairfax's regiment.' She relaxed a little and unwound her bright silk scarf.

'I am glad to meet any hero of our Parliamentary forces, Sir. Our Finny's fame must have spread to your hearing—in which case I am not surprised at your visit.'

'Mistress Grahame I am not here as a client. Finny's sister Sally was found dead yesterday at Ely Hospital.'

I noted her shock. And something else—fear. She put

a gloved hand to her mouth. 'Dead? How?'

'We found her in a washtub—apparently drowned.'

'You do mean Sally don't you—the plain one? Poor girl.'

'You know her?'

'London is full of stray children Mr Lockyer, in case you hadn't noticed. My sister and I try to assist. I take the pretty ones and she takes the others. Sally was undersized and plain, so she went to the laundry. I kept the older one, Finny.'

'Mistress Cattell is your sister?'

'I see you've met. The parish authorities think highly of her. By the way, Finny's beginning to make a good living for herself.'

'Is that what you call it? Working here?'

Mistress Grahame was indignant. I was reminded instantly of her sister. 'I do indeed Sir. Don't act the Puritan with me! This is a whorehouse of the Republic! Everyone—army officers, Justices of the Peace, even preachers come here. Some of our gentlemen are great lords of State. They pay good money. A wise girl can save enough to make her way. It's well for people with lands and titles to preach to us, but I believe everyone deserves a chance in this world.'

Even a whore-mistress preaches politics these days, I thought.

'I'd like to speak to Finny.'

Dicky shook his head. 'No. She's upstairs asleep. We don't disturb our girls.' He smirked.

'Has she had any visitors recently?'

'Day before yesterday, her sister Sally arrived with a parcel. Finny said it was a present. Later that day Finny had to prepare for… an entertainment.'

'Entertainment?'

Mistress Grahame smiled.

'Finny is good at dressing up. She poses as the Cavalier Count of Finsbury—that's why we call her Finny, not her real name. The gentlemen enact a scene with her. It's popular with Parliament's army officers.'

No doubt, I thought. I tried and failed to stop myself imagining it. 'Did Finny perform this entertainment?'

'She did. There were four gentlemen in the room wagering against each other. And no, I will not say who. But I will say one was very sweet on Finny, he'd already had her the previous two nights in a row—for the whole night!'

That must have cost him, by the look of Mistress Grahame's lace and velvet gown, I thought.

'It is important I speak to Finny. Her sister's death was… well—unusual.'

'How do you mean—unusual?' she said sharply.

'I simply mean that whilst we are used to deaths of sick patients, when something happens to a healthy young woman—'

'I see. Very well, Dicky—go rouse Finny.' As he stumped upstairs, she added, 'Dicky keeps better watch than a flock of geese.' There was a noise and a moment later Dicky came down again as fast as his short legs allowed.

'She's not there, Mistress,' he gasped. 'How did she get past me? She must have gone out the back and down the walkway.'

Mistress Grahame looked concerned and seemed uncertain.

'Is it usual for one of your girls to leave suddenly?'

She managed a laugh.

'Not if they know what's good for them! But I can't chain them here—and with a free spirit like Finny who knows her worth... she could have gone anywhere. Perhaps that gentleman who is taken with her asked her to go with him. She'll be back.'

'That's right,' Dicky chipped in. 'She may have felt like a break in the routine. Being Count of Finsbury can get a bit rough.' He grinned and shook his little cudgel. Mistress Grahame frowned at him.

'Do you think I might speak to Finny's sleeping companions?'

'They told me they didn't know she'd gone.' Dicky grunted, scowling.

'I see you run a careful establishment—but the sister of a dead girl is missing from here. It begins to look odd.' I could sense her resistance, but I was determined to press on. 'It could merit an inquiry from the justices or the Army.'

She smiled benevolently. 'Clearly we must help you Sir.' Her voice was soft and sweet. 'Dicky, bring Humility and Charity down. Perhaps a glass of something Sir, whilst we wait?'

I shook my head and she moved closer. I noticed a pulse beating in her neck.

'They will be disappointed that you do not see them at their best. I only have beautiful girls here.'

She speaks the truth about that at least, I thought. Humility and Charity, despite their undressed hair and sleepy appearance, were lovely young women. They looked at me with wide beautiful eyes and almost in unison shook their glossy heads in answer to my questions. They had seen nothing, heard nothing. Humility gave an elegant yawn which was mirrored by one from Charity.

'Sir it is as I say. Finny has gone. It's quite a surprise but—she's that sort of girl! I do not fear for her—I imagine she will be back soon perhaps with some adventure to entertain us! Go on girls, the gentleman has done with you.'

I heard relief in her laugh. They turned in a flutter of white muslin. I watched, fascinated as Humility's smooth legs vanished at the top of stairs but I was not so spell bound as to miss the whisper she gave her companion…

Mistress Grahame began to follow, but I stopped her. 'Mistress Grahame?'

She turned, frowning. 'Did any customer mention the stabbing of a young woman not far from here?'

'A stabbing? Was there? I've heard nothing—gentlemen who come here only want to talk of pleasant things. I'm sure you understand that. We don't discuss the outside world.' She turned away.

'I have a few belongings of Sally's. Perhaps you would give them to Finny when she arrives.' I handed over Sally's poor rags. To my surprise she handled them gently, then took a small key from her belt and opened a cupboard by the stairwell.

'Thank you, Sir. Our girls don't have many possessions. I will put them with Finny's present.'

'That package Sally brought—might I see it?' She hesitated. 'Perhaps there's a clue as to where she's gone.'

Mrs Grahame pursed her lips then handed me a torn parcel. It was roughly wrapped in discarded order sheets from Ely Hospital. I even glimpsed my own handwriting.

The package was soft and light. I had to know what it held.

'Mrs Grahame, this could contain something stolen from Ely Hospital,' I said.

Alarmed, she pushed it away.

'Then take it Sir! I want nothing that should not rightfully be here. I don't tolerate that! Take it away now!'

Then another surprise: she pressed a silver coin into my hand.

'I suppose there will be a funeral to pay for?' Before I could reply she was gone.

Then Dicky grabbed my arm and was steering me to the back door. For a second time, I thought I heard children's voices, from far away beneath my feet.

'Who lives here?'

'That's for me to know and you to find out Mr Lockyer. This is a prudent establishment. I don't allow rascals here! Finny's going like that—a little unusual. But then—so was your admission!' The little man chuckled. 'You may consider yourself introduced to us.'

'Yes, and I've got a nasty wound on my shin to prove it.'

Dicky laughed again. 'Sorry Sir, but it is my duty to defend the house. Feel free to visit us again. Take the walkway, now Sir—lose yourself in the crowd!'

I suppose you say that to all the clientele, I thought. At the end of the walkway was a wooden door that gave out into a narrow passageway. Beyond lay the light and bustle of Aldersgate. I looked out over the long garden and saw a movement in the thick box-tree hedge. The hedge moved again. A bulky figure was crouching, trying to hide. There was no mistaking him.

'Well Thomas, at last! Where have you been? What are you doing here?'

For some reason, it's more pathetic when a big man looks hungry and woebegone. 'Sorry Mr Lockyer, I… I haven't eaten since yesterday, Sir.' I gripped his arm and we crossed the street, heading to The Bull.

'Some rabbit pie will help. How long were you hiding there?' In my experience people were more inclined to confidences when their bellies were full.

'Two nights, Sir, I was watching for Finny. Seeing people come and go. And keeping out of the way of that dwarf.'

I felt a twinge in my wounded leg. 'He is a fierce one is he not?'

Thomas looked serious. 'He is no joke Sir. The other night he was seeing someone off—a fellow big as me, with a cloak as dark as the street. "Mistress says you are to get gone my Lord," he said. "You've been here three nights already. This ain't a lodging house." And he threatened him, Sir—with his club. The man left quick, I can tell you.'

We stepped in Aldersgate Street and felt the dense crush of people. It was unusual, even for the busy route to the North. I tightened my hold on Thomas. Across the road I could see Gibbons, the innkeeper of The Bull, bawling for the doors to the courtyard to be pulled shut. I called to him to wait, but my shout was drowned by drumbeats. There were shrieks and cries of women and a musket was fired. Across Aldersgate Street ranks of London militia, flanked by drummers, blocked the way. Advancing towards them, arms linked, came a line of women, singing. The street was full of people but the space between the women and the militia was empty. The drums beat a tattoo and the militia advanced a pace. The women kept coming, singing as they walked.

'Christ's Spirit is our Truth, we cannot change.
All bloody principles, all strife and weapons
This world doth disarrange.
And thus we testify.
All wars we do deny.
A new Heaven, a new Earth
Will show Our Lord's high worth.'

'Get you home, whores, and do your dishes,' yelled a burly black-haired man next to me. The crowd agreed with howls and insults drowning out the women's song. The drums rolled and the militia advanced again. The line of women had almost reached the ranks of men and their singing increased in volume. I looked at them and to my horror saw Leticia, her cap gone and blood on her cheek.

'Leticia!' I shouted but she was singing her heart out, her eyes shining, and she did not hear me. An order was given, and the front row of men parted to reveal a second row with muskets raised.

'For God's sake, there will be slaughter,' I shouted. I knew that crowds like this could turn in an instant. 'Put up your weapons! Captain—'

I called to the officer in charge, 'Don't make war on women!'

'They aren't women, they're ranting Jezebels,' called a voice and again the chorus of insults swelled. The women and men were now within an arms' length of each other. The crowd fell silent, and the women stopped singing. Their leader, a tall white-haired woman stepped forward and spoke to the militia men.

'Put down your weapons brothers; be moved by the

glory of the Spirit. Join us to make an end to all wars.' The officer was quick to stand between them, his expression between fury and disgust. 'Disperse now, or you will all be arrested and taken to the House of Correction!'

'We have done nothing wrong,' the woman replied. 'We were speaking freely about the Lord and singing his praises, when we were attacked.'

'You are giving out seditious documents—'

'Prayers. Just prayers, brother.'

'Round these women up,' shouted the officer. Militiamen started to close in on the front row and I saw one, laughing, pull Leticia by the hair and grab at her breast. She landed a heavy slap to his face, and he roared with rage. I leapt forward to push through the line and as I did, felt Thomas twist from my grip and vanish into the crowd.

I shouted over the mob, 'Captain, I am Major Lockyer of General Fairfax's regiment.'

The man turned a red heavy face on me. He was not a seasoned soldier.

'Cromwell and Fairfax are Army. The London militia and takes no orders from their sort!' he grunted.

I was desperate. 'That young woman there is my niece.' I pointed to Leticia, who was yelling with anger, aiming blows and kicks at the startled militiamen.

'That little virago! You're welcome! You should keep your womenfolk under better control!' he snarled. 'Go on—take her!'

Leticia looked at me and shook her head. I grabbed her arm and muttered, 'I can see you are having fun Leticia, but this will get ugly. If you don't think of yourself, think of Dr Harvey. You are already hurt—that cut needs attention.'

'I won't go with you!' Leticia hissed, but her words were drowned by shouts of alarm. The crowd parted as a group of mounted dragoons galloped down Aldersgate Street, scattering onlookers, women and militia. Everyone ran as carbine-toting soldiers charged.

As I pulled Leticia, still protesting, inside the courtyard doors of The Bull, I looked for Thomas in the fleeing mob, but all I could see were mounted troopers dispersing the crowd with blows. A fight had broken out between the Army's Red Company and the militia. I could hear loud shouts and cries, whinnying horses, the clatter of running feet and pistol shots. In the melee, Thomas was gone.

'Mr Gibbons,' I shouted, 'there's someone hurt. I need warm water, witch-hazel—and a plaister from your store-cupboard.'

Leticia's face was dirty and bloodied. She looked furious. 'Why did you make me come away?'

I was angry in turn. 'Have you lost your wits young woman? You were within moments of being dragged off—'

'So you dragged me in here instead?'

'—and locked up in Bridewell, which I assure you would be no place for you to relish. Now let me see that cut of yours.'

Pulling off my neckcloth, I lightly bathed her face, wiping the dirt and blood.

'How did you get this Leticia?'

'One of the apprentices threw a stone at me and called me Satan's whore.'

The missile had narrowly missed her eye.

'Thank goodness it doesn't need stitching—there now.'

Gently I laid the silk dressing over the cut. The child was full of apocalyptic fire but had little knowledge of life on the streets, I thought. Nor what being confined in Bridewell entailed.

'You are going to have swelling and a bruise lasting a week. There will be a small scar, I fear.'

'I shall be proud to show it. Tell me Mr Lockyer, why may a woman not preach and pray in a public place? Why must she keep silent? Why is this war being fought if not for freedom? They say that just where we stood there was a temple to a goddess in the old days.'

'Leticia, that was a pagan temple.'

'Well, you and Dr Harvey follow the pagans do you not? Aristotle? Galen? They were not ignoramuses I think?'

First politics with a whore-mistress, now religious philosophy with a girl, I thought. What times these are—only a corpse could fail to feel the excitement of new freedoms, the sharpening of minds and the chance of new ways of imagining the world!

Mr Gibbons the innkeeper bustled over. 'Mr Lockyer that was a fierce to do! Riots are bad for custom! Have a bite to eat Sir, after all the upset.'

He brought me back to earth. The thyme and pigeon pie at The Bull was famous. But there was something more urgent. I needed Thomas to explain an argument with a laundry-maid who was later found dead.

I cursed myself for allowing Thomas to escape, but what could I have done?

Outside the courtyard of The Bull, Aldersgate was empty, littered with handbills and horse-droppings. I hailed a carriage, paid the driver, and instructed him to convey Leticia to Master Eliab Harvey's house in St Laurence Hill.

'You should tell Doctor Harvey what has happened. He will look to you and make sure all is healed.'

'Mr Lockyer, perhaps he might be angry with me.' She squared her shoulders and lifted her head boldly displaying her patched face. 'I'll tell him what I was doing and why. It was for our right as women to speak and worship, but,' she hesitated, 'I couldn't bear for him to send me back.'

'Leticia, you are like a daughter to him. Send you back where?'

'Why, Mistress Grahame's of course.'

Chapter 8

Saturday September 15th early afternoon.

Once alone I realised the riot was a symptom of widespread unrest, particularly the febrile nature of London. The worst threats to the city had passed with the victory at Naseby but there was much uncertainty. Everyone was watchful; fears of plots and conspiracies abounded aided by rumours in gossip and print. Pamphlets were snapped up almost before the ink was dry with a public greedy for news and direction. It would not be long before the Army or some other authority decided to look more closely at Ely and at me. And with my history how could I avoid suspicion? I returned to the pressing questions about Lady Derryn. Thomas knew something about Sally's death, I was certain. Now her sister Finny had gone missing. Had she left Whitecross Street as I'd been told? I reflected on Mistress Grahame's equivocations, and her eagerness to be rid of me. I held the package that Sally had given Finny. Perhaps it contained information that would help. And what was Letitia's connection to Mistress Grahame's? That news had shocked me.

Perhaps Madame O'Brien's inquiries had found something. I decided to get back to Ely. Across Aldersgate lay Little Britain and St Bartholomew's Hospital. I passed the great gates and remembered what Harvey had said about finding me a post at the place where he, the King's Physician, held a senior position. The hospital had many charitable cases. Most of its physicians and surgeons also had a thriving practice in the treatment of the 'foul disease' for there was a fortune to be made offering care in secret to such patients. The treatment, which involved daily inhalations of mercury, while salivating and sweating in a hot box, was unpleasant. I did not want to waste precious time supervising it. Harvey had taught me a better way when he hired me, a penniless student with an unfinished Oxford education, as his anatomy demonstrator. He marked my skill in dissection and helped me to go to Padua to learn more, then follow him to Oxford and collect my delayed MD degree. Then came the war, the Army and the best training any surgeon could have.

But I was damaged and my defection to Parliament threatened my friendship with Harvey who had done so much for me. Anyway, St Bartholomew's was strongly Royalist. Even in defeat, I doubted if the governors would welcome me.

And I had a dependent, the dead woman's child Edward. This was something new for I had no kin. When I left for Oxford, the money Mr Whittier bequeathed for my 'gentleman's' education ran out. I was forced to return to London in the hope of getting an apprenticeship with one of Whittier's old colleagues. Harvey, with his merry laugh open heart and bright intellect saved me.

Everything brought loss and gain, but they are not always in balance. I lost parents I did not know I had but found Dr Harvey. I turned from the King and lost Harvey but found a new career. I found Leticia, but lost Thomas. And if I find Thomas again, what will I lose?

These thoughts preoccupied me so much I almost failed to notice I had arrived at the gate of Ely Hospital. As I passed the gatehouse something made me turn to see a man in a long blue coat, who then vanished into the shadows.

Madame O'Brien looked exhausted. Rather than standing rod straight as she usually did, she was sitting in a chair. On a table beside her a small candle illuminated sheets of ruled paper.

'Mr Lockyer, I hope your day went well because the task you set me took up most of mine. Several people heard the quarrel between Thomas and Sally so that supports what the Ellis girl told you. Apart from that no one heard or saw anything unusual, and no strangers came into the hospital.'

'Where were they on Thursday night or early Friday? Did you establish that?'

She looked at me sourly. I was getting used to it.

'Of course, everyone is accounted for. Nothing stood out. I feel that time has been wasted. I took some notes—here—'

The papers were divided into columns detailing shift times, duties and remarks. Her writing was clear and firm.

'Except for Sally,' said Madame O'Brien, 'only two people were unaccounted for in the hospital late that night—the two of us.'

And her killer.

'Madame, I have seen Thomas.'

'Thomas! You found him? What happened?'

'I don't know; he disappeared again before I had time to talk to him. There was near riot in Aldersgate, and I lost him. But I do believe he knows something about Sally's death.'

'Do you think he killed her?'

'No,' I replied. 'He's been in hiding and he's frightened, but I think he is innocent.'

'Perhaps he killed her by accident?'

I shook my head. Only Aldridge knew all the details of the post-mortem I had performed. 'Whoever killed Sally didn't do it by accident. Her body showed signs of torture before death. I must find Thomas quickly, discover what he knows—he could be in danger himself.'

Her tired face looked despairing. 'What demons have been unleashed in London? Yes, find him, Mr Lockyer. We do not want a third death here.'

I nodded. 'Consider Madame, perhaps someone here in this hospital killed Sally?'

'How can you say that? We are all too busy—or too tired.' She yawned.

'I am sorry Madame. It's late. But I want to know what you think about this.' I laid the soft package on the table and began to remove the layers of paper.

Madame gasped. 'How beautiful! But it's damaged.' She held up the dress of blue silk, threaded with silver. It shimmered in the candlelight and in its folds, the fruit and gold-flowered embroidery were stained with dried blood. Where the full skirt flowed was a ragged hole and the hem hung in tatters.

'It belonged to Lady Derryn Barlow. I cut the hole in it myself, when she was brought here.' This was all I felt capable of saying. I recalled the blood and haste of that night and the squalling baby who against the odds, still lived.

'I thought I might learn something by examining it. But I can make nothing of it except that it is a piece of luxury.'

Madame O'Brien stood transfixed, staring in silence. Then she rubbed the material where it had stiffened with blood. Her words were slow, reluctant. 'I have seen this before. Or something very like it.'

'Where Madame?'

'At my convent in Bruges. We specialised in making the finest silks and embroidery—for vestments and altars, but sometimes for French and Stuart royalty. This is an exclusive print made for a queen or princess. It must have been worn at the French court because it is a recent pattern. I cannot imagine how it came to be here.'

I did not know what surprised me more—her verdict on the dress or revelations about herself. I cannot imagine how *you* came to be here, I thought.

I bundled the dress into its wrapping, thanked her and left. As I went into the yard, I noticed there was a light in Aldridge's room. No doubt the hard-working Colonel was poring over the hospital accounts—fretting about the price of coal, laundry, and medicines. I should worry too, I thought. Being involved with Pembroke is bad enough—if the Stuarts are connected, that's treason. But, I reasoned, they are far away in France. In exile.

Chapter 9

Sunday September 16th

It was Sunday morning, and the Grand Ward was packed. Every patient that could walk had been brought in. The remainder were sitting straight up in their beds. The nurses, even the tired ones from the night shift, were grouped in a corner. It seemed every member of staff was present, except, I noted, Madame O'Brien. Barebon had been true to his concern for the spiritual welfare of the hospital and had sent up a young preacher from his Fetter Street Chapel.

'My text for today is from St Paul's Epistle to the Ephesians Chapter 5 verse 4: Let there be neither filthiness, nor foolish talking, nor jesting, but rather the giving of thanks.'

He paused, regarding his congregation sternly. His fierce gaze was at odds with his boyish features and as he frowned, a haze of pipe smoke caught his throat and he coughed. He cleared his throat awkwardly and began again, *'How often it occurs when men are together, even here in this hospital among the maimed and sick, that the Lord's name is taken in vain? For why has man a tongue? It is a bodily part given only that he may better praise God.'*

The youth was becoming red-faced, but whether this

was from his enthusiasm or because he stood close to the stove, I could not judge.

'I enjoin you to avoid all cursing. For he who is free in filthy speech is but one step away from mischief and sedition!'

I began to pay attention. Most soldiers who could read were avid for anything that the presses churned out. 'Unlicensed and Scandalous Pamphlets' were about to be restricted by a nervous Parliament. Barebon's man was warning his audience.

His voice rose. *'Avoid the idle conversations of those vagrants who sell and cry about the streets to the dishonour of the Commonwealth—Such speaking is close companion to writing of scurrilous works as is a backside to a privy stool—'*

That was enough. As the stove rumbled, I took the chance to slip through the door into the yard. Aldridge was warming himself in the sun and smoking.

'Ah John, you've stayed for longer than I could. I found I needed a draw of my pipe.'

'He began well enough,' I replied, 'but—'

'I know. These fellows make no distinction between the word of God and their own version of godly government. But some good news John—we've been voted the funds to pay our salaries. At last!'

Aldridge refilled his pipe and sighed. Mellowed by the morning sun, he had forgotten all the cares of the hospital including two ill-omened deaths. When all this is over, I thought, he might even agree to pay me more money. But nothing is over. I have not found any knife or another weapon. The tub and the laundry room had been cleaned so there's nothing there. That leaves the three outhouses, used to store coal, candles, salt and wood. There was time while everyone was in church for me to look around them.

The roof of one had partly collapsed. I decided to look there first. The door was half open and the stench hit me. This place had been used as a necessary house and no one collected the night soil. Then I saw the pattens. One rested upright on the floor, the other lay on its side. There were swirls in the dust of the earth floor where something been dragged over it. A length of rope lay in the corner, sliced by a sharp knife or sword that had later found use on Sally.

What a place to die, I thought, in a dirty outhouse open to the rain. The whole peace of a sunny Sunday evaporated.

Aldridge still looked contented, leaning against the wall, so my instinct was to wait before telling him. He had already paid the vicar of St Andrews to arrange a hasty burial for Sally. He hoped to pass off her death as an accident and avoid a visit from the Searchers. Although he wanted justice for her, he thought more about the survival of his hospital. The Colonel was a decent man, appropriated nothing for himself and cared for the welfare of Ely's patients and employees. But the uncertainty of the times made everyone fearful of consequences spinning out of control.

The sermon had ended, and the congregation streamed out into the Yard. I saw Mr Yorke exchange a whisper with Rose Ellis. Colonel Aldridge strode towards the young preacher. His empty sleeve flapped jauntily.

'An excellent text, Mr Greening, Ely Hospital is grateful.' He smiled.

'Yes Colonel, I think I warmed them.'

'Certainly, you did. You did,' continued the colonel jovially, 'perhaps, next Sunday, having made such an impression, your holy labours need not be so long.'

A frown crossed Mr Greening's earnest young face.

'God's humble servants must not slacken in His charge.'

'Oh no, of course not. But you have begun the healing work of the spirit. As with the body, we must be temperate in the administration of medicine to the soul. We have found that smaller doses are necessary for a weaker patient—so also for these men whose spirits are not yet strong in the Lord.'

'I see,' said Mr Greening. 'Well then, perhaps just an hour next week.'

I returned to my room, downcast at the reminder of Sally's suffering, and added my new observations in the outhouse to my growing sheaf of notes. I reread those I had made for my report to Pembroke to see if there was anything I had missed. I could not banish from my mind the image of Sally's butchered foot and the squeaky aristocratic voice of Colonel Algernon Sidney telling me the murderers of Lady Derryn were 'already hanging.'

I decided a walk would clear my head.

Not towards the Thames, though. Mid-afternoon the tide was low, and the stink of the exposed mudbanks stayed heavy in the air. I went outside the city gates north to the windmills of Moor Fields. That wasteland covered in storm-flattened gorse was a haven for fugitives. Perhaps I would find Thomas.

My route took me past Thanet House the most magnificent mansion in Aldersgate. Its owner had rebuilt it as if there had been no war. Above stately Corinthian pillars, the white stone walls were carved with garlands and its glass windows shone. A long line of covered carts stood outside, and a noisy stream of carters and labourers struggled down the marble steps carrying furniture and household goods. A precious mirror of Venetian glass was hoisted into the leading cart. At the head of the line was an enormous carriage, whose windows were protected by heavy otter-skin curtains. My curiosity got the better of me and I lifted one to peer in. The huge carriage was lined with black plush; velvet pillows and beaver skin wraps lay across the long seats. Lamps and foot warmers jammed the central aisle.

'Ah Mr Lockyer, what think you of my coach? Will it carry me in comfort for three hundred miles and more?'

It was the Countess of Pembroke—upright, barely leaning on her stick. A scent of orange flowers wafted towards me. Her black eyes glittered like the jet on her travelling cloak.

'Are you leaving London, Lady Pembroke?'

'You need no longer call me that name, Sir. The Earl and I have parted company. I am going north. I shall never return to London. I sat out the war in gloomy Baynard's Castle, now I'm going to breathe the air of my own green moorland.'

'Then what—'

'This is my daughter Margaret's house. I moved here when Pembroke finally renounced all claims to my land. We are glad to be rid of each other. In any case, he is ill and won't last long.'

'You have a daughter?' I asked.

'I have two, Sir. The fruit of my first marriage to the Earl of Dorset. He died young, worn out with wine and lecheries. Even Whittier, the best apothecary in London, could not save him. Pembroke and I produced no living children.'

'By what name should I know you now, my Lady?'

'Lady Anne, Baroness Clifford, and Countess of Cumberland, reinstated to my five castles.'

She recited their names like old friends.

'Skipton, Brougham, Brough, Appleby, Pendragon. I intend to rebuild them and repair the damage of the war whether Parliament allows it or not!'

But she's old. I thought. Spirited, but old.

'I am nearly sixty. What better way to spend the rest of my life? I shall build churches to God's glory. I have wasted too many years on the men of this world. I tell you truly, Mr Lockyer, the best time of my life, was when I was a child. The old Queen—yes—Great Bess herself, made a pet of me. She used to hold my hand while I read to her. My childhood was happy. Now, with all the obstacles in my life gone, I hope to be happy again in the North.'

Cumberland. To me it seemed further away than Padua.

'A different world.'

'Yes, it will not be easy to reach me there,' she said. Then, to my surprise, she smiled at me. 'I remember you as a small child, Mr Lockyer; you accompanied Whittier several times when he visited my Lord Dorset. What a beautiful dark-eyed boy you were!'

'Mr Whittier was my guardian. I apologise Lady Anne, but I do not recall you.'

'No matter. You were very young,' she replied. She lowered her voice. But her tone was fierce. 'So far, your life has been a lucky one—luckier than most. It could have turned out far worse. Listen to me. Earl Pembroke and the Sidneys are fearsome enemies. These are two of the most powerful families in England. If they move against you, even the Army cannot protect you. Do you think Pembroke was taken in by your attempt to deceive them? He and Colonel Sidney know there is a living child. They intend to find it. They will find you first, and may God help you then, John Lockyer.'

Chapter 10

Sunday 16th September

I hurried back to Ely in turmoil. My scheme to conceal the child had failed. According to Lady Anne I was now in danger. For whoever killed the mother would try to kill the child—and me too if I got in the way.

I pushed open the door to the Great Ward, still trying to order my thoughts. Days ago, I was a simple Army surgeon who survived the war. Damaged but functioning. I had employment that interested me and time for research. Now I had powerful enemies and was involved in the deaths of two women. Their killers remained unknown, but I had to find them and protect the child who depended upon me.

But there was no escaping the present moment and its demands. The men here needed my help, that at least I could do.

'Surgeon Lockyer, Sir! Over here,' called one young man. His face swollen and red. 'I'm in great pain Sir—it throbs like the devil pulling 'is tail.'

I stood over him. 'Open your mouth.'

The man let out a blast of rotten breath. I turned his head towards the window for a better view. His gums were red and inflamed and several teeth had rotted to black.

'Point to the pain, trooper,' I said and gently tapped one tooth. He let out a shriek that produced mingled laughter and grumblings from his fellow-patients.

'That one must come out and probably the others as well,' I said and reached for my pelican, a clever instrument with one flat prong to hold the tooth and a curved one for extraction.

'We'll have to do it straight, trooper Samuel. It will be worth it. Any volunteers to hold him to his seat?'

'I don't need that. I made no sound that time you cut that musket ball from my leg after Maidstone.' It was true, I remembered him. There was no point in reminding Samuel that was in the middle of battle, where a treatable wound sometimes meant a trip to safety behind the lines. Often in those circumstances, a soldier's sense of pain was dulled.

But trooper Samuel was as good as his word and minutes later, three rotten teeth lay in a small dish, and he sat staunching his gums with a bloody cloth.

I opened the cupboard to get vinegar to flush the man's mouth.

'You have a good prescription coming,' I said, 'a mouthwash of vinegar and brandy every day for a week to reduce inflammation.'

'Must they be mixed? Can't I drink 'em separate?'

'Mixed, soldier. One draught in the morning and one before sleeping.'

'I'll take my evening one out in the yard—pretend I'm on the town. Thanks, Mr Lockyer.'

'Be careful out there, Samuel,' said another voice. 'The yard is haunted with the ghosts of dead soldiers Mr Lockyer and Mr Yorke sent to the next world.'

There was general laughter, but the speaker became serious.

'In truth, I've heard noises and seen shapes and shadows in the yard more than once.'

'When was that?' I was alert. 'What did you see?'

'Three nights ago, late at night I see a tall feller moving about. And I see a smaller one, pullin' something on the ground, I couldn't see what. 'E was by the garden gate.'

'The tall man—what sort of build?'

'Sir, about yours. He had a cloak, though.'

Not Thomas then, I concluded. 'Did you see faces?'

'No, Sir, when the smaller feller turned—well he—he had no face. Just a black emptiness.'

The room fell silent. The men were listening to every word.

'What time?'

'After eleven of the night. I heard St Andrew's clock chime the hour. I'd waked with all the noise that madman was making—howling fit to raise the dead.'

'Why didn't you tell this to Madame O'Brien yesterday?'

'She might laugh at me. I won't be mocked by no woman. But they were not of this world. The one that had no face—and the other I never saw but his back—perhaps it was the Devil 'imself. They say he walks near places like this hoping to snatch our souls and drag us to hell!'

'Your mind is running away with you,' said trooper Samuel sharply.

There was an uneasy laugh and the men looked anxious. They feared the dead.

'Thank you, soldier, for this information, I assure you I take it seriously, ghosts or not. Nearly supper time! Good evening gentlemen.'

From the steps of Grand Ward, I stopped to view the yard. I could see both garden gate and front gates easily. I tried to remember if three nights ago the sky had been clear or cloudy. It was calm tonight, the horizon a delicate pale red with one star shining brightly. Something glowed in the darkening doorway. It was Aldridge, smoking his pipe. After a lazy exhalation of smoke, he tapped it on the heel of his boot and beckoned me.

'Ah John, it's been a long day. Come upstairs and take a glass. I'll have supper sent up.'

A new fire flickered in Aldridge's sitting room, reflected on two decanters and crystal glasses on a cherry-wood side-table.

'Port wine or brandy?'

I nodded at the brandy. I always preferred it. As Aldridge poured, I said, 'These glasses are beautiful.'

'A wedding gift from Susannah's uncle. No need for them at home now. I might as well enjoy them here.'

I sipped, then leant forward.

'I found Sally's pattens today, in the outhouse at the end of the herb garden.'

'Does that help you to know who killed her and why?'

'No. One of the patients said he saw figures in the yard the night she was murdered. Thought they were ghosts.'

Aldridge snorted. 'Ghosts indeed!'

'He gave little description except to say that one was small and had no face and the other was tall but not stout—which means neither could be Thomas.'

'Where is Thomas? I thought he was under suspicion—he and Sally quarrelled.'

I hesitated. 'He thought so too. I think he is innocent.

He has been in hiding. I saw him briefly, but he disappeared again.'

Aldridge stared at me over the rim of his glass.

'You know where he is?'

'He has been at Mistress Graham's.'

'Hmm—a happy place for a man to conceal himself.' Aldridge chuckled. 'What else have you discovered?'

'Sally and her sister were foundlings.'

'Yes-yes, I know. The sister works at Mistress Graham's I suppose. But in the matter of her death?'

'Early on Thursday morning she visited her sister with a package. Later she was heard quarrelling with Thomas. According to Rose and Madame, she went about her work but seemed upset. She was last seen after supper. Perhaps her killer or killers came in through the garden gate. She was taken to the outhouse, killed there and her body hidden in the wash tub. And there's something else—her sister Finny is missing.'

Aldridge shrugged. 'Perhaps there's no connection. John, I think I can manage to keep this quiet for the moment. I have not told the parish authorities, so no meddling searchers—the fuss they made over that other dead woman! Sally will be buried tomorrow; let's hope that's an end to it. You haven't found out anything definite. I don't see what more we can do.'

I was silent. I had seen the damage to Sally's frail body. A tortured child. Aldridge drained his glass and shifted in his chair. He wished to change the subject. For the moment, disturbed by that memory, so did I. I took a gulp of brandy.

'How goes your work with Yorke?' he asked.

Aldridge does not miss much, I realised. Yorke was

sergeant-surgeon, and technically I outranked him. But at Ely, these distinctions were less important. Yorke had worked through the Parliamentary ranks to assistant surgeon. He had fought in two bitter campaigns in Wales. He was deeply committed to the Parliamentary cause and suspicious of my background and loyalty.

'He's an excellent surgeon.' I meant it. We worked together successfully. I admired Yorke's skill and energy. The latter grudgingly returned the compliment. But Yorke was a coarse-mannered man and no puritan, as everyone at Ely knew.

'That pretty Rose Ellis is his latest conquest,' Aldridge remarked. 'I saw them the other evening in the Yard. They'd clearly been together.' He laughed 'It must've been the quickest of fumbles for he still wore his surgeon's smock!' Then Aldridge looked more serious. 'His behaviour could cause difficulty. He sees all women as his rightful prey. Except perhaps for one. What think you of Madame?'

'Madame O'Brien?'

'How many others are there? What do you think of the woman?'

He had caught me off-guard. 'I—er—I think she is remarkable,' I replied carefully. I wanted to say arrogant, bad-tempered, and clever. Good at her job. Complicated.

'Yes, John, she's remarkable,' said Aldridge, getting up to carve the chicken. 'Eat well John. You have earned it— you are not a bad comrade for a quondam-Royalist.'

So, I thought, no one ever forgets that. Well, it is better than traitor.

Chapter 11

Monday 17th September very early morning

It was very early morning and the knock on the door was unexpected. I had not asked for an early call and was barely awake. In my dream I chased someone in a dark coach, but although the coach was small and I was large, I could not catch up, however big my strides. As always voices pursued me urging me to move faster before it was too late.

The door was pushed open. Madame O'Brien stood there. Her pale face stood out in the dark of the stairwell.

'Madame is this urgent? One of the patients?'

'No Mr Lockyer. I am visiting the poor man who was so disturbed the other evening. Would you like to come with me? You may judge if he has improved.'

I cursed inwardly. 'Madame, of course. Give me a minute.'

Outside Ely's gate, Madame O'Brien said, 'I ask that this visit is not made known to Colonel Aldridge.'

You can ask I thought. I'm not promising. I felt rather out of temper.

She walked silently beside me as we headed towards the Thames. Streets filled as the day began, a white sky, streaked silver. Sweepers and night soil men emptied the kennels, yelling warnings to keep out of the way. Whiffs of raw sewage mixed with breakfast smells. My stomach rumbled—we had left before the kitchen was open. Years in the field taught me never to undertake an early assignment on an empty stomach, a rule that served me well during long hours in the surgical tent.

We were outside the Black Friar, a sailor's tavern whose upper storey hung unsteadily over the tar barrels outside. Several windows had been smashed but the door was open, there was a fire, and the scent of hot broth. I hesitated.

'Madame O'Brien I need to eat. Is this place suitable?'

'I'm hungry too. I was a soldier's wife; I have seen far worse.'

Within minutes the innkeeper produced two bowls of eel soup. A film of saffron oil gleamed on top and chunks of white flesh bobbed under the surface. The soup smelt sharp and hot. The man slammed down a loaf of hard bread. I reached for my knife, but Madame O'Brien was already slicing expertly with a fine-bladed dagger. She saw my look.

'For protection.' Still unsmiling, she carried on cutting. After a few mouthfuls, taken in silence, I felt better. I looked at Madame O'Brien. She stared right back. My glance fell first. I was not by nature talkative, but I was unused to meeting someone similar, especially a woman. Usually, they chattered, and I listened with half an ear.

I was curious. 'Madame O'Brien, that's an Irish name. I suppose it was your husband's since you are not Irish.'

'Correct, Major. I'm not.'

Silence fell again. Then she said, 'I discourage questions. The less is known the less there is to gossip about.'

On the contrary, I thought, the more people make things up. At least that's what they did about me. She leaned over and rubbed a clear spot on the dirty window.

'I love to see the water. I was born in Marseilles—'

'I know Marseilles,' I interrupted excitedly. 'I sailed from there to Genoa, when studying in Italy. You are very far from home.'

'Yes.'

Fool, I thought. If you want her to talk keep quiet.

'Please—go on, Madame.'

'My father was a naval surgeon. He taught me bone-setting. My mother died of smallpox in the Marseilles epidemic. I was sent to the English Nazarene convent in Bruges. I met Turlough O'Brien, an Irish volunteer. We went to Ireland. He fought for the King and was killed there.'

Her story had been recited like a well-learned lesson.

'Please don't repeat any of it,' she said sharply. 'I can fall under suspicion very readily. They already know I am a Catholic.'

I had never been this close to her before. Now I noticed the light stippling of pockmarks. They ran down the left of her face from her high cheekbone to her firm jaw. Her eyes were unusual, a clear dark blue. But it was her hands that interested me most. They were large and strong. Bonesetter's-hands.

I felt her fear. And I realised what it must be like to live as she did—always on the verge of condemnation at best, imprisonment or death at worst. When I had changed sides, I had to confront the darkest suspicions of others. Now I understood that Madame and I shared a common dread. I was terrified of being accused of misusing my skill and knowledge to serve the enemy. To have it said that my aim was to cause death instead of working my utmost to preserve life. She could be suspected of crimes, perhaps even witchcraft, against the sick and it would not take much to arouse hostility against her. I was even more intrigued. Why, then, did she stay?

'And what of you surgeon-major? How did you come to be here?'

Foolishly, I had not expected the question. Most people at Ely knew I was a turncoat.

'I arrived here after the siege of Oxford.'

'I suppose you must have seen much during these recent wars.'

It was my turn to be monosyllabic. 'Yes.'

Awkwardness had descended on us both. She stood, a spare tall figure, and pulled on her brown worsted cloak. Her long fingers quickly knotted the leather fastenings.

'We should go. I shall have to get back to Ely soon.'

Quickly, silently, she led me to the last dwelling in a street of low houses. At the side yard and wharf was covered. Behind, barges loaded with wood clunked against each other as they floated at anchor. The smell of sawdust was thick.

The door was opened by a slight white-haired man in workman's clothes. Madame O'Brien spoke to him quickly and then beckoned me to come in.

'This is...' she hesitated a moment, '...Father Southworth. This is Surgeon-major Lockyer.'

Father Southworth nodded and led us to a small room at the back of the house. There, sleeping peacefully on a truckle bed, was Ely's madman.

'I am afraid your patient is not much improved Surgeon-major. He needs to sleep a lot; he still babbles and cries for most of his waking hours. Time will help him—time and the new mixture. Have you brought any?'

'We are not supposed to take medicines from our stores,' said Madame O'Brien.

'Well, you may soon have to. Our refuge is becoming something of an outpost of Ely. What about the other one of yours? He arrived, bloodied and beaten. He's in the workshop.' We entered and I saw Thomas lying on the floor, his mighty legs spread, his head buried in his huge hands.

'I did it Mr Lockyer. I put Sally in the washtub.'

I brushed aside sawdust and curls of wood and knelt next to the big man.

'What do you mean, Thomas?'

Thomas lifted his head.

'There's a fox, it often runs between the gardens and the yard. Patients feed it sometimes. It was still dark. I heard it barking and saw it run by the garden gate. I went through, past the outhouses and I saw her. The fox was sniffing her. I ran over. She was a terrible sight. Her foot—'

'I know.'

'I couldn't just leave her out in the open, I didn't want any animals—you know…'

'Yes.'

'So I carried her into the laundry room. I thought I could wrap her in something. But there was nothing except the sheets in the tub. I put her in and lifted the sheets on top of her.'

'But there was lye in the tub.'

'I did not see it—it was dark—only the sheets—I thought… I was going to come back and take her away. To be buried.'

'Why?'

'Because she is of our faith—the old religion,' Thomas answered simply. 'I prayed for her. There was blood everywhere. It was on my jerkin and shirt. I washed it off. It took time and by then there were others about. I was frightened and ran. I abandoned her. I'm ashamed.' He wept again.

Father Southworth stood in the doorway. 'Mr Lockyer say you believe him. Thomas has done no wrong, and his soul is full of pain. Please help him.'

That's your job, I thought. I deal with the body. Thomas's anguish had aroused an uncomfortable memory I wanted to supress.

'Thomas, I don't believe you are responsible for Sally's death. But you must tell me what you know.'

Thomas sat up now. He squared his shoulders and looked more like the seasoned surgeon's assistant I knew. 'It was the dress. The one the noblewoman wore the night you saved her child. It was slashed and stained but still a fine dress, Sally asked me if she could have it. She wanted to wash and repair it for her sister, who likes fine clothes.'

'You know the hospital rules, Thomas—all clothes are stored for re-use or sold for income,' said Madame O'Brien.

'I know, but I wanted her to have it. Later, she told me that she'd unpicked the hem and there were gold coins sewn into it and papers. I said she'd have to give them up. I told her we must take everything to Colonel Aldridge, and she said, "Too late. We're keeping the money and if you say anything, I'll tell the Colonel that you stole it!" I knew she'd already handed the dress to her sister. We parted badly.' Once more his eyes filled with tears.

'Her sister was more important to her than you,' I said bluntly.

'Then Sally was found. I went to tell Finny at Mistress Grahame's, but she was not there. Then you arrived, Major Lockyer. Here—have this—' Thomas reached inside his shirt. 'It's the packet the papers were in; Sally threw it at me.'

He handed me a small purse of waxed cloth. As I shook it open a scrap of paper floated to the floor. Before I could touch it, Madame O'Brien had picked it up. She rubbed it between her long fingers.

'This is French whitepaper. It's rare.'

'That's what's left of the papers Sally mentioned?' I was working it out. 'Someone wanted the papers, gold, or both. I think Sally cared so much for her sister she refused to say where the dress had gone, which is why her killer hurt her.'

I tried to focus. That dress of rare material, and the coins and papers sewn into it with such care, linked the murders of Derryn Barlow and Sally Watts. Sally's love for her sister, her wish to please Finny and then to protect her, had led to her death. Finny could be dead too—or if alive, in danger. I remembered Mrs Grahame's apparent apathy at her disappearance and felt a pang of alarm. I must go back to Whitecross Street—and quickly.

'Thomas, I don't believe you are guilty of any crime. Will you go with Madame O'Brien back to Ely?'

'Mr Lockyer, I prefer to stay with Father Southworth. This place suits me and there is much good I can do here.

I am done with Ely.'

I gritted my teeth in annoyance. Now I would have to escort Madame O'Brien at least as far as the safety of St Paul's.

'Father Southworth, you are costing me an excellent surgeon's assistant. What is your purpose here anyway?'

'Just a workshop,' Southworth replied. 'We produce simple carpentry—floorboards, ship's cupboards, cart shafts and sides, spindles for wheels and staircases. There is demand with transport needed for the wars. The work helps those with troubled minds and souls. Our Blessed Lord was a carpenter.'

'And died on a wooden cross.' The man's meekness and the general atmosphere grated on me.

'We do not make crucifixes,' said Southworth stiffly, 'that has been forbidden for many years.'

The door was closed firmly behind us.

As we made our way along narrow passages and pushed through the crowds around St Paul's I thought I should break the frosty silence, obviously caused by my tetchy behaviour.

'Madame, thank you. I'm glad to see our witless patient is well cared for and grateful for the kindness Father Southworth extended to Thomas. And I hope we may be nearer to understanding what happened to Sally.'

'You may be. I am not.' She turned abruptly to walk west towards Ely.

As I watched, I saw someone behind her in the crowd. The man was close, almost touching. I tried to elbow through the crowd to warn her but was blocked by a phalanx of troopers out for morning drill at the cathedral's entrance. When I doubled back both had disappeared. I was disquieted; why had I spent so much time worrying about the past when there is enough present danger?

I was walking faster even than my usual quick pace. I wanted to question Mistress Grahame. This time, I resolved not be put off by her blandishments. I had arrived at the corner of Chiswell Street. With a shock I realised I was only yards from the house of Edward's wet-nurse. I had not seen him since the night I had cut him from his mother's body. So, despite my pressing desire to advance my inquiries, I felt an equally strong wish to see the child. It will only take a minute. Just to make sure all's well.

Hope-Anna had described the house as two-storeys, three small windows and a door painted blue. I rapped on the door. Almost immediately it was opened by Hope-Anna herself. She looked at me with relief.

'Oh John, I am glad to see you. They left. They said that you must be busy at the hospital but would be along later.'

I was puzzled, then uneasy. *They?* 'I have come to see Edward. How is he?'

Hope-Anna's eyes widened. 'He's well. But they said you would know all about—'

Edward had gone.

He had been taken by a respectable looking couple who had shown his wet nurse a letter from Surgeon-major Lockyer. The letter gave permission for Edward to be given into their care, prior to being reunited with his true family.

'It had a great seal attached Sir and your own signature,' protested the wet-nurse.

'How do you know it was mine? Can you read?'

Mistress Martindale sobbed.

'Peace John,' said Hope-Anna. 'It was your signature; I

saw it myself. I have seen you put your name often at the hospital. I questioned them and said I should ask you to come here. They said you were on your way and would arrive shortly.'

'And you let them go?'

'John, they were pleasant, gentle people.' There was apprehension in her voice. 'As well as your letter, they had a copy of Edward's birth certificate from St Giles. They said Edward's family was known to you.'

Pembroke! Of course. I remembered I had signed the post-mortem report at Baynard's Castle. They had forged my signature. So easy!

'What did they look like, Hope-Anna?'

'They were a couple called Brough. She was dressed very clean and seemed kindly. His clothes were plain but good material, like the steward of a rich house. He was polite. They seemed to know all about you and Ely hospital. This is terrible! What have we done? Is Edward in danger?'

At this Mistress Martindale's sobs became louder. 'Oh Sir,' she wailed. 'Forgive me! I believed them! The seal, Sir—and the money. They paid me ten pounds, nearly a year's wages for Master Martindale.' She put her head in her hands.

'And that didn't make you suspicious? Stop howling! Is there anything else you can tell me?'

'They came in a coach—it had a cradle.'

'Did the coach have a livery, a coat of arms?'

'I didn't notice—perhaps there was something painted on the side, I can't be sure.'

Pembroke's arms are distinctive, but she was a hopeless witness. I turned to Hope-Anna, stricken, her tears barely suppressed.

'Hope-Anna, comfort Mistress Martindale. There's no point in reproach.'

For indeed there was not. What a stupid pair! I believed Hope-Anna had more brain. The consequences could be terrible. Leaving them to wail, I ducked out the door as fast as I could. I intended to return to the hospital to check on patients and then go to Baynard's Castle and confront Pembroke. The 'respectable couple' must have been his agents. For now, Whitecross Street and its formidable owner would wait.

As I sprinted towards Cheapside, I was thinking hard. After all, Pembroke had claimed Lady Derryn Barlow as kin, so her child was kin also. Was it not I, Lockyer, who had acted impulsively by concealing the child? I thought he was in danger from those who had killed his mother. I remembered the red wriggling infant, using all his strength to cry and suck air. Had Pembroke taken the child to destroy him? Why should Pembroke go to this trouble—why not simply put forward a rightful claim?

The shops in Cheapside were hung with flags and flowers and the paving had been swept clean. Strange how life goes on even when you are in the middle of a terrible crisis. The street was even busier than usual. As a shabby dog's meat man retreated into Foster Lane, I stopped him.

'What's happening?' The man set down his reeking basket.

'There's a banquet tonight at the Guildhall to celebrate General Cromwell's victories in Ireland. When he returns, the Common Council will present him with gold and silver plate worth thousands!'

Everyone loves a winner. The City powers, in general

hard-headed and practical had backed Parliament and lent money for the wars. And the investment had paid off. For the time being, the City loved Cromwell.

Crowds streamed east from Temple Bar to the Guildhall. I hurried west against the flow, towards Holborn Bridge. As I entered under the gate arch of Ely hospital the bells of the surrounding churches rang the midday peal. The yard itself was quiet.

Without warning both my arms were gripped from behind. Two men held me while a third manacled my hands. I shouted for help but heard only the grunts of my assailants as they pushed me to the ground and despite my kicking secured my legs in the same iron cuffs.

I was then pulled to my feet and a pistol pressed hard behind my ear. All the time I was thinking why is there no one here? Then I understood. In the shadow of the gatehouse stood a small troop of armed men. I recognised the squat man who was their leader—Captain Burrell. He stepped forward, stuck out his chest and brayed, 'Surgeon-major John Lockyer, acting on information laid before the Justices, I place you under arrest on suspicion of the murder of an unnamed female and her unborn child. You are to come with us.'

I looked desperately around the yard and saw Colonel Aldridge over by the old wall. He looked grim. Rose Ellis and Mr Yorke were there, standing together, whispering. Yorke was smiling.

Burrell turned to Aldridge.

'I also seek the fugitive Thomas Holden, surgeon's assistant, to arrest him for complicity in the aforementioned murder; and for the murder of Sarah Watts, laundry maid of Turnmill Street.'

Rose Ellis ran over to Burrell and spoke urgently.

'I further seek the arrest of a female, named O'Brien, a known papist, living illegally in the City of London contrary to the recent order of banishment of all Papists.'

'This is monstrous!' roared Aldridge. 'It's all lies! Release Major Lockyer!'

'Colonel Aldridge, you are no longer in charge. That post is now held by Surgeon-sergeant Yorke.'

'By whose authority?' Aldridge raged.

'The Council of State, the highest authority of the Army and Parliament.'

'Be damned to all of them!' Aldridge cried. 'Lockyer, I shall go straight to Colonel Harrison, to Lord General Fairfax, to General Cromwell himself. I'll make sure you are freed!'

'I doubt any of them will come to the aid of murderers,' Burrell sneered. 'Be silent before I charge you with sedition and blasphemy.'

Chapter 12

Monday 17th September late afternoon

They had placed me in a covered cart and hooded me; I tried to work out where I was going. If it was to Newgate Prison, I could languish or die of jail fever. But the cart trundled downhill before turning east. Surely, they cannot mean the Tower I thought. Ideas of treason and grisly execution almost unnerved me until the cart stopped and I was dragged out, my protests met with blows and kicks, as I walked still hooded like a man about to be hanged. But no one spoke, even to curse me.

My hands were freed. My captors had gone. I pulled off the stinking canvas hood. I was standing in darkness, below ground level. The shock of my arrest had mostly suppressed my fear—until now. I held to the belief that arbitrary arrest could not happen in the Republic. Then I realised Burrell had probably obtained sworn witnesses and intended to find more. This had all been planned. Who was holding me here? This was not Wood Street Compter where I would have been robbed and beaten already. All my clothes were still on my body. The harsh cries and fetid smells of a common Pound were absent. In fact, I was alone.

My eyes accustomed to the dark and I distinguished

the chamber's vault. Against the wall a flight of stone steps led up to a door. I remembered being hustled down. There were no windows. I could hear a faint rushing of water. If I am near some outflow, the desperate hope that perhaps I might crawl to the river did not survive the aspect of the massive dry walls. The place was old, very old. A stone channel was cut into the floor, but the room was so large I could not see to the end of it. I was gripped by panic that I must be deep underground. Yet, although still hazy from my beating. I knew this was not the Tower. I was still near Ely. Then I knew. Baynard's Castle, Pembroke's stronghold.

As if to confirm, the door atop of the steps scraped open. Torchlight illuminated a flash of yellow hair and van Prin's tall figure.

'Surgeon-major, the Earl wishes to speak to you.'

'Good.' I straightened despite my bruises. 'I'd like to question him.'

'*He* will be asking the questions. *You* will supply the answers. Come.'

I climbed towards him trying not to wince. I was sure the beating had damaged my knee. After a long time climbing and stumbling along corridors, trying to keep up with van Prin's enormous stride, I was once again in the panelled room overlooking the river.

Pembroke sat upright in the same chair but seemed weaker; his robes were bundled round him like sheets. His face was wasted, and his once-fine head of auburn hair was matted and thin. There was nothing left of the beautiful youth to whom the works of the greatest writer of the age had been dedicated.

When he spoke, his voice was hoarse. 'Sit down

Surgeon-major. I heard you were beaten on the way here, that was wrong. I apologise for my men. Before I proceed, let me say I know full well that you did not kill my kinswoman.'

'Then why am I here? I have been accused and I could be convicted while the real killer stays undiscovered. What do you want?'

'You are here for your safety and the evidence you have about her death' The Earl coughed. 'Knowledge has spread in London. The Council of State has let it be known that, with your arrest, Parliament has the situation under control.'

'As under control as when your kinsman hanged four innocent men a week ago?'

'Irish rogues. Don't waste a thought on them. They were far from innocent. Colonel Sidney merely advanced their inevitable deaths.'

'Must I expect the same summary justice?'

'All will go well Surgeon-major if you assist us with information.' It was the high clear voice of Algernon Sidney. Hearing it enraged me.

'What a pair you are—noblemen seeking advantage, using the authority of Parliament to pursue your family squabbles and conceal scandals. I'll not help you with anything!'

Neither looked surprised. Van Prin straightened the Earl's covers. Pembroke gazed impassively at the Thames.

'You are under our protection, Lockyer,' replied Sidney brusquely. 'You are in greater danger than you imagine. Whoever killed my kinswoman Derryn will want you dead too. For your safety, it may be necessary to remove you out of London altogether, perhaps to Dover Castle.'

'Ah yes, your consolation prize from Parliament—to keep you away from doing anything too stupid!' I was furious. 'You called me turncoat—yet everyone knows how *you* changed sides because the King did not trust you to run Ireland. In less than half a year you were fighting for Parliament!'

This time I got a reaction. Sidney had gone pale. 'Is that what they say? I have upheld the honour of my family! We, the old nobility with our blood and treasure, provide the continuity and liberty of England. At least I did not sell my beliefs for bandages and piss pots! Or a chance to better myself in the surgeon's trade!'

We were interrupted by a violent coughing fit from the Earl. I saw the bloody froth at his mouth but resisted the urge to step forward and wipe it away. The Earl struggled with his words, hunching his shoulders with effort. 'Surgeon-major Lockyer, Colonel Sidney outranks you in the army and as a civilian. He is the son of the Earl of Leicester—'

'I know who he is. We all do. Is this why the war is being fought—so earls can go on as they were —but more greedily with the King out of the way?'

'By God what side are you on? Are you for the King yet talking like a Leveller?' exclaimed Sidney.

I felt sick. I did not want to talk about sides anymore. Nor to debate with these men. 'I have seen many men wounded and dead—ordinary men who needed those piss pots and bandages you sneer at and who are fighting this war for you.'

Algernon Sidney was quiet a moment. Then he took a deep breath. 'You are right Surgeon-major. The war is being won by plain men with plain beliefs. Yet I fear we tear down our house without making a new one in which to lay our heads. That is why in this uncertain time, we need order and leadership. Cromwell thinks the same—and you cannot find a plainer man than he!'

Except for a few fanatics, most of whom lacked battle experience, the country was tired of war. The loss of life had been enormous, no family was untouched. Yet it was still going on and plots and revolts confused what was already an uncertain future. Sidney was right. Nothing was settled yet, and Cromwell was more conflicted than Sidney acknowledged. The rising star was torn between his heart's desire for ordered harmony and his soul's wish for Godly revolution.

Pembroke meanwhile had recovered his breath.

'Save this discussion! There are other matters. Lockyer, in your report on Lady Derryn's death you left my question unanswered. Did you mean that had she not been so cruelly stabbed she might have died by other means?'

How do you convey a balance of probabilities to a layman? He wants yes or no. 'The liver and bowels looked unhealthy and scarred, but whether this was disease or a deliberate attempt to poison her, I cannot say. I don't know enough about poisons.' For a moment I thought the Earl might ask for his money back. I decided to change tack. 'Was there anyone who wished her harm?'

'Yes,' replied the Earl. 'The Lady Anne hated her from the moment she arrived here last May.'

'In May! I thought she was a member of the household.'

'She was, beginning of the war. One of two distant Royalist kin from Wales we Sidneys sheltered. My brother Robert conceived a fancy for them and took them to Holland. They were maids-in-waiting to the Princess Mary,' Sidney replied.

Princess Mary of England was daughter of the executed King, married aged nine to the Dutch Prince of Orange and now his widow. After the war turned in Parliament's favour her court at The Hague was a refuge for fugitive Royalists. Sidney continued, 'Early this year, Lady Derryn was forced to leave The Hague and I asked my kinsman the Earl to take her in. Apparently, she had offended the Princess.'

'In what way?'

Sidney laughed. 'Does royalty have to give reasons? It is against such arbitrary authority that I am fighting!'

'Why would the Lady Anne hate Lady Derryn?'

'Perhaps for the same reason as the Princess did. It seems there was someone greatly in love with her, a gift neither the Lady Anne nor the Princess Mary have ever received,' Sidney replied.

Much good it did her, but I was surprised to hear this from a hard-bitten soldier. Pembroke did not respond to Sidney's comment on his wife, simply coughed again and pulled his covers closer. 'I must summon van Prin to carry me to my chamber. I am a teller in the debates and need to be fit for Parliament tomorrow. Lockyer, this is the only chance I will give you. Where is the child?'

'What?' Of all the things he could have said, I least expected that.

'I should ask you! This very morning you sent your servants to take him, using a forged letter from me. Don't lie to me! You have him here!'

'I… It is you who are lying Sir; I have done no such

thing! Why would I bring you here? What treachery is this? You will be punished, Lockyer, you will be hanged, I swear.'

The Earl trembled so violently I feared another apoplexy. Ignoring Sidney's angry stare, I stretched my arms to prevent Pembroke from falling, but he pushed me away with surprising strength, righting himself. Sweating, he gasped to van Prin. 'Take this man back down. Lock him in. Keep him there!'

Tuesday September 18th before dawn

Derryn Barlow sat opposite me, her infant in her arms. I looked at the huge leaking wound in her belly. She held out the blood-covered child to me and moaned in a language I could not understand. I felt fixed to the floor unable to move or speak. I was surrounded by endless linen sheets soiled with old bloodstains. They filled the room and smothered me filling my mouth until with great effort I found my voice and called for help.

No one answered.

I lay awake in the deep blackness and felt the horror of being far underground with no way out. I was back in the siege at Gloucester. A tunnel full of explosives collapsed. The miners and sappers were brought out and I treated those still alive but half suffocated, choking on blood and soil. Since then I had feared the dead weight of the earth.

To calm myself I recited the bones of the human skeleton, beginning with the neck and working down. It was my method of inducing sleep. When I got as far as the feet, I was wide awake and reminded of Sally Watts.

I explored my surroundings, remembering the dry

channel that ran across the floor. I crawled until I felt the floor dip. The channel was about a foot in depth. Slowly I edged along, thinking to use my body as a measure of length and map the size of my prison. It was then I noticed the room was not as dark as it had seemed and looking up, saw at the top of the stairs the door was ajar.

It must be a trap. They intend to catch me and claim I was killed escaping. I had no weapon. Yet the open door was too good a chance. I climbed the stair, emerging into an empty corridor. I could sense no breathing human, no silent watcher, only dead and empty space. It was as if the whole of Baynard's Castle had fallen under an enchantment with even the guard dogs asleep. Then, above the moan of dawn wind through the draughty apartments I heard it—footsteps on stone, impossible to muffle. A large velvet curtain was pulled open. Van Prin stood with a pistol in his hand.

At this distance the man could not miss. 'I was wagering how long it would be, but I knew I could rely on you.'

In his left hand was my dagger. His own, curved and sharp, was lodged, Turkish style, in his belt.

'You will have a use for this I think,' van Prin said and tossed my knife towards me. The weapon clattered. So that's the plan—a more convincing execution if I put up a fight.

'Pick it up. I don't want to fire this and wake the household. Surgeon-major, I deserve your thanks.'

I picked up the dagger and lunged, but he was quicker. He had already changed hands and drawn his sword. He cocked the gun.

'You don't understand do you Major Lockyer? I'm

setting you free. Of course, you're not truly free—for where would you go? There's no network to hide you. But I am freeing you from Baynard's Castle. Someone more powerful than my Lord Pembroke wishes to see you. He is an early riser and doesn't like to be kept waiting. So please, come along. We'll go by water.'

Tuesday September 18th dawn

A high-sided dory built for speed was moored at the foot of the stone steps. My hopes of escape faded when I saw that an armed guard stood on board. Van Prin eased his long body onto the plank beside me.

'The *Venetia* is kept here always for my Lord's use—he takes it when called to Parliament, which is not so often these days. His influence wanes with his health.'

'I suppose you will be looking for a new master before long.'

Van Prin smiled. He stroked the heavy sword that lay across his knees. 'Perhaps. Perhaps not. There are many opportunities in this country, but I would hope to stay with the family. I am trusted by them.'

'Then you must know all their secrets—like what happened to Lady Derryn.'

The boat rocked heavily as the oarsmen turned to take advantage of the current where the Fleet entered the Thames. When it had righted van Prin replied, 'You will not find out who killed her by asking me. Be assured, it was not my Lord Pembroke. In any case she was a worthless sort of whore.'

I was not surprised by the violence of his words—he worked for a vicious household. Cruelty was probably their daily discourse.

Van Prin leaned forward and spat. 'The woman is rotted meat now and buried. Forget her. Tell me while we have time. Where is the child, Lockyer? My Lord thinks you know.'

I felt a wave of distaste for Pembroke's man and was glad to frustrate him.

'The child has been taken, I do not know where or by whom. Is that what this is about—to hold me in a secret cell until I spit out the truth? Even if I knew I would not tell you or your master.'

Just as suddenly van Prin relaxed and became his usual nonchalant self.

'Not at all Surgeon-major. Perhaps we both are equal in ignorance. As I said, you're free although you would be a fool to run now. You're being given another chance.'

The boat scraped alongside the stone jetty. We had reached Westminster stairs.

Tuesday September 18th very early morning

Three men sat at the table. Van Prin took the guard position by the door. The room faced east, and morning light poured through the tall window. A saying of Harvey's, 'whenever possible, examine the patient in an easterly light' came into my mind. I thought of him, old and ill, who had often given me as good counsel as a father would have done. With what I hoped was Harvey's acumen, I scrutinised the men sitting opposite.

One I thought I had seen before, a dark-haired man in a silk jacket. Another sat at the side, ready to take notes. He rubbed his eyes in the sharp light. In the centre, short haired and round—shouldered, with a careworn face—sat the person in charge.

'You are observing us keenly Surgeon-major Lockyer. My name is Thomas Scot, Secretary of State for the Republic.' One of the regicides. Scot had signed the King's death warrant. He seemed so ordinary.

'What do you want?'

Scot gave a narrow smile.

'Well, what could we want from a man who, if he leaves here, will probably be hanged for murder.'

Hope drained. This was not to be an opportunity for me to prove my innocence, just more of the same.

'The accusation is false,' I said wearily. 'I did my duty as a surgeon and—' I realised I was unprepared for this interview, but I was certain about one thing: I would not reveal that Lady Derryn's child lived. Not to these men, whose motives I could not fathom.

'We are also holding your assistant Thomas Holden.'

'He, too, is innocent. We tried to save a woman who was brought to our hospital, and we failed. She died. Is that why I'm here?'

'Mr Lockyer, we don't care about a woman who is dead and buried. We know your history,' Scot replied. 'You have been three years in Parliament's service and that would seem to wipe out your previous loyalty to Charles Stuart the Man of Blood. But you still maintain contact with the Royalist William Harvey.'

'Not really.' A denial to protect us both. 'Although recently I consulted him on a scientific matter. He was my teacher. He is an old man—no threat to the Republic.'

'We can judge that,' said Scot. 'Surgeon-major, when you look at a man you observe his bones and blood. I watch where his thoughts lie. If I cannot observe a man directly, I have a network of people across the country that can. Our clerks prepare files on all Royalist sympathisers. Dr Harvey's is quite extensive, believe me.'

The door opened and another man entered. He was thin faced, dressed in lawyer's black. He was bursting to speak as he threw his papers on the table.

'Tom, I've received another urgent despatch from our people in The Hague. They want to know when we will send a new envoy to seal the alliance with the States General—if we can find anyone to take it on after what happened to the last one.'

'Assassinated—at dinner!' said the man in the silk jacket, indicating that this made the crime even more heinous.

'Mr Thurloe,' said Scot, 'meet Surgeon-major Lockyer.'

Thurloe glanced at me and then at Scot.

'Is this the man? Then let me tell you Tom, I think your plan is a grievous waste of money, I cannot see what benefit comes from sending an agent to France.'

'Because that is where the Stuart court sits in exile,' replied Scot.

'The princes are there *now*, but The Hague is where everything happens. That is where the Royalists murdered our envoy, where they plot, the Princess of Orange is a clear ally to her two brothers.'

'I know you have your own men in place in the Dutch network, Mr Thurloe. A pity they did not foresee the killing of Dr Dorislaus,' Scot said. 'I want something more long term than agents hanging around in taverns buying drinks for those penniless young gentlemen who fought for Charles Stuart.'

'That's not what—'

'Peace Mr Thurloe. I control the budget for intelligencers, and I don't want all my eggs in one basket. The plain fact is that within the three kingdoms, most Scots, Irish and many within England are still loyal to the Stuarts. Charles has already been proclaimed King in Scotland. He and his brother are committed to regaining the throne of England. Behind them is their mother the Queen, a daughter of France and a Catholic. The Stuarts are the greatest threat to the Republic.'

'Ah, they have such passionate attachments, brother to brother, mother to son—son to mistress! Division and jealousy are always possible.' The silk-jacketed man again. He spoke in clear accented English. 'Never a day passes without turbulence in the Royal household.'

'Exactly! Thank you, Monsieur Janvier,' said Scot. 'You see? We must turn them one against each other until envy and frustration defeat them. The Stuart tendency to pleasure and favouritism is legendary. They love easily. It is said that Charles lives openly with his mistress even under his mother's eye. We can use that.'

'So, you are determined to place an agent in their Court to feed on women's gossip and Cavalier injured pride! This won't bring us sound intelligence!' Thurloe was fiercely disapproving, his prematurely lined face frowning even more.

I was fascinated. Intelligencers? Stuart Princes? A heady world, one I knew nothing about.

'As to that,' his superior replied, 'I already have someone there. Now I will have another.'

He looked at me and nodded.

Surely, he was joking. Was this an elaborate ruse to get

rid of me? And why me? As Monsieur Janvier turned towards Thurloe, I remembered him—it was the man whom I had seen twice on the day I did the post-mortem at Baynard's Castle. The man with expensive shoes. My apprehension grew. Scot was serious.

Scot laid both his knobbly hands, palms down, on the table. 'Lockyer. I want you to help us. As a surgeon, you may offer your services to the Stuart Court. French physicians they have—but an honest English surgeon who fought for the King? You'll be welcomed with open arms! What do you say? Will you report to us? Will you go abroad to help the Republic?'

What a terrible idea. 'I would not be an honest English surgeon. I would be false.'

'Nonsense,' said Scot. 'You are no stranger to deceit. No turncoat ever is. Don't pretend to be an innocent. Look at what you did in Oxford.'

So, he knew. Not everything, probably enough. I felt exhausted. I could try one last manoeuvre.

'I did not murder the woman. There was no way I could have kept her alive. I'll take my chance with the laws of the Republic. Hand me over to the justices. I will not help you.'

Scot shook his head and smoothed his few wisps of hair.

'Oh, but you *will*,' he said. 'When I see you next you will agree.' He gestured to van Prin. 'Show him what I gave you. We'll meet tomorrow at the same time.' He turned to the note-taker. 'Mr Milton, you can begin making arrangements for Major Lockyer's journey.'

He rose and everyone followed him out of the room.

I was taken to a side room with the door unlocked. By

now it was mid-morning, and I felt a sharp longing for the sights and sounds of Ely hospital. I should be finishing my round of the Grand Ward and making a start on the walking wounded in the Yard. Yet it was my own action that led me to this room. Scot was asking me to abandon Ely and my work. More—to give up on Lady Derryn and Sally. To change into a grubby shadow man.

There was a knock and van Prin entered with a folder in his hand.

'Secretary Scot asked me to give you this. He would like you to read it. You should.' He laid the folder on the table. 'Goodbye Surgeon-major. I must return to the Earl; he is unaware of my absence. I don't suppose you and I will meet again.'

I will not lose sleep over that, I thought, as van Prin, with an easy movement, pulled the heavy door shut.

I opened the folder and read. There were many documents. I was amazed to see how far back they went, even before the war. There were pages copied from books, reports in the subject's own hand, communications from universities in France and Italy and sheets of observations of movements and meetings right up to the present day. It was a shock to see my own name there with a note scrawled at the side: *1645 Oxford. Changed sides.*

I had no idea that such information existed. In a section headed 'Dr Harvey: Family Connections' one phrase caught my eye—'*irregularities in the way Dr Harvey lives.*' It took me hours to read the folder, but before the end I knew I was caught in a trap laid long ago. Scot was right. I would do what he wanted.

Wednesday September 19th early morning

The same seat, the same men. This time Scot was smiling. If anything, it made him look worse. His teeth were discoloured and two of his upper incisors were missing, giving him a piratical appearance.

'*Cor animalium, fundamentum est vita. Rex paritor regnorum fuorum fundamentum,*' recited Scot.

'The heart of creatures is the foundation of life. Likewise, the King is the foundation of his kingdom,' I replied. I knew the sentence by heart. Mr Milton gave a schoolmasterly nod. Scot leant forward as if to impart a confidence.

'We would like to encourage Dr Harvey to publish *de Motu Cordis* in English. Sadly, sentiments like that do not help him. Have you have read his file?'

'Yes.'

Scot raised an eyebrow. 'As well as his many royalist contacts and seditious comments, his assertion that the soul is part of the blood could be taken for heresy. For when the blood dies, it implies, so does the soul, which we know is not true. If that is not enough, there is the young girl. We have enough to arrest him.'

'The girl is innocent and so is Dr Harvey!' I knew I sounded desperate. I was.

Scot's smile was disbelieving and dismissive. 'Surgeon Lockyer, I do not care about that matter. I would simply point out that the association is unusual. Your debt to him is great and your attachment is strong. Now you can repay him, ensure his liberty. May I assume that you have come to a decision?'

I had thought hard about someone to whom I could appeal. The College of Physicians, St Bartholomew's—but these were all suspect now as containing enemies of the Republic. And Harvey's uneven temper and brilliance had ensured there were others who might assist him but from envy or dislike, would not.

His voice was hard. Scot had signed the death warrant and killed a king. He would not hesitate to crush a frail scholar. Harvey would die in prison.

'I have no choice, have I? I must do as you ask.'

Scot pressed his gnarled hands together in satisfaction. 'I praise God that is settled. You sail from Tilbury this evening. Mr Milton has prepared your documents. Show him.'

Milton handed a set of papers across the table. I saw letters of introduction and commendation bearing the thick seal of the Earl of Northumberland and written in English, French and Latin.

Scot said, 'He can write them in Greek and Hebrew too, if needed. His command of languages is a wonder.'

'Whatever language he uses, they are not true,' I said.

'They do not need to be true,' Milton replied softly. 'Just convincing.'

Questor: Two

Chapter 13

Palace of St Germain-en-Laye, outside Paris
Gregorian calendar Thursday 21st October 1649 afternoon

I watched from behind the balustrade on the long staircase of the Great Hall. As courtiers filed in, bowing, servants came and went, dragging in gilded chairs and padded benches, carelessly slamming them on the uncarpeted stones. They were labourers who maintained the terraces, lawns, and ponds of an elaborate park. Formal parterres, laid out fifty years ago for the pleasure of Henri IV, were now in poor shape. His grandson, the eleven-year-old King Louis, urged by the boy's mother the Regent had ordered restoration, but the work was faltering. Meanwhile the palace was surrounded by a sea of mud and leaking canals.

At the top of the stairs, I shivered. A thin suit of dark grey velvet had been put in the trunk which had accompanied me to Tilbury docks. Some less than generous trimmings of silver lace and a pale blue silk sash completed my court dress. The spy's version. I sensed the chill and was about to go down and find a congenial spot near the great fireplace when I felt a hand on my arm.

'Wait up here if you can—you will obtain a better view.'

It was the man with whom I'd shared a stinking cabin on my cross-channel journey. He had proved the ineffectiveness of Aristotle's remedy for seasickness—a pint of salty wine. Between bouts of vomiting, he smiled cheerfully. He remarked that such malady was simply a hazard of his occupation.

'For I am obliged to travel frequently by sea between our two great countries,' Monsieur Janvier explained. 'My humours are still unbalanced, and my condition never improves.'

He was also the man I'd last seen in Scot's three-man conclave. During the restless night at sea, I learnt Janvier's mission was to buy some of the King's paintings Parliament had auctioned. Cardinal Mazarin, apart from the Regent and the boy-king, was the most powerful person in France and this man was his agent. I had noticed the fuss he made when his large boxes were loaded at Tilbury. But given his association with Scot, I doubted it was Janvier's only errand in London.

I now accepted I had to carry out Scot's assignment. I watched the crowd below closely, curious and keen to understand the Court. I knew nothing of royalty. The first time I saw the King was his execution day. The Parliamentary surgeons had been told to stand close, but I felt out of place and stayed at the back of the crowd. I saw his dripping head held up as the mob surged, I walked away wondering whether regicide marked the end or the beginning—and of what? And all the events since had not made the future clearer.

The massive limestone fireplace was now crackling and blazing. A small stage stood decorated with garden evergreens. A blue backdrop hung from a long brass rod and a trio of braziers gave off scented smoke.

I was in a French palace full of my country's enemies, and in its Great Hall, two queens sat side by side. They did not look at each other. 'Those two!' said Janvier, 'Sisters-in-law and not a word exchanged since they arrived. They can't agree on who is the more important.'

Precedence was clear enough to me.

'Queen Anne is the Regent of France for her son Louis. Queen Henrietta Maria is an exiled fugitive, almost penniless. Her son Charles is without a throne. The whole family are dependent on the charity of the French.'

'Don't underestimate Henrietta,' said Janvier, 'She's a fighter. Daughter of the King of France, with a dagger-wielding Medici for a mother. You know, I suppose she wasn't the first choice for the future King of England's bride?'

'No,' I growled. I was annoyed at Janvier's mocking tone. Later, when I knew him better, I knew he made fun of important things and saved his reverential tone for trivia.

'Oh yes. They asked for the Infanta first, but the Spanish were not impressed by Charles. The Infanta happens to be Anne's sister. She's now married to the Holy Roman Emperor. You English ended up with Henrietta of France. I bet your Parliament didn't anticipate the trouble she would cause! And Henrietta is Anne's sister-in-law. Her brother was the late King Louis. I hope I've made everything clear.'

'Yes, everyone is related to everyone else and royal women are currency. They must be as hard and durable as a gold piece.'

'Oh, they are. To look at Anne you would not think that in Paris now there are riots against her. She's had to flee here! Henrietta's been on the run since King Charles was beheaded. But for one to show weakness to the other would be unthinkable. Queens must preserve *sang-froid*.'

Musicians had entered and tuned their instruments against the chatter of the court. A group of young women in gauzy costumes assembled by the great fireplace, laughing, and rubbing their naked arms.

All noise stopped. The boy-king Louis had entered the hall. The company bowed; the two queens inclined their heads. With a flourish, Louis bowed to them both.

'Your Majesty *Maman*, Your Majesty *Tante Henriette*.' His voice was a child's, clear and melodious. He paused, looking around. 'Why are there no candles lit?'

Queen Anne smiled. A tigress smile. 'Why, Your Majesty my son, your clever *Tante Henriette* has arranged the masque as an afternoon performance. So, there is no need for the expense of candles. Am I not right dear sister?'

Queen Henrietta made an almost imperceptible turn of her head. Her eyes flickered but her body stayed rigid.

'Very well,' said Louis, 'let it begin.' Musicians picked up their instruments and the girls hurried to the makeshift stage.

The masque was brief, barely two hours, and I enjoyed it. The young women who played aspects of Virtue such as Patience, Charity, and Chastity, denoted by the colours blue, red, and white, were sweetly pretty. Queen Henrietta's jester, Jeffrey Hudson, appeared in his customary role as the Evil Imp, pinching the girls' legs and amusing everyone. Finally, Peace was restored, Evil banished and in the closing chorus the company raised green branches as they sang a hymn, praising the unity of God, King, and People. Whatever the defects in production, the show was faultlessly Royalist.

During the performance, I observed Henrietta. She kept her head upright, but her eyes were bright with tears. Was she remembering happier times when she and the King had played in such masques? She had appeared as Queen of the Amazons and danced bare-breasted, clad only in a cloak of iridescent feathers. Now she was *La Reine Malheureuse*, the title with which she signed her letters. Despite myself I was moved by her tears and the sentiments of the masque. At that moment I wanted to believe in peace and harmony.

A space was being cleared and dancing began, stately then more hectic as the company whirled and glittered, trying to recreate the golden sheen of the court they had lost.

A few card tables were set up and alongside, a modest buffet was being served. Janvier headed my way, pushing through a crowd of laughing young women. I helped myself to a glass of burgundy. Here I was, a surgeon of the New Model Army, drinking with the Stuart court in exile. Only weeks ago, surrounded by pain and blood I'd been content cleaning pus-filled wounds and amputating limbs. Now among bottles of champagne and the sight and scent of pretty women, I felt uneasy, sensing danger among the silks and brocade but unable to read its signs. I turned to him.

'Queen Anne has left,' he remarked, 'but you might as well get to know faces. Over there—the fine-looking man in the bronze silk suit, that's Sir Henry Jermyn. Queen

Henrietta does nothing without his advice. Look—she's whispering to him. Some say she is the only woman in his life. I've heard he has huge gambling debts she helps with—although she has no money to spare!'

I saw how the tiny Queen was clinging to Jermyn's arm. His head bent over her, listening, and laughing.

'He's been away on a mission; I don't know where. It looks as if his visit was successful,' muttered Janvier.

'Who's the big white-haired man with the sad face?'

'He fancies himself a sort of doctor, Sir Kenelm Digby. His father was one of those who tried to blow up your King James and Parliament, but the Queen trusts him because he's a Catholic. He says they're writing a medicinal cookery book together if you believe it!'

'Sir Kenelm Digby.' His name was familiar. 'I heard he poisoned his wife with one of his concoctions, trying to preserve her beauty forever. Dr Harvey thinks he's a quack.'

Saying Harvey's name reminded me of why I was was standing drinking expensive wine in this freezing castle—to save the dearest friend and father I never had from imprisonment and likely death. If I had doubts, I reminded myself *this is for Harvey* who genial even in infirmity, was still as sharp as a pin. I had to protect that kind heart and keen intelligence for myself and the world. Perhaps Scot had another reason for his blackmail? Sending me to France would get me out of the way in case a public trial revealed too much of the doings of those great families who ostensibly supported Parliament. But that was over-elaborate. Easier to deploy an assassin—there were narrow alleyways around Ely if all he wanted was to be rid of me. No. This mission was real.

And although he did not know it, Scot was aiding my own private quest. I looked at the courtiers, men and women who whirled like a flock of bright birds; had Lady Derryn danced among them in a dress fit for a queen? For the same dress, a poor laundry maid later paid the ultimate price. Perhaps here in France I would find an answer to those deaths in faraway London.

Without warning, I was surrounded and swept up by a laughing crowd of ladies but before I could delight in their frills and sweet-scented warmth, they parted as if moved by a hidden force. The Boy King had approached.

I bowed as low as I could. Louis grinned, pulling his velvet jerkin tight.

'Monsieur, I understand you are the celebrated English surgeon who has come to tend to his poor brethren in France. There are too many doctors in France already! I detest doctors, monsieur, and surgeons even more! I suppose you are a Protestant—*Maman* the Queen hates Protestants. Still, it is a great consolation when one is ill to have someone who speaks one's native tongue.'

With that he turned and walked away.

'I think he likes you,' said Janvier.

Chapter 14

Friday October 22nd early morning

Friday, a fast day, was always miserable and this one was no exception. Queen Henrietta and her Catholic courtiers were at Mass. Fires stayed unlit and the Palace felt even colder than usual. I sat in my damp room hunched in a blanket. My heavy army cloak had been left in London, probably lost forever. As I shivered, I scribbled my third report for Scot in a month. I hoped he thought he was getting his money's worth. Janvier, whose job it was to transport my letters to London, said nothing either way.

I used a book of ciphers Scot provided. With its shabby leather cover, it looked nondescript, but I had lost no time finding a secure place to conceal it. Using the codes was not difficult, typically depending on the substitution of a letter for a number or another letter together with a set of numbers and phrases that referred to special individuals. I enjoyed encrypting the reports and found my command of ciphers became faster with each one.

Scurrilous information about members of the Parliamentary government and hypocritical acts of the Godly Republic were relayed from spies in London. I was able to indicate to Scot who they might be. As with any group confined under one roof the main subject of interest at St Germain was their own doings: who had quarrelled with whom, who was sleeping with who. Although it was richly entertaining it was nevertheless only the 'courtier's gossip' to which Thurloe had scornfully referred that morning in Scot's Westminster room. Of the King's execution, military strategy, alliances, and funds, little was said. I knew this meant I was not getting to the inner circle, which worried me. And my mind was alert to any mention of a young noblewoman late of this court, murdered in London. But there was nothing.

Today was an exception. I had something useful to report. The Queen had been overruled. Despite Cromwell's victories, some of Charles' advisors still thought Ireland was the best place to launch an invasion to restore his throne. The Queen had quarrelled violently with one of the Irish commanders and was urging an alliance with the Scottish Covenanters, but Charles hated the Covenanters whose Puritan elders had a low opinion of him. His response had angered the Queen further. Striding up and down her tiny figure vibrated with fury as she reminded her son how at the beginning of the war, she had raised money and arms from the Netherlands and as commander in the North had led a Royalist army in the field, sustained a barrage from Parliament's guns and marched triumphantly into Oxford to shouts of 'Generalissima!'

To escape her anger, Charles decided to take refuge in Jersey. There, he was treated like a king already and could continue his affair with the governor's wife. I quoted Janvier's sly observation: *'Whenever he has a problem to solve, he goes and finds a woman.'*

I sighed and stretched; the damp made me sluggish.

Since arriving at St Germain days had passed in a succession of impromptu parties, masques, dances, and hunts. Without the physical demands of work, I lacked exercise. I feared my skills might atrophy but an unforeseen route opened in which I could, partly recreate my old life. Accidents among labourers on the estate were a daily occurrence. Rheumatism from the damp, sprains and bruises, and wounds to hands and feet from spades and pickaxes as they dug out terraces and canals were regarded as normal suffering. No one cared what happened to the men. Janvier had remarked that there was always another worker. I was reminded of the Royalist commanders in Oxford who had shown contempt for their men's welfare. Without asking, I had a room near the laundry cleared and almost every morning found someone waiting for treatment in my makeshift infirmary.

Janvier found it amusing. 'We shall soon see you in wooden shoes, Monsieur Lockyer, and the labourers will be throwing their daughters at you,' he teased. Then a thought occurred to him. 'It could be useful, however, to have somewhere to meet away from Jermyn's eyes.'

It was time for me to go to my *salle de medicin*. As usual someone was waiting. A young woman was standing half-hidden inside the doorway, a baby in her arms. Hearing my steps, she turned quickly clutching the baby. Her long black hair, hanging uncombed, gave her the appearance of gipsy. Her wide brown eyes were worried.

'How can I help you, Madame?'

The woman answered in English. 'Please look at my baby, Sir, he has not slept and seems to be very hot.'

I peered at the baby, wrapped in fine shawls. Babies make me nervous—give me a burly beery soldier with a leg to hack off, any day.

'I am a surgeon, Madame, I know little about the care of infants. If you are part of the court, you would be better asking one of the Queen's doctors.'

'I am asking you, Sir. I do not wish to consult the Queen's doctors,' she replied firmly. Then her words tumbled out. 'I won't let anyone care for him I do not trust. I have many enemies here, but I think you are not one of them for I have not seen you with the Queen's party.' She became insistent, almost ferocious. 'Take him Sir. You must examine him.'

She was prepared to trust me. There was a strength about her, a fierce focus on her child. Reluctantly, I took him from her arms. As far I could judge, he was a little over six months old. To me he seemed healthy enough. His little body felt warm but not hot.

I spoke cautiously. 'How long has he been feverish? He seems alright now.'

The woman looked defiant. 'He was crying all night.'

I looked inside his mouth and ears and felt relieved. There was no inflammation, dryness, or foulness.

'He has no fever now and seems ready to sleep. Perhaps he needs more pap. He's growing, after all. Let him sleep and if he wakes again, feed him a little more than usual. Make sure he drinks enough, as well. I see he is almost out of swaddling bands. Give him a wash in tepid water—and perhaps fewer wrappings?'

She smiled. 'Thank you, Sir, but our room in the Palace is cold. We stay there for safety when his father is away. He's in Jersey at present. Thank God he will be back here soon.' She hugged the child, whose eyes were now closed.

'Is he attending upon Prince Charles?'

She let out deep warm laugh. 'No, Sir, he *is* Prince Charles—His Majesty King Charles since the beginning of this year. King Charles is my husband. I am Lucy Walter his wife and this little boy is our son. He was born in March. We were married last year in Liege.'

Chapter 15

Friday 22nd October mid-morning

I was furious with myself. How had I missed that? Was this gipsy woman truly the King's wife? No one had mentioned her. All the talk had been of Queen Henrietta's attempts to marry Charles to her wealthy niece, Anne-Marie de Bourbon. Queen Anne was naturally opposed but as the gossips said, at twenty-three, La Grande Mademoiselle was not getting younger. Why had I not listened more closely? I'd failed to heed hints and silences.

'Monsieur, you must be more careful!' A sardonic voice. 'You have been keeping company with *la maitresse en titre*. Men have been broken on the wheel for less!'

Janvier walked towards me. Beside him trotted a man in the uniform of a Royalist captain.

'You mean Lucy Walter? Why didn't you tell me about her son?'

'You didn't ask. I flatter her with the title *maitresse*, since she never shows her face and a true *maitresse en titre* is far from reticent. Queen Henrietta hates her. She barely conceals it—acts as if Lucy doesn't exist.'

'The Queen has a horror of bastards. Her father spawned at least eight. They and their mothers were an endless source of trouble when she was growing up,' drawled the soldier.

Janvier said, 'May I present Captain Joseph Bamfylde—friend of Prince James the Duke of York. Meet Surgeon-major Lockyer.'

The short man had a shiny face and a tuft of wispy beard. I'd seen him before dancing vigorously and acting the fop. He held out his hand. '*Surgeon*-major, is it? Not in the front charge, but hacking men up afterwards, eh?'

'I must assume you fought in that leading position,' I said, feeling the man's small, smooth hand. He looked malicious and intelligent.

'My work for His Late Majesty was too specialised to allow me to run such risks,' said Bamfylde, smiling. 'Good to make a new acquaintance! I hear you were Northumberland's private surgeon. I must have missed you at Syon House—but we can explore that over a bottle or two. Come and take wine with me this evening. Janvier will tell you where to find me.'

When Bamfylde was out of earshot, Janvier asked, 'Is the report for London ready?'

'How long have you known about the son?'

'I heard only recently. I don't think Scot knows; tell him if you like. In any case the child is just another royal bastard.'

'No, you're mistaken Janvier. She says they were married last year.'

Janvier scoffed. 'Absurd idea! Bamfylde says she is given to making up stories—like her claim to be descended from ancient Welsh royalty. The girl is of middling gentry stock; she's not clever and royal attention has turned her head.'

'That's Bamfylde's opinion, is it? I'm not sure I'd believe

everything *he* says. I won't be taking up his invitation.'

'Foolish of you, Monsieur Lockyer. You need him to get you close to the Stuarts.'

'I'll find some other way, Janvier. I'm going to amend my report—it will be ready in an hour. You are leaving soon to catch the evening boat for London, so I wish you safe passage. When you arrive, please inquire about Dr Harvey's welfare.'

Friday 29th October evening

Although our exchange had been brief, I had taken an instant dislike to Bamfylde. As someone said, it saves time. Most of the cavaliers hid their grief and disappointment with frantic gaiety, but Bamfylde was far too contented. Perhaps it was his closeness to Prince James that gave him that cocky air. The Queen and her two sons were like planets, each encircled with its own collection of advisors and hangers-on. These factions were bitter enemies united only in the fact that Jermyn, the Queen's closest confidante was hated by everyone.

I walked back to my rooms, easier now the mud had recently been covered with gravel. The main balustrades were built and the largest of six fountains was working. Wind blew the cold spray everywhere and I was obliged to dodge it. I could hear shouts and music and noticed, two storeys up, torches flaring in the Great Hall. Silhouetted against the light, a young man swayed on the window-ledge, drinking from a bottle to cheers and shouts. Then, others climbed out. Moonlight caught the gleam of bottles, buckles, and the silver slash in a velvet sleeve. Three young men waved and grabbed unsteadily at the smooth stone arches of the window. The yells and whoops intensified to the sound of breaking glass. More windows were filling with figures gesturing and leaning perilously.

Every young man, including me, has made a drunken dangerous walk. Most are lucky. I knew that at that height anyone falling would be badly injured or lose his life. I ran inside and saw Bamfylde running too, from another direction. He yelled loudly as we raced upstairs and entered the Great Hall neck and neck.

'Jamie! Jamie! Jamie!'

Everyone turned, the musicians stopped playing and the room went quiet. I strode to the pack of young men. One had a pistol, another a short sword he was jabbing in the air. They were all drunk. During what seemed like a long minute I glared at them.

'Gentlemen, no man of honour wants to die falling from a window,' I said.

My height, stern look and because they had no idea who I was, had an effect; one by one the youths climbed inside. I was relieved but it didn't last. An angry voice shouted, 'Who are you? Did the Queen send you? It's my birthday party, Bamfylde, I'm sixteen. Why does she want to spoil everything?'

The voice was young but commanding. A tall, fair young man, with a rosy face in which sweetness and sulk were mixed was its owner. Prince James.

'Your Highness your safety is as important as His Majesty's your brother. You are precious,' replied Bamfylde.

The boy flushed. 'Oh yes, very precious, very precious indeed. So precious as to be left behind in Oxford, to be left behind in England—'

'From where your Highness made a daring escape' interrupted Bamfylde.

'—to be left behind in Flanders, passed over at Sluys, told I can't command a Navy, left again while my brother makes war plans in Jersey…' As he recited these humiliations, he was close to tears. This wasn't simply a young man's petulance.

Bamfylde put his arm around the prince. 'Your Highness, my duty is to protect you for I know how much you wish to restore your family. You cannot do that if you are maimed or killed. Enjoy yourself of course but exercise care.'

The music had started again. The company was quieter now and I noticed some young men and girls were already slipping away in pairs as the mood of the evening shifted.

Bamfylde glanced at me. He had lost very little of his complacency.

'Thank you Surgeon-major although I think I might have managed. You see what I must deal with! I should stay and watch the prince this evening. You are welcome to stay too.'

He held out a gold rimmed glass of claret. I took it and sipped. On the dance floor Prince James and a plump girl in white silk were laughing together and I remembered how easily young men are distracted.

'He was quite unhappy earlier,' I said. 'Why is that?'

Bamfylde considered. 'The Queen is angry with him—with both her sons. Lockyer, best you hear this from me, there is so much untrustworthy gossip. The princes love each other but something happened that nearly ripped them asunder. Things have still not quite recovered.'

I leaned closer, alert. Bamfylde seemed eager to confide in me. 'In February after the late King's murder,' he continued. 'Both Charles and Jamie were at his sister Princess Mary's court in The Hague. That creature Lucy Walter was there pregnant with Charles' bastard. There was the usual flock of fly-by-night young women and Jamie fell in love with one. Deeply. But Charles wanted her as well.'

'Did James step aside for his brother?'

'Of course not. They quarrelled—they almost fought. Charles had his way, he always does. But his sister was furious. She knew a scandal was brewing. She felt the family had to stay united, so I was asked to get the girl away. Send her to London.'

He gave a self-satisfied shrug.

'Any difficulties it's "*Bamfylde will attend to it.*" She has relatives in London, supporters of the English Republic—the Earl and Countess of Pembroke. I brokered it with the Sidney brothers—you know there is one on each side of this war? Robert commands for the King and Algernon's a Parliamentary hero! Opposing sides but you'd never know.'

Not when it comes to hiding a scandal.

'Noble families stick together,' I remarked. 'That is how they survive.'

Bamfylde gave a knowing laugh.

'Oh yes, blood counts. While men like me sort out the mess. Not had a word of thanks from anyone of course.'

One more question, I thought. Then I can be sure. 'What was her name?'

'Can't remember. Something Welsh and outlandish.' He yawned.

'Good company is scarce here. We must have a longer talk. Come to my rooms—let's make an evening of it soon!'

So Derryn had been here, I was almost certain! I felt elated. No, I didn't like Bamfylde; I was sure he felt the same. To me he was a typical royalist sycophant of whom I'd seen many. Yet I must use the fact that he wanted to impress me with his insider knowledge to keep him close.

As I walked back along the Great Terrace, I felt large, cold drops of rain on my bare head. Black water lay in the half-dug lake below the terrace and beyond lay flooded fields. Damp hung in the air, and I knew I would not sleep well.

Derryn did not come into my dreams at first, but I lay thinking of her. I remembered the night she had been carried from the street, moaning and blood-stained. I recalled the gasp of her last breath. I had held her living child. Despite the assurances van Prin gave, I believed Pembroke must be involved in her murder. Why did the Earl want her dead? Bamfylde had played his part too. I wondered what it could have been.

Saturday 30th October midday

I'd been roused by a fierce knocking at dawn and Bamfylde's urgent call. Now I was sitting by the bed of a young courtier. I was not optimistic; I had treated chest wounds before on the battlefield. A few men had lived. Most had died. The lungs could collapse or if they didn't blood could set in clots inside the chest or an infection might take over.

Earlier that morning, a duel had taken place. Bamfylde

came to my chamber door, his face twisted with anxiety, hissing that all must be kept secret as duelling was forbidden. One of the young men had superficial injuries to his arm. The other had a sword still sticking out of his chest. I left the sword in place; pulling it out would cause the boy to bleed to death. Then to cries of alarm from those watching, I took my square-headed lancet and cutting just below the boy's armpit managed to drain the blood which was causing him to suffocate. The wound was deep and I had packed it with rolled lint to allow the humours to breathe and to soothe damaged nerves. But he had lost blood and was in deep shock.

I fed him sips of water. Now I could only watch and wait and wish that Ambroise Paré was at my side! That bold surgeon's calm and cheerful words, full of experience and practical good sense were what I needed.

Instead, it was Henry, Lord Jermyn who barged into the room. His face was thunderous, and his voice was haughty; this was the first time he had deigned to notice me.

'Surgeon-major I suppose I must thank you. We are lucky you were there. My nephew Richard will be punished for his foolishness.'

'My Lord, compared to the other boy, his wound was not severe; however, his sword arm is damaged. He'll have pain and some loss of movement for a while. That should be punishment enough.'

Jermyn clearly had something on his mind.

'Surgeon-major, duelling is forbidden in France as it is in England-but the French have severe laws, feebly enforced. Instead, occasionally someone is selected for exemplary punishment—it must not be my nephew!

When all is said—we are precarious guests here. I'm told Prince James was present.'

Jermyn took a step closer, and I was enveloped by the nobleman's over—scented breath. I saw the muscles of his arm under his silk shirt. He was staring at me intently.

'I don't really *know* you surgeon major. I assume you are a faithful servant of his Majesty. I believe you know your duty in this matter.'

'You want me to keep quiet. Is that it?'

'I command your loyalty, yes.' Command indeed! The man was just a bully.

Then, in an instant Jermyn's manner changed. He looked worried.

'Is the boy going to survive? It was my nephew who wounded him. I beg your discretion.'

'My Lord, news has already spread. The boy's name is Owain Hopkins—everyone knows he's a friend of Prince James and will draw their own conclusions. In any case he is likely to die before the day is out.'

Chapter 16

Sunday 31st October morning

Owain Hopkins did not die that day or overnight.

Prince James came to visit, watching me as I fretted over the boy. The large lint roll with which I had packed the wound was still in place but leaving it for too long would delay healing and closure. He'd developed a fever, as so often happens. And his survival was still uncertain. Observing me, James looked thoughtful.

'Mr Lockyer, I want to apologise for my boorishness the night of my birthday. I was celebrating.' He looked over at his friend.

'I think I would like to be a surgeon. It's useful—will you teach me?'

'It's mostly blood, bone and bandages—and lots of screams,' I replied. 'Not a job for Princes.'

He laughed his young face full of the sweet knowledge of being special.

'Well, as I'm a Prince let me do the job I can do—come to the chapel tomorrow and after Mass I will present you to the Queen,' he said.

The next morning at Mass I prayed for Owen. I prayed for myself too, that my soul would be healed. At the end of the Last Gospel James brought me to Queen

Henrietta. I bowed to the little Queen, charmed by her enormous smile and brilliant black eyes. Her diminutive arm rested on Lord Jermyn's sturdy one.

'Did you not think the music splendid?' she said.

'Beautiful, Your Majesty. The choir has a rare sound.'

She had already turned away to greet Queen Anne.

'Your Majesty my sister, the music was exquisite, sung with unusual sweetness and reverence,' she said, too brightly. The Regent remained unsmiling.

'Yes, dear sister, the choir is from my convent in Val de Grace. It includes several Englishwomen sent here for safety; such is the disorder of your God-forsaken country. And you seem to be bringing it here. I am told there was a duel among your young men!'

'I fear Your Majesty is misinformed,' said Jermyn smoothly. 'An accident during rapier practice, that's all.' Henrietta nodded.

Queen Anne pulled on her deerskin gloves and glared.

I ducked away and James caught me up.

'Perhaps you're right about surgery Lockyer, it is rather lowly. I want to be a soldier or a sailor. Do you know I was made Lord High Admiral when I was nine? The sailors love me—they said so. Bamfylde says they love me better than my brother.'

'Those are dangerous sentiments.' I spoke sharply. 'He was unwise to say that, don't listen to him. Your brother is the King.'

'I know,' he replied sulkily 'I am always second.'

As we arrived at the *salle de medicin*, I heard singing. Lucy Walter was sitting by Owain's bed and holding his hand. She broke off.

'He is so hot. I washed his face,' she said. Seeing James,

she stood up and curtseyed.

'Your Highness.'

'Good day madam,' said James coldly. As soon as she had gone, he rushed over to Owain.

'His fever is worse.' The boy moaned.

I wrung out more cold cloths. Prince James laid them gently on Owain's face and neck.

'Was that a Welsh song?' I asked. 'She has a sweet voice.'

'Owain Hopkins is her kinsman. His Majesty my brother loves Madam Walter in his way. She is a beauty for certain, but she causes trouble. That duel yesterday— Richard Jermyn was drunk as usual and when he saw Owain he shouted that all the Welsh are good for is making bastards. Owain couldn't let that go.'

'I see.' It was a clear provocation from Jermyn's nephew. He had all but issued a challenge.

'She makes things up. She says she's married to my brother. She's even called her bastard *James*. That is a royal name. That is my name! Yet everyone knows that Robert Sidney had her first.'

Sunday 31st October late afternoon

Lucy had returned. Owain was awake and suffering a lot of pain. Between spasms, he muttered in Welsh. I was worried; his fever was stilling, not to a healthy calm but to a clammy coldness. His breathing was short, and he dribbled blood.

'Sir Kenelm has asked me to give you his wound salve. It is very special and he's sure it will help.'

She smiled and held up a green jar. I peered and sniffed

at the green mixture inside and decided it was yet another of his doubtful concoctions.

'Thank Sir Kenelm, but none of that is to be smeared on a patient of mine.'

'No, Mr Lockyer that's not how it works! You mix some of the foul matter from the wound into this liquid and it will heal.'

Owain groaned. I lifted the soiled dressing from his side. A massive blood clot had ripened, and I caught the whiff of corrupt matter.

'Help me to turn him over the edge of the bed-then hold his nose. Now Owain, deep breath, deep, deep, breath. And hold.' He gasped.

'Your life depends on it,' I urged. With a massive effort the weakened man took air into his lungs and held it.

As I'd hoped, at the change in pressure blood and clots gushed from the wound. I reached in with my finger and felt more lumps as the contaminated fluid flowed away and Owain, released from suffocation, coughed weakly as we laid him back on the bed.

'Je le pansay, Dieu le guarit,' I murmured Paré's words under my breath.

I looked at the pool of fetid blood and turned to Lucy. 'You might as well mix it with Sir Kenelm's wound salve. It cannot harm.'

She unsealed the jar snapping the wax with her nails. It was the first time I had really looked at her. She was truly beautiful with lustrous black hair, dark eyes and glowing skin. But not the wife of a king surely! Lucy had none of the courtier's affectations. Her claim must be mistaken, merely a comforting fiction.

After she had finished her task, she left. I put the jar

aside and cleaned Owain's wound. Then I covered it with a loose dressing and left it to drain. Now I could only hope, leaving Nature, the greatest physician to do what she would.

There was a tap on the door. Bamfylde entered looking embarrassed. It was, I guessed, a feeling unfamiliar to him.

'Surgeon-major Lockyer, forgive me, I'll say this plainly. The Queen has made it clear that she strongly disapproves of Prince James' visits to your—er—*salle*. She forbids any further contact between yourself and the prince.'

I wasn't offended—just curious. It was a setback to my task as a spy.

'She doesn't mind that that he associates with a rascal like yourself!'

Bamfylde frowned. 'There's no comparison between our positions. I take care of him on her behalf and sort out any scrape he gets into. Don't forget I helped Prince James in his escape from London. No matter. I have delivered my message. I hope this will not mean bad feeling between us.'

'Out of interest—why does she disapprove of me?' Lockyer asked.

'You have been seen in the company of Lucy Walter, who has visited your *salle*. And you appear to be on close terms with Monsieur Janvier, a servant of Mazarin and therefore Queen Anne. Shall I go on?'

'No need.'

Bamfylde extended his hand. He smiled.

'As I told you, good company is scarce here. Why don't you visit me tomorrow evening? We can drink and talk about past times—our memories of the war.'

'Very well, if you want to spend an evening discussing smashed skulls, burns and amputations.'

On balance, my mission was turning into a mess.

Chapter 17

Monday 1st November Feast of All Saints late evening

That evening as I arrived at Bamfylde's apartments, the first thing I noticed was the freshly opened brandy bottle. Then, that it was half empty. Nor did his greeting put me at ease.

'Come in Surgeon-major or doctor or whatever you are,' he gurgled. 'In fact, *what* are you exactly? No one seems to know! Never mind–have a drink and hear my news!'

The disorder in Bamfylde's room made me feel uncomfortable. Discarded and dirty garments were piled in one corner, books and papers were spread on the floor. Bamfylde himself sprawled on a large sofa, his boots off, hat and cloak carelessly discarded. I noticed a fine pair of pistols in an open case, and a sword leaning against the wooden sideboard. I'd not been offered a chair, so I poured a large helping of brandy, pushed a bundle of clothes together and sat, ready to listen.

'What's your news Bamfylde?'

My host leered tipsily.

'A woman of course, Lockyer. From Eve onwards, are they not the downfall of us all? There is a woman to whom I owe a debt.'

'Of money?'

'Of love. And it must be paid—and shortly will be. I am returning to London to be married.'

'Married?' Truly the thought of Bamfylde as a spouse was not credible. 'Now you have surprised me.'

'I have surprised myself, Lockyer. I'm not a man for entanglements. There is only one person who has my loyalty—'

He lurched towards the table and grabbed a silver-framed miniature.

'Jamie, my young prince. Lockyer, you wouldn't believe what I have done for him.'

He threw his arms wide in a maudlin gesture. I knew the story but decided to humour him.

'I outwitted all Parliament's agents and—helped by the lady mentioned—brought him to France.'

'I hear she bought a woman's travelling dress for him and convinced the tailor of the unusual size of the wearer.'

'She did! It was bravely done. For the Stuart cause and for love for me.' Bamfylde drained his glass. 'So, I must honour my promise.'

'I am not sorry to leave,' he continued. 'Jermyn commands everything here. Ireland is lost. The King returns tomorrow from Jersey and an alliance with the Scots looks likely. Their leader Argyle wants to marry his daughter to Charles. It will be hard for the Stuarts—they'll have to curb their ways.'

Charles must be feeling desperate to ally with the Scots. It meant nothing substantial in arms or money was coming from France or any other power.

'The Scots sold his father to Cromwell! How can he bear to treat with them?'

'He can't. But he's putting on a virtuous front. Mistress Walter and her bastard are being packed off to Paris. I had to convince the poor girl that the King would be joining her.'

Tottering, Bamfylde refilled our glasses. The liquid glowed amber.

'Armagnac! From Normandy. The locals there drink a tumbler a day to keep them healthy. Confusion to Jermyn!'

I saw again the big man in silk and felt the power of his arrogant gaze. He would harm anyone who tried to hinder him and had been accustomed all his pampered life to getting his own way.

'I'll drink to that.'

Bamfylde wiped his mouth.

'I do the dirty work around here. Jermyn doesn't. Remember that girl that both princes were after?' He gave a sly look and giggled. 'Princess Mary knew that both dogs had mounted the bitch—with a consequence. You know what Her Highness said? *'One bastard is enough.'*

'What did you do Bamfylde?'

'Made travel arrangements for the girl—with the Sidneys, as I said. And broke the news to Jamie who raged and moped for days. I told the Princess it was all dealt with.'

All dealt with. A laughing flirtation of laces and silks ends in screams and blood on the dirty banks of the Fleet. Bamfylde, you dealt with it alright.

'Tell me again who she was.'

'I told you–a lovely Welsh pigeon. I sent her back to her coop!' And he roared with laughter.

I hit him.

I could say it was the brandy, but truly it was his laugh, coarse and grating. Ragged like the cut I'd had made in Derryn's belly. In a rush of memory, I heard Sidney's voice and recalled Pembroke's haughty manner. No one cared about her. *All dealt with.*

I hit him again. And before I knew why I had Bamfylde by the throat. I was a head taller and stronger, and I shook Bamfylde like a pit bull shakes a rat.

'You murdered her, didn't you? You killed Lady Derryn!'

Bamfylde struggled and wheezed.

'Killed her? Why would I? I helped her! Dead—how?'

'Stabbed to death in the street two months ago—and you know it!' I wanted to go on squeezing until the man's life was gone and my grip tightened.

'Please—'gasped Bamfylde, 'please—I'm not—I gave her money—lots of it. Gold!'

That stopped me. Gold? Would a murderer do that? I let go—just in time. Bamfylde fell to the floor. He lay gasping, rubbing his bruised neck. Then to my surprise, he rallied. He suddenly appeared quite sober.

'That is a powerful grip, Surgeon-major,' he croaked. 'I suppose it comes with the job.' He looked at me earnestly.

'I planned carefully; no one wanted her harmed. Just a discreet removal. I thought I had taken her to safety returning her to the Pembroke household. Now you tell me that I was badly mistaken.'

He shook his head. 'I did not foresee this. Jamie will be distraught—he must not learn of it.'

He grabbed at the flask of Armagnac and took a slug. His elbow dislodged a pile of books from the table. As they crashed to the floor, I glimpsed something lying underneath that I recognised immediately: a brown octavo volume with a worn leather cover.

Now Bamfylde was standing straight. He swayed, but his head was up, and his eyes were hard and suspicious.

'You were never in the service of the Earl of Northumberland, were you?'

I countered swiftly.

'What about you? That daring escape of Prince James—has no one asked how you slipped under the Parliamentary guns at Deptford without any check? Perhaps they *allowed* the escape. Then James couldn't be a rallying point for rebels.'

'That's a ridiculous idea,' Bamfylde said, 'trying to draw attention away from your own treachery.' He flung his arms wide dramatically. 'I'll make sure everyone knows that you are a spy!'

I reached for Scot's leather code book and shoved it across to Bamfylde.

'If I'm the spy who gave you this?'

Bamfylde was silent a moment. He looked at the little book then at me. Then he laughed.

'If you recognise that, then you know who gave it to me. If you also possess one, then you'll realise we are on the same side.'

It was all downhill after that. I drank too much. Bamfylde showed no hard feelings, indeed acted as if the violence sealed our friendship. He opened more bottles and tried to entertain me with lewd stories about the Stuart court. I'd heard most of it before. Then he started on powerful Parliamentarians using information which he said came straight from Scot. In the end I tired of him. I needed some fresh air and got up to go. He grabbed my arm.

'Merely out of interest, how much are you being paid? Just to make sure I am not undervalued.'

'My payment,' I replied, 'is the life of a friend.' It sounded dramatic, but I was drunk. And it was true.

'Oh, you outdo me in humanity, Surgeon-major.' He gave a mocking bow as I opened the door.

Outside I took a lungful of cold air and looked up at the night sky. I could see the misty sisters, the Pleiades and below them the brilliant Aldebaran, named The Follower by the Arabs because it tracked the Seven Sisters faithfully across the winter sky. And I thought to myself, tonight I lost control and almost killed a man. I'd seen so much slaughter, but I'd hoped to use surgery to mend, heal and remove harm, to repair the damaged men before me. Now, I was reminded that I was no one special. I too could murder—and do it with bare hands.

Bamfylde is Scot's man here at Court, I thought. It had been Scot's plan to set each of us to watch the other. Bamfylde claims that he only made travel arrangements. What other arrangements might he have made? He's a professional. I'm an amateur and he knows my identity. In a soldiers' vocabulary acquired over several years of war, I soundly cursed myself.

Bamfylde is an outright liar, cunning and deceptive, perhaps he will expose me, but he could betray himself. Above all, he's a survivor. Safer for him to keep quiet and head back to England.

I pitied the woman waiting for him there.

Next day, Owain improved. He was weak, but the fever had gone. He had not been alone. Lucy Walter sat for many hours with her kinsman spooning broth into him, talking softly in Welsh. Once Owain slept she turned to me. She smiled a conspiratorial smile and whispered, 'Mr Lockyer, my dearest Charles is returning from Jersey this week. We shall soon be together again in Paris, away from here! Captain Bamfylde is arranging it.'

I said nothing.

Prince James arrived to visit his friend. He scowled at Lucy, who put the feeding cup down and hurried away. James took her place at Owain's bedside and in a few minutes the two young men were laughing together, James heartily, Owain rasping and weak. Then James stood up and grinned at Lockyer.

'I know my mother does not wish me to associate with you, Mr Lockyer. She thinks you are barely a gentleman. But I hope I know the worth of a man. She doesn't like the fact that Owain is my friend, either—she knows it was Lord Jermyn's nephew who nearly killed him. Richard Jermyn is a loud-mouthed bully.'

Like his uncle, I thought. 'Rivalries and dislikes are widespread here,' I observed. James laughed.

'No one can avoid them—not you or anyone. In this little kingdom, all are subject to the rule of gossip. Don't believe half of what is whispered—the trouble is knowing which half,' he said.

'Yes indeed. That is the most difficult,' said a third voice. Janvier had entered the *salle*.

'I'm going,' said James. 'Before Her Majesty my mother sends Goody Bamfylde to summon me for a scolding.'

Janvier bent over the fire and warmed his hands. Then turned his backside to do the same. 'I need your latest report. And I have two letters for you. One from Dr

Harvey.'

'William! Did you see him? How is he?'

'Read his letter.'

I tore it open.

Harvey reported that his gout was bothering him and his feet *'are as if held to the fire by a torturer. I immerse my legs in cold water for hours to ease them.'* Leticia, who had been skilled at making soothing plasters had left the household in St Laurence Lane some weeks before. *'London has many temptations. My brother persuaded me that Leticia is well of an age to need a woman's care. She has joined the household of Countess Ranelegh, a woman of great learning and unquestioned piety, to continue her studies. I miss her. I am finishing my labours on the development of the embryo. Return quickly, John, I need your judgement on the length and order of the manuscript.'*

To hear from him lifted my heart. It seemed our friendship remained undamaged. I was also relieved that Letitia had departed. Without her, life for Harvey might be bleaker but less risky. Scot's agents would know she had gone. I lifted the seal of the Commonwealth on the second letter.

'We have learned from to our agents in The Hague that the brothers Charles and James Stuart will be joining Mary, Princess of Orange there by January. The wife of the late Charles Stuart, Henrietta Maria of France will remain as a guest of the Regent of France Queen Anne and her son King Louis.

Charles Stuart may then attempt to land on these shores and foment rebellion.

At present there seems no advantage to your continued presence at the Palais St Germain and you are hereby instructed to return as soon as transport is available and report to me within a fortnight at the latest.' The letter bore no signature, but one name—'Jo; Thurloe. Assistant to the Committee of Examiners.'

'I suppose you are wondering what has happened to Scot,' Janvier remarked. 'As the plots of the Royalists grow more complex, Thurloe is adding more to his brief. He and Scot will soon collide.'

My mind still full of Harvey's news, I'd had failed to notice something obvious. The letter was in plain secretary hand, not encoded.

'How do you know that?'

'Forgive me Monsieur Lockyer. I know it is wrong to read letters addressed to someone else. I wanted to discover the latest codes you English are using. They are not quite as advanced as ours. I transcribed your letter from Mr Thurloe. You must have suspected me before now. Surely?'

True, but I had hoped he was generally benign.

'So you *are* more than a courier who sells art.'

'My chief talent is my ability in codes and ciphers. I was impressed with how quickly you picked them up.'

'Thank you. I suppose this means that everything in my reports is known to Cardinal Mazarin.'

Janvier smiled apologetically.

'He doesn't think the Republic will last, but like Richelieu before him, he distrusts the Stuarts. Mazarin wants to ensure that England never rises again to threaten the supremacy of France. Come Monsieur Lockyer—John—we are almost friends. I have been frank with you. You will be going home soon and will see your beloved Harvey again. Let me offer an unusual *divertissement.*

Come with me and watch King Louis at Mass this evening.'

'Mass? Again?' I protested.

'Today is the Day of the Dead. Catholics pray for them a lot,' Janvier replied.

Chapter 18

Tuesday November 2nd Feast of All Souls early evening

The young king had made two orders: only black or white garments were to be worn and there would be no reserved places. All ranks would be mixed to symbolise the equality of death. Courtiers had already tried to huddle separately but were being forced to mingle. Black velvet stood incongruously next to the unbleached linens and rough wool of the workmen. The voices of the choir soared up to the lofty darkness. At the *de Profundis*, King Louis, dressed in a surplice of white satin, walked slowly across the nave and prostrated before the altar. At the words 'let perpetual light shine upon them' he rose and simultaneously nine great candles flamed. The solid gold monstrance on the altar shimmered in reflection and all the jewelled cups and altar plates glittered. As the choir sang the magnificent Office for the Dead, I observed Sir Kenelm Digby. The old man was weeping openly. Was that for his beautiful wife, I wondered?

'Louis loves a religious spectacle especially if he's at the centre,' whispered Janvier.

'You are irreverent Janvier.' I was slightly shocked.

'France is the eldest daughter of the Church—we are allowed to mock,' he said, laughing. I had been impressed.

Say what you like about General Cromwell, he wouldn't be able to put on a show like that.

The crowds streamed out of the Chapel. Bamfylde, with one arm around Prince James' shoulders waved cheerily across as Lucy Walter hurried by, her cloak pulled tight. Members of the choir, clad in long grey cloaks, were filing out, eyes downcast. As they came abreast, one of the women raised her head and I found myself looking directly at her. She returned my gaze and, in an instant, had passed by. The line continued and quickly vanished in the winter darkness.

There had been no hint of recognition from Madame O'Brien.

I was stunned. Had I imagined it? Janvier said, 'John, what is the matter? You look as if the ghost of old Henri Quatre has appeared, with all his stab wounds bleeding!'

'Where in the palace are the members of the choir housed?' I asked wildly.

'Probably somewhere behind the Queen's apartments I suppose, near the east wing. Why?'

'I thought I saw someone...'

'What!' Janvier laughed. 'Val de Grace is a foundation for aristocratic widows. Some say that is why their singing is so rich and sweet—not a bunch of piping virgins! John, you hunt dangerously—first Charles Stuart's mistress now some mysterious lady under the Queen Regent's protection. Can't you be satisfied with light-headed jades?'

'What jades? Any one new?' Bamfylde had pushed his way across, his arm linked with the Prince. 'Let his Highness know, will you? He's tried all the current crop! Am I right Jamie?' He chuckled and Prince looked uncomfortable. He beamed at me expectantly. 'Surgeon-major dine with me tonight—I've—'

'I must go,' I said and headed towards the eastern turret of the Palace, determined to find her.

Tuesday 2 November evening

Under the massive arched gate, Madame O'Brien was waiting. Another woman, equally tall, was at her side. Wrapped in the grey cloaks of the Val de Grace Order, they stood together in the biting wind. I shivered.

'Can we go inside?'

Madame O'Brien shook her head. 'No men,' she said. 'We can talk in the lay sisters' niche.' The three of us entered and stood among the brooms, buckets, and mops. It was too dark to see the stranger's face, so I felt, rather than saw, something familiar in Madame O'Brien's companion.

'Madame O'Brien what are you doing here?' She was the last person I wanted around, in fact I wished her a hundred miles away. She could ruin the final few days of my tattered mission.

'I can't tell you that. Mr Lockyer, this young woman is in danger. There's someone here who could do her a lot of harm. She needs immediate help to leave for Paris.'

'I am not able to move freely here.'

The other woman laughed softly.

'Come Sir, a doctor has more freedom than most. He can go almost anywhere; no one will question him.'

Her voice had a tinge of London's streets. A bell sounded directly above, and the door opened.

'We must go,' said Madame O'Brien. 'The choir has to prepare for Vespers.'

'Not more singing!' complained the young woman.

'It has saved you so far,' Madame replied sharply. 'Mr Lockyer, where can we meet safely and when?'

I described the location of my little infirmary.

'Come tomorrow mid-morning. If there are any patients, they will have gone by then.'

As light from the galleried courtyard fell on all three of us, I got a proper look at the stranger. By some devil's trick, her drab nun's garb flattered rather than concealed her beauty. I was sure of one thing—a pretty woman was a complication I did not need.

Wednesday November 3rd before dawn

I left Madame locked behind her convent gate and immediately ran into a posse of young Grooms of the Bedchamber who cheered and pestered me for war tales. This resulted in another night of heavy drinking. I fell into bed without bothering to undress and my sleep was deep and dreamless. Waking, I groped for my bedside water flask and took a long gulp. Then I heaved myself up and lumbered towards the chamber-pot. It was still dark, and the air felt damp. I was scratching around to light a candle when without warning, the door opened.

Before I could stop her, she was standing inside.

She moved closer and stood next to the bed. No longer dressed in the dowdy habit of Val de Grace, she wore a blue travelling cloak with a red fox trim. The hood was down, and as my eyes focussed, I could see a gleam of dark blonde hair.

'I hope I don't disturb your morning prayers, Mr Lockyer,' she said, smiling.

'What do you want? I asked you to come later with Madame O'Brien.'

'Later is too late. I have some private business to discuss with you, Sir.'

Her skirts rustled as she gave a half—curtsey.

'Finny Watts, sister of Sally. From Mistress Grahame's—I expect you've heard of Whitecross Street.'

I was right, it is her. She resembles Sally—except she is far more beautiful and unmistakeably alive.

'What do you want Miss Finny? Money?'

Finny laughed. 'A whore always wants money—is that it? No, Mr Lockyer, I want something else. I want *you*.' She moved closer to me, and I backed away hoping the stench of me would put her off.

'Me? Is someone hurt?' She was only a few inches away.

'Hurt? There might be!' she said. 'Sir, I need get out of this dreary place! I'm not going to moulder in a convent choir. A whore's worth goes down fast—Paris is the best place for me. Listen, we could set up together—you could make a lot of money there from the rich—treating the foul disease! I hear the French are rotten with it!'

She was in earnest. And it was not a bad plan. Although my head hurt, I could not resist grinning at her.

'How did you get to France?'

She sighed.

'Clothes of the dead are bad luck. When Sally was killed, I was scared I might be next. I ran to Father Southworth's. A few days later Madame O'Brien came there needing to hide. I begged her to take me to France with her.'

'There was a small fortune sewn into the hem of that

dress. Did you take it?' Finny pursed her lips and frowned.

'You know about that?'

Her closeness and warmth were distracting.

'After Sally was killed, I tried to find you, Finny. I met Mistress Grahame—an unusual whore mistress. I thought. Tell me about her.'

'Must I?' said Finny impatiently. 'Mistress Grahame doesn't just deal in flesh. Men come there for other reasons, women too. After dark. Now, will you help me?'

'What did they want?' Whitecross Street had been full of muffled sounds and shadows.

'How should I know? Mistress Grahame would take them into her room and lock the door.

'I've always wanted to get away—I wanted to be free— as free as those gentlemen who came and went as they pleased! As high as them! I want that now!' She clasped her hands and the big ring on her forefinger flashed fire.

'You made it to France—so what is the danger here?'

'Alright, I made that up to stop Madame O'Brien. The woman is hoping to convert me! But I am in danger—of dying from boredom! In Paris, there is so much—gowns, wine, music. The theatre! A new life where I will be loved and respected. Will you take me to Paris?'

A young hopeful woman! Perhaps she believed that she could have everything, but I knew that these days, especially in Paris, love and respect were in short supply.

I was tempted. She was such a beautiful supplicant. For a moment, her pale face filled all my senses, the narrow room looked full of seductive corners, my rumpled bed widened and smoothed. Even my soiled surgeons smock hung alluringly along the back of the settle. The sight of it brought me down to earth and I began to laugh at myself.

It was not the time or place for adventures. They belonged in another life—for on my mind now was a summons from Thurloe. If I disobeyed what would happen to Harvey? No.

'No.'

She stepped back and looked puzzled.

'It can't be because you've a fancy for Madame O'Brien. She's quite old you know—she must be all of thirty, and all she cares about is her runaway Catholics and worn-out priests.'

'Finny, my future is not in Paris. England is my home. I must go back there.'

'In England they still think you killed that woman—you are up for a hanging!'

She reached inside her cloak and took out some fragile sheets of white paper. 'Sally found these sewn into the hem with the money. I can read but these are in code. Take me to Paris and they are yours.'

Thomas told the truth. I had to see those papers. In my excitement, I reached out to grab but she jerked her hand away from me.

'I learnt a lot at Mistress Grahame's Whorehouse,' she said and began to loosen the fastenings on her cloak. I watched for a moment, fascinated, as it slid from her shoulders.

I had not expected to be looking down the barrel of a pistol. Her hand was completely steady.

'Touch me if you dare. I *will* blow your hand off. You won't be worth much as a surgeon then.'

She stood back, unsmiling now.

'You'd have to learn what it's like to make your way with nothing. Pity—we could have been a good team.'

'Finny, the papers are no use to you.'

'What do you know about it? Turn around, hands behind your back.'

I turned slowly. The pistol gleamed in Finny's hand. My head ached.

'I know several ways to render a man helpless,' she said. 'Keep very still.'

Chapter 19

Wednesday November 3rd early morning

'Madame I can't ride—not like you do, with your legs apart. It's indecent!'

Finny's face was twisted in an expression of disgust at Madame's suggestion that she climb onto the spare horse left by their dead attacker. There was a smell of lead and flint in the dawn air. But Madame held the pistol—the same one, I saw, that Finny had used to threaten me earlier. She had retrieved it from the seat of the carriage in which Finny had begun her escape. Finny had used it sometime earlier to good effect, fatally wounding one of three ruffians who had attacked the coach shortly after it left St Germain on the Paris Road. They had not expected a fight, nor that Madame and I would arrive in pursuit of Finny and the papers she carried. It seemed like a random attack for with the Fronde disturbances in Paris, the roads were unsafe. But I wondered.

Inside the coach sat Lucy Walter and her infant. Lucy still had her arms clasped fiercely round her sleeping son. Clever of Bamfylde to have arranged an early morning departure for the King's mistress and sharp of Finny to have hitched a ride. Now she did a dance on the spot and threw her head back, laughing.

'I showed 'em,' she crowed. 'On the horse, Finny ordered Madame, "Quiet. Listen!"'

The clatter of hooves was unmistakeable. Four mounted men rounded the bend in the road. It was now light enough to see that they were armed and in uniform.

Bamfylde dismounted, sliding from his saddle.

'I wondered what you were up to Lockyer,' he said. 'What are you doing running away with three women, one of whom is the King's mistress? And I see you've killed someone too.'

'That was me,' interrupted Finny and made a clenched fist.

'Well, Bamfylde, you 're too late to face any danger,' I said, 'The coach was attacked. Why was Mistress Walter allowed to travel without an escort? The coachman ran away.'

'There's an escort now—the palace guard from St Germain. Mistress Walter, please stay in the coach. You can resume your journey.'

'Not you,' said Madame O'Brien as Finny moved to join her.

Bamfylde beamed.

'This charming lady can ride with me,' he said. Finny pulled a face to Madame who simply glared back and pointed her pistol. Finny heaved herself onto to his horse and he followed sitting close behind her. She jabbed him with her elbow, but as we turned back to St Germain, I noticed Bamfylde whispering urgently in her ear.

When we returned to my clinic, Finny made her disgust clear slamming her leather holdall so hard on my rickety elm table that one of the legs shuddered visibly. A stone pestle rolled to the floor and cracked.

'I know you are angry, but please don't wreck the place Finny. That was quite a conversation you were having with Captain Bamfylde,' I observed.

'It was not a conversation. I won't repeat his dirty talk before Madame,' Finny replied with a pious air. She'd decided to try and soften Madame's heart.

'Oh, for goodness' sake Finny,' Madame replied. 'I know all about places like Whitecross Street. I'm trying to help you. Do you want to end your days a as a toothless nightwalker, haunting the back alleys for customers? You could make a new life here at Val de Grace.'

'And spend it as a skivvy to those high-born nuns—not me, Madame. I'd rather take my chances with the high-born men! You wouldn't know this Madame Purity, but I attract them like wasps to a honeypot! If Lucy Walter can get a king, there's no limit to what I can do! Lucy said she could help me. She asked if I knew her friends in London the Sidneys and their kinsman Earl Pembroke! Imagine!'

'What did you say?'

'Course, I've never met them—although I have met Pembroke's man. He came to Whitecross Street.'

My mind gave a somersault.

'What did he look like?'

'Blond man. Tall—foreign voice. He brought someone with him.'

'Who?'

'I didn't see—her hood was pulled down. I think she was young; her clothes were expensive—a maroon silk.' Finny stood up, brushing the mud from her skirt.

'I'm going back now to find Lucy. She's not tough or worldly—she needs me to look out for her. The King is using her.'

'Do you believe they are married?' I wondered if Lucy had confided any details to her new friend and protector.

Finny shrugged. 'Lucy does. She says that there were witnesses, one was her kinsman Owain Hopkins.' And he had nearly died.

'Witnesses can lie. Any record of the event, a license?'

'How should I know?' said Finny. 'Papers can be forged, too, I suppose.'

The reason I'd chased after Finny in the early morning mist and mud.

'Let me have those papers, Finny. They are no use to you.'

She began to rummage inside her bodice, pulled out the bundle and held it defiantly above her head.

'Still warm too,' she mocked and laughing bent as if to tuck it in her drawers. Then, just as quickly she tossed the fragile packet on the table.

'You can have it. I don't want nothing from that dead girl's dress. I wanted nice things for Sally and me, but Sally's killed, and I have no one!' Suddenly all her bravado had gone, and her young face was sad and angry.

'Why did you make me leave Lucy? You'd no right to take my best chance away from me!'

'Stop it Finny.' Madame was impatient. 'Mr Lockyer wanted those documents. Now he's got them. I want something too Finny—a promise. I helped you to escape. I took a great risk for you, a risk with other people's lives. You know our routes and safe houses.'

Finny shook her head.

'Come on Madame—you're joking! Damp old manors in wet fields—could a town girl like me tell one from the other?'

'Can I trust you? You must swear to me that you won't reveal what you know.' Madame's voice was so intense and serious that Finny's expression changed, and she replied earnestly.

'Madame, I promise. I'm of the Old Faith like you! I am an honest whore. Go and count your money Madame,' said Finny, 'I had plenty of chances to take it. It's all there to pass on to Sir Kenelm.'

Madame O'Brien opened her mouth, but no sound came out.

'You let his name slip. I guess he's part of your plans. Don't worry I've forgotten his name already.' Finny began to hasten towards the door.

There are few who can silence Madame, I thought. So, she is up to something here but I must postpone my curiosity. I haven't finished with Finny.

'Stop! Please Finny wait! The woman who arrived with Pembroke's servant—I think she was Lady Derryn Barlow. Can you remember anything—anything at all about her visit? When did it take place?'

Finny halted and turned.

'You mean the *dead* woman? The dress I—? It was late summer the first time. Perhaps twice after that, I think. I didn't see her properly or pay much attention—Mrs Grahame shooed us out of the way when she came. If you ask me, she—'

But she was unable to finish. At that moment, the door was pushed open Lord Jermyn stood there. His big body filled the entrance.

'Lockyer, get your surgeons' tackle and come with me. You are needed *now*. Hurry man!' he bellowed.

I saw Finny retreat into the shadows.

Chapter 20

I kept pace with Jermyn's long strides as we squelched together through the mud.

'Is it your nephew?' Helped by the cosseting attentions of half-a-dozen young ladies, Richard Jermyn was making a good recovery. I didn't want to waste any more time on the arrogant puppy.

'No. Not him,' Jermyn answered shortly and said nothing more. I followed him back to the royal wing of the palace. The panelled chamber was huge and crowded with courtiers. Dead air smelt of old sweat overlain with the stifling sweetness of musk-roses. Queen Henrietta sat in a gilded tapestry chair. In the gloom, I caught sight of Prince James and lounging next to him on the sofa, a tall, dark man with a lean face, handsome and sensual. The candlelight flared and I saw a forehead lightly pitted from the smallpox he had suffered the year before. His black hair hung to his shoulders in thick ringlets. He had a half-amused yet watchful look. A heavy amethyst bracelet hung on his wrist.

So, that must be King Charles. Finally, I was seeing the man on whom the hopes of so many depended. The man they wanted restored. How many of them knew that only months ago he had written to Cromwell, begging for the life of his father. Cromwell did not reply. Now, Charles spoke, and his voice sounded older than his nineteen years. It was deep, with a mocking note.

'The Queen has a fever and needs to be bled. Jamie insists that you are a very superior surgeon and the man to do it.'

'If it is the correct remedy, Sire, yes.'

'It seems to work for most things from pox to gout.' Charles laughed. I tried not to show my anxiety. Henrietta had already made clear that she did not like me. In my experience that meant that she did not trust me either.

The Queen was shivering and breathing heavily but continued to sit upright. She looked hot in her heavy gown and her black eyes held an expression of distaste. Jermyn hovered nearby.

I bowed.

'Your Majesty. How long have you had the fever?'

'It has come on only in the last hour. Her Majesty was reading some letters from London,' Jermyn replied. One of the French physicians, fussily bewigged and robed in fur, stepped forward.

'Her Majesty's pulse is very irregular,' he said. 'I am not sure that bleeding will be effective. My almanac says the day is inauspicious. Monsieur—perhaps a purge is in order?'

It was, I remembered, the feast of St Winifred, a Welshwoman beheaded for refusing a Prince's advances. Lots of blood there and after all she was miraculously restored to life and lived fifteen more years. The day itself was not, in principle, unlucky.

I should have expected a posse of interfering French physicians, but it was irritating—the more so because I actually agreed with the pompous little fellow that bleeding was not necessarily the best treatment. Although I cared little for the Frenchman's almanac which specified the appropriateness of bleeding for certain conditions at planetary phases, I had begun to doubt whether excess of blood, a *plethora* as Galen and Hippocrates maintained, was the cause of any bodily disorder. Harvey had clearly shown that the amount of the blood in the body stayed much the same and was pumped around by the heart. Taking blood, especially in the quantities that were customary, merely weakened the patient. However, my old friend was circumspect and did not condemn the practice on which surgeons' incomes and patients' expectations depended. He agreed that 'breathing a vein' had its uses— usually because everyone hoped it would.

'I shall do nothing until I have examined the Queen,' I said firmly. 'Your Majesty—I need to look at your ankles and your neck.'

'Heavens!' said Henrietta. She turned to Jermyn. 'Don't go Harry, please, I need you here.'

Jermyn looked uncomfortable. The Queen stretched out her hand to him. He took it.

'The Queen needs space and quiet,' I said. 'Sir Henry you may stay—and one of the waiting women. Everyone else must leave.'

'I too will stay with Mama.' It was King Charles. I did not argue. Henrietta shivered again.

'You are right surgeon,' she said. 'There is always so much noise—I seem to have been surrounded by it all my life, with my father's bastards fighting, pulling my hair and stealing my poppets!'

I looked at her closely. More than anything she looked tired and older than her forty years.

Her pulses were sluggish and uneven but did not indicate fever.

'Your Majesty, how do you feel?'

'Feverish.' I thought there was something more.

'Your Majesty's courses—when was the last one?'

'Ended ten days ago. I have been well.' She was tight lipped. I wanted to explore further.

'Before I proceed, I must ask—does the sight of blood trouble you?'

'Do you mean my own or that of others? Surgeon, as with noise, my history has been full of blood.'

She inhaled sharply as if in sudden pain. I noticed that her tremor had increased.

'May I ask if your Majesty has endured any shock within the last twenty-four hours?'

The Queen's eyes widened. She pressed her hand against her chest.

'No,' she replied 'None. Surgeon, could we please get on with it?'

While her waiting woman unbuttoned the Queen's gown and rolled up the sleeve of her silk undershirt to just above the elbow, I prepared my tools—tourniquet, measuring bowl and my little silver fleam in its tortoiseshell case. The Queen eyed the blade but did not flinch. I had already decided that I would take only a tiny amount of blood—just enough to make everyone feel that something was being done. For I was certain that whatever ailed the Queen, it was not a fever and would not be easily relieved.

The King watched me keenly. As blood poured into the measuring bowl the Queens lapdog yelped and ran towards me ready to lick up any spillage. Charles gave the tiny Papillion a gentle kick. The Queen's blood ran steadily but slowly. I took no more than two ounces then bandaged her arm. She announced that she felt better but wanted to rest.

The King stared quizzically at the contents of the measuring dish.

'Why you've barely got a cupful, surgeon. Are you sure you've removed all the bad humours?'

'A little at a time Sire. I do not want to make the Queen insensible,' I replied cautiously.

'Hmm… I thought that was the point.' He turned to Jermyn. 'Having her insensible for a while could be a relief for all of us.'

'I heard you, your Majesty, my son,' was Henrietta's surprisingly vigorous retort. 'Everyone can go now. Thank you, surgeon.'

'Yes, thank you, Lockyer. Would you like to have a drink with Jamie and me?' There was a wry smile on the King's lean features. It was not quite noon, and this was a command.

I took some time to clear my and wash my instruments. I emptied the bowl and tried to calculate how much blood I had seen over the years. Now I was pouring away royal blood—which looked, smelt and stained like any other. It *was* like any other and that thought reminded me strongly that we are all human and mortal. I had seen the equality of the grave too often to have any other view.

By the time I reached the King's apartment both Prince James and the King were already drinking. Both held bumper goblets of red-gold Rhenish and looked settled for the rest of the day. The cracked marble table was covered with an array of bottles and dirty glasses. Two long-eared puppies were wrestling on the floor and there was a strong smell of dog. I poured a beaker of yellow Moselle.

'It's too wet for hunting,' Charles said, wiping his mouth on a grubby square of lace. 'Well, Surgeon-major you have delivered my whole family, and it is barely afternoon! There's my mother, who seems to have calmed since you relieved her of a dish of her royal blood, then Mistress Walter and the child. We found the coachman, and Bamfylde has told us how he came to your rescue this morning.' I supressed a smile. Trust Bamfylde to turn events to his advantage.

'As you know I am a king without a throne and I have no money either, so I cannot repay you. I could offer to marry you Lockyer, it's what my mother usually proposes for me when we are in a tight spot. Failing that—for I'd be an ugly bride—I want to bestow the Order of the Unicorn; it is an ancient Scottish Order of the Stuarts for faithful service. I think Sir Kenelm Digby was the last one to receive it so he can tell you the details.'

'Thank you Sire, but no reward is necessary,' I replied. Secretly, I was touched.

'Oh, don't deny me the chance, Surgeon. Fate does not often give me the opportunity.'

King Charles finished his glass, reached for the Moselle and poured himself more wine.

'Charlie—don't forget you are King of Scotland! We'll soon beat Cromwell and the English rebels!' said Prince James. Charles smiled and put a hand on his shoulder.

'Ah, Jamie, you may not have noticed, but the Scots haven't crowned me yet and are likely to ask for all sorts of ridiculous things before they do. And Argyle their leader—'

'Don't trust him Charlie—he sided with rebels before!' shouted James.

'I know he's a snake—curse his Covenanting rogues! But at present they may be our best hope.'

Prince James was undeterred.

'What of the Irish Charlie? They fight bravely for sure.'

'Yes. But Cromwell will crush the Irish and some of their leaders have changed sides to fight for him—'

'The traitors!' James was in a fury. 'I swear we will hunt them down and one day Cromwell's head will be spiked on London Bridge—and all the turn-coats too! Don't you agree Mr Lockyer—traitors deserve only one fate!'

'Ah you are a true warrior, Jamie—I thank God you are on my side,' said the King.

I was beginning to feel very uncomfortable. The Stuarts had welcomed me, treated me as one of them. I hated to think how they would react if they learnt the truth.

'There's a brace of woodcock moulting in the kitchen. Stay and dine, Lockyer, we do not have great ceremony here.'

'*Maman* won't like it,' said James 'She's told me to stay away from Mr Lockyer.'

'I am King and shall dine with whom I please. I want to hear more about this morning—getting the better of those ruffians and saving my dearest Lucy and my son.'

'I was not alone,' I said. 'It was Miss Finny and her pistol that made the difference.'

'Oh! And who is Miss Finny? She sounds quite a woman! Is she handsome?'

'Yes, very.'

'Then bring her here.' commanded Charles 'She can dine with us as well! What interesting acquaintances you have, Lockyer.'

'Your Majesty, Miss Finny belongs to the congregation of Val de Grace.'

'Even better,' exclaimed Charles. 'It won't be the first time I have had one from there!'

His tone had slipped easily from comrade to absolute monarch.

'Sire, I regret that I am unable to stay. I must attend to my clinic.'

Charles gave a knowing laugh and his black eyes glittered.

'Ah Surgeon major—I see you do not want to share Miss Finny, even with your King! I like you though—I declare I'll invite you to The Hague. Surely you long to get away from St Germain? There's more interesting work to be had than labourers' thumbs. Leave them to Sir Kenelm!'

I felt a stab of anger. My work was not a pastime to be picked up and abandoned at will.

'I fear Sir Kenelm's refined remedies wouldn't work, Sire. And a labourer needs his thumbs. Daily, men are injured in the work they do here. Last week a youth of his Highness' age was crushed by an overloaded cart. I could not save him. He died in great pain.'

I noticed Prince James had stopped smiling. I continued relentlessly. I wanted to wake these boys up.

'The labourers here get sick because they are poor-however many hours they work. But you and the Court know poverty too, you said. It is a hardship to be unable to buy an expensive weapon or an elaborate costume! Sire, Your Highness, good afternoon!'

I drained my glass. At that moment, the ringing as I set it down hard on the marble, was the only sound in the room. I bowed deeply and turned to go.

'Tell me, Surgeon-major,' said Charles, 'how have you lived so long?'

Chapter 21

Wednesday November 3rd late afternoon

As I left the eastern turret, I knew that no patients waited for me. But I was still angry. How I wanted to get away from the seductive Stuarts, with their open-handed charm and air of entitlement. We are right to be rid of them because they are so easy to love I thought. Why are we so moved to desire servitude and abandon freedom to put ourselves under the rule of another? Why had I mentioned Finny? Because I was in a preening contest with the two of them—at my age I should know better. I admired how brightly Finny shone in her fierce refusal to accept the position Fate had handed her. Finny was a hard-headed young courtesan yet the idea of her being made into a king's plaything distressed me. Charles had been right. I did not want to give him that chance.

My exchange with him had tipped the balance. I wanted to get out of Palais St Germain without delay. Yet Thurloe's letter ordering me back to London contained no hint of what awaited on my return. I was going into the unknown and the murder charge still hung over me. I wasn't sure that Scot or Thurloe could afford me protection Perhaps both would want me out of the way. Thurloe would crow that he had been proved right.

It was an uncomfortable truth with which I had to agree. As a Commonwealth agent, I had provided little of obvious value. No invasion plans or lists of secret supporters of the King. But my time in France hadn't been wasted as far as my own interests went. For I now knew for certain that there was a connection between the Stuarts and Lady Derryn. I had uncovered two vital pieces of evidence, and these might serve to clear me of the murder charge. First the papers sewn into the dress, which Sally had found, and I now held; second Finny's assertion that Pembroke's man van Prin—for it could be no one else—had visited Whitecross Street and brought a young woman with him. I could not be sure it was Derryn but I already had a suspicion as to the reason for her visit.

I was surer than ever that although they had denied it, Pembroke and possibly Sidney were involved. But *why* would they want Lady Derryn dead? The child? Pembroke knew the child lived. How had he learnt that? I could think of no one in Ely, Hope-Anna was not false, nor Aldridge. But perhaps I should be looking elsewhere—searching here in the shabby gilded environs of the palace of St Germain. Charles and James had been rivals for her—perhaps someone at the Stuart court disapproved and wanted her destruction. One thing was clear to me—there was more than one person with a motive to kill her. And what of Sally? Evidence from the dress suggested both women's deaths were connected. All these speculations passed through my mind. If I were mistaken the consequences would be fatal for me.

Finny could mention van Prin's visit and confirm the Pembroke connection—if she could be persuaded to return with me to London. I could defend myself in court and Scot's hold over me and Dr Harvey would be weakened by Leticia's departure from his house. The political situation was changing daily. Both Scot and Thurloe had much bigger fish to fry for Parliament itself was struggling to maintain its power against pressures coming from Cromwell and the Army towards the creation of a Godly Kingdom. They wanted a truly revolutionary republic not merely a Parliament without a king and this conflict between the real power—the Army—and the current Parliament was leading to frustration and inaction on all sides.

Suddenly I felt the weight of a gloved hand on my shoulder. It was Janvier.

'Surgeon-major, everyone is talking about your heroic adventures and your fair accomplices! Is it true they are runaway nuns?'

'No.' I put my arm through his.

'Janvier, I want to leave here.'

The Frenchman shrugged. 'Monsieur, who doesn't? It's full of damp and evil humours. I hear even Queen Henrietta is afflicted. What's the matter with her?'

'Ask one of your spies amongst the ladies-in-waiting.'

'Yes, but I want to know from you—is she ailing?'

'I don't think so. Disturbed, yes, ailing no. She's as strong as a horse.'

'Mm, Queen Anne will be disappointed. She pays her a pension you know.' Janvier paused. 'I'm leaving next week to take a boat from Le Havre. Bring as much money as you can. I'll have to bribe you aboard.' As he bowed a leavetaking he almost collided with Madame O'Brien rushing out of the choir doorway. She was flushed and looked anxious—the first time I'd ever seen her like that.

'Finny is gone,' she said. 'As soon as you left, she ran out and I couldn't stop her. But she forgot her travelling bag. It's full of money. Would she do that if she were leaving? I wonder what she's up to. Could she…' she hesitated.

'What Madame?'

'Could she be meeting Captain Bamfylde?'

'But she claimed the ride with him had been unpleasant,' I said.

'Finny has many faces,' said Madame. 'You have seen only a few.'

Finny. I needed her evidence—my freedom depended on her story.

'I must find her now. Do you want to help me?' I asked.

'Are you so sure she is lost?'

We inquired at the obvious places, the gates, stables, but there was no word of her. It began to rain, water streaming down the walls of the palace.

'She's probably warm indoors, laughing at us,' Madame said.

As we tramped through the mud, any tension between us dissolved. Madame O'Brien was part of my former life, a life to which I longed to return. Gradually we began to exchange fragments of information. Surrounded by the intrigues of the Stuart court in exile there was relief in sharing confidences with a familiar person. Forgetting all caution, I told her about my arrest and the threats against Dr Harvey which had resulted in this secret mission. And she began to confide in me. Madame's aim was bold—to enlist Sir Kenelm Digby, who still had influence with both sides, on behalf of the English Catholics. She hoped to save Father Southworth who presently lived under sentence of death. In his twenty years of serving the poor and outcast, he had survived four arrests, protected by Henrietta Maria.

'Now she has gone into exile we don't know how long things will stay quiet; we seek an understanding with Cromwell and the Army, about a softening of the Penal Laws.' She spoke in earnest, shaking the rain from her sleeves.

'For Catholics? With Cromwell? Surely not after Drogheda?' The news of those massacres had begun to filter back to England as I left.

'Not all Catholics are to be found in Ireland! Before Queen Bess, the name for England was Mary's Dowry and many still have a love of the Old Faith even if it is outlawed,' said Madam O'Brien. 'You would be surprised how many profess in secret. Nor are they all grand folk with priest-holes in their manors, or gentry recusants—most Catholics are working people—labourers or dairywomen, farriers and farmers no different from their neighbours but subject to harsh restrictions on their faith.'

I nodded for I knew from my own experiences in the war, that she was correct. A stream of water trickled down my back, distracting me from a terrible memory.

'Cromwell is an Independent. And they are a growing force in Parliament,' she resumed, tipping her head forward to drain the rain from her hat.

'He is neither Presbyterian nor for the English church. He commands the Army. It is his source of power against Parliament. Last year we made secret contact with him. We think there's some future for English Catholics in the English Republic—as long as they don't plot for restoration. We don't need kings; we need fairness and freedom of worship. Cromwell could give us that.'

'So, you'd abandon the Stuarts?'

'The Stuarts are a burden. Sir Kenelm knows this. He can negotiate for us—Cromwell respects him.'

'You keep odd friends, Madame.' In the dimming light her face stood out white and stark, gleaming with rain. I saw how that enhanced her. She was a woman not conscious of her beauty which was rare enough but even if she was, she cared nothing for it, even rarer. The tension of her mission showed in her face. It was her sole preoccupation. Her heavy boots squelched on the grass.

'The old loyalties are upside down.' She shivered suddenly and pulled her shabby cloak tighter. During our early morning ride, she had abandoned the dull coif of the Val de Grace and her black hair hung loose and damp. Not, I noticed in the fading light, a glossy Mediterranean blackness, but one in which there was shade of red like an occult fire. She smiled and her face relaxed.

'It's getting dark. One last search—the pump house. Shall we?'

Thursday November 4th morning

Early in the morning a messenger from King Charles had arrived reminding me of the presentation ceremony. I now found myself back outside the royal apartments, shivering in my only good suit. I had made the mistake of not taking Charles seriously. No—one else had shared my view. I was embarrassed to see most of the court were up and present. Janvier was there too, smiling in a doublet of amber silk slashed with dark green satin. I felt distinctly underdressed as I tried unsuccessfully to pull my limp lace cuffs into shape.

'Well surgeon-major,' said Janvier, 'It's a chance for a king to behave like a king. Everyone likes a ceremony, they feel reassured.'

Long mirrors of Venetian glass reflected the elements of the exiled court—some frayed satins and dulled velvet, fragments of worn lace. But I noticed how cleverly these were concealed. Every buckle and sword gleamed. Charles and James were dressed in flawless uniforms of summer's day blue. Their weapons shone, their cockades were dazzling white. The King's fingers were heavy with gems and the heels of his boots gleamed silver. He looked happy.

'Prince Rupert lent the uniforms,' said Janvier. 'I see Jermyn is here—without the Queen. What's happened to her, I wonder?'

I glanced at Jermyn. As always, he looked haughty and ill-tempered, but I detected something else, almost an air of triumph.

'He seems even more pleased with himself than usual. The beauty next to him—could she have something to do with it?'

Bare shouldered in a gown of carnation silk, black satin ribbons in her blonde hair, stood Finny. She was already attracting admiring glances and more than one young red-cloaked gallant jostled to be near her. Jermyn distanced them with a single glowering look.

A dumpy man in an oversized robe hastened towards the King. He waved a parchment protocol list. Charles let out a laugh that silenced the room.

'Good heavens Mr Hyde, my grandfather knighted a joint of beef in Lancashire! Don't tell me we need all the fobs and finery to do this small act of gratitude. And Sir Kenelm has charitably offered us the loan of his pendant so I may bestow the Order of the Unicorn on Mr Lockyer here. Now could we get about the business?'

'Surgeon-major Lockyer, you may approach His Majesty,' announced Hyde, and summoning all the dignity of a senior courtier, he beckoned me forward.

I came as bid and Hyde read the words of the investiture. Out of the corner of my eye I saw Jermyn smirk as he heard the Wiltshire twang in Hyde's voice. When Hyde stopped speaking, the King stood up. A smile on his long dark face, he placed a green velvet collar decorated with linked figures of eight in silver over my head. A silver medallion fretted with the image of a unicorn hung at the centre.

'The unicorn is fierce and gentle. Be thou also in the service of thy King. *Virescit vulnere virtus*—strength grows from the wound.' Charles intoned and cinched the collar into place. 'Despite your insolence Surgeon-major,' he whispered. Then he embraced me. Simultaneously, I felt the grip of a man as strong as myself and the collar's heavy weight.

The Court burst into polite applause and Charles looked hungrily towards the long table where plates of cold game and bottles of Moselle and claret were laid out.

'I rose without breakfast,' he declared.

'Your Majesty! Your Majesty, this is urgent!'

Jermyn's big rippling bulk had forced its way to the front, dragging Finny alongside. The King looked annoyed.

'My Lord Jermyn what is it? I hope there is no point of protocol that should put off our breakfast?'

'Your Majesty, treachery is not a matter of protocol. Hear me out! You too your Highness.'

Charles sighed and stretching his long perfect legs sat back in his chair. James came and stood beside him, hand on the hilt of his sword, his bright eyes searching the crowd of courtiers.

'Your Majesty, you have been grievously deceived,' Jermyn said, 'You have given honour and favour to a man who has betrayed you, who has wormed his way into your confidence and that of your brother.'

Oh. Then it was all over for me, and I measured the distance from where I stood and the door. If I made a dash now, I could escape, but it would be a brief freedom to be followed by a humiliating death.

'I have information by Miss Watts lately arrived as a refugee from London.'

Finny made a deep curtsey, leaning well forward and gave her carnation skirts an extra rustle. Charles eyed her and smiled appreciatively. Courtiers surged forward, blocking me in.

Jermyn resumed. 'According to Miss Watts, who has been close to our agents in London, he is also implicated in the heinous murder of a young woman known to Your Majesty from the Hague court. Her name was Lady Derryn Barlow.'

I noted the shock on both royal faces as Lady Derryn's name was mentioned. Of the two, Prince James looked the more stricken, his rosy face suddenly pale.

'A murder! Who is this villain?' he shouted.

'One who has stood closer to you than I am now,' said Jermyn slowly. I saw that James was about to draw his sword. This is it, I thought. I don't want to harm him, but

I won't go without a fight. My hand was ready at my scabbard.

An anxious silence fell. I glanced at Finny. She stared back at me without expression.

'What name he goes by to his Parliamentary masters I care not,' said Jermyn. 'At this court we know him as Captain Joseph Bamfylde.'

'Bamfylde! No, it can't be—' Prince James was unbelieving.

'We searched his quarters Your Highness. There was clear evidence—documents, codebooks,' said Jermyn.

'Then—arrest him!' exclaimed King Charles. 'I never liked the fellow.'

'Unfortunately, Your Majesty, he has fled—sufficient proof of guilt indeed...'

'Yes, yes. I know. Jamie, my dear boy—'

The King put his arm about his brother, but the Prince shook him off angrily. I could see that James was holding in his tears. My first reaction was relief that my own flimsy disguise had not been penetrated but I was puzzled as well. I had believed Bamfylde's claim that he was not involved in Lady Derryn's killing. I could not credit I was so wrong about him. Liar yes—professional double agent—of course—but killer? My instincts said no, and I clung to that judgement. But I had been wrong before, especially when women were involved. Finny. Everything seemed to begin and end with her.

Janvier was again at my elbow.

'Well, that was a narrow escape Surgeon-major,' he murmured. 'Bamfylde. Who would have suspected it?'

So, I thought, even Janvier does not know everything. Unmasking a traitor had stimulated appetites. Once the

King was served the crowd fell on the feast scooping up game pasties, carving jellied ham and slicing chunks of flame coloured Mimolette cheese. The room was soon full of chatter and laughter. Jermyn presented a glass of wine to Finny with a bow and a smile. I looked around to thank Sir Kenelm Digby and return the borrowed Order of the Unicorn. I found the old man sitting alone, his white head bent forward, turning a half-empty glass in his hand.

'Sir Kenelm—'

He looked at me blankly then seemed to recognise me and a look of intense hostility passed over his wrinkled face. 'I have nothing to say to you.' Digby growled. He called to a servant. 'Get me to my feet, young man. Now the rain has stopped, I wish to go outside. I dislike crowds.'

'May I help you?' I offered my arm. 'It was gracious of you to lend the Order.'

'His Majesty requested it. I did it for him. Pleasing you was not my objective.'

'Even so I am grateful Sir Kenelm,' I said, persisting. 'I understand you have a laboratory here and a telescope. I was hoping you would let me pay you a visit.'

'Then forget that hope, Sir. I want nothing to do with you. Leave me alone' Sir Kenelm turned away abruptly and hobbled through the glass doors. I was at a loss. Perhaps he had heard what I said about his precious wound salve. But his reaction seemed excessive for a professional injury. Janvier splendid in orange-tawny was at my side.

'That went well,' he remarked. 'He's *very* possessive about his telescope. Lady Cavendish kept making the same request and the only time he let her in she declared that matter was composed of atoms and wanted to set up experiments to determine the mass of the moon! He threw her out and called her mad. I'm afraid that unlike here in France, your English nobles have no respect for women's learning.' He surveyed the busy room.

'If I'm not mistaken, your next encounter won't be any better. Dr Le Barre is furious that you were asked to bleed the Queen.' The queen's physician stood too close, his belly straining against his brocaded jacket.

'I believe she has summoned you again,' muttered Dr Le Barre. 'I cannot think why since you failed to find out what was wrong! I recommend a regular cold-water clyster. Have you considered a supporting corset for Her Majesty?'

'Learned monsieur, I think of little else,' I replied. 'But I shall not be giving any robust treatment. *Vis mediatrix naturae.*' I bowed to Le Barre. 'Depending on how matters develop, I have the services of an excellent Frenchwoman who can, in all modesty, provide a relieving massage of the spine.' I smiled to myself as I imagined how Madame O'Brien would react to this suggestion.

'Massage!' fumed Le Barre 'You English know nothing!' And he stomped away.

'Henrietta's trying to avoid going back to Paris with the Regent and King Louis. Once there she'll be under the eye of my master, Cardinal Mazarin,' Janvier observed. 'The whole court is on the move—the King and Prince James to The Hague, Hyde to Spain and Jermyn's leaving too. I haven't discovered where he's going. You have picked a good time to leave.'

Chapter 22

Thursday November 4th afternoon.

I quit the gathering with relief. After Finny's revelation about Bamfylde I wondered what had caused him to take flight. If he had forewarning from someone, I could not imagine who it would be. I needed to try to decipher the minutely written bundle of papers Finny had tossed at me earlier. Perhaps there would be something to link Bamfylde and Lady Derryn. Back in my room, I unrolled and smoothed the flimsy pages, then reached for writing paper and extracted my codebook from a crevice in the deep wainscot. I worked for hours scribbling and crossing out trying to find a pattern in the jumble of letters. There was one number in the whole package: '1649.' Could this indicate the key or was it simply a date—or was there some other significance that I could not imagine?

My original pride in my skills began to evaporate as I realised that this was a task far more difficult than I had imagined. None of my cipher-keys was the correct one. I did not even know if the original text was in English. It could be Latin or French, or even Arabic. Madame O'Brien had said the white paper was French. But no recognisable word in any language emerged.

I decided to keep trying, surely it must yield something

eventually.

It was no use; the letters stayed meaningless. Finally, I knew there was only one person to whom I could turn for help. But I would be taking a risk—how big I could only guess.

He was the picture of comfort, seated in front of a lively fire, decanter at his elbow, his short legs resting on a footstool. In one hand, he held a book and in the other a mirror. His feet were plunged into velvet slippers. On a stand in the corner hung his cloak of amber silk.

'Ah Monsieur Lockyer, good evening, I may look *en pantoufles*, but I am in Purgatory!' Janvier said cheerfully.

'How so?' I asked. I could not help smiling at the relaxed figure whose repose I was about to disturb. The letter was tucked inside my jerkin.

'Cantica Two sees the blessed Florentine working his way through the seven deadly sins. I have reached Sloth. He has interesting things to say about reflection, too. For example—how is that image we see in the mirror actually made?'

He was talking about *The Commedia*, of which I had heard much but never had time to read. I was told it made tantalising use of the number three and its eleven syllable *terza rima* was perfect relaxation for a cryptographer. I'd no time for any such games however diverting.

'I need your help to decode a letter,' I said bluntly. 'I've no idea what it contains. It could be something of great importance or—nothing. I might betray some secret that should be kept from your master Mazarin.'

Janvier smiled and rested his book.

'A difficult problem. What is the source of this letter?'

'It was found on the body of a murdered woman.

Before I left England, I was accused of killing her. The letter might help to prove my innocence.'

'Yes, I remember surgeon major. That accusation, and a threat issued against your old friend Dr Harvey are what forced you here. I didn't like Scot's tactics that day.' He leaned across. 'Let me see if I can identify the type of cipher.'

I held out the letter. With the gentlest of movements, Janvier's small hands unrolled the thin sheet.

'French white paper. Whoever wrote this intended that the message should be well concealed, as this paper is made fine to be hidden. And it was not written in England, such paper is unavailable there.'

He stared at the letter. And stared again. After a quarter of an hour, he said, 'Thurloe's codebook is new. This is an old Royalist cipher, but more sophisticated than usual. I think it's a transposition cipher. I would guess that 1649 as well as being a date is a clue to the way in which to read the letters. See they are in blocks of four. So first, try letters 1,6,4, and 9.'

'Good!' I exclaimed. 'We are getting somewhere.'

Janvier laughed. 'You are a long way off yet. This one has a twist—it uses a cipher phrase as its base. Unless you know the phrase, you cannot discover what the letters stand for, even if you discover the order in which they should be read. No wonder you could not break it.'

He smiled, waiting.

'Are there standard phrases? Shall I try the codebook? Would it be something like 'God Save the King?'

Janvier shrugged.

'There are, but that one's unlikely—too obvious. See how quickly you thought of it!'

He saw he'd put me in my place. Then relented.

'One grace to the cryptographer is that amateurs always think they are being original when they are not. They often choose things close to home and I've noticed Royalists tend to use something grandiose. Now, I could help you to work out the phrase, but then I'll know the content, won't I?'

I nodded. I could not risk that.

'Please forgive me then, surgeon major if I leave you to your challenging task. I must get back to my sins and my glass of Armagnac—a gift from the unfortunate Bamfylde. Good night!'

I was seized with a dull familiar sense—every time I thought I was getting closer to the truth another obstacle would appear.

Sunday November 7th early morning

The Hague 1649
The Tenth day of May, to Colonel Algernon Sidney, residing at Baynard's Castle, Demesne of the Earle of Pembroke,

Beloved Brother. as you asked here is all the matter concerning Lucy Walter, our purest love and care for many years.

On August twentieth of Our Lords Year Sixteen Hundred Forty—Eight I accompanied our much beloved to the pilgrims Eglise de Saint Jaques in Liege, Flanders. Then in the side-chapel was a party assembled, namely Lucy Walter, Monsieur Thomas Barlow (whom we know as Charles Stewart, King of England, Second of that Name), Monsieur Owain Hopkins, a Welsh gentleman, Lady Derryn Barlow friend of Lucy

Walter, myself your loving Brother and a Roman Catholic Priest. I witnessed an exchange of Vows and Rings between Monsieur Thomas Barlow and our beloved Lucy. This was not a Nuptial Mass, but a ceremony of such that those within that Faith would consider a true Marriage. A written record was taken by the Priest. Afterwards we repaired to an Inn. I could not be merry to see our dearest Love so united to another. Monsieur Barlow (for so he wished to be called) was presently very happy saying Lucy was his Wife.

As you know in March of this year beloved Lucy was brought to bed of a son. Many tongues have wagged since. We know the Truth. But here lies the greatest scandal: for her sister Lady Derryn, the fair messenger of this letter was most wrongly prevailed upon by the same Charles Stewart until she was forced to yield to him. She now carries the fruit of that wickedness.

It has been the custom of this man like his father before him to act as if neither Nobility nor Commons meant a jot and pour scorn on our House. We owe him nothing and I say to You my Beloved Brother, nothing shall he have. I vow it and so must you.

Your Brother in Love, Robert Sidney.

I had worked all night until the bird that sings first in the morning is joined by other birds. As the winter morning opened with a pale sky, I stared at the sheets of paper that lay across my bed as light and white as flower petals. On the table, inked and crossed out were my versions of the letter. My back ached and my eyes felt they had been squeezed from my head. Now, after over two days of solid labour I knew something of the truth. Yet of one thing, I was sure. I was still far from knowing the whole of it. I fell asleep.

Sunday November 7th afternoon

Finny had accused Bamfylde of Lady Derryn's murder. What did she know? I had to find her. The afternoon sun was drying the sodden ground and small wisps of vapour rose from the muddy path. Striding past the royal apartments I saw her. She was lifting her mulberry velvet gown clear as she hopped on peasant-girl pattens. She pretended not to see me, and kept her eyes fixed on the ground. I called out.

'Miss Finny, you look very fine.'

She halted and smiled her golden smile.

'Compliments from you are rare, Mr Lockyer! My Lord Jermyn has been ever so kind.' The smile turned into a cat-like yawn. Looks like business as usual I thought— Finny has made quick work of Jermyn. Or is it the other way around?

'This dress belonged to the Queen. And I'm wearing it! Course she is a deal shorter and stouter than me. I ain't had time to alter it properly. If only Sally was here, she would have helped. She was better than me with a needle.' She hesitated for a moment. 'I miss her.'

I pictured again the beaten girl in the yellowing waters of the washtub.

'Finny, Jermyn used your testimony to accuse Bamfylde before the whole court of treachery and murder. How can you be sure?'

Finny took a sharp breath.

'My Lord Jermyn was already suspicious of him.'

'Spying, perhaps, but why add murder of a woman in

London to the list?'

'Bamfylde knows all about the Princes and Lady Derryn. How could he know all that? My Lord was *sure* he must have done it. He said Bamfylde wanted her out of the way for good to protect his own work as a double agent. Lord Jermyn said he should expose the villain the Prince had trusted.'

And strengthen his own hold over the Court. The revelation of Bamfylde's spying had certainly done that and Finny had been Jermyn's willing instrument. She looked thoughtful and fiddled with the black satin ribbon around her neck. I wondered if she might have lied to please Jermyn.

'Did Bamfylde ever visit Whitecross Street? Did he even come to London? You said it was the Earl of Pembroke's man you saw at Whitecross Street with a young woman, not Bamfylde.'

'Bamfylde *was* there as well,' she said sulkily. 'He did not bring her, it was one of the times she came alone without the Earl's man, but they were there at the same time. Don't you see—' Suddenly her voice sounded urgent.

'She knew who he was and must have wondered what he was doing there—perhaps she asked him? Alright, I only saw his back—he went straight into Mistress Graham's inner room. He had a message for her-I heard his voice.'

'Are you certain it was him?'

'Yes, I am certain!' she declared. 'I rode back with him the other morning to St Germain. I am not mistaken!' Finny was looking about her, impatient to be elsewhere.

She might be telling the truth. Bamfylde's rich voice was distinctive. But he had denied the murder only a few days ago.

'Well, he would, wouldn't he?' Finny retorted. 'He's a spy after all. You can't trust him.'

Nor you, I thought. But perhaps the identification of Bamfylde by Finny and the links I knew he had with Derryn could suggest to any fair-minded Justice in London that questions could be raised about the murderer's identity. A reasonable doubt? It was a slim chance to prove my innocence.

'Finny if you returned with me to London and told the Justices all you know about Bamfylde, and Whitecross Street, you could set me free! Tomorrow, I'm riding to Le Havre. There is a Dutch ship bound for England and I can get you aboard. Come back with me. Please.'

As soon as I'd said it, I realised how ridiculous I sounded. She looked amused, then shook her blonde curls and laughed.

'*You're* asking *me*? Who'd believe a whore? Mr Lockyer. I can't come with you. I ran away, remember?'

'But Finny, if Bamfylde killed Lady Derryn—he may have killed Sally as well—the murders are probably linked. Worse—since you've seen him before in London—even if you didn't know who he was—then your life is also at risk. You denounced him publicly!'

'I wish I'd shot him back there in the forest! Anyway, he's gone now and good riddance to him.'

She looked doubtful but only for a moment.

'I'm sorry Mr Lockyer I can't do what you want—I must go where my chance lies. The Queen won't mind me if I only wear her second-hand dresses.' She turned away in a swish of mulberry velvet and then was gone, her quick short steps tapping through the mud. And as I watched her leave, I wondered if I'd really wanted her to return with me only for her testimony? Perhaps I just wanted her, as simple as that, like the morning she came to my room. She remained a desire unfulfilled.

'Mr Lockyer!' It was Madame. She advanced towards me with swift purposeful strides, unrolling her long linen sleeves. She placed both hands on my shoulders gripping me hard.

'You need to get away from here quickly. I was giving the Queen her massage. Then Jermyn came in. I was sent out, but your name was mentioned. There was an argument between them. I heard her say "Finish it!" he said. 'Young Hopkins has already been sent away; I don't think that meddling surgeon knows anything.'

Owain Hopkins gone! No one asked me if he was fit to leave. I had the feeling that everything was running away from me out of control.

'And there is something else—very serious. It could change the future for all of us.'

Madame looked grave 'There is a report from London. Cromwell is dead.'

Questor: Three

Chapter 23

Julian calendar Thursday October 26th, 1649, evening

I was staring at the black water of the English Channel. Astern lay the last lights of Le Havre. I was onboard the Dutch merchantman *Prinses Amalia* and going home at last.

The palace of St Germain had been in a state of uproar. Everyone had heard the news about Cromwell. Cavaliers were cleaning their weapons with heady talk of revenge on the whey faced murderous rebels and cowards who had somehow defeated them. Prince James was in a high state of excitement. King Charles was ready to delay his trip to The Netherlands and the meeting with the Scots. Finally, Jermyn had persuaded him to leave, before setting off himself. As Jermyn's carriage turned out of the main gates, I had spotted Finny seated inside, peacock feathers nodding in her hat.

Now my thoughts moved ahead to the situation in London. Would Scot and Thurloe still be in charge and able to protect me? Hearing Madame's warning I decided that to leave the Palace immediately would be the best strategy. She showed neither sadness nor surprise at my going, nor did I expect she would. After the brief interlude of confidences exchanged in the damp Palace gardens, matter of fact had remained Madame's preferred style with me. As we parted, I gave her the key to the *salle* with a request that she might carry on my work. She looked straight at me with her dark blue eyes and surprised me again.

'John Lockyer, I trust you. I hope that you are restored to your post at Ely.'

'Thank you, Madame. I value that opinion.' It almost annoyed me to think that I cared of what she thought of me, for I did.

'And what of you Madame? You were so valuable there. Will you try to return?'

'That would place my greater task at risk,' she replied.

'Something greater than the work we did at Ely? What's better than that practical good?'

She shook her head. I did not say what I thought. She is another fanatic, a product of the times: implacable, courageous, and ultimately capable of anything. I feared she was lost, and it troubled me to think what might happen to her. But she had chosen her path whether from faith, ambition, or grief I did not know.

Now as I grasped the *Prinses Amalia's* rail, I was excited. With every gust of wind that drove the merchantman nearer to England I felt a new energy. I longed to be back in London, to the crowded streets and the busy river, a place where everyone seemed to have something important to do and not enough time to do it.

The ship bucked in the strong easterly. *Prinses Amalia* had reached a trough in the Channel. I felt the cold spray on my face and breathed in the salt-laden air. There was a little moonlight and looking along the deck, I saw someone grasping at the rail. The figure crumpled to the floor and lay there. As the ship pitched the body slid dangerously close to the side. I made my way along and heard a moan.

I poked the heap with my foot.

'Come Janvier let me walk you up and down. It will help.' He seemed far sicker than he had been on the outward voyage six weeks ago, but the sea had been calmer then.

I pulled him to his feet. He lurched to the ship's side and vomited. I dodged out of the way but kept my grip as he fought to stay upright on the slippery deck. Janvier cursed.

'Surely this terrible Channel is your country's best defence,' he gasped.

'Yours too,' I replied. 'Take some deep breaths and walk with me a little. We'd best stay on deck for a bit. Autumn is not a good time in the Channel.'

'Wrong monsieur!' he croaked. 'No time is a good time in this hell, Oh *Mon Dieu!*' He retched again.

Waves and spray surged over the deck, and I felt wetter and colder. Janvier gulped the frigid air and sea spray as if it would save his life. After some time, he seemed better. I loosened my hold and with my arm steered him around coils of rope and sacking back in the direction of our quarters. Walled off by rough planks, it scarcely deserved the name of cabin, but there were two hammocks and room for the small chest that contained our goods. As I came down the steps, I saw a sudden movement in the dark. Someone scurried away like a ship's rat. I called out but the person was already lost in the gloom at the far end of the ship. The chest was closed but the clasp was loose. Janvier was alert instantly.

'I must check if anything is missing—you too Monsieur Lockyer. Are all our papers safe?'

I peered inside at the parchment invoices Janvier had so carefully tied. None were undone. Our white linen shirts were as neat as when I'd folded them laying them on top of several surgical textbooks, whose weight was the main contributor to our heavy luggage.

'As far as I can see nothing has been disturbed. He was probably looking for money.'

I had ensured the letter whose contents were so explosive was always in my pocket. I was leaving nothing to chance.

The bell sounded for the next watch. There were roars and grumbles. I lit a candle stub.

'Put that light out!' Someone growled. I regarded my poor travelling companion who had climbed into the nearest hammock. He was pale and shivering but wide awake. The night sea was calmer now and the water gently slapped the sides of the ship.

'You need sleep to recover,' I said. 'Have some brandy. Here.' I too swallowed a mouthful of spirits and fell asleep in seconds.

Janvier and I were standing on deck to catch the weak morning sun. The Frenchman was looking better. He was able to look out over the green waves without heaving.

'I knew it was a good idea to travel with you,' he said. 'You have cured me, Monsieur! My thanks.'

No birds circled overhead, and a mist was rising from the water. We could not see either coast and as the sky darkened and the faint sun failed to disperse the haze, I had the feeling of being cut off from the world. The sea lapped gently along the sides.

Janvier stared down.

'I understand that the waters of the Channel are among the most saline,' he said. 'So wreckage is preserved. The remains of many warships must lie on the seabed.'

'At an inn near Dover they have what they say is the dragon-head prow of a Viking ship,' I said, recounting a tale from a patient whose weathered skin indicated a long service at sea.

Janvier shivered. 'Truly those were terrible times. Pure savagery. Thank God we are more civilised. I should not like to have been alive then!' Then he smiled.

'Did you see the gift that Queen Anne sent to Queen Henrietta before she left for Paris?'

'No. What was it?'

'It was a silver salt cellar, filled to the brim!'

'An odd present to give to an invalid.'

'Ha! Don't you see? It's Queen Anne's way of saying she doesn't believe a word about Henrietta's illnesses. I think her message *cum grano salis* will have been understood. Do you know why Henrietta was so anxious to stay?'

'I have no idea,' I said. 'But in the days before we left, she was very disturbed by something. Her Majesty neither likes nor approves of me. I am not privy to her confidences.'

At that moment, a cry went up from the tops and I saw a boy hastening down the Jacob's ladder. Through the fog two ships had been sighted, still some leagues away but closing fast.

'Too far away yet to make 'em out,' said one sailor. 'Pray they are not privateers, or our throats will be slit for sure.'

Things had been too peaceful, and I should have

known it wouldn't last. Why did I let myself believe it was going to be easy to return? The Channel is crawling with French privateers out of Dunkirk. They sail out under the noses of the English garrison to prey on rich Dutch ships. I knew the *Prinses Amalia* had a dozen demi-culverins and was relieved when I heard the Captain shout orders to the crew. I had never been in a naval conflict and was doubtful as to the outcome. Our ship could see off one marauder perhaps, but not two. Meanwhile it was clear that we were being pursued and that the hunters were getting nearer.

Across the waves came the unmistakeable sound of cannon being fired. As all on board *Prinses Amalia* peered through the fog, one of the ships turned about and headed off in the opposite direction. Her mainmast was sheared away, and the remaining sails hung in tatters. The crew of the *Prinses Amalia* gave a cheer but fell silent as they observed the speed with which the other ship continued its approach.

'We are not that far from the coast of England. Could we not put in at Dover?' said one of the passengers, a thin man in the crowd of portly merchants. He was poorly dressed in a green cloth coat.

'London is our destination,' said the Captain bluntly. 'Our course lies beside the English coast for many miles still. This route was chosen for greater safety.'

'Well, it doesn't feel safe now Captain,' complained one of the merchants.

I stared at the oncoming ship which was now less than half a league away. I could not yet make out the flag, but before long it would be well within firing range. I noticed the captain open a wooden box and remove a brass spyglass. Despite the circumstances, I was immediately curious. I remembered watching the King as he used one at Edgehill; it was a new toy to him then.

'What d' you see?' I asked the captain. The Dutchman grunted and handed the instrument to me. Fluttering from both mainmast and stern I made out the double flag of the Commonwealth of England, the white half displaying the red cross of St George, the blue bearing an Irish gold harp. Steadying myself against the movement of the deck I could make out the elaborate carving on the prow—*The Constant Warwick*. I knew of it. A frigate originally built and commissioned as a privateer for the Earl of that name, it was less than five years old. The Republic had commandeered it and it was now the fastest ship in the Navy, built to outmanoeuvre and with its 32 cannons, outgun the French privateers.

There was great alarm as *The Constant Warwick* closed in. The merchants went below to secure their possessions and ready any small arms they carried.

'We need not assume that the ship is hostile,' said the Captain calmly. 'We are a merchantman of the Dutch Republic, and we are not at war with England. When they hail us we shall know their intention.'

Within the hour, it became clear that that *The Constant Warwick* wished to send a party aboard 'for inspection' and that denial was impossible.

'These are English waters,' explained *Prinses Amalia's* Captain. 'The sooner we allow them, the sooner we can be on our way.' Grumbling, but relieved, his passengers agreed and gathered in a nervous huddle on the deck. I watched as the inspection party came aboard. It included an officer and eight armed marines. The officer, whose rough blue uniform bore no insignia introduced himself as Captain Nehemiah Brooks. He gave a short response to the Captain's affable greeting. On hearing that Le Havre had been their port of origin, Captain Brooks nodded unsmilingly and said, 'You have lately been in a Catholic country. We must carry out a search for Popish items and literature. These are forbidden in our Godly Republic.'

'Sir, we are Dutch Protestant merchants! You will find nothing here,' the captain protested.

'Nevertheless, we shall search. I advise you all to sit quietly. It will take some time. Is everyone on board a Dutch citizen?'

Before embarkation in Calais, I had told the captain my name was Peter Brink from Leyden, a dealer in medical books. I still felt the need to keep my identity and mission secret. Whether the Captain believed me or not, an extra sum of money had changed hands.

Janvier stepped forward and bowed to Nehemiah Brooks.

'Your servant, Sir, I am Alexandre Jean-Marie Janvier, gentleman of France and a happy subject of His Majesty King Louis.'

'Kings!' said one of the English sailors. He cursed and spat on the deck. Nehemiah Brooks glowered.

'Anyone else?

'Isn't one Frenchman enough? Come and have a glass of good Geneva and smoke a pipe with me while your men search' the captain urged.

Brooks shook his head.

'Be sober, be vigilant. Wine is a mockery and strong drink is raging. Proverbs, twenty, verse one.'

'I will take that as no,' said the Captain. 'Well, please

yourself.'

'It pleases the Lord,' replied Nehemiah Brooks. 'You men—go below and search. Bring up what you find.'

Friday October 27th early afternoon

The merchants were becoming hungry and restless, complaining loudly. But I noticed one, a thin man at the edge of the group who remained silent pulling his green coat around him. The sailors had carried trunks and box from the hold and the fact that ours was heavier than most evoked some curses. Captain Nehemiah Brooks silenced his men with a glare. The marines now proceeded to open the goods and spread the contents on deck. Janvier saw his precious invoices being blown about and groaned in frustration. Suddenly one of the sailors let out a shout of triumph.

'Mr Brooks, here! Look at these!'

In one hand, he swung some sets of rosary beads. The other clutched a small gilt statue of the Virgin Mary.

'They were in here Sir. Bottom of this trunk.'

'Empty it,' Brooks ordered.

It was our trunk. Janvier looked over and shook his head. More prayer books and pictures were discovered. The sailor tossed them on the deck and the little gold statue rocked back and forth.

'Romish idols!' roared Brooks. 'To whom do these belong?'

There was no reply from the shocked passengers.

'Good Protestants, eh? Sailor—piss on these baubles of the Whore of Rome! Now!

The sailor untied his breeches to do as he was ordered,

but as he did so, the thin man cried out and threw himself forward. He held a knife and before anyone could stop him he had driven it into the sailor's arm. In a moment, Brooks ran his sword into the man's side. He shrieked and fell to the deck, his green coat darkening with blood. It leaked from his body, forming a red pool on the deck.

Some of the merchants gripped their pistols. The remaining sailors had all drawn their weapons. There was a shocked and fearful silence in which the only sounds were the hiss of a coming squall and the creak of the shrouds.

'Stay your swords,' said Brooks wiping his own. His face was white but whether with indignation or alarm I could not tell. 'Captain you must explain this. I am holding your ship until you do.'

The captain, shaken though he was, drew himself up.

'Be assured Sir, I had no knowledge of this. We are all peaceful merchants here.'

'Where is your ship's surgeon?' Brooks shouted at *Prinses Amalia's* Captain.

'He was obliged to stay behind in Le Havre.'

'Ours has fallen sick himself,' said Brooks. 'I did not expect—You!—What are you doing?'

This was to me. For I was not going to allow a man to bleed to death in front of me and was already kneeling beside the thin man and tearing at his clothes. A hair shirt was revealed, thick with lice. I saw the wound was a clean one but deep and the man was groaning. Although he fought to supress the sound I could see he was in great pain. I hoped there was opium in the ship's medicine chest. Someone tried to pull me away, but I resisted.

'Let me help. I have some skill. If his wound is not

bound this man will die. It must be done now,' I roared at Brooks. 'The same for the other, although I think his wound is less serious. Staunch the bleeding! Press a pad there, I'll get to him in a few moments,' I shouted to the sailor's comrades.

'May the Lord guide your hand,' said Brooks. 'I shall ask you later why you did not declare yourself an Englishman.'

The Dutch merchants had gathered in a group by the side of the ship. They talked briefly and looked across at me. Then one of them spoke up.

'That chest filled with Papist trinkets belongs to him and the Frenchman.' He pointed a fat finger at me. The man beside me was gasping for air and I was too busy to care what these fur-clad overfed burghers were concocting to release themselves from blame.

'Then they are both under arrest,' said Brooks. 'But leave this man to finish his work.'

Friday October 27th near midnight.

We had been taken off the *Prinses Amalia*, which after payment of a hefty fine, some boxes of nutmeg and several bolts of rare cloth, would be allowed to continue to London. Janvier and myself, together with our heavy incriminating trunk were hustled aboard *The Constant Warwick*, my French companion's protestations of innocence going ignored. Brooks ordered that he be confined below deck. I on the other hand was allowed some freedom of movement, albeit under the eyes of two armed sailors.

'You may do the Lord's work for the wounded men,

but we are watching you for Papist tricks. Don't try to baptise them into your so-called Faith,' said Brooks.

It was not worth arguing. I knew that a long night lay ahead of me where I would have to keep close watch and attend to the needs of two injured patients. The sailor's wound was skin deep, the man had been lucky. His attacker, the thin man in green, was critically ill. Brooks' sword had pierced his bowels, and his spleen was damaged. The wound could prove mortal. Above all, he did not seem to wish to continue to live. He bore the pain and refused the wine and opium cup I offered. With an effort he whispered to me that he wanted his mind to be clear then continued to mouth words soundlessly and supress his groans. At the end of the second watch of the night he called out weakly to me.

'I want to speak to the man who wounded me.'

Brooks was wakened and at first refused. When he arrived, he was in a fine old temper but fell silent when he heard the man's words.

'I am a Catholic priest.'

Brooks stared at him, his blue eyes now wide awake and full of horror and disgust.

'I ask forgiveness of the man I attacked but I could not allow the desecration of the image of Our Blessed Mother. I ask you to pray for my soul.'

The priest's hands scrabbled at his sheets.

'Pray? I should interrogate you! And if you survive, I fully intend to do so. You Papists are a constant trouble. You lie low in hiding; you keep secret places and plan rebellion. You and the King would have turned free Englishmen into slaves of the Pope! All our ancient laws and liberties crushed!'

Brook's rage was both genuine and out-of-place.

'Be quiet,' I remonstrated 'The man is gravely ill. He needs rest.'

'Tell me your name, priest,' demanded Brooks. There was no reply and with an angry gesture of dismissal, he turned to go.

But the man was struggling to speak. 'He knows nothing of the relics.' He pointed to me. 'I hid them in his goods when he was on deck. His friend was sick. They are both innocent.'

'Your name, priest!' Brooks brought his face close.

'Sir—are you a Christian?' I shouted and pulled him away. At that moment the man made a sound somewhere between a breath and a cough.

It was a sound I knew well; I had heard it often.

'It's over. He's dead,' I said.

'His life for a painted statue! Can you understand that?' said Brooks. 'Well, one thing he can be thankful for—he died a cleaner death here than if he'd been caught in London. He'd be drawn and quartered at Tyburn.'

'I think he suffered enough even for a Papist.' I was angry at Brook's intolerance. 'His words have cleared me. It is a dying man's testimony.'

'If I believe him,' said Brooks. 'He probably had some Romish twist which means he does not have to speak the truth. That is how those priests argue in court.'

'That was after torture in the old Queen's time.' The man's pitilessness was beginning to tire me. 'Are we not more civilised in the new Republic? Let me cover him.'

Chapter 24

Saturday October 28th early morning

Six bells had sounded and as the ringing died away voices resounded over the water. The sailors were singing at the beginning of Morning Prayer.

'An Ark of Virtue is our Ship
Well-ordered for the Lord
Against His Foes we boldly smite
In keeping with His Word.
Through Grace we broke the Tyrant's Rod
O praise the Mighty Works of God!'

I turned over and tried to get back to sleep but could hear the voice of Nehemiah Brooks echoing across the deck. I dragged myself up to catch the end of his sermon before the crew.

'Here begins our lesson from Deuteronomy Twenty-three: *When the Host goes forth against thine enemies, then keep thee from every wicked thing.*

'In the early hours of this morning, the Popish Malignant who yesterday attacked one of our sailors died of his wounds. We commend him to the Lord to undergo his just punishment in the next world. As it says in Maccabees *It is a holy and wholesome thought to pray for the dead that they may be loosed from their sins.'*

The priest's body wrapped in canvas and weighted at the head and feet with culverin shot was let slip over the side. It bobbed for a moment and then disappeared under the water. Brooks had already turned his back and his preaching recommenced.

'Now I speak on the matters of discipline in which failures have occurred…' I was turning to go back to bed but was brought back with a start. '…I condemn all uncleanness against women. No woman whatever her station in life should suffer indignity from this crew. Those who were guilty of such action yesterday will be severely punished. How can the Lord favour us if we do not keep His Commandments?'

Someone cried out from the assembled crew, 'We don't want a woman on board! Throw her over the side!'

'Silence,' bellowed Nehemiah Brooks, but his words were drowned out by hostile shouts. In a moment, the officers had reached for their clubs and blows were being dealt. They shouted furious orders and threats until the men dispersed. I guessed that the prayers were a little shorter than usual that morning. I was wondering about the identity of the unwelcome passenger when Janvier appeared, twinkling and alert. Unlike me he was freshly shaved but then, he hadn't been up most of the night.

'Good news, Surgeon-major. They let me out! That man Brooks came in looking very bad-tempered. He said I was free to walk about the deck and that you should look at the ship's surgeon, see if you can find out what is wrong with him. There's more.' He paused. 'A flogging later this morning, three men. Apparently, they tried to violate a woman although where they found her I don't know since this ship has cruised the Channel and North Sea for the past fortnight.'

Then it's true, I had heard correctly. What of this woman? What injuries has she suffered? And if men are being flogged a surgeon must stand by. I hurried to get my kit together and once assembled I made my way towards a bulkhead. The ship's surgeon was normally housed there next to the gunroom. A gangling freckled young man barred my path.

'You can't come this way,' he said. 'No passengers allowed here.'

'I seek the surgeon. I believe he is sick. I am a surgeon and may be able to help.'

The youth swallowed and his pale eyes widened in relief. I realised he was terrified. 'I beg your pardon Sir. I am Mr Hodgkin's mate.'

'The surgeon's mate?' There had been no one to help in my struggle with the two wounded men. 'Where have you been? You should have helped me last night.'

The boy assumed a hangdog expression.

'Sir I have had trouble of the bowels. I thought to keep away while I still had the looseness.'

'You must see to it before it spreads among the rest of the crew.'

'I got it from them Sir. Some of them are pressed men and don't know the customs of a ship. They don't use the heads. Worst is, I had to give up my cabin to that *woman*.'

'How is she? What happened?'

'She was put aboard two days ago. We were escorting the English packet out from Calais, and she was taken off and brought to our ship. Some of the lads got wind of it and three of them broke the door and made a grab for her, but I believe she held them off with a pistol. A real virago Sir! They were a bit drunk. It was just high spirits.'

'Really? I doubt she saw it that way,' I said. 'How is she?'

'No one knows Sir, she won't let anybody past the door even with food. She's barred herself in.' He grinned. 'Women are bad luck on a ship. The crew want her put off but Captain Brooks says we have to complete our duties first and can't put in to harbour.'

We reached the surgeon's door, and the boy pulled it open awkwardly. Something was blocking it.

Mr Hodgkin was lying on a makeshift mattress on the floor. He was curled up, knees almost touching his chin and appeared to be asleep. There was a stink in the room. I shook him gently.

'Mr Hodgkin. Tell me the trouble.'

Hodgkin stirred and grunted.

'I can't get an answer,' said the youth. 'He's been that way for over four days.'

'Does he complain of pain?'

'He groans a lot Sir and holds his belly. He has made very little water.'

'Any stool?'

'No Sir. Not for two days Sir, before that he shit his breeches.'

'I'll have to examine him. Is that the surgeon's chest there?'

'Yes, Sir, but most of the tools are kept in my cabin, And that woman is there so I cannot go in.'

I bent over Mr Hodgkin who opened an encrusted eye. He was a heavy man with a mottled complexion and flaking lips.

'Luke is that you? Where are you, boy? Bring me water, I stink like a privy. Who are you Sir?'

'I need to inquire your sickness, Mr Hodgkin. I am a surgeon and Mr Brooks has asked me to look at you.'

'Brooks be damned, the whore's son,' said Hodgkin groaning. He rolled over on his back displaying his soiled clothes.

I felt Hodgkin's belly, then pressed firmly. Hodgkin groaned again.

'Devil take you! My belly is hard as iron, and I cannot shit.'

Either the flux or costiveness I thought. This poor fellow has both. Who'd go to sea? I turned to the mate.

'Look in the chest for a clyster syringe—the one that takes a pint of liquid.' The boy slowly obeyed. He rummaged and brought out two objects which immediately aroused my disgust. I walked over and looked at the jumbled instruments—all sizes of saws and pincers thrown together. In some, the blades and screws were rusted, others were clogged with dirt.

I was furious. Who lets their precious equipment get into such disorder?

'Is this how you serve your surgeon, boy? Look at the state of these—how can they be used? Go and find a bucket of seawater and scrub them until they shine!'

I suppose the medicine chest will be a mess as well, I thought. But first things first. I called the boy back.

'You can do cleaning later. Just scour the syringe for the moment and prepare a warm wine mixture for it. Make sure you oil it well. And get a change of linen for Mr Hodgkin and some clean water.'

The patient had returned, wheezing, to his curled-up

position. His breath stank worse than his britches.

'Mr Hodgkin, I must relieve your costiveness. It may be hiding another condition.' Hodgkin gave a weak nod.

A bell sounded above. Luke's pale face coloured up. For once that sorry morning he looked animated.

'It's the floggings Sir, may I go and watch?'

'No you may not! Stay and do the job you are supposed to,' I snapped. What was he thinking of? The boy looked petulant.

'You are hard, Sir. All hands are supposed to attend a flogging,' he replied sulkily. I reached across and slapped him hard on the side of the head. The boy staggered, and tears sprang into his eyes.

'Do as I tell you or you'll get another one,' I growled.

The sky had begun to darken and rain clouds were piling up. All the crew had been summoned to witness the punishment of the three wrongdoers. For a ship's crew they did not look as sorry and ragged as I expected. Most had the pale complexions of new recruits, but there were older sunburnt men. Their rough blue jackets were clean and they looked healthy and whole. No sailor can stand still for long and they jostled each other in an uneven line.

'Leviticus twenty—six—*And they shall bear the punishment of their iniquity.*' Nehemiah Brooks intoned. He read out the charges against the men. Although he spoke of extreme drunkenness he said nothing about the attempted assault. The sentence was six lashes 'according to the customs of the sea.'

'That's very light.' Janvier had appeared at my elbow ready to provide a commentary. He sounded rather disappointed.

'Why has he not mentioned the attack on the woman?'

I asked.

'There is a lot of grumbling amongst the men. They say she is a jade who deserved it. Brooks could have ordered up to twelve lashes but he's afraid of how the crew will react. He'll be glad when this expedition is over. Surgeon-major I seem to be getting sea legs. I feel very well!'

Janvier's joviality was mirrored by most of the crew; it was a break from the tedious labour of the morning, and many were humming or grinning in anticipation, while others looked sullen.

I watched the bosun's mate bring the knotted cords of the lash whistling down on each of the three in turn. The youngest, not more than a boy and already incontinent with fear, was last. They cursed freely and screamed as their backs split open, pierced to the raw. Buckets of saltwater were thrown over them. As each was drenched a cheer went up, with shouts of encouragement from the spectators. I came forward to inspect the injuries. They were not the worst I had ever seen inflicted. The bo'sun knew his work. Two were cursing still, but the boy was very pale and seemed almost insensible with pain. I knelt beside him.

'Get some brandy for this boy,' I ordered. 'He is in shock.'

Saturday October 28th noon

'Is Mr Hodgkin clean?'

'Yes Sir,' replied Luke, 'I washed him. I have scrubbed all the dirt from the syringe and the mixture is there in that brass pot.'

'Very well,' I said. 'The men who have been flogged

may need dressings as well. The young one seems quite lacerated.' These wounds could turn ugly. That was why the salt seawater deluge, though brutal, was cleansing.

'I know him Sir, we enlisted at the same time. They were jesting him Sir saying it was time he had a woman.'

'I see. That's no excuse. He could have disregarded them.'

'Disregard those two? No Sir!'

'Well, the sentence has been carried out. Now Luke, wrap the syringe in tow, oil it and show me how you administer a clyster.'

'To Mr Hodgkin Sir?' Luke was horrified. 'I have never done it before,' he said, his voice trailing off. I felt sympathy, for I remembered my own early and clumsy attempts.

'You are very young for this position. You don't like the work?'

'I hate it Sir. In an engagement, I must work at great speed with the lints and the wounds are horrible. I'm only here because after my father was killed at Preston, we could not afford a proper education. My pay helps my mother and the younger ones.'

I sighed. Another of war's unintended victims. The poor and middling sort always suffered, their small dreams easily trampled.

'I'm sorry. While I'm here I will try to teach you some skills. And Luke.'

'Yes Sir?'

'Forgive the blow I gave you earlier. It is not my custom. Let us get on. Help me to turn Mr Hodgkin on his side then bring me the *speculum ani*. He may have a fistula there. I can demonstrate how to introduce it

gently.'
Saturday October 28th afternoon

The wind was bitingly cold and a shower had made the deck slippery. It was busy with sailors seeing to sails and rigging and rushing the length of the vessel. I was arm-in-arm taking a turn with Janvier and getting cursed when I got in their way. I'd had shown Luke how to fill and insert a clyster syringe, then after getting him to carefully oil the steel exterior, I let him try. Mr Hodgkin proved a difficult patient, moaning and resisting and it took us both to complete the job. It is true that doctors make the worst patients. But Luke was proud of what he'd done and I was pleased to see him some time later with a brass pail ready to dump the contents over the side. Whatever else is wrong at least Hodgkin's bowels are clear, I thought, and that was a start. I'd better take another look at him. Over the noise of flapping canvas, I called to Luke.

'How is he?'

'Still drowsy Sir. I've been giving him water.'

'Have you dressed those backs yet?' I did not intend to let the lad relapse into bad habits. Luke scurried off.

Janvier was sheltering from the wind. He held out his hand.

'You are working hard surgeon-major. And I can see that the death of that priest weighs heavily on you.'

He was right. I had been moved by the priest's courage. What Brooks had found incomprehensible I had respected. Why else might one engage in bloody and dangerous business if not for a deep attachment to something beyond oneself? Not simply veneration for the products of reason whether they were practical like good surgery or abstract like justice and liberty. I understood those sentiments. They were the counsels of the great Erasmus. This was something else—something I had never had, or if I had, had lost long ago without even a memory of its going. An unquestioning faith. And beyond that I knew there was another lack, a void. The emptiness of being alone.

'I'm no seaman, but we seemed to have changed direction,' Janvier observed. It was true. The ship was closer to shore than it had been some hours ago.

'Perhaps Brooks wants to sail up the coast for safety. Janvier why did that priest choose to hide his objects in our trunk?'

'Old smuggling trick. Get someone else to take in your contraband, then steal it back on landing.'

'Risky though.'

'Nor did it pay off. I wonder what happened to the stuff. I suppose it was thrown overboard.'

'I think Brooks will have kept it as evidence of his devotion to duty. I'd better get back.'

I entered Hodgkin's cabin. The sick man was asleep. My foot hit something. In the mess on the floor was a brown glass bottle, one of several. I sniffed it and called Luke.

'Have you seen this before?'

'Laudanum, Sir. He said he had terrible pain and flux and it helped him.'

'Explains his chronic costiveness,' I said. 'He also has ulcers where he has been scratching himself. He needs ointment.'

'All the ointments are locked in with that woman! Don't make me go near her!' Luke looked terrified.

'Watch him,' I said. 'I'll go myself.'

I walked over to the mate's cabin and gave a gentle knock on the door. There was no response. I could hear nothing from inside but above the creaking and swaying of the ship I knew that the room was not empty. I tried again.

'Madam I understand why you keep this cabin barred. I'm a surgeon. Just now I need medicines from the cupboard. A man is very sick. Please open the door.'

A few moments passed and I heard a small movement. Then there was a scraping sound and the door inched open. I stayed quite still as the occupant emerged and stood in the doorway.

'Thank you,' I said. 'Thank you, Finny.'

Sunday October 29th early afternoon

'Sir it is time you told me who you are. You are no bookseller.'

In the sparsely furnished captain's cabin, Nehemiah Brooks and I faced each other. The most prominent object in the room was a black covered ship's bible bound in brass and chained to a shelf. He had invited me stiffly, to share a meal. We ate in silence from pewter plates although I noticed a tarnished silver charger which bore the arms of Warwick. There were few remains and only thin beer.

'I will tell you,' I said, 'but—since this is my first chance to ask—I want to know if it's true that General Cromwell is dead. Is that why have we changed direction?'

'Where did you hear that? I assure you the General lives. He is in Ireland where he has had glorious victories.

God's Providence favours us. Such rumours are often spread by the Royalists. *The Constant Warwick* is here to protect the Republic's shipping from privateers and to engage with Royalist forces. We change direction as needed. It is believed among the crew that you and the Frenchman are Royalist spies.'

'How can I convince you? I'm a surgeon and served under the command of General Fairfax.'

'Fairfax is not Godly,' observed Brooks.

'He ensured, with Cromwell, that the King was defeated,' I replied. 'I have recently been employed at Ely, a military hospital. I want to get back there. I went to France to buy surgical books. They are in the trunk.'

'And the Frenchman?'

'He is a dealer in paintings. He carries letters from Mr Thurloe and Sir Arthur Hazelrigge. They carry the seal of the Republic. Inspect them.'

Brooks shook his head. 'Too late. It's time you left this ship. I am calling at Deal. I shall land you and the Frenchman— and the woman. I want rid of her. She will make her way—that sort always does.'

'How did she come to be aboard?'

'At Calais a Royalist lord approached me—he said he had permission from the Republican government to return to see what remained of his estates. He wanted to offload the woman travelling with him—she was an embarrassment. I said that England did not need such whores, but he offered a good price, so I agreed.' Brooks tapped his nose.

It seems Jermyn had abandoned Finny. Did she realise?

'Captain Brooks, you should also land Mr Hodgkin, he is very sick—I think he has an ulcer of the guts, he cannot work. The boy Luke is inexperienced and unable to look after a ship's crew alone.'

'Then he must learn. We must all manage as best we can. I have had no ship's cook since the last tour out.'

I looked at the table. There were a few fragments left of the cabbage, potatoes and boiled chicken that we had eaten.

'The meal was excellent all the same. Thank you.'

Nehemiah Brooks smiled for the first time since we had met.

'Use hospitality to one another without grudging,' he said.

All well and good, I thought. The first thing I'll do when I get to London is go to The Bull and order a rabbit pie. I speared one of the remaining potatoes.

Wednesday November 1st morning

My last sight of *The Constant Warwick* was of three black masts outlined against the moonlight as we were rowed ashore. It was a hard row—the November gales were up as we scraped up the shingle beach at Deal. Defeated Royalists there had already found a profitable new occupation—smuggling. The three of us stayed the night at a ramshackle inn, where sleep was disturbed with much coming and going and the sound of boxes being dragged along the ground. Next day we set out for Canterbury, hoping to get to London. Finny had been silent despite Janvier's attempts at courtesy. Finally, I intervened and said that Finny should be left alone.

It was not until we were waiting in Canterbury, that she began to speak. Her voice was low and full of anger.

'I know what you think! I heard what they told you—

just high spirits—ain't that what they said? It wasn't like that at all. I knew what they intended, and I thought they would kill me as well, Mr Lockyer. There were three and I couldn't withstand them. I heard them coming and I was terrified. I had the pistol, but it wasn't loaded.'

'Oh Finny.'

'Then some others came and the three of them were dragged off. They'd bragged of their intentions beforehand. It was Captain Brooks who ordered their arrest.'

'Well they were punished.'

'Not enough!' cried Finny. 'They should 'ave been gelded! And the young one to whom I cried mercy—he was the worst!'

She clenched her fists.

'So much wrong! So much is wrong in this world! I haven't the words to say it!'

'Finny I am sorry. That was a terrible occurrence.' I did not say I understood her feeling but I certainly recognised it. I remembered the anger and distress of another woman who had been brought into my care after marauders had surrounded her isolated cottage. She would not let me near her and ran away to I knew not what.

'I was a fool about Jermyn, too!' Finny replied. 'As we were boarding the English packet at Calais, I was arrested—Queen Henrietta's orders! They said I was a well-known thief and whore wanted in London. My Lord Jermyn was nowhere to be seen! I was taken off and put aboard the warship. You know the rest.'

'Truly, Finny you have been very badly used.' I did not, in truth, know what to say. She did not reply and looked away.

Janvier had gone to secure a passage to London but without success. Despite showing the signature of Sir Arthur Hazelrigge on his *laissez-passer*, the men of Kent accepted only the authority of gold. On returning, he beckoned me to an adjoining room.

'These rogues are extracting the maximum and want more to carry our fair companion. Must we keep her?'

'Yes,' I said firmly. 'She needs protection.'

'So be it,' sighed Janvier. 'I hope you have thought about a roof over her head in London. I invite you to stay at my lodgings in Hosier Lane, but she's not welcome.'

When we returned to the main room of the inn, Finny was gone.

Wednesday November 1st midday

My search for her was fruitless. Like the woman of my memory, she had vanished, and I feared for her. The streets were closed or patrolled by soldiers, who stopped and questioned passers-by. To avoid them, I was forced back to the inn. There I found Janvier smiling, barbered, and wearing clean linen under his new leather jerkin.

'Monsieur Lockyer, we leave when the bells strike the half hour. You have just time to use the services of the excellent barber of this inn. I am glad our companion has gone. Stay easy. We should reach London tomorrow evening.'

Finny is lost to me, I had failed her. Perhaps, despite her denials to Madame O'Brien, she remembered a safe house nearby, some remote manor on the windy chalk Downs where the old Faith still prevails. Would she be safe there? Tomorrow I would be in London and my firm intention was to abandon spy masters and intrigue and to renew my proper occupation. Doctoring was where I belonged. But first I would visit Thomas Scot and deflect the scorn of Thurloe who had thought my mission useless. And then I remembered that I could not cut loose so easily. I must begin the search for Edward. I might not be the only one hunting him.

Chapter 25

Thursday November 2nd early morning

'Have a pilchard, Surgeon-major.'

Thomas Scot scooped one and dropped it into my dish. My early arrival had coincided with his breakfast. 'They are from Ireland. You'll find them a bit salty but excellent. After Cromwell's successes there, trade is starting up once more and ships are anchored at the wharves. None too soon, I should say.'

'Cromwell is definitely alive? At St Germain I was told he was dead for certain of the ague.'

Scot grinned showing his cracked teeth. 'It is true, he suffered the ague in Ireland and had a few weeks ill of it. He was probably born with it in those pestilential fens. For him, it flares up at surprisingly convenient times. I use such rumours to unmask plotters who show their hand the moment they hear,' replied Scot.

'The news caused uproar in France.'

'What news?' John Thurloe had entered the room, his gown trailing and a bundle of papers in his hand. 'Have you something useful to add to your reports?'

'We were talking of the rumoured death of General Cromwell,' replied Scot brusquely.

'I suppose it is different when you are Chief

Intelligencer,' Thurloe remarked. 'Normally, such speech would merit a fine or worse. The alehouses are still open and it's high time they were shuttered. My men report of seditious stories, toasts to the King and declarations that all members of Parliament are sons of whores. Even here—in London! However, I can assure Mr Lockyer that General Cromwell is in excellent health.'

'That must be taken as truth coming from one so close to his family,' said Scot.

'I do a little legal work for the General's son-in-law. Should I be embarrassed? We all take second employment. Look at Surgeon-major Lockyer here. We know he's a good surgeon but he has also proved himself a conscientious and observant agent. And—my apologies Lockyer for my scepticism—his information has been useful and brought us up to date on the doings of the young Stuart gentlemen. And that witch, their mother. You have a talent Sir!'

'It is one I would prefer not to exercise,' I said, as wary of Thurloe's praise as I was of his criticism. 'I did what you asked. Now I want to go back to Ely.'

Scot and Thurloe exchanged glances. Sitting on either side of the table they looked like two black crows. Scot said, 'After reviewing the evidence, I am prepared to declare you innocent of any misdoing.'

'Prepared to? But I *am* innocent. And I was arrested in accordance with no law. I was deprived of liberty contrary to the laws of England. Replacing one tyranny with another—that is not what I fought for!'

Scot banged the table with his knife. The plate of pilchards shook.

'Are you living in this world? England is at war. The

Republic is threatened by all those who want to bring back a king to reign over us. There are enemies and conspiracies everywhere. To add, France and Spain would see us brought low. As for you—a turn coat—even now I doubt whose side you are on! Understand this—I can have you set free or re-arrested this day. Do not challenge me with talk of the liberties of England.'

I stood up, placed both hands on the table and shook my head. I wanted to be far away from the pair of them.

'I did everything you asked. I carried out your mission.'

'And Dr Harvey has remained free and safe,' replied Scot. 'I have kept our bargain. But you need to understand this. You are one of us now. You cannot leave. The Republic needs your skills.'

I felt the chill in the unheated room.

'In France I came across Joseph Bamfylde. He was a sly creeping worm of a fellow. Is he *one of us*, too? His codebook suggests he is your agent and has been for a long time—is it so?'

Thurloe leant forward and picked up some paper with a deliberate gesture. 'Oh, you made contact in St Germain? That was not supposed to happen!' He glanced across at Scot then said, 'You'll be interested to hear that our gallant Captain Bamfylde is at present not fifty yards away imprisoned in the Gatehouse.'

Bamfylde could always guarantee a surprise.

'His offence?' I asked.

'It seems he has accumulated some debts.'

'He's your man, can't you help him out?'

'It suits me for the moment to keep him where he is. He'll be released shortly. He needed a sharp lesson in loyalty,' replied Thurloe. 'You fellows—are sometimes inclined to keep matters a little too close. I need to make sure he has told us everything.'

A silence followed. Outside Scot's gloomy chamber, I could hear the seagulls' angry shrieks as they fought over foul things that littered the riverside.

Scot smiled, the smile that never reached his eyes. 'Let us begin again. Tomorrow, you will be re-instated at Ely. About the dead woman—that matter is finished. You yourself provided the post-mortem report. Renegade Irish Royalists were found guilty of the murder. Under the laws of war, they were summarily executed. Colonel Sidney himself ordered it. Have you forgotten?'

'I have forgotten nothing,' I replied. 'They were executed, then I was arrested and imprisoned for the same crime.'

'A blunder,' said Scot. 'Our intelligence was wrong …just two old ignorant women, the parish Searchers. They said the wounds they saw could only have been made by a surgeon. Swore to it. We still have their deposition. Nonsense of course, but it could be material should you want to pursue the matter.'

Thurloe leaned across the table. It was his turn to smile.

'Surgeon-major, don't fall into the trap of conducting your own investigations. Leave that to us. We have a report that before leaving for France you visited a whorehouse in Whitecross Street.' He giggled. 'It wasn't for the usual reasons. You went there asking questions. Please don't do that.'

'What Mr Thurloe means,' said Scot, 'is that naughty houses are the concern of the City justices. We only step in if there is sedition. Leave such matters to our direction.'

There was a clatter of crockery as Thurloe's thin hand held out a plate. His eyes were greedy. 'If you were to upset things Surgeon-major, Ely Hospital would be deprived of your skills even longer. Close the door behind you. Tom, may I have a taste of those pilchards?'

Thursday November 2nd late morning

After leaving Scot's office, my first action was to hail a wherry to Holborn dock. I wanted to get to Ely as fast as possible, dogged as I was by the fear that my re-instatement would be cancelled by those two devious men. I stared at the weather-beaten necks of the oarsmen and watched the regular movements of their arms, routinely noting stiffness, injury and the white marks of old wounds. It was a cold, calm morning—winter was almost here. The tide was full. We slid over the grey-blue water past the wharves, warehouses and gardens towards the dense heart of the city. With the rhythmic movement across water, my thoughts began to settle.

I remembered Thurloe's remarks about *'you fellows'* who keep the secrets they have learnt. He's right I thought. I have said nothing about the letter although the intelligence within it is shattering. I was silent about the missing child Edward. I'm going to keep these matters to myself and choose my time. Then there was the warning to keep away from Whitecross Street. *'Leave that to us.'* To them? I almost laughed aloud. Keep quiet, wait until you are told what to do?

No. Nothing is going to keep me away from Whitecross Street.

Friday November 3rd morning

I was wrong.

As soon I he entered the yard at Ely next day, Colonel Aldridge shook my hand and began talking as if our last conversation had been only briefly interrupted.

'Good you're here John, we're a surgeon down and the work is piling up.'

'Where's Yorke?' Aldridge barked a laugh.

'Gone! After he married Rose Ellis, they were throwing money around and some hospital funds disappeared. Then he came in here one evening saying he followed the prophet Ezekiel and now all women were to be held in common including his wife!'

'A novel idea! I wonder what Rose made of it?' I was glad that Madame was not in earshot.

'Now, he and Rose are working as itinerant preachers, travelling from town to town with doom-laden prophecies saying that in the coming Apocalypse the Elect will reign and the mighty will be brought low and suchlike nonsense.'

I tried to imagine dissolute Mr Yorke and sensuous luxury-loving Rose Ellis as messengers of the Word of God. I failed. Aldridge was having none of it.

'Religion, John, can drive people mad. Even someone as level-headed as Madame was up to something, I'm sure.'

I knew that Madame had hopes of an England where the Old Faith could be freely practised.

'And that pest Barebon has been back preaching that England is a Godly Republic and that these are the Last Days before Judgement.'

'Well as for putting down the mighty,' I said, 'the common people have spent much blood in the battles just past. No doubt they will be asked for more. Have their lives improved? The powerful have simply changed hats. Birth. Blood. What do they mean? I've seen inside many men—guts and hearts and limbs are the same and precious for all.'

For a moment Aldridge looked angry, then reverted to his kindly bluff self.

'Do you really think so little of what has been achieved John? I'm not one for preachers either-or for hypocrites. I know things are turbulent at the moment but I'm an Army man—with some discipline the country will be restored. Just now there's a lot of fear about. Much talk of traitors and conspiracies for between you and me the Republic doesn't feel secure, and you can't tell friend from enemy. So be careful what you say, there are informers everywhere, even here. You may not be out of trouble yet.'

I put my arm around his solid shoulder.

'Don't fear for me colonel. Tell me what else has changed since my—er-absence.'

'Ah John—always the practical surgeon! Well, the new boiler has been installed and we're doing many more sweating treatments for the foul disease. Dr French will need your help, it's a big part of our income these days. We've got many casualties still and you are the only fully qualified surgeon.'

'Are operations and dissections still made in the afternoon?'

'When we can. Hey corporal—over here!' Aldridge called to a stocky man in a bloodstained gown.

'Corporal Rowland is a new surgical assistant—' I smiled and shook Rowland's hand. I knew by the feel of the man's grip, that he would be dependable. A podgy woman with a sulky face was slowly crossing the Yard. She barely acknowledged Aldridge's greeting and carried on past, unhurried. Aldridge grunted.

'Mrs Faulkner our new Matron. Madame was worth ten of her. Papist or not—Madame knew what she was about. No detail left to chance when she was here.'

I could only nod agreement.

'And her bone-setting!' The colonel enthused. 'Countless men left here able to take up a trade again. I miss her John. We all do.'

I said nothing about our meeting in France. Instead, I glanced up at the window of my room. The shutters were closed. Aldridge looked embarrassed.

'I'm sorry, John but your room has been converted to a chamber for our private patients. You're welcome to an outhouse. I can get one cleaned for you.'

I had a swift memory of Sally's pattens lying at angles in the dirt.

'No thank you Colonel Aldridge. I have a place nearby,' I replied. A truckle bed in Janvier's lodgings in Hosier Lane to be exact.

'At least you have your books,' said Aldridge. 'I managed to stop Yorke and his rapacious wife from selling them after you were arrested. I was able to save your old Army cloak too.'

I was moved by the old Colonel's kindness and care.

'I thank you from the bottom of my heart for my books. I thought I should never see my cloak again.'

'You'll need it. They say now we are only at the beginning of a very hard winter,' said Aldridge.

Chapter 26

Saturday November 4th morning

As I walked into Ely the next day, I was thinking about what I should do next. I was ready to start work but my other tasks had not gone away. Should I go to Whitecross Street and try to get Mistress Grahame or Dicky to tell me more? Or go to Barnards Castle and confront Pembroke? I did not relish the thought of another stay in the underground cell. And now the weather upset my calculations. Aldridge's words of the previous day were proved right. It was bitterly cold, and the Yard was full of ice.

The patients gave only a feeble reply to my greeting as I entered the Great Ward. The fire was out, and the air was chilly. I went straight out and ordered more fuel, but the porter shook his head.

'The boiler, Sir for the sweating rooms—it uses such a lot now. Our stock is low, and Colonel Aldridge says we must delay a few weeks as the price of wood is so high, and the coal deliveries from the North have only just re-started.'

'Prices will go up even further if this cold continues,' I said. 'I will speak to Colonel Aldridge.'

Aldridge was reluctant. 'John, it's difficult. I must

admit I thought the boiler would pay for itself. General Cromwell is asking for more money and Parliament has just voted him a massive sum to crush the Irish once and for all. There's an allowance for a surgeon to replace Mr Yorke but we have nothing to spare.'

But I persisted and by the end of the day, the fire in the Great Ward was blazing again. At suppertime, the soldiers, their spirits restored drank to my health. For the first time in many months, I felt a sense of achievement and the rightness of things. It made me feel extraordinarily happy.

Tuesday December 18th early evening

Days of unrelenting work had passed for me and now I was seated by the fire at The Saracen's Head. Janvier sat opposite. Having finished our meal, we were smoking. Outside, it was still freezing but the sky was clear and brilliant with stars.

Janvier stretched and yawned pleasurably. 'I must get down to Somerset House later there is another sale of the King's pictures. The Council of State are hoping to pay off debts with a Correggio here and a Van Dyke there. My master has his eye on something by Titian, so I must get there before the Spanish ambassador. His gold has no limit.'

'Aldridge said we should try and get something for the hospital to enliven the spirits of the men. See if you notice a suitable painting. He warned me off anything naked or Papist.'

Janvier laughed. 'Others aren't so reluctant! Colonel Hutchinson bought Titian's *Venus del Pardo*. General

Cromwell's got two paintings of the Virgin Mary, although I hear he turned down Titian's *Salome*. Apparently, he didn't like John the Baptist's severed head—raised some awkward parallels, I expect! Perhaps you should buy it for your Grand Ward!'

'I fear it might prove a little too stimulating.'

'Pembroke's man was there last night, bidding for the Earl. You know him—tall blond Dutchman?'

'Van Prin.'

'Yes, him. We spoke a little. The Earl is dying.'

The fire crackled and let fly a shower of sparks. People talk before a fire, the embers prompt reflection. I said, 'Before we met for the first time in Scot's office, you had been following me. Why?'

Janvier frowned. 'Following you? You are mistaken, John. Why should I do that?'

He has answered a question with a question. I thought. He's guilty.

For a time, we both stared into the fire. To break the silence, I asked, 'So how goes your enterprise?'

'Well, the usual, John. Hurrying back and forth between counting houses and wharves; arranging paperwork. I've seized some good bargains.'

Janvier sucked on his pipe and blew out a long curl of smoke.

'I've another job to do, but I don't wish to do it.'

'Oh. What's that?'

'Just now you asked me if I followed you in London. I denied it. I was not telling the truth. Haven't you noticed how smoothly my business goes? No permit is ever withheld or questioned. That is the favour I enjoy from Scot—as long as I keep him supplied with information.'

I stayed silent.

'Back then, Scot asked me to watch you. I think he wanted to recruit you. He said you had an interesting history, but I found you rather unexciting—apart from your visit to the Whitecross Street whorehouse. He was interested that you called on Harvey.'

'Does he know that I went to Baynard's Castle?'

'I am not sure. I didn't follow you there, my shoes collapsed in the mud.' Janvier looked embarrassed.

'You've told Mazarin about me in France and Scot about me here. What next?'

'Scot wants to use you again.'

'I want nothing more to do with him—or that twisting lawyer Thurloe.'

'Nor do I John. You and I have become friends. You share my home, my food. You cured my *mal de mer*. I will file no more reports about you for Scot.'

Do I believe him I wondered? He seemed sincere. But once a spy it corrupts the heart.

Yet I couldn't help liking him. I'd got used to his lively face and bright quick gestures.

'What if we made a bargain with Scot?' I suggested. The idea had just come to me.

'With the Chief Intelligencer?'

'I mean offer him some valuable information. Say it's for him alone to give him the edge on Thurloe. You know that they are rivals—Thurloe hopes to take Scot's place. Play one off against the other.'

'Do you have something in mind?'

'I think I have.'

Thursday 20th December late evening

Back at our Hosier Lane lodgings, I unrolled the fragile sheets of paper and laid the transcript alongside. Janvier leant over and begun to read. As he read, he let out grunts and whistles of incredulity.

Then in the side-chapel was a party assembled, namely Lucy Walter, Monsieur Thomas Barlow (whom we know as Charles Stewart, King of England, Second of that Name), Monsieur Owain Hopkins, a Welsh gentleman, Lady Derryn Barlow cousin of Lucy Walter, myself your Brother and a Roman Catholic Priest.

'In Liege last year?' he said. I nodded.

'I witnessed an exchange of Vows and Rings between Monsieur Thomas Barlow and our beloved Lucy. This was not a Nuptial Mass but a ceremony of such that those within that Faith would consider a true Marriage.'

'Incredible,' said Janvier.

In March of this year our beloved Lucy Walter was brought to bed of a son.

'The King has acknowledged the child,' I said.

But here lies the greatest scandal: for her cousin Lady Derryn, the fair messenger of this letter was most wrongly prevailed upon by the same Charles Stuart until she was forced to yield to him. She now carries the fruit of that wickedness.

'So this is what you deciphered in France,' said Janvier. 'A letter from Robert Sidney to his brother Algernon. Have you told anyone?' I shook my head. Re-reading the letter had been an eerie experience.

Janvier had a question.

'How did you find the key phrase?'

'I took note of what you said about royalist ciphers

being grandiose. The phrase was in plain sight—'*Quo Fata Vocant* "Whatever Fate has in store" the Sidney motto'.

Now Janvier was as excited as I'd ever seen him. 'How have you kept this so closely? It could blow the Scottish alliance sky-high if they discover there's been a Catholic marriage. That makes Lucy Walter's son a legitimate heir. And the murdered woman was a witness!'

'It's clear Derryn carried a Stuart child too,' I said. 'Is Charles Stuart his father? You can see why several people might want her and her child out of the way.'

'General Cromwell would not be pleased to see more Stuarts.'

'But if Lady Derryn had been alive, she could have given evidence herself. Who wanted to prevent that?'

Janvier thumped the table. 'This is a good bargaining hand,' he said gleefully. 'We must extract a high price from Scot—freedom from his commands.'

I still felt angry about the tactics Scot had used on me. But I was not convinced that my own freedom and that of Janvier were identical in shape. The letter provided clear motives for murder but did not prove—as I'd originally hoped—that I was innocent. What it did reveal was a motive for murder for someone dedicated to the cause of the Stuarts.

'Scot shouldn't have threatened me. I am not his man. I've taken a risk showing you this.'

Janvier said, 'I'll inform Mazarin, but you knew that. What do we do now?'

'When I came back to England, I had two intentions. The first was simple—to return to my work at Ely. The second has overwhelmed my life—to find out who killed Derryn Barlow and Sally Watts and to find Edward.

These purposes are in conflict. I'm not sure I can do both. I don't think my life can ever be what it was before.'

Janvier nodded.

'I'll get no help from Scot—more likely the opposite. That's why I've held back on revealing the letter's contents. Exposing his origins to Scot may put the child in danger.'

Janvier spoke quietly. 'Is the child alive? It's unlikely. The women are dead and buried. Your job is with the living—you have important work. Think on it.'

I stretched out and pushed away the footstool. I needed fresh air. 'I'll see you back at the lodgings—I need a walk.'

I needed to think about the whole problem and my next move. Janvier was right—the Republic did not need more Stuart children—whether they were legitimate or not.

Coming out, I turned right down Hosier Lane. There were few people about; the sweepers were finishing, and the men of the night watch had begun calling the hour. Carts and traffic going north out of the City had ceased and Aldersgate was barred for the night. I tried to work out the next step. A letter written eight months ago had been intended for Algernon Sidney. For some reason Derryn never passed it on. She must have known it was important.

Am I wasting my time? I allowed myself to think that for a moment. Then I remembered defenceless Derryn, her vigorous child and the wounded half—starved laundry maid. No. I was not wasting my time.

Tomorrow, I was going to deliver the letter to where it was meant to go.

To Baynard's Castle. I would find Algernon Sidney.

Friday December 21st

Over breakfast, I told Janvier of my intention. I no longer cared that Janvier worked for Cardinal Mazarin or that he urged me to treat the State powers more seriously.

'Give me a day to confront Sidney and see what he can tell me about Lady Derryn Barlow. Then I promise, we will take everything to Scot.'

I set out for Ely in rapidly worsening weather. A freezing wind was blowing and as I entered the Yard, I saw new piles of logs. Ice had been swept aside. Hurrying across the Yard came Hope-Anna muffled against the weather. She rushed over.

'The cold John, today! The Thames is already freezing solid. Mistress Faulkner is in a fury over the laundry and has had a great stand-off with Mistress Cattell over the costs. She's told us to limit the number of changes a man can have in a week—but we cannot keep them clean! The boiler is having problems—I don't know if Jonas can fix it.'

It seemed as if a dark cloud had settled over the hospital. The men were complaining; the soiled sheets were piling up. The boiler stayed inert. The buck tub had frozen overnight, and no one was in a mind to thaw it out. More fuel was sent for, but the logs were damp. The bandage supply was insufficient and despite Mistress Faulkner's protests, I ordered more sheets to be torn to create a makeshift. By the evening, I was exhausted, but I knew I could not leave. If only Yorke's replacement would arrive.

Finally leaving the Yard, I noticed that the normally dark street was lit up. Coming up towards Holborn

Bridge a torchlight procession was moving towards the City. As they came nearer, I saw that many carried emblems of the sun, moon and stars. The flames made long shadows in the gutters and on the walls of houses. The procession was silent, and this had the effect as it advanced of silencing the people who had come out to watch. At the end came a painted horse-drawn cart. A woman stood upright carrying a scroll in one hand, a gold disc in the other.

At the foot of Ludgate Hill, the procession halted. More torches were lit. As they flamed, the woman held the gold disc above her head. Its brilliance was reflected in the faces of her many watchers and they too shone. She began to speak.

Her voice soaring high and pure in the night air, told of the Last Days as foretold by the Prophet Ezekiel, where the earth would be consumed with fire and stars would rain from the heavens. Men's wickedness was so great, she cried, that the Lord had chosen to put an end to His creation. In these final times those who put themselves up would be pulled down and the humble would be raised on high. And for those who believed, all their sins would be wiped away, for none of those things that the kingdom of men called transgression mattered now. Each was free, man or woman to do as they pleased for the Chosen were already Chosen.

I listened in alarm and fascination. I recognised the speaker.

It was Rose.

The crowd was attentive, shocked into silence. But gradually they too found a voice and the intensity of their cries, punctuating her soaring phrases, rose in intensity until they were baying in excitement and anticipation and Rose, responding ecstatically to the mood threw back her head and let out a long rapturous cry which seemed to shake the very cobblestones and make the torches flare up. It was then I noticed a small troop of men threading quickly among the crowd. Rose had spotted them too and hastily called on her companions to douse their torches. Instantly, the street darkened, and she disappeared into blackness. But she was too late. She was surrounded, and before she could cry out, speedily bundled from her cart. It was over in a moment; Few people had seen and fewer realised, the crowd shifted uneasily, unnerved by the sudden darkness.

The Republic's grip is tightening, I thought.

The darkness and cold of the evening meant that after a brief time the crowd, deflated and muttering in confusion, melted away. I decided to head for Baynard's Castle. What I had just witnessed confirmed my fear that there were many forces at work both to create and quell dissent—and they were growing in intensity and power. My visit to Sidney carried a new urgency.

Baynard's Castle stood immense against the night sky. The great oak doors were shut fast. At an entrance in the wall the porter sat by his brazier and behind him, guards patrolled the inner wall. The porter was unimpressed by a man who had arrived on foot without coach or horse, but I was determined, saying I had a message for Colonel Sidney. After a long wait, during which the porter's coals burned low and the evening star appeared, I was summoned and found myself once again in the upper-floor room overlooking the Thames, where I had first encountered the Earl of Pembroke.

Colonel Algernon Sidney arrived, unannounced and alone, in the uniform of a colonel in the New Model Army. True Republican—or disappointed second son, with only the prospects he makes for himself? I wondered. His lean face wore an expression of weary caution.

'Surgeon-major Lockyer, I can't imagine what your message could possibly be. I thought our business was done.'

'Read this first, Colonel. It is meant for you. It was found on Lady Derryn Barlow's body.'

I handed over a copy of the letter. I had kept the original. Sidney took it and was immediately surprised.

'From my brother Robert? But he died last year of a disease of the lungs. How did you come by it?' He began to read. When he had finished, he sunk down in Pembroke's worn chair, his head in his hands. I waited.

'Last year, in The Hague, Robert hinted about this marriage. I wanted to know more but he wouldn't say. So I did not pursue it.'

He looked at me with bleak eyes.

'I have loved Lucy Walter since we were children together in Wales. My brother Robert loved her even more. Now I know he died because his heart was broken. How I hate and curse the House of Stuart!'

He leapt from his chair in a sudden passion.

'Why did you bring this to me? What are you about? You are that damned surgeon who anatomised Lady Derryn. You all but accused us of poisoning her! How do I know this isn't some trap?'

'No trap, colonel. What would be the point?' I was puzzled.

'No point, no point?' raged Sidney. 'These are times

when any man may betray another. Perhaps you are in the pay of General Cromwell—or of my elder brother Philip who hates me. Oh, yes, we Sidneys are a family divided many ways in this war.'

He glared at me.

'I shall say nothing more. You will not entice me to speak treason and then report it.'

Those who had spoken of the violent temper of the Pembrokes' and the Sidneys were right. I'd been on the receiving end of both, so nothing to lose.

'I came here because I want to know who killed Lady Derryn Barlow and why. Was it you? And I beg you not to return to that tired story about Irish vagrants.'

'I did not kill her! How dare you question me surgeon!' Sidney was white with fury. Still, I persisted.

'What about the Earl of Pembroke?'

'Of course not! My cousin is a dying man!'

I said nothing. The silence lasted as Sidney poured himself a glass of *eau de vie.* He drained it and sat down heavily. There was silence again. Then Sidney spoke more quietly.

'What is your part in all this surgeon-major? My uncle had you detained because Derryn Barlow had a child which thanks to you survived her death, then disappeared. Because you tried to conceal what happened, my uncle thought you were involved.'

'Concealment was a decision on impulse. To preserve the child from harm,' I said.

'When Lady Anne found out that Derryn was pregnant, Cousin Pembroke and I suspected that child might be a Stuart bastard. The letter confirms it. But it also suggests that Charles is the father whereas I thought it might be James. That could be a complication.'

Sidney paused, then added 'My mother looks after the younger children of the late King, Elizabeth and Henry at Penshurst Place. Before that my uncle Northumberland was responsible.'

'When James escaped,' I remarked, not without malice. Sidney ignored me.

'Our family task is to turn the Stuarts for Parliament. The Republic trusts us to do it.'

Quite a task! The chief aim is to show that the Republic is not a barbarian bunch of rebels. And some still hope to bring the Stuarts to a negotiated settlement.

'We have a common interest, Colonel Sidney. We need to find the child-and whoever killed his mother. Tell me all you know about Lady Derryn Barlow.'

Sidney shrugged. 'She was some distant kin of ours. Not content with seducing Lucy, Charles Stuart took Derryn from his brother. James—not more than a boy—was in love with her. The great libertine thought he should enjoy some pleasure while his 'wife' Lucy was pregnant. It caused a scandal, and she was banished from The Hague. This letter rounds off the story surgeon.'

A bell rang somewhere in the house, and I heard hurrying feet.

'When she was staying with you, van Prin said she was sick. It doesn't sound like the usual sickness of pregnancy. That is in the early months—but she was near her term. What was the cause?'

He frowned dismissively.

'No idea—I was in Dover. Pembroke was anxious about her, so a midwife was engaged. I think van Prin found someone just to keep Cousin Pembroke quiet. I never saw the creature.'

'Did she come from Whitecross Street?'

Sidney hesitated for a second, then stiffened.

'I've never heard of Whitecross Street. Why do you expect me to know every hovel in this wretched city?' He was in a fury again.

'It's been suggested that a man called Bamfylde killed her. Is that possible?'

Sidney snorted.

'Bamfylde the Stuart's fixer? Who suggested *him*? — that two-faced villain gets everywhere! I wouldn't be surprised at anything—'

There was a noise in the corridor outside and Sidney looked around irritably. It was van Prin.

'I have come from Westminster, Colonel. The Earl fell ill about an hour ago during one of the debates. They carried him to his room in Whitehall Palace, but he is still senseless.' Sidney's face changed and he was full of concern.

'He shouldn't have attended the chamber today. I told him so! Major Lockyer, I beg you to assist.'

Chapter 27

Friday 21st December later that evening

The Earl of Pembroke was lying on a truckle bed. He had already been bled eight ounces of blood and the local surgeon was ready to drain some more.

'Surgeon-major Lockyer will take over,' said Sidney, dismissing him. The Earl's eyes remained closed, and his breathing came in heavy snorts.

'Enough blood has been taken for the time being,' I said. In current theory, bad humours had risen to Pembroke's head and must be expelled. But I agreed with Ambroise Paré, that this condition could be caused by a blockage in one of the great arteries. Paré observed that the patient usually falls asleep.

'There is nothing to be done?' Sidney was indignant.

'Most remedies are based upon drawing down the phlegmatic humour from the head,' I replied, 'where it can be bled from the body. A clyster will also expel humours along with the body's waste.'

'Well, do what is necessary,' said Sidney impatiently.

Pembroke remained unconscious throughout the night. I watched him and slept little. In the morning, I instructed that he should be given a warm infusion of garlic and ginger. As I made ready to go Sidney followed me to the stable yard.

'Stay with us Major Lockyer. We need someone we can trust,' said Sidney. 'Help the family and you will be well rewarded.'

'The Earl is beyond help,' I said. 'I don't think he will live much longer. You can best reward me and yourself by helping me to find the killer of Lady Derryn and recover her son.'

A call came from above. 'Major Lockyer, the Earl has woken up.' I ran back up the stairs.

Pembroke's head lay against the tangled sheets. His eyes opened and he appeared to recognise me. He made a weak movement with his hand.

'Ca-aa sh…ca-a-shel,' Pembroke mumbled. Then with great intensity 'CA-AA-A-SHEL!'

'I cannot make sense of it,' said Sidney. The effort had exhausted the Earl. Saliva drooled from his mouth.

'Make sure he rests,' I said to the attendant. 'He may be bled a small amount tomorrow by the palace surgeon, and then do nothing for three days. Keep him clean and fed.'

As we clattered down the stairs together, I said to Sidney, 'There is not much more that can be done without doing such violence to his person, he would suffer needlessly.'

'We have still the other matters to discuss,' said Sidney.

'Yes. The child,' I said. 'If he's alive he would be nearly four months old. Easy to dispose of in a large city. I think the search should begin at Baynard's Castle. Someone there forged my signature to remove the child from his wet-nurse.'

'Nonsense,' said Sidney, angry again. 'No member of my family would do such a thing! What about someone at Ely hospital—in the pay of the government? I suppose you think one of us killed Lady Derryn as well.'

'I do not know what to think. Your family has motives for abduction *and* murder. You all seemed anxious to deflect suspicion at the time. You called me in as a safeguard. Perhaps you were simply trying to ensure that I got the blame—which I did.'

I remembered my arrest and my fearful imprisonment underground at Baynard's Castle. In some way that dark palace was implicated in what had happened. Impatient with Sidney's protestations of innocence and feeling a rush of sleepiness, I left Whitehall and turned towards Westminster Stairs and the frozen Thames.

Sounds of singing and laughter drifted up from the ice, busy with crowds of skaters. Portly matrons skimmed between ragged young boys. I could see the lighted booths, brightly garlanded, that had been set up at the river's edge. Christmas celebration was forbidden but Londoners do not so easily relinquish their pleasures. The hot pie stalls were busy. The smells of crust and rich beef gravy floated on the air and I felt urgent pangs of hunger. I had taken nothing since last night's *eau de vie*. My route took me past the Gatehouse outside Westminster Abbey, and I remembered that Bamfylde was incarcerated there. I'm sure he is in a fine chamber, with books and a large fireplace. Then I thought of Rose. She's in Bridewell with a lecherous jailer and rats for company. I wondered what had become of Mr Yorke and his crusade to announce the end of the world.

A movement caught my eye as a figure emerged from behind a pillar. It was Janvier.

Well, he gave me the day I asked for to the minute, I

thought; he could hardly wait.

Janvier was whispering urgently.

'John we must go back to Hosier Lane. There's something you need to see.'

'You have seen Scot and shown him the correspondence?'

'An hour ago. He accepted it was genuine. I also told him that I would not spy upon you again and that you wished to be relieved of any future service.'

'And his reply?'

'That Mazarin is my master, that your objections are noted and that he does not bargain with the safety of the Republic.' Janvier was speaking rapidly, as if he had not breath enough.

'Did he ask about the child?'

Janvier looked puzzled.

'No, he didn't seem curious. He must have assumed Edward died along with his mother I suppose. I thought you would prefer me to keep quiet about that. He was very interested in the news about the marriage. And he wants to see you.'

I groaned and shook my head. Scot was as persistent as a terrier and my stratagem hadn't worked. It was only desperation that had made me think it would.

Janvier continued insistently.

'John there is something else far more important I did not tell him—something neither of us realised.'

He would not say more until we arrived at Hosier Lane. Once inside, I saw that he had laid out on a table the original coded message from Robert Sidney. The thin white sheets sat anchored under a pot of ink. Janvier picked up a fair copy of his transcription.

'John, when I looked at the original letter you had deciphered, I noticed something you had not.'

'Did I mistake the key phrase?'

'No—not that. We both missed this,' said Janvier. 'There was writing on the back of the letter, but I had thought, as you did, that it was simply the front text appearing through thin paper. Even when I looked closely, I did not see it. It's written in a particular ink.'

'See what?'

'Do you remember back in France when I asked you how the image of a mirror is made? It was the wrong question but relevant. When I held the text of the reverse side against a mirror, I saw another letter! I copied and decoded it.'

The Hague 1649. The Tenth Day of May, Year of Our Lord Sixteen Hundred Forty—Nine to Colonel Algernon Sidney

Beloved Brother You asked me to give my Opinion as to the Temper of our English Soldiers serving in the Dutch Service once commanded by our illustrious Father, I will say that the most Part will not admit to whom they are loyal. In The Hague are many Soldiers who fled England among them a part very dedicated to the cause of His Majesty now as before the Murder of the late King. They speak hotly of the new Commonwealth as Rebels.

Among these is a faction known as The Special Force ripe for any Venture on behalf of His Majesty. The aim is to raise a storm in the Eastern counties of England, not by large Armies but by Assassination to thereby spread Fear among the Populace and give them to think that their Force is greater than it is. It will meet with dissident elements and Phanaticks and make common cause. This Special Force is to be based in

Holland but it plans to spread Murder and Riot in London, and the eastern ports.

My Beloved Brother, I beg you to be aware of this Likelihood in the Months ahead and prepare yourself. Van Prin will be our contact as he will shortly resume his service in the Household of our kinsman Pembroke at Baynard's Castle, where I hope this Letter finds you well.

Beloved Brother you above all should be aware that the division in our Family is found in some others of the Nobility where some serve His Majesty and others, like you, have taken Arms against Him and fought for Parliament.

I stopped reading. I was puzzled.

'It does not refer to a specific plot. It names van Prin. I did not realise how deeply he was involved—but does it get us any further?'

'Read on.'

But where is the Good to our Country if we are so divided? Or the Fortunes of our Family? Cpt. Van Prin has knowledge of that certain House in Whitecross Street near St Pauls where those of both sides can meet to do what they are able to make Unity within our Country. But there is much Danger in that place as they risk a Traitor's Death.

Treat the Fair Messenger as she deserves.

Your loving brother

Robert Sidney.

'A certain House!' said Janvier. I nodded. What had Mistress Grahame called her establishment? *Whorehouse of the Republic.*

'Janvier, I can't believe this,' I said.

Janvier was delighted with himself.

'What have we discovered here? Nothing less than a—' he hesitated. 'In France we have a vulgar phrase to describe it—but I will call it a back channel.'

'What is that?'

'It is a means by which secret negotiations can be carried on between parties who are apparently hostile to one another—like Royalists and Parliamentarians.'

I sat for a moment, digesting the news.

'Janvier you are amazing. So, this is the business—the true business of the Whitecross Street whorehouse?'

The Frenchman nodded.

'Yes John, that is correct. You did the hard work, I merely trudged in your footsteps.'

He added modestly.

'But unless you wish to be a traitor to your English Republic, Scot must be told.'

Sunday 23rd December late evening

I had begun to believe the gap-toothed Chief Intelligencer possessed almost occult powers. As if he had overheard, at dawn a message came to Hosier Lane from Scot demanding my presence 'In the name of the Republic.' Nevertheless, I was determined to keep to my schedule of operations for the day. It was late and dark when at some expense, I took a sled along the frozen river from Temple Bar. I was forced to share with three other men who had drunk heavily against the cold. The journey proceeded in a haze of sweat and brandy and I was glad when it was over.

Scot's rooms were along one of the darkest and narrowest passages that surround the Palace of Westminster. My feet crunched on the frozen mud.

Scot was hunched over his desk, his shirt grey and

worn and his thin hair uncombed. When he raised his eyes at my approach, they stood out red-rimmed against a face pale with fatigue.

'I see we both keep late hours Surgeon-major. That is what I like about you. You work tirelessly for the things that matter to you. For you it is the sick. For me it is the health of our Republic. You say you no longer want to serve in that great cause. But I have a task for which only you have the correct knowledge.' Scot placed a paper neatly in a pile.

'You are not too tired for flattery, Mr Scot,' I replied. 'I am not the sole surgeon in the Republic.'

Scot ignored my remark. He frowned.

'Royalist plots. There are assassins on the loose. There has been a gunpowder attempt in Ipswich. The explosion killed ten people, but the news-sheets are banned from publishing that.'

Perhaps this was the work of the Special Force Robert Sidney mentioned. Did Scot know about it already?

'Who did it?'

'We think at least one of them was among those killed. I want you to identify him.'

'Wasn't that done locally?'

'No,' Scot replied, 'for two reasons. The body found at the scene was that of a tall and dark man. There is a growing rumour that the body is that of Charles Stuart himself. He has been expected to land on that coast for some time. You are the only one who can reliably identify him. You must go Ipswich.'

'And the second reason?' I asked. Scot made a barking sound which I realised was a laugh.

'In the explosion, the head was blown clean off.'

Chapter 28

Wednesday December 26th early morning

I could tell Parson Knipe was unhappy. St Stephens day was probably the one day of the year that he looked forward to, the day he gave presents to his servants and perhaps felt for a brief time that they liked him. He did not want to be up and about dealing with the grisly remains that had been lodged in his crypt. He wrestled with the big iron key as he grumbled that 'things like this do not happen in Ipswich.'

I ignored him and concentrated on what might be waiting for me on the table downstairs. Parson Knipe looked askance when he had been asked for some buckets of sawdust and then horrified when he realised why.

'I hope you will not make a slaughterhouse of my crypt, Sir,' he gasped.

'It may not be necessary.' I hoped so.

I found the body wrapped in a linen shroud, the fabric heavily clotted with blood. As I cut it open, I was surprised to see that except for the raw tatters of skin and flesh on the neck, the body was relatively undamaged. Was this the corpse of Charles Stuart? Scot said that letters had been intercepted a week ago suggesting that the King might attempt to make landing on the east coast.

I sighed. 'Let us have a look at you,' I said to the decapitated corpse. The man was tall—about the King's height. And his copious body-hair was jet black, the King's colour. It was only a short time since I had last seen Charles. I began to observe and compare. This man was well built, but recently had become thinner. His skin sagged. He was an active man. I examined his feet. The hardened skin suggested a walker. I continued my search for similarities. As I did so the strangest apprehension came over me that the body before me was familiar.

Whereas the King was barely twenty this man was older, in his late thirties, and had lost some teeth. The feeling of familiarity persisted. This was not the corpse of Charles Stuart, I was certain. Yet I felt I knew it.

I tried to imagine the body fully clothed, the strong arms and shoulders clad in good quality broadcloth. Under that, a well starched shirt with cuffs turned back over long capable hands. I noticed the fine dark hairs on the fingers and my memory did a cartwheel. Of course! I had seen those hands many a time. I remembered sleeves rolled up, a bloodstained smock, a surgeon's blade poised. It was Mr Yorke.

Thursday 27th December early morning

The morning was dark and icy cold. I looked ahead over a road that was frozen hard, the bushes stiff with frost. My horse's hooves sounded on the hard earth. Two sturdy soldiers accompanied me to guard the coffin, which was wedged against the rough sides of a lumbering cart. Mr Yorke was going home.

Parson Knipe had made no objection that the body

must be brought back to London. I supposed he was glad to be rid of the whole business and able to lock up his freezing crypt. If he was curious as to the identity of the corpse, my grim face and abrupt manner prevented him from asking questions. Thus, although I did not at the time know it, rumours continued in Ipswich for several years afterwards that Charles Stuart had met his death there and his body had been removed for secret burial.

Meanwhile I contemplated two days on the road with a headless corpse for company. I was glad it was the middle of winter.

Monday 31st December morning

'General Cromwell is most anxious to hear the outcome of your investigations!' I heard a bullying note in Thurloe's voice. Scot sat quietly for a moment, then he said, 'The Council of State gives me my orders, John Thurloe and you take yours from me. Surgeon-major Lockyer is convinced that the body is his old colleague Mr Yorke and not that of Charles Stuart, but because he is a cautious man, he suggests additional verification from Mr Yorke's widow.'

'She was arrested some days ago for illegal preaching,' I said. 'She's in the Bridewell. We need permission to have her released.'

'I will arrange it. Afterwards she can go back again,' Thurloe said abruptly.

'Mr Thurloe, she may have information about plots against Parliament—the Ranters threaten us daily with divine vengeance. We should treat her carefully.' Scot continued to speak quietly. 'What is more, Mr Lockyer knows her. I think he should speak with her.'

'Surgeon-major,' Thurloe raised his eyebrows, 'you never cease to amaze me. Truly you are a great asset as an intelligencer. You seem to be connected to everyone of interest.'

'I've told both of you that I don't wish to be an asset. I will speak to Rose Ellis—Mistress Yorke—then I want no more of it.'

But I was curious.

'Tell me what Yorke was doing. Was he one of yours too?'

Scot frowned. Thurloe replied, 'Just a hired hand. Soldiers talk among themselves and wounded ones even more. He kept me informed of their mood from time to time and any other events at Ely. I rather lost him to the Ranters.'

'So when Yorke and I were colleagues at Ely he was already spying for you?'

'What?' Scot sat bolt upright. Thurloe was silent.

'Informing on weak, wounded men!' I felt a surge of anger and disgust. 'I suppose he reported on me too.'

'You are right, Surgeon-major,' said Thurloe, 'of course.'

Tuesday 1st January 3pm

During the time spent viewing her dead husband, she had kept the golden disc clutched to her breast. Her face was bruised, her dark ringlets covered in dust. She was just able to stand upright.

'The stars have gone but I have kept the sun,' she said, holding it up. I saw now it was a circle of gilded wood, scuffed and chipped, but still bright. 'I got it when the

Cockpit Theatre in Drury Lane was raided. It has been useful. People like shows.' She laughed distractedly, and I noticed a missing tooth. I pointed to her damaged face.

'What have they done to you, Rose?' I asked.

'What do you think happens here? For the jailer, I'm part of their wages. Mr Lockyer, can you get me released?'

'Well, they can't keep you here much longer just for preaching. What was Yorke doing in Ipswich?'

'We went our separate ways after—' she hesitated. 'Mr Lockyer, these have been the best months of my life. Preaching to crowds, telling what is to come—for it will come, Mr Lockyer believe me—the cheers, men tugging at the hem of my cloak, women shouting blessings! I was always soaring up on their hope, rising above the city, flying over the river, the earthly temples, bearing the sun as if to plant it in the sky.'

'I've heard you preach, Rose. Your words amazed me.'

'They have returned me to the Bridewell Mr Lockyer, but I have already left this earth; they can do nothing to me. Nothing will bring me back to the smell of blood and filthy sheets. I am clean. White as snow. I am a woman of gold. Mr Lockyer, if in the old times you had forced me, I would have had to submit. But soon you will kneel before me and beg to touch the strings of my garment. All who are high shall fall.'

She tried to walk towards me and staggered. I caught her. I saw the shine of sweat on her skin and smelt her sour breath. I felt a pang of pity and said gently, 'Now that you have identified the body of Mr Yorke, he can be buried. Colonel Aldridge has arranged with the vicar of St Andrew's Holborn. I hope you think that is right.'

Rose started to laugh again. Her laughter went on and

became wilder, as she bent double and coughed.

'Well then he'll be in the same churchyard as Sally Watts. They can rise together when the Judgement Trumpet calls. It won't be long now! Will his head be back on his shoulders and Sally recover the toe he sliced from her foot?'

I stopped.

'How did you know about that?' Only Aldridge knew about Sally's wounds.

Rose coughed again then recovered her breath.

'I was there when he did it. She was a stubborn little brat. I hit her few times myself, but she wouldn't tell us where she'd taken the dress. Her own fault—she had been boasting earlier to that clod Thomas that there was a fortune in gold pieces sewn in the hem. I wanted them. To be a drudge no longer! No more Madame O'Brien and her punishments! Yorke was after the papers, too—they might be valuable. It was a way out for us both!'

With an effort, I kept my tone flat. Rose just wanted money. But Yorke—he must have hoped the papers contained something he could sell to Thurloe.

'What happened to Sally?'

'We grabbed her in the evening as she was leaving to go back to Mistress Cattell's. It was dark. No one saw us.'

Wrong. But the man who glimpsed them thought they were ghosts. Later, Aldridge had thought they were returning from a tryst.

'Go on Rose,' I said quietly.

'We took her into an outhouse and tied her up. When Yorke took out his knife, I thought she would break but she didn't. So, he started to cut. It didn't take him long; she was so small and starved. But she fainted away and then—

she was dead. Of fright!'

I was silent for a moment.

'Are you going to get me out of here Mr Lockyer? I have work to do! You always liked me, didn't you?'

I shook my head. But she did not see. Rose was standing and her eyes were shining.

'I am of the Elect; my sins are all forgiven. In a little while I shall walk on rainbows to the Heavenly Kingdom. In the last days of this earth I shall pass through the cleansing fires, I feel their heat even now upon my skin!'

I looked at Rose. I could see the tell-tale blotches that had already developed on her arms. Outside, I pressed four silver coins into the jailer's hands.

'Take this for the female preacher. Leave her alone. See that she is cared for.'

In the flickering rushlight I saw his dirty unshaven face. He growled, 'Who are you to tell me what to do here? I've had the best of her anyway—and now I'm paid for it too!' He laughed and tossed the coins in his hand. I looked at him.

'Indeed, you are. She is tainted with the jail fever and will not live long.'

Tuesday 1st January

'John, I know your clothes are not the height of fashion, but why do you have to burn them? We are in the middle of winter! And why are you wearing my housekeeper's bedcover?'

There was a small bonfire in the back yard where a pair of breeches smouldered. Inside, I was boiling my shirt and small clothes. The Hosier Lane lodging was steamy enough for a laundry. On returning from Bridewell, I had stripped and examined myself for lice. All jails are lousy especially the Bridewell, packed with prisoners. Everyone knew that body sweat made lice. When mixed with poisonous air the result was jail fever which saw off more prisoners than the hangman.

Janvier was suddenly anxious.

'Have you dried your skin thoroughly? Closed all the pores? Rubbed yourself with spirits and vinegar? Do you need me to lend you a shirt?'

I laughed. 'Yes I have and no thanks. Your shirts are too good for me to wear when doing my sort of work.'

'Ah, John, I forgot. You may have touched royal persons and be learned in Latin, yes—but you need to wear workmen's clothes every day so you are not quite a gentleman, are you? Now, you resemble a washerwoman of easy virtue. They go about half naked you know.'

'I know,' I said. 'What to do about my army cloak—'

Janvier interrupted. 'John, I come from a high plateau in the south of France, the winters are cold. My grandmother made the servants hang our clothes outside on freezing nights to delouse them. The lice were all dead in the morning. I'm sure in this winter the goodwives of London could do the same. Hang your cloak in the yard overnight. Lice resemble us, they do not like it too cold, nor too hot. I recall when I was soldiering in Spain—'

Someone was hammering on the door. Janvier got up and received the handwritten note addressed to me. He handed it across and I saw it was another message from Scot.

'Come at seven o'clock tomorrow morning to my office in Westminster.'

What does he want now? Perhaps finally, he is going to discharge me, I thought with relief.

'Seven? As late as that?' Janvier scoffed 'The old warrior is getting soft! Don't forget to put your cloak out. There's a nail hammered into the ash-tree. You can hang it there.'

Chapter 29

Wednesday 2nd January early morning

Scot and Thurloe sat at either end of the table. They looked, I thought, like a married couple who had just had an argument.

I did not sit.

'There is someone who would like to meet you. Someone of distinction,' Thurloe began pompously. Scot looked sour.

'You gentlemen are quite distinguished enough for me,' I said. 'I did not come here to make acquaintances.'

'Wrong.' Thurloe was definite. 'General Cromwell can make a great difference to your prospects.'

'He certainly did to yours,' Scot remarked.

Thurloe ignored him and continued, 'No more blood and sawdust, unwashed soldiers, laundry concerns. Your own chemist's workshop, well equipped. How does that sound?'

It sounded like a trap.

'I like blood and sawdust. I prefer it to secret letters, lies and creeping about.'

'But that letter is doing the Republic a great service,' said Scot soothingly. 'A copy detailing Charles' secret marriage to Lucy Walter is already on its way to

Edinburgh. It will create a fine commotion amongst the Covenanters and damage the alliance his mother wants so much.'

'What if no one believes it?' I asked.

'Enough will,' said Scot. 'Charles Stuart is a dissolute and undeserving youth. Like his father he tries to play the Covenanters—a big mistake. That letter will make the Scots even more unreasonable in their demands and will sow rancour on all sides. It could delay matters long enough for General Cromwell to ready himself for an invasion of Scotland by the summer.'

'Mr Scot, that is a plan, but I do not make these decisions myself. I must await the crack-farts in Parliament, the Council of State and the blessing of Providence.'

The voice was loud, the speaker broad rather than tall. His hair was thin and looked uncombed. He was dressed in a dark leather jerkin and carried a pair of heavy riding gloves. Both Scot and Thurloe rose quickly to their feet. General Cromwell had entered the room.

My impression was of a man possessed of both physical strength and fierce purpose. At Naseby, as I waited behind Royalist lines, I had seen Cromwell a long way off riding furiously along the front line of Parliamentary horse. Even at that distance I had sensed the energy coming from the Parliamentary side, a vitality that occurs when men are following a leader in whom they believe. He had fired their conviction that the Army was the instrument of God and enjoyed divine favour. Now the General stood less than a foot away. His blue-grey eyes were fixed on me with a quizzical expression. A waft of cinnamon caught me by surprise. I looked at the general's face and observed that coloured pastes had been applied to Cromwell's skin, rendering it smooth and free of broken veins and blemishes although the great wart on his forehead still dominated. Yet despite the hardships of war and his thinning hair, he looked younger than his fifty years.

'If you are to believe the pamphlets you may think that the invasion is decided upon. It's my view that we hit the Scots before they invade us on behalf of the young Stuart. The lying fellow has already publicly agreed to the Covenant – not everyone believes that he is sincere. He won't stay long under the yoke of the Kirk. Still, some fools here think we can settle with him in some way.'

'No!' I was surprised at the ferocity of Scot's denial. He had sprung to his feet full of republican fire. 'I say no, Lord General; we do not want a return of the Stuarts however tamed they seem—shall lives and suffering go to waste?'

Cromwell laughed.

'There is more to come. Despite their doubts about him the Scots will march south in his support. In numbers their army is greater, and David Leslie is a wily commander. Parliament is divided. Tom Fairfax is against an invasion—he's sick of war, which means, I suppose that I shall assume total command of our forces if we move against Scotland.' Cromwell did not look as if he was reluctant.

General Fairfax had rescued me from Oxford and given me a new life. He had fought many engagements in the war. Principle, tradition, and Yorkshire stubbornness kept him going, but he was without any religious sympathies or grand visions of a new world.

'I suppose he wants to return to Nun Appleton, for he

feels he has given all he can,' I said. Cromwell swung round to look at me. His eyes gleamed with energy and power.

'These days no man can feel that until we have brought together our nation in a new Commonwealth in which all must play their part. Surgeon-major, Mr Scot has told me you changed sides at Oxford. If there is a right time for turning, that was probably the occasion. Since then you have rendered faithful service to the Commonwealth. The Army esteems you as a surgeon. He has asked me to support his request to the Council of State that you be offered a permanent position.'

After his speech, I knew I would anger him; but I wanted to pursue my work unhindered by politics. Like Fairfax, I hated the wrangling over belief and the jostling for position.

'Sir I have made no such request myself. I do not want one. I like my work at Ely.'

Cromwell looked annoyed. For a few seconds his eyes narrowed as he appraised me. Then he began to draw on his gloves.

'I see that you are not one to whom it is easy to do a favour. But this is no small matter in the affairs of the Republic. Explain to him, Mr Scot.'

Scot straightened his shoulders. His voice dropped a couple of tones.

'This is an honour which we are offering to you Surgeon Major, a chance to serve your country in perpetuity. Many of the most prominent medical men—Dr Bathurst, Dr Goddard, Mr Trapham and others have enrolled in the service of the Republic. Save for a few reactionary gentlemen at the College of Physicians, service with the new Commonwealth sits well with a medical temperament—exploring the new—throwing off old ideas and testing new ones—working to heal our nation. You can continue your excellent work at Ely, however as you are aware, the Republic is not at peace—'

'Yet!' growled Cromwell.

'O, exactly, Lord General,' said Scot hastily, 'but there may be sensitive instances, like the events in Ipswich, where a trustworthy person with the right skills is required and—er—although a part-time post it carries a stipend, and a title worthy of the Roman Republic—Questor *General.*' He gave the designation heavy emphasis.

'I don't care for titles,' I said. I saw Cromwell's mouth form into a firm line. I thought this might be a danger signal, heeded by those who knew him. Yet the voice stayed steady.

'No airs and graces will be required! I remind you, Sir, respected surgeon or no, that you are still a part of the Army. The Army is the most powerful body in the Commonwealth because its members *obey orders.*'

He leant his formidable body towards me.

'I don't have time to waste with you Major, nor do I think your hesitation does you credit. At this difficult time, I am trusting you to serve God's Republic. *Christ's bowels!*' he suddenly roared. Thurloe jumped. *'Do what is being asked of you!'*

As his voice reverberated, Cromwell turned and strode out of the room. Thurloe stood, mouth open. There was a long silence, then Thurloe recovered himself. He adjusted his black lawyer's gown, settling it firmly in neat folds around himself.

Scot said, 'You will be your own man Surgeon-major, free to investigate any matter that touches the safety of the Republic. My authority will support, but not direct you. The letter you found and deciphered—we may be able to make that young woman's death serve us—er the Republic, I mean— Find her killer—it will show how the Royalists are divided amongst themselves.'

My ears were still ringing with Cromwell's words.

Thurloe coughed loudly and handed me a sheet of paper. The meeting was over.

Chapter 30

Wednesday 9th January

It was the morning of Yorke's funeral. As we walked the along freezing street to St Andrew's churchyard, I told Aldridge about my new position as Questor General and what I had learned about Sally's death. The colonel looked grave. He was determined to maintain the fiction of an accident. I agreed that to protect Ely hospital, Yorke's actions would not be made public. Aldridge was less pleased about my intention of using my newly acquired powers to re-examine Lady Derryn's death.

'No good comes of raking this up, John. It may set hares running that cannot be stopped. That young woman's death has caused enough trouble already.'

'I am not likely to forget that,' I replied. I was thinking about what my new post meant. The link with Scot's office made me uneasy but recent events had reminded me of the advantages of having power. It gave me a measure of control. If it led me into trouble, so be it; at least it was trouble of my own making. And I could use my power to search for Edward.

There had been another advantage: I had access to records and the services of clerks. In the past week I had learned, by their diligent scrutiny of ships passenger lists, that both Henry Jermyn and Joseph Bamfylde had been in England during September. Bamfylde had arrived in August and stayed until the end of September. Jermyn had come earlier and left towards the middle of October. This put both men in England at the time of Derryn's murder in mid-September. Both had ample motive: had they acted together?

We reached the graveside and after a short official prayer, earth and stones rattled into Yorke's open grave. The wind was fierce enough to bend the dark yews at the entrance to the churchyard. I jammed my hat on my head and as I did so, caught sight of Finny standing by the gate. She turned quickly.

'Leave me alone Mr Lockyer. I've been to visit Sally's grave and a poor pile of turned earth it is, too.'

'Finny, I must speak with you. I have information about Sally's death.'

Quickly and without holding anything back, I told her. Finny stood cold-eyed. Then she said, 'You picked the right place to give me the news—her body's not a yard away and her killer's close by! They could almost be sharing a bed! What a joke!' She began to laugh. 'Oh God!' and brushed a hand across her eyes.

The wind tugged at her thin cloak. All her French finery had vanished, and with them her carefree veneer.

'May I walk you where you want to go?' I asked.

'I'm back at Whitecross Street. You and that Frenchman were glad to get rid of me, weren't you? Don't say anything. I don't want to hear your bad opinion of me.'

'Wrong Finny. I admire you. You are courageous and ambitious. I have never met a woman like you.'

'Born a man, I might have been a General instead of

sleeping with one! And you Mr Lockyer—a funny job, cutting people up. But you are honest and kinder than you look.'

We were hit by another gust of freezing wind. I pointed to the hospital entrance across the way.

'Come and have something warm to drink. A hawker arrived today selling Dutch biscuits.'

Finny smiled at the prospect. I watched her thawing out, her hands around a mug of hot ale. No diamonds sparkled on her fingers now. Her chin was covered with crumbs of cinnamon-cake. She brushed them away and said, 'I have news of Madame. She's gone to the Benedictine convent in Ghent. The Queen dismissed her. It was your fault.'

'My fault? She is an expert masseuse. I can't believe there was any defect.'

'True, but she spent too much time in that clinic of yours with the working people. The Queen wanted her as a personal servant, she refused. No one says 'no' to Queen Henrietta.'

Except Madame.

'My Lord Jermyn told me—he had a letter from his nephew.'

'Jermyn is here now—in London?' Of course, he had boarded at Dieppe, when Finny was put aboard *The Constant Warwick*. But that had been over a month ago. I didn't think he would be staying, for fear of arrest.

Finny grinned. 'I bet you'd like to know where he is and so would Parliament.'

'Do you know why he's come?'

'Perhaps to check on his London property. He had a big house here before the war. I expect some Parliament man has got it now! I'm just happy that he is close by. I suppose you find that odd.'

'After how he behaved to you…'

'That was the Queen's orders, not my Lord. She was jealous when she found out that I knew him before in England. I was his favourite—until Mistress Grahame stopped him calling.'

'I see.' I was thoughtful. Was Jermyn the 'gentleman' Mistress Grahame mentioned who had kept Finny '*nights in a row*' last September? I walked her to the Fleet bridge, and Finny turned off south. It was not the way to Whitecross Street. She saw my glance and responded with a defiant look.

'He wants to meet me and I'm going to him. Don't follow.'

Thursday January 10th 3pm

I was outside the house in Whitecross Street. The afternoon sun was low and red in the sky, forecasting frost. The stallholders had packed and gone. Mistress Grahame's establishment was shadowed, shuttered and silent. I now regarded it with different eyes. At my first visit I had realised that it was no ordinary cunny house. It was a place of assignation for sure, but not of the obvious sort. Here members of opposing sides met in the utmost secrecy to plan the future of England. The Whorehouse of the Republic—I knew now what that meant.

I rapped at the front door. There was no reply.

I remembered a door in the alley at the side. It opened into a grassy plot. It was empty except for two large earthenware pots. I walked over, pushed their wooden lids aside and immediately recognised the pungent leafy smell. I did not see Mistress Grahame appear. She smiled and held out her hand. The gold lace on her dress glowed in the late sun.

'Mr Lockyer is it not? These are not our hours of business, Mr Lockyer. But of course, for a gentleman like you I can always make an exception. Come inside, sit by the fire and have a glass of Madeira wine. I will summon a girl.'

She took my arm pulling me to her in a companionable way and I was aware of her breast, firm against me. She was guiding me into an antechamber, and I brushed against the thick velvet drapery. The house was warm after the frosty street.

'I do not seek a girl,' I said. 'I want to ask you about a young woman—' She stopped me by placing her palm against my mouth. It tasted of musk-rose.

'Your last visit cost me one of my best, Mr Lockyer. What do you want to know?'

'At the end of last summer a young woman, visited here with a servant of the Earl of Pembroke's household. Her name was Lady Derryn Barlow. She also came here alone. Shortly afterwards, she was killed.'

She was smiling. 'Killed? Mr Lockyer, you have quite lost me.' She raised her eyebrows. 'I thought it was Finny's sister who was dead. Drowned in a washtub, wasn't it? Then you came here, sneaking like a thief and—yes, now I remember you mentioned another girl was dead too. Very unpleasant.' She smiled. 'I forgive you for that Mr Lockyer. Here, let us have a drink together.' Again, gripping my arm, she leaned towards the dresser and offered me a brimming glass of red wine.

'Do sit, Mr Lockyer. It is a pleasure to see you.'

I sipped the wine. It was delicious with a musky burnt sugar taste. I looked around the room. The panelling was stained black, made I guessed, of Irish oak. Walnut furniture glowed with polish, and I noticed the sheen of silk rugs on the chequered marble floor. Mistress Grahame sat very still, watching me. I could hear nothing except my breathing and the crackle of the fire. Through the shutters I could see the daylight fading. Suddenly I felt the need of rest and comfort. Surely this was the place to find it?

Sounds roused me. There were swift light movements pattering across the floor of the room above. I could hear soft thuds, as of a group of nimble children jumping.

'That's Dicky with the younger girls,' she said. 'We have a few here whose mothers wanted to keep them. He teaches them how to trip a man, dodge a blow, slip from a grasp, to tie a knot securely, or wield a small weapon. The streets can be dangerous as you know.'

I recalled Finny's ways with pistol and rope.

'In truth, they are useful for all sorts of tasks around the house, and most will gradually grow into whoring. Although one was acquired by the household of an elderly gentleman, and I hear that now she is companion to a noblewoman! We are not all bad Mr Lockyer.'

She began to rock gently in her chair. The faint creak and movement made me want to nod my head in time.

'I suppose you have travelled in France and Italy. Tell me, how does my establishment compare with the ones there? Are they finer, the women prettier?'

'Mistress Grahame, I was a poor student; I could not afford to visit a grand house like this. I remember in

Padua, that the main bordello had a herb garden and kitchen for making medicine. They may not have been taught how to use a dagger, but most of the women knew how to prepare medicines for conditions related to their occupation.'

She leant forward with a look of interest.

'What herbs did they grow?'

'I think you know,' I said. 'You grow the same ones here in your garden; rue, wormwood, and in summer, pennyroyal, tansy.'

'Burdock and savory,' she added. She lifted the lid from a white china jar. 'Sniff that,' she ordered. 'A tincture of it does wonders for a man. The Bishop's Palace used to grow a field of it.' I inhaled the powerful scent of dried saffron.

'You are an enterprising woman, Mistress Grahame, like your sister. You make up syrups to increase desire, salves to heal a pox and most importantly, a mixture to bring down a woman's courses when her flow is stopped. We all know the commonest reason for that complaint. I suggest you have quite a flourishing trade in these, carried out, naturally, in secret.'

'Then make a report to the Grocers Company, Sir. Expose me to the Apothecaries.' She laughed softly.

'I'm not interested in their fines and restrictions. I want to know why Lady Derryn Barlow came to this house. Was it to purchase a remedy to end her pregnancy?'

She said nothing. I felt sweaty and impatient.

'Mistress Grahame am I right? Believe me, it is in your interest to answer. I can pay you well for information.'

'I don't need your money Sir,' she retorted. 'I run good trades here and people get what they pay for. The Earl's man came to me saying he needed help for a lady friend.

The medicine failed, just made her sick. I didn't know at first how far gone on she was. Finally, he asked if I would find a place for her to hide away until the matter was settled one way or another.'

'And then?'

'I agreed, but she never arrived. I heard nothing more until today.'

I felt sleepy and forced myself to concentrate.

With an effort, I said, 'You lack curiosity Mrs Grahame. Did you not wonder what had happened to her?'

She shrugged.

'Some things are best left alone Mr Lockyer. I'm surprised you've not learned that, given your own history.'

My mind felt foggy. I made myself ask her.

'You admit administering a poison to this young woman?'

'Not poison, Mr Lockyer but a remedy of which she was in need.'

The noise upstairs had stopped. I heard Dicky coming down. The grille rasped back. The front door was opened, and someone stepped inside. I heard a brief exchange, but it was enough. I knew the voice and the man.

My knees buckled, and I fell to the floor.

Chapter 31

Thursday 10th January early evening

It was cold. It was dark. It was damp. I felt hands exploring my body and tugging at my bonds. I felt the ropes loosen on one arm, then tighten on the other. There were two or three people close to me. Suddenly I felt the sharp point of a blade in my thigh and yelled.

'He's awake,' whispered a voice. 'Here let me have a turn,' said another and a second pinprick came, this time in my arm.

'Is this the right way?' said the first voice.

'Stop it,' I roared, twisting my body away.

'Careful, he'll fall in.' It was a third whisperer. 'We're only supposed to be watching him.'

'We can still practice,' was the soft reply. 'You know we've been told to practice.' Suddenly the knots on my ankles were tightened and a red-hot pain seared my legs. I groaned. My tormentors sniggered and I heard a handclap.

'Again! Do it again! We must practice in the dark.' Feeling the hands on me once more, I rolled away and shouted in desperation.

'Who are you?' The only reply was a series of muffled whispers followed by laughter.

Above my head, a trapdoor rasped open, and someone called. For a moment, I could glimpse my surroundings. I was lying on a stone ledge in a tunnel. At one side a channel of water flowed rapidly towards a portcullis. Beyond, only darkness. I watched helplessly as three shapeless creatures scrambled up a wooden ladder and the trapdoor was slammed shut.

I lay there for a long time. As hours passed, occasionally I heard a splash as if something had leapt into the water. There was a salty muddy smell and I felt rather than saw that the level in the channel was rising. I realised it was tidal, connected to the Thames and would rise and fall accordingly. Enough to drown me?

The pool of water at my feet was growing. I wriggled and strained against my bonds. I realised, my shirt strings had been untied, trousers unbuttoned. I stretched my fingers to feel the knots at my wrist. One felt slacker than the other! I set to worrying the knot until my fingers ached. I felt it work loose. A long time passed as I laboured to release my wrists. The hot pain went deep below my skin until at last I succeeded in freeing my hands and bent to work on my ankles.

There was a scraping above my head. The trapdoor opened and I saw light glint off a blade. I lay completely still. Someone jumped lightly down next to me. With one hand, I grabbed the figure by the throat to stifle any cries, while my other closed around its dagger hand. My captive threshed and squirmed. I realised then that my opponent was small—a young girl not much more than a child. I held her firmly and hissed, 'Keep still or I'll cut your throat and throw you to the rats.' She gibbered in fear. I slashed at the cords around my ankles and still holding my prisoner, lurched to climb the ladder.

I pushed aside the trapdoor and found myself underneath a stone sink. The girl banged her head as I pushed her through the opening and I was obliged to gag her cries again with a hand across her mouth and throat. She spat and tried to bite my fingers. I threatened her again and she was silent. I realised she was terrified. I set her down.

She began to cry. 'Everyone's run away,' she sobbed. 'Please find Finny.'

I heaved the door open and saw a flight of stone steps. I had been imprisoned very far underground. Pulling the girl with me, I climbed up to another door, opening this time into the panelled corridors of the house. As she had said, the place seemed empty. I heard a door open and a shuffling movement. It was Mrs Grahame. One arm hung limply. Her sleeve was torn and soaked with blood.

'Help me,' she whispered.

Her right arm bore a gash on the underside, but the bleeding had stopped.

'This should be covered,' I said. 'Do you keep any bandages?' She nodded.

As I cleaned and wrapped her wound, Mrs Grahame began to speak.

'You were looking for something. Others would follow you—I needed time to think. I was not trying to kill you.'

'But if the tide down there swept me away you would not be greatly concerned. 'Where is everyone?'

'As soon as you fell unconscious, I sent them all away. I thought we were to be raided and I did not want to be arrested.' She stopped and took a gulp of breath. 'My women went through the tunnel. It leads to my sister's laundry. They all passed you as you lay sleeping Mr Lockyer.'

'I am glad to been the source of amusement.' I finished bandaging her arm and gave the dressing a tug to firm it. She gasped.

'That hurt Sir!'

'I thought you were made of stronger stuff, Mistress Grahame.'

There was a loud wailing sound coming from the corridor.

'That's where she is! Finny took two with her, but that one disappeared. Get up girl' Mrs Grahame ordered.

I looked at the thin white-faced child who had tormented me for fun.

'Mistress Grahame, tell me what happened here. Someone arrived at the door and demanded entry.'

'That gentleman never takes no for an answer,' said Mrs Grahame, '—sniffing after Finny like a dog after a bitch. Last year he hired her night after night! He was demanding to stay *here*! I tried to throw him out and he drew his dagger and slashed at me.'

Jermyn! I had recognised his voice.

'He should not have come here again—a Royalist—I could be imprisoned. I could not bear imprisonment.'

'Jermyn came here because he wants me to leave with him—to the Americas. This is my chance!'

It was Finny who spoke. The girl rushed over and clung to her.

Perhaps, I thought, Jermyn has finally got tired of the whole thing—the exhausting Stuart cause, the exacting, ageing Queen, the desperate search for money. Above all, his bungled murder of Lady Derryn Barlow. He had been in England at the time and arranged it. He murdered to get rid of the evidence of the Catholic marriage and please his Queen. That much was obvious now.

But why had he returned? Could it really be for Finny? Mistress Grahame got there first.

'Don't be a fool Finny. You've always made too much of him. Have you heeded anything I've taught? Great lords do not commit themselves to whores.'

Finny shook her head.

'I have seen great lords close—aye and great ladies too. They are no different from me. You don't understand— My Lord Jermyn cares for me.'

'Nonsense Finny! I warn you, if you leave this time, I'll not have you back.' Mistress Grahame had recovered her composure and was once again in command of her House.

I had to warn Finny. To tell her the truth.

'Finny listen to me. You are in great danger. Lord Jermyn is sure to be hunted down. He is on a mission for the Stuart Queen. Soon he'll be arrested for the murder of Derryn Barlow. You could be his accomplice. You'll hang.'

The child screamed and clutched Finny.

'But I've done nothing! Stop it Mr Lockyer!' Finny protested.

'Whatever feelings Lord Jermyn has for you they do not amount to love. When you were put aboard the navy ship at Calais it was at Jermyn's request. He paid Captain Brooks to take you.'

'I don't believe you! It was the Queen!'

'He told them you were an embarrassment of which he wanted rid,' I continued remorselessly. 'I'm not lying to you Finny. Help me and help yourself.'

Finny had gone pale. She stood completely still, gazing

at me. Then, she put her arms around the shivering girl.

'We have to get the children away from here. If there's a raid they could be in danger. They have information about Lady Derryn. That's why you're here isn't it?'

'You gave me a story back in France. It was all about Bamfylde then. Is there more? Do you ever tell the truth?'

Finny pushed the child forward.

'If you don't trust me, listen to her.'

The girl trembled and stared at me for a moment. Then she said, 'Uncle Dicky said not to tell nobody.'

'You can tell Mr Lockyer,' Finny said.

The girl's milky skin and pale blue eyes seemed to glimmer in the dark. She sniffed, then spoke in a near-whisper, 'It was night. Uncle said we should go out to practice. We were going to follow a woman and steal from her. We followed her from the bridge down to the river. It was easy, but then we lost her and we feared Uncle would angry. Then we found her again, she was climbing the bank. At the top by the hospital some men caught at her. One poked at her with a dagger until she fell.'

'Did you—'I could not restrain my question.

'Hush!' said Finny. 'Let her finish.'

'There was a light and a shout, and they ran away and left her. There was a lot of blood on her dress. She was on the ground. I think she was dead.'

'Did you see the men? What did they look like?'

The child stared at me in terror. Then she gave a cry and threw herself at Finny.

Monday January 14th early morning.

I woke up angry and rage fuelled my feelings of cruelty. Finny was the chief object of these feelings. I could not decide whether she was a cunning liar, a misguided fool or both. All my sympathy for her had evaporated and my admiration had turned to contempt at her persistent belief in Jermyn's affections. Well so be it, I thought. My best tactic now is to use her as bait and threaten her with imprisonment if she does not co-operate.

In my mind I began to rehearse scenarios which would crush her resistance and force her to help in trapping Jermyn. I was beginning to enjoy the process as much as the consuming rush of energy my anger gave me. To solve the problem once and for all; to end my bloody dreams of Derryn and Sally and other dreams as well. To end the voices that came with them.

That the end might be in sight made me even more impatient as I arrived at Whitecross Street a second time.

Finny was waiting. She was dressed for outdoors with the severe simplicity of a puritan wife. Her dull travelling dress was finished with a modest white collar and covered by a thin wool cloak of indifferent brown. Black gloves and drab leather boots completed the picture.

'Are you going somewhere?' I inquired.

'I have a plan Mr Lockyer,' she answered coolly. 'After what you told me I thought I might as well assist you in the capture of My Lord Jermyn. As you say, he cares nothing for me. If you are offering gold, I'll take it.'

Surprised and rather deflated I realised there was no need for my angry rhetoric, my winning arguments, my irrefutable logic.

'I can see by your face you agree, don't you? I've already sent him a message saying I'm set and eager to leave. I do think ahead.' She was smiling.

The arrangement was for Finny to meet Jermyn after midday at Smarts Quay beyond London Bridge. There the water ran more freely, and small boats could pass downriver, to take passengers to the larger sea-going craft making the long and dangerous passage to the Americas. Normally, Cheapside would have been clear, but the frozen Thames upriver meant that many who would have travelled by water were now on foot or in a coach. The mass of folk stumbling and weaving between carts meant that everyone moved at a snail's pace. It was snowing.

I walked some paces ahead of Finny, making a way through the crush. As we came towards Poultry it seemed impossible to go any faster. In the press of the crowd I suddenly felt someone touch my arm.

'It is good to find you at last Mr Lockyer.' The huge figure was muffled in wool, face and eyebrows covered in snowflakes. It was Thomas.

'I followed you to Whitecross Street. Waited all night like I've waited there before—it was colder this time! You need looking after Mr Lockyer—you and Finny.'

'Thomas!' I embraced him. 'But I cannot stay—'

'I am coming with you,' said Thomas firmly.

We had reached Walbrook. Alongside the fast-flowing stream was a wide street open to the sky and I felt a sense of relief as I glimpsed the Thames. But the route to the river was blocked by carts unloading. Finny gestured impatiently.

'Mr Lockyer, I told him one of the clock.'

'Let's try Swan Lane, it may be clear. Finny your boots are soaked.'

The snow was now settling in dirty clumps but despite

it we begun to walk more freely. Then we heard shouted orders carried on the wind. Everyone turned to look. A troop of mounted musketeers blocked the road as they accompanied a straggling group of ill-clad captives. Citizens were forced to stand aside to let the column through.

'Scottish prisoners going to the Tower,' said Thomas. 'Bottom of the river's a better place for 'em.'

There was a general dislike of the Scots and all their doings. Londoners resented having to feed them. Some were clearly suffering from wounds and even when these were dressed, the bandages were ragged and bloody.

'Where are your pike men now?' A passer-by jeered. The men did not turn their heads but looked ahead and continued their trudge eastward.

I glanced down at Smarts Quay. There was enough clear water for small boats to anchor. Ice floes bobbed against the wooden piles.

'I said I'll wait at the landing house,' said Finny. 'Mr Lockyer—Thomas, stand back a little.'

'Yes we do not want to frighten him away,' I said.

'You promise Mr Lockyer? I shan't be accused of any crime?' Finny was insistent. 'I'm only helping you for the money.' But her motives no longer mattered to me.

That morning, I had sent a hastily written note to Whitehall. I was asking for help in the capture and arrest of Henry, Lord Jermyn for the murder of Derryn Barlow. Thomas and four mounted troopers from the Billingsgate militia were now concealed behind the counting house. I scanned downriver for some time. I was puzzled. There was no boat approaching the Quay. The snow had stopped but it was still very cold. I wondered how long Finny, in her thin cloak and sodden boots would last under the biting wind. She looked fragile and nervous.

Without warning, a horse and rider clattered past, inches from where I was hidden. A big man in a fine beaver cloak. It was Jermyn. He rode straight at Finny and as she swung around, I heard a pistol crack and a fierce shout. Jermyn lurched forward, raked the sides of his horse and took off at speed.

I broke cover.

'Get after him,' I yelled to the troopers. 'Thomas stay here. Hold Finny! Don't let her out of your sight!'

For it was from Finny that the shot had come. She, who never missed her target, had fired a warning into the air.

In those seconds, Jermyn had turned away from Thames Street towards the river. He was heading upstream to where the ice could bear him. I pushed an astonished trooper aside and seized his mount. At Fish Wharf, just short of the bridge, I saw Jermyn wrench his horse's head sideways, scramble down the snow-covered bank and ride out onto the ice. He was making for the centre of the river where he would be free of skating crowds and tradesmen's booths. I followed, calling the militiamen to follow.

Jermyn had reached clear space and was riding away towards the south bank. I could see the circular walls of the bear pit. Without warning, Jermyn's horse slid and staggered to a halt. A fissure in the ice stretched from the south side. It collapsed, tipping horse and rider into the water. I slowed my mount as Jermyn frantically tried to pull himself out. I shouted to the pursuing militia men to heave Jermyn from the ice and bind him fast. In the struggle, two of them fell in beside the thrashing man and suffered a drenching. They expressed their fury in oaths and blows against their prisoner.

I was glad that I had avoided the water. Authority sometimes has its advantages. Then came another thought: I suppose I shall have to see if Jermyn is wounded. Patching up a murderer? I hate the man.

Chapter 32

Tuesday January 22nd early morning

'It has been a week, Lord Jermyn. We need a confession from you.'

Thurloe was in a rage. His eyes seemed to have shrunk. I noted that the black hairs in the deputy spymaster's nostrils were quivering. The object of his annoyance sat back casually in his seat, one leg looped over the arm of the chair. His black velvet suit showed no stains from the foul waters of the Thames; his linen was snowy and his red-gold beard well-trimmed.

Instead, Lord Jermyn's gaze was directed at me.

'Sawbones, you were never quite the gentleman, however I'll admit, you deceived us well. I may have thought you a low fellow, but I never doubted your loyalty. Of all of us, the Queen was less convinced, but there again she is a woman of remarkable insight.'

Thurloe spoke in almost a growl. 'Sir, I think you need to remember where you are, a prisoner of the Commonwealth. One who works for the return of Charles Stuart. The scaffold is where you are likely to end.'

Jermyn laughed.

'You think so, lawyer? No doubt you can cut off my head on any charge you wish. But your Republic,

Commonwealth or whatever you are pleased to call it, will be short-lived. You have no power without the Army. Informers and agents swarm over England like the plague of lice and frogs in Egypt!'

He turned back to me.

'The King will return believe me and what will you do sawbones? Change sides again?'

I was silent. It was Thurloe who said, 'Surgeon-major Lockyer is an officer in the Army of the Republic. He holds the official post of Questor General. Please address him correctly.'

'Questor General! How magnificent!' Jermyn sneered.

Thurloe folded and re-folded a paper in front of him.

'You killed the woman because of what she knew didn't you?'

Jermyn hesitated, then frowned and shook his head.

Behind him, Thomas Scot had drifted into the room as silently as a barn—owl swooping on its prey.

'You took a great risk coming to England to organise a murder. Once it was done why did you return?' he asked Jermyn.

Jermyn turned in his chair to face him.

'Thomas Scot, king-killer. You look almost like an ordinary man for one so blood-soaked.'

Scot continued in the mildest of tones.

'Perhaps you came to do further mischief, Lord Jermyn. Your allies the Scots who would have us all under the strict rule of the Kirk, are outraged by the loose behaviour of the Stuart court. I have ensured that they are aware of it.'

'No doubt you have. But the Scots are not allies; they are subjects of His Majesty. Unlike your rabble of upstarts and regicides, His Majesty does not require or need an Oath to the State to ensure loyalty.'

Thurloe struck the table.

'Stop this! It is not our purpose here to discuss politics! We demand your confession to murder, Lord Jermyn.'

'Nonsense! I came here to see to my house which your "godly" men have ransacked. Why don't you ask Lockyer and his hospital accomplices?'

At this reminder I decided I could be more use binding the limbs of maimed soldiers. I got up from my chair.

Tuesday 22nd January, afternoon.

Immediately on my return, I was faced with a decision on a young man who had developed an ugly wound infection. The soldier had been hastily treated following a skirmish in Ireland, but the field surgeon had been unable to extract all the fragments of metal and bone. The man was so thin and underweight; I began to worry about whether he would survive amputation.

I was conferring about it with Kershaw, the young burly northerner who was Yorke's replacement when I received a message saying that I was needed urgently back at Whitehall 'on the matter.' I hesitated. Kershaw said he could manage the work himself. As I set my surgical instruments aside, I felt irritated at these peremptory commands from Scot. Not what I would call a part-time post.

When I arrived, Scot was sitting alone, frowning.

'Jermyn refuses to make a formal confession. He says we have no right to arrest him. In fact, we have. —his *laisse-passez* is out-of-date and probably a fake. Perhaps you could talk to him. You know him better than anyone here.'

Scot's voice held an almost pleading note.

I protested that my dislike of the man was an impediment, but Scot was unmoved.

'See what you can do. I'll have him brought up again.'

'Wait. Keep him standing outside. And remove the chairs here.' I was thinking.

There was something I was not sure about, and it bothered me. Had Jermyn's sole purpose when he first came to England been to get rid of Derryn Barlow? Did he have more than one reason for going to Whitecross Street? He said he returned to check on his property. Yet that put him in danger.

When Jermyn entered, he looked in vain for a seat. His face could not have been more scornful.

'I do not bow to regicides and their servants.'

'Forgive me if I do not bow to you, either,' I said. 'That belongs to your world.'

'Yes,' said Jermyn. 'And I want my world back! You had a taste of it, didn't you? A world of beauty, nobility, and grace. Visions of empires beyond the seas. Not sour-faced squires and soiled apprentices—Bibles in hand and no thoughts beyond the shoreline of the Godly Republic!'

With such intransigence, I thought, could Jermyn really be one of those looking for 'a middle path 'between King and Parliament?

'How you love the Court,' I observed. 'Yet you were not born a nobleman.'

'At least I know who my parents were.'

I had heard the insult before, and it had long ago ceased to trouble me.

'Tell me why you wanted Derryn Barlow dead. She was a victim of the corruptions of the Stuart Court.'

'Nonsense,' said Jermyn. 'Or if she was, she was a willing one. She and that other Welsh trollop, Lucy Walter.'

'She did you no harm.'

'How do you know what harm she did?' replied Jermyn fiercely. 'Or what harm she could do? As to that so-called marriage, that farce of which she was said to be a witness—it is a lie. The King is not married to anyone.'

'Yet you fear the story is true. Is that why you hired thugs to have Lucy Walter killed as well?' I asked.' And why your nephew attacked Owain Hopkins?'

Jermyn looked impatient. 'Surgeon-major Questor—what a ridiculous title—why should I talk to you about the death of that little fool? When Princess Mary decided to send her away, she made a mistake, that's all. We did not know then her part in that marriage charade. The whole matter should have been dealt with in Holland.'

'With a paid assassin like the one that killed Ambassador Dorislaus?'

Jermyn smiled lazily.

'His Majesty needs to be rid of barriers to his rightful Restoration.'

'A rightful Restoration?' I paused. 'From the tangled gossip, I heard in France the Stuart princes are not even Stuarts. Some say you fathered them.'

He drew a sudden breath. He took a step forward and his languid manner deserted him.

'Your slur demeans you Lockyer. I've never married. I never will marry. *I have no heirs.* There is a Queen, a woman who stands at the apex of my world, for the Stuarts are the future of England. If you want to talk murder interrogate that hag and her dregs in Whitecross

Street!'

'And what of Finny? Is she a dreg too?'

'Don't speak of her! You know nothing about her!'

'Finny helped in your capture. She'll have to testify against you,' I said.

'The Count of Finsbury's a whore. That's her occupation,' Jermyn answered. 'But be assured, Finny will never speak against me.'

'You were in England last September when Lady Derryn was murdered. Where were you on the evening of her death?'

'How do you expect me remember? I was here to check on my estates.'

'Jermyn, you are nothing more than a slaughtering servant. You have tried to keep the hands of your mistress spotless. A Queen may wish murder, but she does not have to commit it herself. One of the advantages of royalty.'

'I don't need to say any more,' Jermyn replied. 'You have me prisoner here. Cut off my head.'

Wednesday 23rd January mid-morning

I had thought to spend a quiet morning writing notes. I reflected briefly on the disappointment my failure with Jermyn had caused Scot and wondered if he might decide against the necessity of a questor who lacked inquisitorial talents. A call came unexpectedly from someone I had impressed with my skills—Sidney wanted me to check on his cousin Earl Pembroke. Following a further stroke, he had remained bed-ridden in the vast Palace of Whitehall. The Earl's apartments overlooked the Privy Garden, a once-formal space of grass and bushes, dominated by a giant sundial. I climbed the stairs. Pembroke was out of bed and sitting in a chair facing the window. Next to it was a fresh pitcher of wine and barley-water. At his side, van Prin was reading aloud. He stopped as he saw me.

'Has he spoken at all?' I asked the big Dutchman.

'Nothing intelligible. Sometimes he tries to speak. He can certainly hear,' replied van Prin.

I approached the chair and greeted my patient. Carefully, I tried to raise the Earl's left arm, followed by his right. There was no strength in them. The legs, too, had only dead weight.

The Earl let out a groan and turned his head. As he saw me his eyes brightened and with great force he said, 'Br-r-ro-'

'Brother?' I asked. The Earl shook his head.

'B-r—r-o—' The Earl was sweating with effort, but his mouth would not form the words and his third attempt ended in a groan.

'Does he desire some broth?' I asked.

'He has said that before but refuses anything when offered. He has not the strength to drink it.'

'Well then let him rest. Keep reading Captain van Prin, it will console him.'

Van Prin shifted his large body and bent his blond head over the book. I listened to the rise and fall of his soft Friesland accent:

'God hath made no decree to distinguish the seasons of His mercies; In Paradise, the fruits were ripe the first minute, and in heaven it is always Autumn, His mercies are ever in their maturity...'

I recognised one of Dr Donne's sermons. It would do

Pembroke better than any work of mine.

And that word. I wondered. Could it be 'brothel'?

Wednesday 23rd of January late afternoon

Kershaw had worked hard that afternoon treating two soldiers who were suffering from serious burns. I was pleased with the new surgeon, who was deft and gentle. Then I went to talk with the hospital carpenter. One of the amputees needed new buckles and spare pins for his artificial leg and another wanted a softer harness; the one he had was chafing his thigh.

While I was dealing with this my mind was also nagged by the Earl's speech. His words made no sense—but then why would I expect them to? I worried at the thought some more, for I thought against all the odds that Pembroke recognised me and had been trying to tell me something As I walked back to the out-patient room, Hope-Anna, her arms full of red cotton bandages, caught up with him.

'John, someone left a message for you at the gate an hour ago, but we know you don't like your work interrupted.'

The porter held out a paper. I read: *'The Earl of Pembroke died just after two of the clock today 23rd January 1650'* Captain Tjaard van Prin.

Chapter 33

Wednesday 30th January afternoon.

Pembroke was dead, his embalmed body removed to Wilton House, the family's main estate. I had declined an invitation from Colonel Sidney to accompany the Earl on his last journey, pleading work at the hospital. I wished to distance myself from these aristocrats. I hesitated about accepting the substantial fee offered for my services, but in the end practicality prevailed. I owed rent to Janvier.

It was sunny, and the wind had dropped. Seagulls foraging the mud banks were mewling overhead in the freezing air. I took in deep breaths and walked briskly, as I reviewed events. What secrets had Pembroke taken with him? I felt again an anxiety that I almost refused to recognise—for the lost child Edward, saved at such cost. Was he still alive, somewhere in England? I had to find him. Jermyn might be in prison awaiting trial but there was unfinished business. I would have to return to Whitecross Street.

This thought pre-occupied me as I walked along Snow Hill. By St Paul's Cathedral the print booths were busy. The newest edition of *Eikon Basilike*, the dead King's testament, was on sale and piled next to it *Eikonoklastes*, the Republic's response. I realised that today was the first anniversary of the King's execution. A detachment of soldiers armed with muskets passed at the end of the road. They must be on the streets because the government expected trouble. I picked up *Eikonoklastes* and glanced at the author's name. It was the same Mr Milton who, in impeccable French and Latin, had forged my references for the Court in St Germain.

One hawker thrust a broadsheet at me. It bore an engraving of a huge pair of spectacles. '*In the First Year of Freedom our Sight has been restored,*' I read. Despite my mood I smiled. My own prescription for clear sight was to stay focussed. But how much I have missed, I thought.

I turned north. I knew that in a quarter of an hour I would find himself outside the Whorehouse of the Republic.

She was not pleased to see me but hid it and gave a smile of welcome. She did not offer me anything to drink. I was glad; I remembered the last drink I had received from her hands.

'Mistress Grahame I know what you have tried to conceal. I suppose you are paid handsomely for your discretion.'

She looked puzzled. 'Are you talking about my trade in simples and potions, Sir?'

'No Mistress Grahame, nor your trade in flesh. Something else.'

Her face was stony.

'I don't know what you mean.'

'A house of pleasure is good cover for men who may wish to meet secretly. Men who would normally be enemies. Who should not be seen together? A place where discussions can happen that must never come into common knowledge?'

She was silent.

'Did you plan it like this? Or did it happen because of someone who is very high in the Council of State? It is treason to discuss how a king may return.'

I watched her. The sheen of white powder made her face appear ghostly.

'Equally, those who love a king may not love the one that birth has entitled. Kings' defects sometimes outweigh their rightful claims. But that can't be said in public.'

She brushed an imaginary speck from her velvet sleeve, then got up and walked over to a walnut cabinet. She took out a gilded box studded with pearls. I watched as she opened it and shook out a square of rust-coloured muslin. It was badly creased, and the colour was uneven.

'Do you know what this is?' She held it up. 'Some would say it's a holy relic. A handkerchief dipped in the blood of the King, moments after he was beheaded. The crowd rushed to soak up the gore. Many still love that King.'

'And many do not love his son.'

'Loyalties and treacheries,' she mused. 'Exactly what is it you think you know about my house, Mr Lockyer?'

I decided to risk it. 'Enough. I know that Royalists— perhaps your best customer Jermyn—have had clandestine meetings with leading Parliamentarians.'

At the mention of Jermyn, her lips tightened.

'Secrecy is important to the successful running of this house. Perhaps Lord Jermyn threatened you to make you hide the murder of Lady Derryn. It was he who needed her killed, not you, I know that.'

Mrs Grahame walked to the window and put her hand

on the dark shutters.

'I knew you would bring misfortune the first time I met you Mr Lockyer. I deal in human weakness and yours is that you act as if you have none. But you have jumped to the wrong conclusion. The young woman came to me for help. I knew she was Pembroke's kin and I should have refused. She was supposed to return one last time, but she never came. That's all I know of her.'

'Perhaps your memory will improve when you are summoned to speak at Lord Jermyn's trial.'

Her jet earrings swayed and glittered as she moved cat-like towards me. She stood close and I was aware of her scent and her heat.

'I used to be afraid of you Mr Lockyer. Now I have your measure. Even with your new title you are just a man after all. When you say the girl was killed Lord Jermyn was here; he did not stir from Finny's arms until I told him to leave.'

Once again, I had come up against the impenetrable barrier that was Mrs Grahame. Why was she protecting Jermyn?

She started to laugh.

'Your man who was skulking in the garden bushes—Thomas is it? I hear Thurloe had him jailed. He saw Lord Jermyn leave—ask him.'

It was true. Thomas had said he had seen Jermyn quit the house, threatened by Dicky. But I could not believe that Jermyn was simply there as a client of Finny's.

'Who else did he meet when he was here?'

'Your ideas about my house—you have no proof. Whip me through the streets as a whore-mistress if you want.'

'That could happen,' I replied. 'You must furnish me

with a list of your political visitors, Mistress Grahame. I want to know who visited last September.'

She did not answer. Instead, from a nearby table she picked up a pair of heavy military riding gloves.

'They never treated you as an equal, Mistress Grahame, did they? You don't owe them anything. Your visitors are good at lying.'

She smiled faintly.

'That men are liars is nothing new Mr Lockyer. If there is such a list, it's Deputy Thurloe who keeps it. Perhaps he has not shared it with you.'

Friday Friday 15th February morning

'As a leading Royalist, Jermyn deserves to be summarily executed,' said Scot, 'but justice in the Republic does not proceed that way. He is right that we have no proof linking him directly to murder. Those children are hardly credible. Lockyer tells me that the inhabitants of Whitecross Street either cannot be found or refuse to testify. There are no documents. In the absence of a formal confession, it may be difficult to make the charge stick.'

But Thurloe was as usual, clutching a folder of papers. 'Tom, we don't need any of that,' he said jubilantly. 'We have him! Listen. Nine years ago, he and some others were involved in a Royalist plot. They proposed to seize the Tower of London. They were betrayed and Jermyn fled to France. In his absence, he was condemned to death by Parliament and the order still stands!'

Scot sat silent at this news. Then he closed his eyes. Thurloe became impatient.

'This trouble about the girl, Lockyer and his doubtful

witnesses—they are all unnecessary. We can take another route! Let's act now and get it over with!'

'Yes. I see.' Scot appeared to be thinking deeply. Then he sat upright and pulled a sheet of paper towards him. Instead of his usual pallor he looked flushed. His normally limp hair seemed crisp with life.

He looked at his Deputy.

'John Thurloe, who runs this office?'

'Why you of course Tom, under the Council of State.'

'Yes. I hold the authority of Parliament. Can you explain to me why you have set up an independent source of information in Whitecross Street?'

'I, John? That is the house of ill-repute—Lockyer understands it better than I.' Thurloe was gabbling.

'I know all about it,' said Scot.

'I—I thought it could be useful to us.' Thurloe no longer looked so cheerful.

'Us? Or you?' Scot's voice was relentless. 'Encouraging royalist spies John Thurloe is a treasonable offence. Let me be clear. Even if they agree to be ruled by Parliament, we will have no more kings here! No further bloodshed in England! I have fought the Good Old Cause for the Republic and will not have it overturned with soft compromises.'

Thurloe seemed to have shrunk and his eyes darted around the room. They rested on me with a look of extreme dislike. I knew from that moment I had made an enemy for life.

'As of now there will be no more brothel meetings with royalists,' said Scot firmly. 'Do you understand, Thurloe? I am directing policy here. Very shortly, the invasion of Scotland will begin. We need no compromises with the enemy. You will turn all your files over to me.'

He twisted the piece of paper in his hand.

'Oh, and Captain Bamfylde—'

'In jail!' crowed Thurloe.

'No longer. I have released him. He is not your agent, but *mine*.'

Or anybody's, I thought.

'I know you tried to involve him—he has confirmed to me everything I had learnt about Whitecross Street.'

Then to Lockyer's surprise, Scot joined his arthritic hands together as if to offer a prayer of peace. The Chief Intelligencer smiled.

'But sometimes one must exercise statecraft. I am sorry, Thurloe that you found that paper. Bury it again. I am thinking of letting Jermyn go.'

There was silence. I was astounded. Even Thurloe could find nothing to say. Eventually, after a long minute he spoke.

'Why, when you have him here? Is it not a triumph for your office? Can you give me one—just one—good reason why Jermyn's head should not end up on the block?'

'I can give you thirty thousand reasons. That is the number of livres sterling the French are offering for him.'

Thurloe shook his head in disbelief.

'Does Queen Henrietta love him that much?' I asked.

'Someone does,' Scot answered, 'according to your friend Janvier.'

Friday February 15th midnight

If I fall asleep, I thought, I will have bad dreams. Derryn. She will come to me again—this time it will be with a bloody face.

As I lay there restless and sweating, I saw the door open very quietly. In a moment, I had seized my dagger and forced my arm around the intruder's throat. The man struggled and choked.

'John it's me! Let me go!'

'You traitorous bastard Janvier! I'm going to kill you!' I started to drag the Frenchman out towards the yard. Janvier flailed but I was far stronger.

'Just like your grandmother said—to get rid of a louse hang him out overnight in the cold!'

'John—'

I did not listen. I bundled Janvier into the freezing yard.

'You can explain to me in the morning—if you are still alive,' I said, and locked the door.

When at last I fell asleep, it was of Jermyn I dreamt. In the dream, I had asked him a question but could not remember what it was. Jermyn, elegant in black silk leant indolently towards me:

'I have only ever loved the one with tricks and charms…' he said. His smile was knowing. I heard myself saying *'Do you mean Finny?'* Then Jermyn turned away and I could hear his voice faintly echoing as if down a long corridor. *'The Count of Finsbury was always my mermaid, she fired that shot.'*

When I awoke, I felt thick-tongued and sweaty. I could not explain to myself why I felt the urge to weep.

Saturday February 16th early morning.

'Don't, whatever you say, tell me I do not understand high

politics.'

'I've not said a word.' The Frenchman was by the fire, drinking hot soup for breakfast. He was unshaven, and his nose was running. After being locked out in the yard he had sought refuge in the Saracens Head. He had caught a chill. Through coughs and wheezes he remarked, 'Scot didn't tell Jermyn about the ransom offer. He allowed him to think that he could go free if he agreed to spy for the Republic.'

'Did he agree?'

'Of course—I suppose he thought he could change his mind once he was back in France.'

'After all we spies have no honour-code.' Janvier's voice was self-mocking.

I was still angry with him.

'You said you were done with spying.'

'This was *negotiation*—almost diplomacy,' Janvier protested. 'In any case, what I said was *I* would not spy on *you*. For Scot. As Scot pointed out, Cardinal Mazarin is my master.'

'Jermyn escapes justice and you call that diplomacy?'

Janvier frowned.

'In fairness John, although Jermyn had a strong motive for murder you were not able to prove anything conclusive, were you? Yes, Jermyn was in the vicinity; Certainly, he had a powerful motive. But he has never confessed.'

'Jermyn *is* guilty. He almost admitted it—*I must remove barriers to His Majesty's rightful restoration* he said. He did it or—perhaps at least—arranged for it to be done. And after all the evidence—the letters—all of it, Scot sets him free!'

I was suffering outrage and disappointment that all my efforts had come to nothing, and that Lady Derryn's killer was unpunished. It was a ragged ending. Not one I was proud of.

Janvier's face remained untroubled. I suppose it is all in a day's work to him, I thought bitterly. The Frenchman said gently, 'John, you did everything you could. You were as sure as possible. But you do not understand high politics.'

'Then explain.'

'This is about France. We are the biggest power in Europe, and we are going to remain so. No Spaniard, Englishman, or—heaven help us—Dutchman can prevent that. Charles Stuart has worried Mazarin by sending envoys to Spain. He wants King Charles indebted to France alone. Mazarin will make Jermyn work for *him*. He has not paid that money for love of the man.'

'That seems to give Jermyn the advantage if he is so much in demand.'

'Not really. Jermyn now must play a double game wherever he is. Finally, everyone will suspect him of working for everyone else and he will not be trusted. He will die of grief and gout.'

'I think he will live to a ripe old age. Although I hope his greed and ambition may yet destroy him,' I said.

Sometimes, I thought, people just get away with it. The bitter thought gnawed at me.

Chapter 34

Saturday February 16th morning.

The talk in the streets was of victory—in Ireland, castles had fallen to Cromwell's siege guns. The Scots would be next, people assured each other, it would be their own fault for supporting Charles Stuart. Rumours had been circulating that a high—ranking Royalist was in prison and would shortly be put on trial for murder. Many who enjoyed a good hanging were disappointed when it was learnt that there would be no execution after all. As if to compensate, the streets were littered with copies of a terrifying handbill. It proclaimed that the 'Papist Queen', directing matters from France, was sending horrid murder to London's streets and had set loose a secret force of assassins to kill pregnant women. I was surprised at the accuracy of some of the detail.

At Ely's gate, I bumped into Hope-Anna who carried a crumpled copy of the newssheet. She looked worried.

'Have you seen this, Mr Lockyer?'

'It's scurrilous rubbish Hope-Anna. Don't be concerned.'

'I know that.' Hope-Anna placed her hand on her swollen stomach. 'I do not believe there is a threat to me or my baby. But has this anything to do with the poor young woman we took in?'

'Yes, but not directly.'

'And what of the infant—Edward? There will be questions—I could be blamed—lose my midwives' licence.'

'Hope-Anna you are not to blame. No one except Pembroke tried to claim the child.'

'Was it he who took Edward?' There were tears in her eyes.

'No, Hope-Anna. And the Earl is dead. I am no nearer to knowing who took Edward. Can you remember anything more than what you told me at the time?'

'John, they were decent people. Honest servants acting they said on behalf of the family. There was nothing odd. The coach was equipped for all—'

She stopped.

'All what?'

'All you would need for a long journey.'

Her words were almost lost in a babble of noise. Several women were gathered in the hospital yard. More were streaming through the gate. I guessed they were soldiers' wives and widows. They looked in a dangerous mood. Parliament paid a sum to every sick man to support his family, although it was less than he would earn as an able-bodied soldier. Patients and their wives often complained that the money was insufficient. Since the Treasury Offices for the Sick were based at Ely, it was a focus for angry demonstrations.

Aldridge was forcing his way through the crowd. He was exasperated.

'When we had a king, they got nothing. Now we assist them, and they do naught but complain! John I am glad to have caught you. I must have a word.'

We climbed the stone stairs together in silence as the noise increased. I could hear the women arguing with the clerks below.

Aldridge sat down heavily.

'Things are about to change John. That crowd down there is only the half of it. Although Parliament is generous to the Army, everything is always in arrears. I must scrimp on coal and laundry, yet Parliament has voted Dr French fifty pounds to take some of the patients to the healing waters at Bath! Can you believe it?'

'I can,' I replied. 'Committees are always more willing to give money to dazzling projects than those which are mere routine.'

'Dr French is anxious to develop all kinds of new treatments. The Committee for Sick and Maimed Soldiers has decided that Ely should become the main hospital for medical cases and those poor souls disturbed in their wits. Surgery is to be centred on the Savoy Hospital which has more surgeons.'

'Which means?' I asked.

'They are expecting a lot of extra wounded. Casualties from Ireland will be replaced by those from Scotland. An invasion can't be far away. And—it means a transfer for you. They want the Questor General to join the other surgeons at Savoy. You must go there immediately.'

'Now? But I've only just returned, and the work is going well.'

Aldridge looked pained.

'I don't want to lose you either, John, but there is more: Barebon and Burrell have never forgiven you for the incident earlier this year. They say your loyalty to the

Republic is suspect. They oppose your appointment at any hospital and also your questor role. They want you out altogether.'

'But Cromwell himself appointed me!'

'Cromwell is in Ireland. You have enemies—you weren't careful to cultivate the godly faction and if it's a choice between Ely and you—'

I knew the answer.

'John, you must get over there now before anyone can stop you. Your appointment comes up soon formally before the Council of State. If you're already working, it will be more easily ratified. And John—'

'What?'

'Remember Cromwell must keep friends with the godly in the Army whose influence is very strong. I have not asked you what you did in France, I've ignored those men in the shadows who think they own you. Make sure of your position. I am sorry, but one mistake and you could lose everything.'

Monday 18th February mid-morning

'At last, someone talks some sense to you, John. Colonel Aldridge is quite right—you must secure your position. What friends do you have? I know! Speak to Colonel Sidney—he's a member of the Council of State.' This was Janvier's immediate advice.

'Jean—Louis I know a man must rely on friends and influence as well as skill, but I hate to ask favours from Sidney.'

'Do you think you are the only man with pride? Swallow it. Lord General Cromwell was right—you are difficult to please! You must not only secure your position but turn this to your advantage. Savoy is an enormous hospital and the best surgeon in the land, Mr Trapham is in charge.'

Thomas Trapham who had prepared the King's body for public view after his execution. 'I've stitched the head back on the goose,' he said. Then he cut a lock of the King's auburn hair to keep. Did I want to work with such a man?

Janvier was fizzing with enthusiasm.

'Unlike Ely, Savoy is upriver away from the stench of the city, surrounded by houses of the nobility and,' he added mischievously, 'only five minutes' walk from Scot's office in Westminster. He'll be close at hand if you need him.'

'Reason itself for staying away from the place.'

Nevertheless, the next day, I set out for the mansion of the Earl of Leicester, Sidney's father. It lay just north of Westminster, the largest house in London. Twenty years ago, the Earl had enclosed land where commoners had enjoyed the ancient right to pasture sheep and have their pigs forage. The people objected, and it was finally agreed that a small portion of land, Leicester Field, should be available to the commoners and that the Earl's house should be surrounded by a high wall, behind which extensive building continued. The wall made the huge house look like a fortress; I could see this was only the beginning of what would be the encroachment of all the common spaces within Westminster.

Sidney had been living there since the death of his cousin Pembroke. Whether or not he had successfully defended to the old Earl his part in the regicide, was of less importance than the family's urgent need to prevent the house being taken as a billet for soldiers as General Fairfax had threatened.

Sidney welcomed me and invited me into a high roofed hall. The walls up to the ceiling were covered with green mohair and lower down, striped silk hangings of emerald and cream. I saw an elaborate chimneypiece of green marble with silver plaques inset and around the lower wall a wainscoting of cedarwood. All costly work. He saw me looking and remarked, 'As a family, we like the colour green.'

An emerald swung and glowed in his ear.

'You'll find it everywhere in the house. Personally, I think the gilding is overdone, but my mother likes it.'

The haughty manner had been replaced by one that was cautious and—almost—polite. I could not believe that Sidney was impressed by my new title. I was still the petitioner here, asking favours. But he wanted something too.

Sidney indicated a gilt leather chair, inviting me to sit.

'There is rumour that Lord Henry Jermyn, is under arrest. Do you know of it? What was he doing in London? He is prominent at Charles Stuart's so-called court-in-exile.'

'I've heard nothing—I'm not sure who Lord Jermyn is,' I replied. My response did not remove the suspicion in Sidney's eyes. I glanced around. 'This is a comfortable place.'

Sidney frowned. He didn't want to chat about the richness of his surroundings. But he decided to be polite.

'It is more convenient for Parliament than Baynard's Castle,' he replied, 'and far quieter. I am here to help my father with accounts and lawsuits. My elder brother Philip is spending huge amounts in buying the King's pictures but has no skill with money.' He drained an early glass of port and offered one to me.

Philip, Lord Lisle the heir to the Leicester title, I thought. You're probably working to displace him.

'With such ability, Colonel Sidney perhaps you can assist me. I need your support in the Council of State. Barebon and others are trying to block my appointment at Savoy Hospital. My profession is my life.'

It is the only thing that gives it any meaning now, I wanted to say but I'm damned if I'll beg him.

Sidney shrugged and walked over to a tall ebony—framed looking glass. He spent almost a minute looking at his reflection. When he turned to me, the old hauteur was back.

'I doubt I can help you. In Dover, citizens say my soldiers are out of control because they haven't been paid for months. I say the Army should pay but Cromwell is against it. He knows I suspect him of high ambition. I'm not your best advocate.'

So, there was to be no help from him. I did not show my disappointment. For at last I had Sidney before me. This family has more secrets than Scot and Thurloe's files, I knew. I wanted to ask him again about Edward, the infant who, against all the odds had survived only to disappear.

'The child?' Sidney was momentarily confused. 'Oh, that. It was Pembroke who cared most. I think he was in love with Lady Derryn the old goat! Anything to annoy his wife, Lady Anne!' He laughed and refilled his glass.

'I do not like Anne Clifford.' He continued. 'Too full

of her ancient titles and greedy to control her own estates. But she was right about one thing—from the moment Derryn Barlow arrived, she was making up to my cousin Pembroke and he fell for it—hard.'

'Lady Anne need not suffer any longer,' Lockyer said.

'No indeed! She fought hard and won. She's gone to rule over Westmoreland for what it's worth—sodden moors covered with sheep-shit. And her five ruined castles *Skipton, Brougham, Appleby, Brough, Pendragon.* We knew them off by heart—her rows with Pembroke always ended with the same litany from her.' Sidney continued his recital of Lady Anne's faults, but I was no longer listening.

I was thinking of Edward.

I had saved this child. If Edward were dead, in some secret region of my heart I believed I would have known. But I thought: Edward *is* alive. Perhaps if I do find him all the fragments of my life will fall into place. And now I think I know where he is.

Chapter 35

Wednesday February 20th early morning

There are four great roads out of London. If I was wrong in my choice, I would condemn myself to a week's hard riding in vain and in a cold month. There were few signs of spring as I rode out of the city. The road, broad and lined at first with stone and later with steep ditches was busy with innumerable hide-covered carts carrying calves, corn, fish, iron, coal and all the other wares a city produces or needs. Newly fashioned carriages with half—a—dozen passengers wedged together creaked behind the mounted riders, who like me, were muffled in fur against the chilly February morning. When Cromwell had formed the New Model Army, he said how he preferred the plain russet coated captain fighting for his beliefs rather than a gentleman with none. His regiments of horse, full of such ordinary men had been foremost in defeating the enemy and now horse riding had become open to all. The roads and inns were full, and the people were on the move tasting both the freedoms and hardships of travel previously confined to tradesmen or gentry.

I kept company with the flow, sometimes falling in with a group sometimes heading off on my own. As we streamed out of London past the brickfields and graveyards, market gardens and common lands, windmills and tanneries towards the densely wooded hills, people often sought each other for among the traveller's hazards were highwaymen or armed gangs of renegade deserters. This was how I found myself riding alongside a man on an old horse who had fallen behind a large and noisy group of successful tradesmen returning from market. The man, small boned and delicate-featured with one of those ageless faces, greeted me pleasantly asking if I minded his company. I was a little concerned at the speed of his mount but knowing that we were not far from an inn, I reckoned a little time spent ambling would be welcomed by my horse too, who had done many miles that day. When we finally rode into the galleried courtyard of the White Hart, there was a comforting bustle and the smell of roasting meat and freshly baked pastry. I noticed that he dismounted with difficulty and limped more than his horse. His face showed that he was in pain.

'I am a surgeon, perhaps I can help?' I offered and he accepted gratefully.

As he stripped away his stockings and breeches, I called for hot water and towels which I applied to relax the muscles. He began to show signs of relief as the warmth loosened them. I took a little of the almond oil I carried in my surgeon's pack and had it heated.

'I'm going to rub your limb with this. I will be pressing into it at the same time, and it will hurt when I hit a knotted muscle.'

As my fingers probed deep into the flesh, I noted the wasting of his leg and the old marks of manacles about his ankle. He saw my look.

'Yes, I was a felon, but you need not fear. My crime was

dancing.'

I knew that some thunderous new laws had recently been enacted which sought to reform the population away from 'heathenish and Romish' practices but had not expected such severity. I continued to explore the sinews of his leg.

'I am a dancing master—or was. I doubt that employment will continue for who wants one who is lame—even if there was a call for my services. For dancing is no longer a necessary accomplishment in a genteel house, I will have to find something else.' And he fell silent, soothed a little by my massage and the warmth.

The next day he walked more easily and suggested that we continue to ride together; he saw me hesitate and laughed.

'You are worried that I'll hold you up but don't be concerned. I have negotiated a fresh horse—and there is one for you too—at a good price.'

Seeing the quality of the pair he had already hired that morning, I admired his eye for horseflesh and hearing the price, I realised that the dancing master possessed a talent for haggling far above my own.

We passed through marshland and the number of other riders lessened. The rivers and brooks were foaming in full spring spate, overhung with willows and catkins. The sound of wheels had given way to birdsong, the high cold call of the curlew and the sharp cries of waterfowl, as we forded the great river that went half across England.

During the next days we talked inconsequentially, commenting on the state of the weather, the road or the inns where we stayed. Occasionally, he would sing in a light tenor voice., snatches of Dowland and Campion.

His songs were beautiful and mournful, but when our horses speeded up he started on "Fine knacks for ladies" as we swung along.

'That's a peddler's song.'

'Well, I am a pedlar of sorts.' He smiled but did not say more.

The benefit of my companion's skills became increasingly obvious. He obtained the best rooms and prices and the quickest service, all without the outlay of extra silver. I realised that the dancing master had no more inclination to tell me his business—even his name—than I had in telling him my mission. So, I knew nothing of his war experiences, his family or even his destination. And I think both of us realised that this was unusual.

We were now heading towards mountainous country, the valleys were chequered with small towns and villages where early crops of barley and oats were just beginning to green the narrow fields; we passed gentry estates still bearing the fortifications of war and siege and finally reached the outskirts of the great northern city, the end point of many of those we passed on the road.

I had been attending to his injury every evening. His leg was still wasted but the muscles seemed firmer, and he found walking and riding easier.

'The movement is a little better and with daily massage and exercise it will improve,' I observed. 'Provided you don't overexert your limb, the ability to dance is there—and the skill is something you don't forget.' He did not respond.

I said, 'I shall not go into the city—I must continue north. What of you?'

Something seemed to unfold within him.

'I must enter the city, but I fear it for I was imprisoned there and barely survived. Not just for dancing—it was long before these new laws about ungodly habits, before war came with its terror and loss. I am a Catholic who refused to take the oath or attend service. A recusant.'

That alone was enough to explain his reticence.

'But imprisonment? Surely just a fine?'

'The old Faith is still strong here among the gentry and people. As a dancing master I passed between houses, took messages for priests, carried prayer books and holy objects and helped to keep the Faith alive. I was discovered and imprisoned, lucky not to be executed. But they swore to damage me and ensure that I never went "creeping into houses" again. I am not useful now—I could not fight for the King as my brother did—he lost his life.'

The war had reached nearly every family in the land. I asked, 'Where did he die? In which battle?'

The delicate face hardened with an expression I had not seen before.

'In no battle. He was a prisoner after the siege of Oxford and was betrayed.'

And I felt a blackness fall upon me.

The inn was crowded with ale-drinkers by this time, some rowdy, so I excused myself saying I must make an early start; my dancing master bowed and thanked me warmly for my help, wishing that we might meet again. I could not tell him that I wished the opposite.

A few hours fitful sleep followed when I awoke, aware that there was someone in my chamber, moving silently towards me in the darkness. It was my companion of the road, the dancing master. I feigned sleep but he came and shook my shoulder.

'Wake up, we must both leave now, there's danger. Dress quickly and quietly!'

Was it a trap? But I did as he said and in a whisper he explained.

'I recognised two men, local pursuivants who arrested me in the past. They were asking after a London surgeon, and someone recalled your changing my bandages last night. They carry instructions to find you. I don't want them to find me either. We'll take different routes.'

There was no time to think about who might wish me arrested again and why. We were soon on the road riding fast in the darkness towards the crossroads. There by the gibbet I said goodbye to him. As we turned our separate ways—he to the city, I to the bleak moorlands, my heightened senses became aware of the sound of other horsemen, not far away. I spurred my mount and raced upwards on the stony drovers' trail leading west.

Wednesday 27th February early

I was looking out over massive stone walls. Beyond them the bare hills were green but too austere for my liking. Dark rain clouds moved across the sky. I shivered in the damp cold. That morning, I had crossed the last pass. The high country was boggy, the brackish brown pools fed with constant rain. Streams, white with energy gushed down the mountainside and sometimes my path was obscured by clouds. The poor dwellings of lead and copper miners were squat, small and chimneyless. Higher up there were isolated shepherds' huts, made of rough dry stone. Inns had been few and far between but even the poorest would have a herb-flavoured pottage of peas and beans, perhaps a curd cheese tart, or occasionally a dish of stewed coney, offered with cordiality. The heavy rain and wind had blotted out all sound for many miles, but I was reasonably sure that I had not been followed. I wondered if the pursuivants had caught up with the dancing master. Reaching my destination had taken hours of hard riding and I had arrived saddle sore and weary.

'Mr Lockyer, how like you my castle of Brough? Cromwell had the roof ripped away, but as you see, I am replacing it.'

Lady Anne Clifford stood leaning on her stick, her dark cloak billowing as she studied everything including me with her sharp black eyes. She had offered me the hospitality of her draughty castle and a good breakfast. Now, she wanted me to view her re-building so together we climbed up to the stone steps of the square Clifford Tower. I noticed that water trickled down the inside walls. The wind was icy.

'This site has always had a fortress—they say in Roman times there was a huge camp here, covering many acres. It was for defence against the Pictae tribes. My castle was built over four hundred years ago, by the Normans. It has withstood much and will again.' She turned her indomitable face to me. 'I have four more to repair before I am done.'

We turned out of the wind to descend the narrow steps. Lady Anne refused my arm.

'I am sorry to be slow. But my mind is ahead. Mr Lockyer, we must go and seek what you have come for, must we not? It will take us much of today to get there and back.'

'Are they expecting us?' I asked.

'Of course not! You gave me no warning. But they are my tenants. They will admit us.'

There was a sturdy farm cart waiting in the courtyard. As a concession to comfort, a couple of cushions and a fleece cover had been placed inside. Lady Anne held out a large bottle of French brandy.

'I see you have a stout cloak, but this will also keep out the chill. It is all for you, I do not drink brandy myself.' She glanced at the sky 'We may get some sun later this morning. The landscape will then come into its own.'

I could not care less, I thought. Let us get this done. I helped her into the cart. Under her cloak I noticed she carried a small cotton bag. I plumped a cushion behind her shoulders. Lady Anne was not grateful.

'I have no need of a nursemaid,' she said sharply. 'Drive on,' she commanded the farm-boy. The cart jolted out of the gate and began a steep climb up the fell. It started to rain heavily.

'When that slut arrived at Baynard's Castle, Pembroke insisted that we take her in. He loved doing favours for the Sidneys! She made up to everyone especially him, the old fool. When I told Pembroke she was pregnant he was delighted. He even tried to pretend the child was his although I knew that was impossible. He said it to humiliate me. He said we should look after her and keep the baby. All that affection for a silly girl. Whereas I who had brought him a fortune had to endure the daily insult of his indifference.'

'I am sorry that you suffered such unhappiness, my lady.'

'It is over now,' she said. We sat silently for a while as

the cart bumped its way up the rocky track then turned to go down. I could see we were heading to a low stone-built farmhouse with a slated roof. On this side of the fell there was less wind and after some minutes the sky began to clear. As Lady Anne had forecast, the sun came out and I could see hills covered in snow.

'A splendid view is it not? My own green land.' We bumped along in silence until she said, 'I have always wondered who killed her.'

'My lady, at one time, I thought it might be you,' I replied.

She laughed and did not seem displeased at the suggestion.

'I declare I was glad she was dead! Then, I learnt that you had saved the child. That is when I decided. I took him first to spite Pembroke, I admit. But then I thought about why I hated Pembroke.'

She rubbed the back of her hand.

'Both he and my first husband Dorset were full of vices, for all their lives they were too close to the Court. At last, I had my escape, and I wanted the child to have a chance to be brought up cleanly, away from intrigues and seductions.'

I had been so near and so far, from the solution, I thought. *Mr and Mrs Brough. Brough Castle.* One of her five ancestral forts, protection against the Scots. Pembroke had tried to tell me.

'So you convinced yourself that you were doing a good action.'

'See and judge.'

We had arrived at the farmhouse into a yard whose slate flags and stone walls were green with lichen. Two black and white dogs, slender legged with bony intelligent faces advanced on us, barking and waving their silky tails like pennants They herded us expertly to the low door. A fresh-faced man my own age welcomed us in. I found myself standing in a pleasant stone flagged room, wide with low long windows looking out over the fell. A new fire blazed and the house felt warm and safe.

A young woman, not more than twenty stood by the fire. In her arms, she held a sleeping baby. As I moved towards her, she looked defiant and clutched the child close.

'If you are here to take him, believe me, I will resist you.'

'Peace, Kate,' said her husband. 'The Lady Anne would do no harm to Edward.'

'What about him?' she said pointing to me.

'I mean no harm—I would only like to look at him. I am no relation,' I said.

'This is Mr Lockyer, the surgeon who saved Edward's life,' said Lady Anne.

'Then we can never thank you enough Sir, for this precious gift. Come here. Hold him.' She placed the baby in my arms.

I looked down. I saw black hair and long black lashes, fair rosy skin. I saw peace and contentment. I felt the warmth of the small body as the child stirred but did not wake. I held him a little longer and then laid him again in his mother's waiting arms. I could not speak.

They say that women want children; but so do men. I remembered Jermyn's passionate words when for once he spoke not like a courtier, but like a man:

'I have no heir.'

I watched her as she carried Edward outdoors and placed him in a stone cot in the yard. 'Fresh air is good for him,' she said. I nodded, knowing that London mothers would be horrified at such exposure to chills and smoke. But there was no smoke here, the air was pure.

'Now you must stay and accept northern hospitality.' She smiled and led me to a table where amongst the beer, fresh-baked bread and dishes of yellow butter and white cheese lay a great wheel of hot pork sausage, a pot of fresh redcurrant sauce at the side. Still warm on the plate a pile of scones sang in the heat, ready to be coated with thick damson jam. Lady Anne's appetite was good—we were both of us hungry and cold after the drive. She chattered cordially to Kate but I ate sparingly and stayed silent.

It was not until sometime later we returned to the cart, rattled out of the gate and started up the stony track that led by the barn to the fell beyond.

'You were right,' I said to Lady Anne, 'whatever your reason, you were right.'

'They are good hardworking people who lost a child last summer. He will do well there.'

'I would like to offer—'

'Some money? That is always welcome. Now they know who you are they will not mind a visit, although it is a very great distance. But—' I had never known her to hesitate. When she spoke it was with great intensity.

'You and I Mr Lockyer know that his origins are far above those of farming folk. I have told them he was a foundling whom you rescued.' She looked hard at me. 'Believe me Mr Lockyer that is sometimes the simplest way.'

The cart jolted past a wind-bent grove of ash and

rowan and arrived at the barn.

It was only for a moment. But I saw him. The man was unmistakeable.

I jumped from the cart and whispered to the driver, 'Run back to the house and tell them to bring as many as possible to surround the barn.'

I drew my dagger, wishing I had brought a pistol instead. Although for close work a dagger could not be bettered, I hoped I wouldn't to have to use it.

The boy departed at speed. Lady Anne was immediately alert. Wasting no time on words, she heaved herself out of the cart. Meanwhile I had reached the barn. The door stood half open and I could see sheaves of straw and piles of uncleaned fleeces. There was a strong smell of sheep's wool, lye and dung.

The low barn was dark but light enough to see a figure, who turned, arms full of what looked like a matted fleece.

'I suppose you told them you were an out of—work soldier.'

The man turned for the door of the barn but holding my dagger I barred his way.

My opponent raised the bundle of fleece and made for the barrel of lye in the corner of the barn.

The bundle gave a whimper. I stopped as I realised. It was Edward.

'Don't,' I shouted. 'Give him to me.'

'Then take him,' came the reply and the bundle splashed into the barrel. I leapt to retrieve, plunging my hands into the searing acid liquid. The fleece floated on the surface and I heaved it out wet and dripping. The whimpers became screams, and I was aware of the burning in my hands. I placed the child on the ground, lurched towards the man and held him fast. Matched in height and strength, we struggled. My opponent gave a snarl of satisfaction but as he tried to reach for my throat, he slipped, and we thudded onto the earth floor. The man was breathing heavily. With a tremendous effort, he threw me off and made for the door again but this time someone else stood there.

'Stand back. You will not get past me. Lie on the floor,' she commanded.

Lady Anne's wrinkled hand was steady. The light caught the shaft of the pistol she held. Captain van Prin sprawled awkwardly, one hand pushing back his blond hair, now streaked with sweat and dung. There was a clatter of weapons as the farmer and his workers filed into the barn. Two men caught and bound van Prin as if he were a runaway ram.

I ran outside and plunged my hands deep into the drinking trough. The skin was already reddening and peeling.

'The child,' I called, 'bring him here, Get water! Get water!'

Edward was screaming in pain and fright as I drenched his tender skin. From what I could see, the fleece had protected him. There was one streak on his delicate face which might leave a mark. But he was unharmed. Had the bundle fallen in face down, I did not like to imagine the consequences.

There was a shout. It was Kate, an enraged tigress. 'Let me see him. I want to see the villain who tried to harm Edward.'

She stared at van Prin, amazed. 'Why, it's the new hand we took on for the lambing! What has happened? Give me my child!'

Lady Anne still held the pistol.

'The country, even here, is full of renegades. I thought you were safe from them. I was wrong.'

'Let me kill him,' Kate shrieked.

'No Kate enough has happened. Be thankful your child is safe.' Lady Anne's voice was stern. 'We must lock this man away. If I cannot keep him secure in my castle, then I do not deserve to be a High Sheriff of the North.'

Chapter 36

Thursday 28th February morning

I was staring at my bandaged hands. They would need time to heal. The pain was severe, and I had none of my salve with me.

'Walk with me Surgeon-major.' Lady Anne offered her arm, and I took it, wincing as I did so.

Her wolf skin cloak flapped in the wind. With hood thrown back, her white hair flowed down her back.

'My lady you look like Queen of the Picts,' I said and she smiled. Pale sunshine, wet mist, clean cold air, drystone walls. Green moss everywhere. I felt I was in a different world, where the writ of the south had never run. Would never run.

'My orchards are ruined. Parliament's soldiers cut down my ash woods, dug siege trenches and burnt the earth with their campfires.'

I stared across the ruined fields. She guided me to a stone seat which had somehow survived.

'They will be replanted. My first husband, Lord Dorset was from a family that loved orchards. So, the one thing I brought from the Sackvilles was the knowledge of how to plant fruit trees and this I shall do. We shall have blossom and fruit and cultivate the damson. What is important endures. Now, tell me—how did you find me?'

'The Earl told me—or tried to. I failed to understand.'

'Trust him to try and defeat me even at the last!' she growled.

'Finally, I realised that the servants who took Edward used the name of your castle—Brough. As the Earl realised.'

'It served its purpose,' she replied. 'Now what am I to do with van Prin? The Earl used to call him "my clumsy Dutchman". Mind you he called me far worse.'

'Van Prin has been so present that I failed to see it. For as the Earl's devoted servant, what motive would he have for murder? After all—even if it pains you my lady, the Earl appeared to love Lady Derryn.'

'You really think van Prin is the killer of that silly whore?' Her face flushed with sudden angry memory.

'She was Edward's mother,' I reminded her sharply. 'Don't condemn her. Her death was agonising. Yes, I think it was at the hand of van Prin. For a long time, I suspected Lord Jermyn; he himself had tried to implicate Captain Bamfylde.'

'Bamfylde?'

'A government agent. I think Jermyn made the accusation to kill two birds with one stone—to deflect inquiry away from himself and destroy a spy. Jermyn had powerful reasons to kill her. She carried a Stuart child and held information harmful to their cause. I was wrong. When Lady Derryn was killed, he was—elsewhere.'

If Mistress Grahame was to be believed, he had paid for Finny in his bed the night that Derryn was killed.

Lady Anne was not listening. She looked gleeful.

'I knew I was right! I guessed Edward's parentage was

noble! But I did not think him a royal child.' She looked puzzled for a moment. 'Why should van Prin care?'

'Or why kill her? I shall ask him tomorrow,' I replied.

Friday 1st March late evening

I sat in the dungeon of the Clifford Tower, facing van Prin. The Dutchman was shackled at the ankles, but his hands were free. Before him was a confession which he had just written and upon which the jailer had thrown sand to dry the ink. The torches were spluttering, and the men's shadows jumped erratically across the stone walls. The jailer folded van Prin's document. It would be taken to Lady Anne for her to read and seal.

The air was dank and heavy with the smell of wax, ink and dirty straw. Yet there was no fear in the atmosphere. My opponent was calm.

'You came to finish the job you bungled six months ago,' I said.

'Wrong Surgeon-major. I came to restore the child to Baynard's Castle. It was My Lord Pembroke's last wish.'

There was silence. Then van Prin observed, 'The last time we sat opposite each other, you were the doctor. The time before that you were the prisoner.'

'I have not forgotten,' I replied. 'In a wherry on the way to Westminster. We spoke about Lady Derryn. I remember you said '*You will not find out who killed her from me.* Now you have written that you were her killer. I believed you when you said Pembroke did not order it.'

'I spoke the truth then and now. It was the last thing he would have wanted! I have been a faithful servant. But I can expect no reward.'

'You are deceiving yourself van Prin. How faithful have you been? You betrayed your master Pembroke, consorting with Royalists.'

Van Prin glared.

'Half his family were Royalist!' This was true. Like many families during the war, they had split loyalties.

'I know that escorting Lady Derryn to Whitecross Street gave you a chance to make or maintain contacts between opposing sides.'

Van Prin nodded. 'The worst kind of war is a civil war. Of all wars it is cruel and unnatural. The costs to any country are terrible. There are more than you expect who want a middle path between King and Parliament. That young woman could have destroyed everything. She saw things she should not. She arrived unexpectedly and saw me meet Jermyn, Sidney and others. I knew she would recognise Jermyn from her time at the Stuart court and would tell Earl Pembroke. That put everything in jeopardy. I could not allow it to happen.'

'Sidney was there?'

'Yes, he was. Sidney's politics are all for Sidney. He's never agreed with anyone except himself! Earl Pembroke wasn't against the King; simply, he believed in Parliament. Before his death, he was one of the most loyal members of the Council of State and—' van Prin hesitated.

'I loved the old man like a son. He trusted me. I did not want him to know how I was deceiving him.'

'You killed her for that?'

'You have no idea. She was dangerous—troublesome— she tried to seduce my Lord Pembroke. She made herself the centre of his affections. And I knew she would use her knowledge against me. What better reason did I need?'

Van Prin had been impassive but now his expression was one of hatred, his blue eyes bright with anger.

'You decided to kill her.'

'I detested her. Every minute she was alive. I can't understand why people loved her. She was concerned about nothing except herself—she didn't care if thousands died,' said van Prin.

I regarded the tall blond man. We are the same age, I realised, and both been through the wars. Two lost men. He threw his lot in with a noble family, I with the Army. He relied on personal influence, I depended on my skills. In this new world, it's been the safer way. I narrowed my life, until the chaos in it was something I could control. How would I have I managed with those things I could not control?

'She visits me you know,' said van Prin. 'She comes every day and shows me her wounds. "*Look what hate did to me.*" she says. Her anger follows me in sleep. Sometimes she dances in her blood—soaked dress.'

So we share that too, I thought.

'Interrogation is tiring, isn't it?' said van Prin.

'More for you than me,' I replied. 'I found this on the floor of the barn.' In my bandaged hand I held up van Prin's dagger. Van Prin nodded.

'You came to Ely with a request that I anatomise Lady Derryn's body. I did and wrote a report.'

'That report caused confusion because you did not rule out poison.'

'There was poison—but it was self-administered—drugs that she took to rid herself of the child. Obtained from Mistress Grahame. Only she did not take enough. Perhaps she changed her mind.'

'My lord Pembroke wanted that child. I came to claim him.' There was no hiding from the intensity of van Prin's blue gaze. I looked away from him and continued.

'When I examined her wounds, I noticed that some were unusual. The blade that made them penetrated easily and the wounds were saw-toothed. They were probably made by this weapon. I would guess that there are not many daggers with the cutting edge of yours.'

There was a long silence. Van Prin shifted his shackled feet. Something scurried in the corner.

'Tell me about the night you killed her,' I said.

'She was to be met at St Pauls by someone from Whitecross Street. I followed her with two mercenaries. They grabbed her and I came up close. When she saw, she shouted my name, "*Tjaard!*"—'

Van Prin imitated a woman in terror then threw back his head and his long yellow hair glinted in the light. He was laughing.

'She thought I'd come to help her. A vain creature even at the end! Believed I was her willing slave like every other man she met. But I stuck her and left her to die in the mud.' His manacles clinked and he clenched his long hands together as if squeezing out her life.

Then he seemed to lose the energy with which the memory of killing had infused him. He frowned: his voice dropped, and he said slowly, 'I have this in common with her. Neither she nor I were born under a fortunate star.'

I nodded. And was off guard.

In a moment van Prin had leaned across, stretching his long body and in one movement grasped the weapon and hugging it to him, forced it beneath his own heart.

'No need,' he gasped, 'for you to save me, Surgeon-major.' Grabbing him quickly, I saw the pulsing blood spilling, reddening his shirt. The wound was so deep, even had I wished it, I could not keep him alive.

So, I left him to bleed.

Friday 2nd March morning

'How shall I explain the death of my prisoner?' This morning, Lady Anne was stooped and tired.

'Why do you need to explain? As Warden of the North, you are the source of authority here,' I said. 'You have sealed the record of his testimony.'

'I am beginning to feel pity for her, after all. I should imagine that there is more to it than his brief confession, but I shall ask no further.'

'That is the simplest way.'

She gave a faint smile, and I felt a sense of kinship with this tough old woman. I felt safe with her. I took a breath.

'I want to tell you about something that happened in the war. Something I did. You are not the first to learn of it, but the first to whom I have spoken.'

She showed no surprise.

'It was after the siege of Oxford. I was caring for the wounded of the Royalist defence. We had no supplies or medicines. Some Parliamentary soldiers arrived. I did not know if they were official or irregulars. I didn't care because they brought a much-needed medicine chest. Said I could have it if I pointed out the Catholics. We had six such patients—two officers and four of their men. Farm boys.'

'What did you do?'

'I said there were none. They did not believe me. I tried

to bargain, saying a ransom would be better, but they threatened everyone, pulled the wounded from their beds—'

'So, did you…?'

'Yes. One of them was corrupt and said the officers could buy their lives. I could do nothing. The common men were being dragged away and they called on God to forgive my treachery. One officer offered to change places. For he said his farm boy was married with a family. They hanged them both.'

'And the medicines?'

'Useless. If there had been a poison there of value, I would have swallowed it.'

She was silent. I could not read her reaction.

'I no longer try and justify anything I did. That includes, a few days later, accepting the offer to work on the victorious Parliamentary side.'

'You're right not to attempt to defend your actions. War presents these choices, which are not choices at all.'

'General Fairfax learnt of it. They were irregulars, an extremist sect—there are others in the Army. I identified them and he had their leader executed.'

In the silence, she looked at me with her hard, black eyes.

'Mr Lockyer, for years I have carried secrets as well. Too many. I would lighten the load.'

'*No*! Please Lady Anne. Do not tell me anything.'

The fierce response startled her. She leaned forwards; her shoulders bowed as if under a weight; her mouth clenched with disappointment. But I did not want the knowledge she wished to give me. Ever.

Chapter 37

Thursday 30th May afternoon

Londoners had forgotten the great frost of the early months when ships were stuck in the Thames and oxen were roasted on the frozen river. And the fortnight—long thaw that followed. Winter was far behind them. The weather was warm and mild. In the streets children were selling bunches of pinks and lily of the valley. The Thames was full of wherries and small craft, back to its usual crowded and urgent business.

Despite new laws to punish drunkenness the alehouses were fuller than ever. All the talk was of the forthcoming invasion of Scotland, to be carried out by the Lord General now he was landed from Ireland. 'Take the war to them—kill the Covenanters' was the general sentiment and the armourers, clothing merchants and money lenders were anticipating a profitable season.

On returning from Westmoreland, I had found Janvier packed and ready to leave for France.

'I hope your mission was successful, John, for you have paid a price,' the Frenchman had observed. He was remarking not on my obvious injuries but that in my absence my employment at Ely had been terminated, with no further prospects. My title as Questor General remained unconfirmed. At Scot's office no one wanted to speak to me. Aldridge was dismayed but powerless. Now Janvier was returning to France. I knew that he had been charged with the safe delivery of the diplomatic package known as Henry Jermyn. Janvier promised to return. 'For there are many of the late King's goods yet unsold,' he said, and we parted friends.

My hands were healing. I realised my luck; the lye solution had not been a concentrate and my immersion brief. But puckered white scars remained and some of the feeling in my fingertips had gone. I had despatched van Prin's confession to Scot but heard nothing. I knew I must seek a post soon. But who would want me now? Before leaving Janvier had proffered some advice.

'Scot is furious with you for going away without notice. He thinks you are not treating your official position seriously. So, when others criticise, he has not defended you. He is punishing you. You must go and explain your actions to him. Do it now.'

But I knew that I would not visit Scot and beg for his help. Was I an errant schoolboy to be whipped? So much for the independence the Chief Intelligencer had promised me. Scot would play a cat and mouse game over van Prin's confession. He would ask questions about Edward. And he was not an easy man to deceive.

My new lodgings were in Holywell Street, off the Strand. As I approached the door my way was barred by an armed trooper who saluted.

'Surgeon-major Lockyer, General Cromwell presents his compliments to the Questor General and requests that you take supper with him at his apartments in Whitehall.'

I was puzzled. Had the General ratified my

appointment, after all? He never wastes time I thought. From bed to council chamber. From Ireland to Scotland with barely a rest. What does he want from me?

Cromwell's apartments were modest and simply furnished. Some of the grandeur of the king's palace remained in the velvet hangings and black marble floor. But the furniture was solid and plain, the table scrubbed, the plates and jugs of green glazed earthenware. I looked at the freshly baked loaves and plates of apples, the beer mugs and enormous cold herring pie. Modest food but plenty of it.

There were three men already waiting. The tall lean one was Thomas Trapham, chief surgeon at Savoy Hospital. He smiled and held out his hand.

'You took your time. I was expecting you weeks ago.'

'I understood there were some objections to my coming to Savoy,' I replied cautiously.

'Mainly from yourself as I heard it. The Sidney brothers seem to think highly of you—Algernon in particular. Apparently, you cared for Earl Pembroke. It never harms to have friends on the Council of State.'

Algernon Sidney a friend and ally? Just keep quiet and be thankful, I told myself. Eventually he'll tell me what he wants in return.

'May I introduce the General's physician Dr Goddard from Oxford? This is the man I told you about, Jonathan.'

Jonathan Goddard, with his fair curls and a ruddy face looked like a country squire for whom following the hounds was a more suitable occupation than experimental philosophy. He smiled pleasantly.

'I hear you were one of Dr Harvey's pupils. I did not have that privilege. I shall look forward to discussing his ideas with you.'

'You are welcome, I am honoured to meet someone of your learning,' I replied.

'Well if it is not John Lockyer—your pardon—Q*uestor General* Lockyer. I did not think we would meet again—still less at General Cromwell's request.'

The face was unfriendly but not unfamiliar. A tall pasty-faced man, balding with some remaining wisps of greasy hair, was looking disagreeably at me.

I held out my hand. 'How do you do George. I suppose I could say the same.' George Bates' hand was as I remembered it, soft and clammy.

'Come help yourselves gentlemen; Eat, drink—for tonight I am in a hurry.' It was the boom of an unforgettable voice, and all turned as Cromwell strode towards them, throwing down his gloves so they slapped on the table.

'The Scottish campaign is less than a month away. Our business tonight is your business—doctoring. Many of our soldiers died in Ireland—not only at the hands of Papist brutes but through cold as they lay in dripping tents laying siege to Irish castles. Many were weak and ill-fed! It was only Providence that gave us victory.'

And your heavy artillery I thought.

'The point is gentlemen I will not bring an ill-nourished weakling force to fight the Scots. I want the puny weeded out before any engagement takes place and once in the field proper provision for the wounded. Mr Tresham, you are Surgeon—in-chief, this is your task and I know you'll accept it. As to the rest of you—'

Jonathan Goddard said, 'General Cromwell, I am eager to serve Parliament. I will give what I can of my skill with a willing heart. Physician-in-chief is a great honour.'

There was silence for a moment. Cromwell said evenly, 'That leaves Dr Bate and Mr Lockyer. I've heard you gentlemen met during the siege of Oxford.'

I was thrown off-balance. Why was Cromwell bringing up the past?

Perhaps seeing my face Cromwell remarked, 'The Lord's peace, surgeon-major Lockyer. We all know that at Oxford you came over to us. It took Dr Bate a little longer to see the light.'

To leave the circle of comfort and idleness that surrounded the King, I thought.

'I've got something different in mind from that proposed to Mr Tresham and Dr Goddard. Mr Lockyer, have you ever cut for the stone?'

'I have, General Cromwell. But it is an operation better done by specialists. Mr Molins at St Bartholomew's—'

'I know Molins,' growled the General. 'A royalist. Although I swear when the pain is bad I care not if Charles Stewart himself wielded the knife if he could relieve me.'

'My lord General, I'm sure he'd relish the task!' George Bate giggled. There was an embarrassed silence.

Cromwell turned to face me.

'Surgeon-major, you and Dr Bate are men of skill, honesty and good character. I want you as my personal doctors during the Scottish campaign. Mr Tresham and Dr Goddard carry overall responsibility. But you will be on hand—not as field doctors but part of my personal staff.'

Bate's pale faced flushed, and he seemed to glow.

'Lord General Cromwell, nothing would give me

better pleasure than to serve you personally. I have excellent remedies for relief of the stone and the—er—rare bout of black bile that—er—clouds your Lordship's senses. Or so I have heard…' His voice trailed.

'Thank you Dr Bate. Surgeon-major Lockyer?'

'Lord General, I would never refuse any man who needed my skill. But I would prefer to work for the common soldier in the common soldiers' conditions. That is the work I know, Sir. I should add that the office of questor may also require me. I fear I could not be on hand as you would wish.'

Behind Cromwell's back, I saw George Bate mouth the word, 'Fool!' Yes, I sounded pompous; but I hated an atmosphere where ingratiation seemed the way to behave. The General frowned and then gave a loud barking laugh.

'Well, Lockyer if is hardship you require you will find plenty in Scotland. The food is terrible, the weather worse and the Scots, while not papist barbarians like the Irish, are a canting lot much wanting in brotherly love. I don't seek a tame puppy Sir. I am sure Mr Tresham will be more than glad to use you to the limit.'

He grunted.

'By the Lord of Hosts, I give you my word I shall only call for you if I am in utmost need. And as for the burdens of office, Sir, do not complain to me. For I know what manner of man you are. You are never happy unless burdened. We leave in three weeks.'

Monday 10th of June morning.

Each day I made my way to Savoy hospital, where the rhythms and routines were different to the ones which had been so much part of my life at Ely. Built like a fortress, overlooking the river, three Tudor monarchs had endowed it to house one hundred 'needy men' and offer nightly lodging to the homeless. It was now the largest army hospital. The great vaulted rooms and chapel echoed to the sounds of injured and suffering soldiers and the constant industry of those who cared for them. The work was varied and interesting and I found to my surprise I liked it better than Ely. There was much going on and enough surgical colleagues eager to discuss their work. I was beginning to feel at home. This morning I saw Mr Trapham, Surgeon-in-chief, striding rapidly towards me, the strings of his operating smock flapping loose. Normally stately, he seemed anxious and alarmed.

'Surgeon-major—what a business. There's riot going on in the Long Ward, you'd better come with me. —It's been overcrowded for weeks now, I feared this might happen—'

Shouts and furious voices were raised across the yard. I raced to the door of the Long Ward, with Trapham and a following crowd panting at my heels. We were met by two burly surgeon's assistants holding a patient whose matted hair hung down his back. It was tangled with his loosened bandages. The man was red-faced and struggling. His shouts filled the courtyard, but his rage was so consuming that I could not make out the words.

'That's Trooper Fellowes,' gasped Trapham out of breath. 'I bound him up a week ago. He had a pike wound in his back—it was full of maggots. He's due to return soon to the ranks.'

'You want me back? For what?' roared the man 'Slaughtering women and young children—that's not soldiers' work. Cromwell isn't a general—he's a butcher!'

'They were Papists!' came a shout. A group of patients had left their beds. They carried a motley assortment of crutches and pressed forward close to Trapham. Too close.

'What is your trouble man?' asked Trapham. 'Are you not well cared for here?'

'We don't need officers and sawbones to sort our troubles,' came a reply from the crowd.

'Leave us alone—this is soldiers' business,' called another and there was a growl of assent. The surgeons' men looked nervous and released their hold on Fellowes. Trapham gave me a desperate glance. I faced them.

'Have you a grievance against us here at Savoy? Why is there such disorder—many of you are still infirm.'

'Listen to Major Lockyer—he's fought in the field,' someone shouted.

'Yes—on both sides,' came the reply. There was a gale of laughter.

'This has got to stop,' hissed Trapham. 'They must disperse.'

Trooper Fellowes straightened himself.

'Treatment, I've no complaints. But why make us whole again? We fought for the freeborn people of England. For liberty from the king's rule. Now we fight the Irish and the Scots. Why exactly? No Irishman took the roof over my head! I don't want to fight anymore. We're never going to get the pay that's due to us, so we will take what we need! The earth is God's common treasury for all!'

'Aye.' There was a chorus of agreement.

I had heard about this. Groups of soldiers, calling themselves Diggers had taken over unused pasture and were living communally, working the land. Local landowners had attacked the settlements, and the Council of State was considering the use of troops.

'Mr Fellowes, your beliefs do you credit. But you 're not yet recovered, nor is anyone here. A man needs his strength to dig the earth as much as wield a sword! I'm asking you to return to your beds until you are fit to leave. Believe me, there will be many waiting to take your place.'

Trooper Fellowes hesitated, pushing his hand through his wad of red hair. Then he limped back pushing away all assistance and one by one the others too settled into their beds or chairs. But the Long Ward was far from quiet. Voices rose echoing from the vaulted roof in a wave of intense discussion. Who more than these men knew what sacrifices have been made and what blood had been spilt? From the earliest days of the war my heart had always been with the plain soldier.

'Well done, Lockyer,' murmured Trapham. 'You know how Parliament watches us. Some want any excuse to cut our moneys. I'm due at a meeting now and I'm late.'

He gave me a harassed look. 'Could you go in my place? It'd give you an opportunity to meet the new Superintendent. But hurry. The Superintendent is a stickler for punctuality.'

Another authoritarian, I thought. Along with Days of Humiliation and Penitence, preaching missions and the death penalty for fornication. In the main building I was asked to wait, the Superintendent would be along. Typical I thought. Keep me in my place. Gloom and fury settled in my heart.

'Mr Lockyer, thank goodness you stopped the riot. It could have got ugly.'

I turned.

She looked almost in a good humour. She stood tall and strong, and her large hands held a bunch of shiny new keys. One look at her calm and resolute face and my rage dissolved. I was glad to see her. Very glad.

'Did the Ghent nuns throw you out Madame?'

She laughed. 'No, it was time for me to leave. Sir Kenelm—remember him?—recommended me to Cromwell and—'

'—now you're the new Superintendent.'

'Correct. I have a lot to do to straighten this place out.'

'They've tightened laws against Papists—you are forbidden within five miles of London. How will you survive here?'

'Parliament cares not so much about our beliefs as sequestering our money—but for those who have no grand estates…' she shrugged. 'Well we're more or less safe. But laws against murder are as strong as they ever were. I hope there will be no more corpses to embarrass us! Face it, John—we know each other's secrets. We should keep them.'

How had she managed it? Her schemes seemed to be succeeding. Clearly, she had the Lord General's trust. And she was right. We knew enough to hang each other.

Chapter 38

Monday 24th June afternoon

I walked from Savoy to St Laurence Hill. I was going to say goodbye. After an earlier shower, there was sunshine; the river was at full tide and the sky showed the pale washed blue that follows rain and promises a few fine hours. The house looked much the same although I noticed that the mulberry tree had been cut back. There were some new flags in the pathway, a boot scraper and a new iron knocker. I rapped smartly. After a few minutes, there was a shout, a crash, a shuffling sound, and the door was pulled open. Before me was the small figure of Doctor Harvey, covered in a powdering of white dust. He opened his arms in a warm greeting, releasing a further cloud which immediately transferred to my jerkin as Harvey pulled me close.

'John! What a great pleasure! Did you get my letter in France? Apologies for the dust, Eliab is having the ceilings re-plastered and the whole house is in a commotion. I just knocked over a sack of the stuff. It gets everywhere—I've had to move my study out to the back, come in come in.'

Taking my arm, Harvey led me through the hall, making white footprints.

'Well-well, John, your coming—it's like they say about trying to find a hire-coach in a rainstorm—you wait and wait then two arrive at once! Look who's here!' He addressed me and the figure bent over a table, viewing an engraving.

The thick fair plait I remembered was now smoothed, coiled and decorously pinned. She turned and straightened up, brushing some particles of plaster dust from her black dress. I recalled her smile. It brightened the little room.

'Leticia!'

'Mr Lockyer!' She took a step forward, then hesitated and made a curtsey. As she bent her head I caught a glimpse of the white scar above her eye.

Harvey beamed. 'Leticia can visit if she is chaperoned.' At his words a dumpy figure stirred in the corner, and a small round-faced woman stood up.

'Leticia, how do you like Lady Ranelagh's household?' I doubted that a girl of her spirit would settle happily into a life of prayer and fine needlework.

'She's very kind Mr Lockyer and most learned. She is teaching me her skills as a physician—

'Humph!' Harvey made a noise which he converted into a sneeze. 'Lady Ranelagh favours herbals,' he remarked.

'Dr Harvey, she's helping me to translate Lucretius. It is scientific work Sir.' Leticia was laughing, half indignant.

'All right. Should she introduce Heraclitus, exercise caution,' said Harvey. 'Now John, I want to show you some pages of my treatise on the embryo. Leticia is doing the sketches for the engravings.' Harvey blew the plaster-dust off several piles of paper. I spent the next hour listening to him happily recount his findings. At the end, he picked up the copy of his manuscript and held it close.

'How glad I am to have you both here, who are so very dear to me,' he said, looking from one to the other.

I saw tears in Harvey's eyes. Leticia put her arms around the old man.

'The Shulamite loves you,' she said. 'This book will be another great work.'

'I think it will be my last,' Harvey said, 'but I am finally going to put the cap on that rascal Aristotle. I'm to describe the beginnings of life. You see, it's all in the egg.' He blinked. 'I need a good anatomist. Join me, John.'

I shook my head. 'I shall shortly leave for the war in Scotland.'

'Ah yes,' said Harvey, 'still in thrall to Cromwell.' He chuckled.

It almost removed the sting.

'You know me better than that William.' I glanced at Leticia. 'I will always find days for you. For both of you.'

Wednesday 26th June 1650

I stood in a shadowed corner of the courtyard of Baynard's Castle, staring at a rectangular stone. It carried no inscription, but I knew that beneath it lay the remains of Lady Derryn Barlow. Placed in a little-trodden part of the yard, weeds and grass were already sprouting tall at the edges of the slab. Was she at rest now that her killer was dead and her child in safe keeping? Van Prin had been right, I reflected. Hers had been a short life which ended badly. Was the devoted love of one prince and the greedy attention of another any recompense? Even though she had dominated my life for the last ten months I realised that I still did not understand her. I only knew I no longer heard her voice, and my nights were calm.

I had another grave to visit, and I walked along the muddy banks of the Thames to the point where it joined the Fleet. I headed north up the hill to St Andrew's churchyard. A small mound of turned London clay covered the body of Sally Watts. A pot of marigolds had been placed there, the orange petals still fresh and glowing; Finny must have done that before she left, bound for Jamestown, Virginia. She went with money in her pocket—a government reward for her part in Jermyn's capture. I had omitted some details from my report. She had freedom at last and I was glad. No more whoring, no more 'entertainments. The Count of Finsbury was no more. I would miss her bold heart, and her bright spirit.

As I turned to leave, I imagined I heard the usual rebuke from a familiar voice: 'Mr Lockyer! Where have you been?' I was aware that I must parcel my goods for Scotland. And that a message from the Chief Intelligencer already awaited me. But for the moment, I felt content and without any burden. I made my way slowly past the shaded, mossy urns and out into the sunshine of the busy street towards the hopes and possibilities of London and the world that never stops.

THE END

Bibliography

A very large number of publications deal with the War of the Three Kingdoms, (commonly referred to as The Civil War) of the mid-17th century. Almost as much has been written about Oliver Cromwell himself, and only slightly fewer which focus on the English Republic or Commonwealth and Cromwell's Protectorate. What follows is not a full bibliography but a handful of the works that helped while writing this book. This is a novel, and errors and omissions must, of course, be credited only to me.

Nadine Akkermann (2018) *Invisible Agents: Women and Espionage in Seventeenth Century Britain*
Philip Aubrey (1989) *Mr Secretary Thurloe*
Christopher Durston and Judith Maltby (2006) *Religion in Revolutionary England*
Audrey Eccles (1982) *Obstetrics and Gynaecology in Tudor and Stuart England*
Antonia Fraser (1973) *Cromwell, Our Chief of Men*
CH Frith (1911) *Acts and Ordinances of the Interregnum 1642-1660*
SG Gardiner (1903) *History of the Commonwealth and Protectorate (4 vols)*
Eric Gruber von Arni (2001) *Justice to the Maimed Soldier*
Paul Hardacre (1956) *The Royalists during the Puritan Revolution*
Christopher Hill (1958) *Puritanism and the English Revolution*
Christopher Hill (1972) *The World Turned Upside Down*

N H Keble (ed) (2001) *The Cambridge Companion to The Writing of the English Revolution*
Michael Macdonald (1981) *Mystical Bedlam*
Brian Manning (1976) *The English People and the English Revolution*
Ivan Roots (ed) (1998) *'Into Another Mould': Aspects of the Interregnum*
David E Smith (ed) (2003) *Cromwell and the Interregnum*
Philip K Wilton (1999) *Surgery Skin and Syphilis*
Richard Wiseman (1686) *Several Chirurgical Treatises*
Keith Roberts (2013) *Cromwell's War Machine*

www.ingramcontent.com/pod-product-compliance
Ingram Content Group UK Ltd.
Pitfield, Milton Keynes, MK11 3LW, UK
UKHW031831160125
453814UK00004B/150